# BLOOD IN THE RAIN 4

Edited by Cecilia Duvalle and Mary Trepanier

# BLOOD IN THE RAIN 4

Published in the United States by Cwtch Press
16625 Redmond Way, M-229, Redmond, WA 98052-4444

Cover Design: IndieDesignz

Cwtch Logo Design: Elizabeth Person

ISBN: 978-1-947234-10-9

Print ISBN: 978-1-947234-11-6

To the jaded eye, all vampires seem alike, but they are wonderful in their versatility. Some come to life in moonlight, others are killed by the sun, some pierce with their eyes, others with fangs, some are reactionary, others are rebels, but all are disturbingly close to the mortals they prey on. I can think of no other monsters who are so receptive. Vampires are neither inhuman nor non-human nor all-too-human, they are simply more alive than they should be.

— NINA AUERBACH, Our Vampires, Ourselves

# CONTENTS

**FOREWORD**

Vampires–these blood-sucking, soul-sucking creatures of the night continue to fascinate—no matter how many incarnations they take, no matter how many worlds they inhabit, no matter how many ways they kill. Or suck and fuck. The variety of vampires and their hot, bloody, sexy selves continue to entertain and enchant us.

Vampires are not well-known for consent, kindness, or generosity, so consider their nature as you read this collection of explicitly erotic horror stories. Each tale is expressly written for adults with a discerning nature looking for sexually graphic stories that horrify and delight.

We provide a variety of sexual groupings, genders, and myths as well as writing styles and points of view. Our vampires range from soulless, tortured self-loathing creatures to altruistic keepers of history.

We hope that you'll devour this unique collection with as much relish as we had putting it together.

Cecilia Duvalle and Mary Trepanier
October 2018

# MIRACLE MONSTERS

## SARA DOBIE BAUER

The club *thump-thumped* to its usual melody—a heady mix of music and sweat. Fletch and I sat off to the side, watching the crowd. We weren't hunting, per se, but I personally always kept my eyes open. We sat on a black leather sofa that stank of alcohol and just a touch of semen. My heightened senses allowed me such knowledge, and where others might cringe, I wallowed in the aroma. Being a few centuries old, I remembered the days of prudery in England: the too-polite conversation and backroom trysts. How lovely that modern society had kicked the door wide open on such things. Now, we could say what we wanted, do what we wanted, with little thought to consequence.

Well, we didn't kill, of course. Humans weren't cattle to be slaughtered but instead objects of desire, vessels of pleasure. I spotted one such creature under the moving, colored lights. While I leaned halfway on my husband's lap and played with his long, black hair, I watched the handsome stranger stand off from the crowd, his hip against the bar. He just barely nodded his head to the heavy bass as young men and women shouted at the bartender for another drink and another. He didn't appear to hear them. When he was approached, I understood why.

"Fletch." I squeezed his shoulder. "Look."

The handsome stranger put down his drink and signed. He was deaf. The rapid motion of his hands allowed me a close study of his long, pale fingers. His friend responded in kind, and they laughed together. The stranger had shaggy, dark hair like my husband, so he twitched his head back to clear his view.

"Shall we give him a miracle?" I asked Fletch.

His nose tickled the side of my neck. "You don't even know the man, dear. He might not want to hear; not everyone does. Maybe he's perfectly content the way he is."

I wrapped my arms around him, the leather of our jackets sticking together in the muggy club. "But don't tell me you wouldn't like to meet him at least. Look at him."

"I'm looking."

"He has the face of an angel, but the body of a man."

"A boy, perhaps. He's thin as a rail."

"But tall. As tall as you if not taller." I kissed the side of his face. "Don't dare lie to me, husband. You would love to have him in our bed."

"Your Good Samaritan is showing, wife. You only want to fuck him because he's novel."

"Let me at least meet him."

Fletch gave my thigh a playful squeeze as the stranger watched the crowd.

"Look how he moves," I whispered above the music, right in Fletch's ear. "He can feel the bass but nothing more, yet he watches the way people dance. He moves with them."

"Like a man stumbling in the dark."

"Yet, he is the light."

When a young woman shoved up to the bar, the stranger tilted his body further toward us. Fletch was right, he was thin and delicate in the way flowers are with androgynous features that tricked the eye—every eye—into believing this creature belonged in bed. I could see them all looking, even the rude woman behind him. They all wanted, but we had the advantage: Fletch and I could actually sign.

"Good God, look at that mouth."

I laughed at Fletch's low growl.

"Fine. Go on, go get him." He gave my ass a squeeze as I stood. "Just be sure to bring him back."

I tucked my long, blonde hair behind my ears as I parted the crowd in a slow saunter. The raging club beat was replaced by a slow Massive Attack writher as dancers altered to a slow grind. I was right. The stranger was taller than Fletch up close, and he smelled like cigarettes and scotch.

I tapped his shoulder. He turned to me, smile tight-lipped as though dreading another explanation of his inability to speak. I lifted my hands and shaped my fingers into the language he understood.

"Does this song sound different from the others?" I asked.

The sudden burble of his laugh was opened-mouthed and shining white. He put down his drink and faced me. "How did you know?" his fingers said.

"Less bass. More synth."

"Are you deaf, too?" He gestured to his ear.

I shook my head. "I had a friend who was, a long time ago. I learned how to speak to her. I'm Ivy." I spelled out the letters of my name.

"Like the plant," he replied before moving his fingers at a rapid pace.

"Addison," I said.

He nodded. Up close, his skin was like marble. He couldn't have been much older than twenty-one.

"Would you like to come sit with my husband and I?" I signed and gestured back toward Fletch, who lifted one hand in salute.

Addison had the kind of eyes that made him look either half-drunk or trying to seduce at all times—and yet, they fell at the mention of "husband." Still, he played polite, probably happy to meet someone he could actually talk to. I grabbed onto his hand and lead us through the crowd, back to the semi-privacy of our seat. Fletch stood at his arrival and bowed his head.

"My signing isn't as good as hers," he gestured.

"It's okay," Addison replied, smiling.

Fletch slowly spelled out his name as I introduced Addison.

We sat, Addison in front of me and Fletch practically curled over my back. When the waitress came by with a tray of free champagne, we each took a glass. It was almost like an old English soiree—almost.

"Do you come here often?"

He laughed at the ridiculousness of my comment and shrugged. "As much as I can stand. I love the music, but I get tired of trying to explain myself. Next time, I'll wear a t-shirt that says, 'I'm deaf, but I still like sex.'"

Fletch snorted right in my ear.

"You shouldn't have any trouble with that," I signed. "You're the most gorgeous person here."

His dark eyes widened for just a second before he looked away and hid his mouth behind a sip of scotch and another of champagne.

Fletch reached around me and tugged the cuff of Addison's black blazer to get his attention. He said, "You can read my lips, yes?"

Addison nodded.

"Were you born deaf?" Fletch asked.

One side of his mouth curved down before he shook his head no. "I was thirteen. Car accident." He curled his hands together and extended his fingers suddenly, a mimic of explosion. "I miss music the most. I've tried explaining my frustration to some of my deaf-born friends, but ..." He shook his head. "They don't understand my loss. The closest I can get to hearing music now is at dance clubs."

"What do you mean, hearing?" I asked.

He put down both his drinks and leaned further back in the couch. Where a moment ago, he'd been perched on the edge, ready to bolt, he now melted until my knee touched the side of his thigh. "I can feel the floor shake. In my mind, I try to imagine what the music sounds like." He moved his hands up and down in a pantomime of vibration. "I like watching other people experience the music. The dancing. It's like watching an artistic masterpiece come to life. Everyone is so alive."

Fletch may have nudged me a little considering we were most certainly dead—and lacked the heartbeats to prove it.

"You want to hear music again," I signed.

He took another sip of scotch before folding his hands in his lap. I assumed the conversation was over until he looked up at me and studied my face. "We always want what we can't have," he replied.

Clumsily, Fletch signed, "I want shots."

Addison laughed that silent, wide-mouthed laugh of his as Fletch shifted me over enough to stand and walk to the bar. By the time he got back, Addison and I were deep in discussion over the recent *Twin Peaks* reboot.

Addison was mid-sentence, hands flailing with artful enthusiasm—"I worry that Lynch uses long pauses as nothing more than ego masturbation"—when Fletch handed him a shot glass of something dark green and ominous. Addison looked up at my husband, forehead wrinkled.

Fletch shrugged. "It has absinthe."

Addison shook his head, not understanding, so I tapped his thigh. I spelled "wormwood" and gestured to my ear before spelling "Van Gogh."

He snapped his fingers and nodded. I don't think it was the alcohol, but he kept getting better looking. Perhaps it was the comfort of being with two people he could laugh with while lacking fear of discrimination. We toasted and took our shots, which tasted of black licorice and black licorice, really. I moved even closer to Addison when Fletch sat behind me. I cuddled equally against my husband and the young man I hoped to help —if he'd let us.

"How long have you been married?" Addison signed.

It had been so long since anyone had asked, I had almost forgotten the fake answer. Truthfully, I'd met Fletch—known as Fletcher back then—three hundred years ago at a terribly dull summer ball. Both miscreants, we'd snuck into the hedge maze to kiss. I hadn't known he was a vampire, and he hadn't known I had loved him immediately.

"Five years," Fletch said.

It had been but five months before Fletch had fed me his own blood and made me like him. We had been wed: a pointless, romantic gesture but one I insisted upon for fear of losing him. Young as I was, I'd thought he would stay with me longer if I was his wife. Silly since Fletch was mad about me then and still is.

"Do you have anyone?" I signed. "Girlfriend? Boyfriend? Family?"

He shrugged, and fingers flew. "My mother died in the car accident."

I touched his knee. "I'm sorry."

Addison looked away toward the writhing bodies. "My father lives in Florida. We're not close. He's very conservative, and I'm ..." He shrugged and then waved toward the mass of bodies that practically climbed the walls. "I'm here with my friend. He says I've been grumpy and need to get laid."

I laughed as Fletch reached around me to touch Addison—a

light brush of his fingers on pale cheek. "What's sex like without a lover's noises? How do you know what to do?"

Addison laughed and dropped his head, probably to cover his blush. His dark hair tumbled into his face, and I brushed it back with my hand. When he looked up at us, he chewed on his bottom lip before signing: "I am probably a better lover than you." He pointed at my husband, and Fletch guffawed.

"Tell us why, love," I said.

"Love?" he signed. "Are you British?"

I smiled and nodded. "Now, tell me why."

"There is no need to hear," he explained, "when you can feel. I know when a lover's breath changes. I can feel when the pulse pounds."

That last bit was something we all had in common.

"Without the distraction of noise," he continued, "there is so much to hear." He smirked and mimicked quotation marks. "The way a lover reaches for you—or claws at you. The slide of sweat. The clench of muscles. I don't need my ears to make love. I just need to pay attention." He rested his hands on his thighs.

I signed, "But if you could hear, would you lose all that?"

He grinned. "No. I would become even better."

Suddenly famished, I leaned forward and kissed him. He drew back immediately, before I could even taste his mouth, his hands on my shoulders. He looked at Fletch as though Fletch might punch him, but the expression on my husband's face must have dissuaded any doubt about our intentions.

The tip of Addison's tongue touched his upper lip as his grip on my shoulders loosened. He caressed my upper arms through my leather jacket before tilting forward, closer to me. He hesitated but once before kissing me. I sighed against his mouth and held his face in my hands as the kiss deepened. His mouth was a variance of flavors from smoke to licorice to the gentle vanilla of aged scotch.

He pulled back, smiling softly, and reached behind me for Fletch's hand. He tugged until Fletch got the message and stood, although my husband's forehead still wrinkled in confusion. Addison let go of his hand and patted the empty space on the couch behind him, so Fletch sat. Naughty boy, Addison tilted his head to the side and tapped his neck, eyes fluttering closed. As vampires, that was quite an invitation; as supposed humans, Fletch laughed and immediately kissed Addison's pale skin.

When his eyes opened, I signed, "You aren't shy."

He shook his head, no, and pulled me onto his lap by the lapel of my coat. With Fletch's hand on my thigh, I licked into Addison's mouth until I felt a rumble that might have been an audible moan if not for the club beats. I reached under his blazer to find Fletch's hand already there, rubbing against his abdomen. I felt Addison's blood pounding; he was right—sound was not necessary during sex.

He vibrated … and vibrated until he stopped kissing me and fought to reach into the back pocket of his dark jeans—quite a feat with Fletch pressed so tightly against his ass. The glow of a cell phone screen lit his chiseled face, and he slumped against my husband, frowning. He held the phone up to me: just a message that read, "We're leaving."

Fletch was too busy sucking the side of Addison's neck to notice the text.

I signed, "Can we see you again?"

He nodded and reached back to grab ahold of Fletch's hair before titling his chin up and accepting a rather ravenous kiss from my husband.

"Fletch, he needs to go."

"No." My husband wrapped his arms around Addison's chest, tightly.

I touched the young man's chin before signing, "Drinks at our place tomorrow night?"

He nodded as his phone lit again. He leaned forward to escape Fletch's grip, and I almost giggled at the putout expression on my husband's face. He slumped back into the couch like a child who'd lost his favorite toy. "Give me your address," Addison signed before handing me his phone.

I entered the number of our residence in his notes section as he stood and blatantly adjusted himself. He ran both hands through his hair and smiled down at us, and I handed the cell phone back.

"It's been a pleasure," he signed before kissing us each on the cheek and walking away. Although his body disappeared quickly into the crowd, due to his height, I followed the bob of his curly head for a while before he left.

"Thin as a rail?" I taunted my husband's earlier criticism and cuddled against him.

"Well. His blazer hid that sumptuous ass. I almost went crazy with it pressed against me."

"Shall we give him back his hearing?"

Fletch's fingers played with my hair. "If he chooses, my dear Ivy. In exchange for …"

"Yes." I kissed his palm. "In exchange for."

---

HE SHOWED up at our apartment at eight PM in a black button-down, black blazer, and jeans, his hair an artful swoop that tickled the tops of his ears. I hugged him immediately. Although he still smelled vaguely of cigarettes, he'd worn a spicy cologne that made him all the more edible.

"You look beautiful," he signed.

I bowed my head to his praises as Fletch handed him a glass of scotch and kissed his cheek.

"It's not much," I signed as he looked around our apartment —and it wasn't. Fletch and I moved around a lot, partially because we loved to travel but also because it was dangerous to make personal attachments when one never aged and subsisted on human blood. The only thing that traveled with us consistently was our sizeable music collection.

Addison set his glass on our kitchen counter and walked toward the bookshelves filled with albums. He pulled out Debussy and tickled his fingers across the cover. "I remember this one," he signed. "Reminded me of a rainstorm when I was a child. It looks as though you like music as much as me. Do you play instruments?"

I played five; Fletch played more than seven. Instead of explaining that eternal life meant a life of constant learning to defend against despair, Fletch signed, "Sometimes."

He looked back and forth between the two of us—relics from another age—my husband with his dark, Byronic good looks and me, almost albino in my lightness. "Why me?" he signed.

I understood exactly what he asked. "You're beautiful."

He shook his head and signed quickly. "Many people are beautiful, Ivy. Is it because I'm deaf—something strange and rare?"

"I'm rather fond of your mouth and ass," my husband quipped.

Addison turned a bright shade of pink. "Most men are fond of those things," he signed.

Fletch and I inched closer. I put one hand on Addison's cheek, the other on his chest. He would notice soon, notice that we were different. "We want to give you something," I said.

The most adorable wrinkle appeared between his heavy brows. I leaned up on my toes to kiss him, and I think that was when he sensed it—or, more properly, sensed nothing. He took a step away from me but backed right into Fletch, who put both his hands on Addison's upper arms.

"It's all right," I said.

He froze for a beat, leaned against my husband, before shoving away from Fletch and taking two stumbling steps further into our apartment but at least away from monsters. "You have no heartbeat," he signed. "Why don't you have heartbeats?"

Of course, the club music from last night would have covered our lack of life. In the quiet of our apartment, we had nowhere to hide.

"We don't want to hurt you," I signed, which did nothing to calm him.

Instead, his rapidly moving fingers were more agitated than ever. "If you don't want to hurt me, why are you stalking toward me like hungry beasts?"

He had a point. Fletch and I both stopped moving.

"We can give you your hearing back," I signed.

"I've been to a million doctors over the years. Nothing has ever worked. It's impossible."

I shook my head. "We have performed miracles before."

When his back hit the wall, he had nowhere to go. Although

his blood still sang in a panicked pulse, his dark eyes weren't quite as wide and terrified anymore. "What are you?" he signed.

"Vampires," Fletch said.

"Not real," was Addison's immediate reply.

"Very real," my husband said.

I held my hands up in front of me and signed as though racing toward finish. "But we don't want to hurt you."

"You claim you'll give me my hearing back," he signed. "What do you want in return?"

He allowed me close enough to touch him, so I did—one fingertip down the side of his cheek and over the edge of his sharp jaw. "Your pleasure," I said. "And your blood."

He shook his head and lifted his hands between us. "You said you wouldn't hurt me."

"It doesn't hurt," I signed. "On the contrary."

With shaking fingers, he replied, "This can't be real."

Fletch grabbed his hand and squeezed before flashing his fangs. Although Addison pulled in a shocked breath, he didn't shove us away or try to run. Sadly, I suppose he knew as well as we did that his vocal chords didn't remember how to scream.

"It is a very simple exchange," Fletch said slowly. "We will give you pleasure like you've never known and then give you what you long for. I see no downside."

Addison tugged his hand free of my husband's grasp and signed, "You're not the one who's for dinner."

Fletch chuckled as Addison turned his attention back to me.

"How do I know you won't kill me?" he signed.

I shook my head with such vehemence my vision shook. "No. No." I mouthed the word with great clarity before moving my hands. "We give to those in need."

"I don't *need* to hear."

"But you want to." I kissed his full lips.

His brow wrinkled. "You don't even know me."

Fletch signed carefully, having never mastered the skill. "She knows enough to know you lost a treasured part of yourself, and we can give it back."

"I want you to hear music," I signed.

"I want to hear your voices," he replied.

For a moment, I thought my dead heart might beat.

He looked from me to my husband and back again to make sure we both watched carefully. With big, forceful gestures and eyebrows raised: "Ivy. Fletch. Do not hurt me. Promise?"

I nodded and squeezed his hand while Fletch drew a cross over the center of his chest. Although ironic, I knew he meant well. Fletch always kept himself in check around humans he adored.

We lead him to our bedroom. As the most oft used room in the apartment, it was the coziest with blankets of soft fabric and pillows upon pillows. Addison's eyes took in the expensive silk that adorned our king-sized canopy bed. It probably looked like something out of *Arabian Nights* to him, but Fletch and I always had loved India.

I pulled my long, black dress off over my head. I wore nothing under it, so I revealed all my pale skin to Addison's dark eyes. He reached for me immediately, with his hands on my hips, and kissed me—a touch so sweet, I tasted sugar. I buried my hands in Addison's lush curls as I heard the slide of fabric: Fletch removing Addison's suit coat. His hands only left my hips for a second before returning and squeezing. His acrobatic fingers dug into my flesh, and I thrilled at the thought of what else they might do.

To hurry things along, I pulled my mouth away and focused

on the buttons of his shirt. Fletch kept Addison otherwise occupied by kissing up the side of his neck—and then rubbing his hand over the front of Addison's jeans. I froze when Addison made a noise, something between a grunt and a groan, so small I almost missed it. My entire body tingled at the unexpected sound, and I gazed up at my husband, whose eyes were half-lidded with lust.

It became a rush to divest garments as Addison kicked off his shoes and unbuttoned his jeans. Within moments, he was as naked as I. He tackled me onto the bed beneath him. I laughed against the side of his face and pushed his hair back off his forehead before nuzzling our noses together and welcoming his tongue into my mouth. We rolled across the bed, him on top one second and me the next—but my legs never loosened around his hips as I pressed myself against his hard length.

"Care to share, wife?" Fletch's voice was closer than I'd expected. He hovered above us, standing at the side of the bed. His bare skin was as translucent and flawless as the day we'd met.

I turned Addison's face toward Fletch, and he apparently got the hint since he flopped off me and onto his back. He extended his arms up as though seeking a hug. Fletch actually snarled. He knelt between Addison's spread thighs, pushing them open further before diving in for a kiss that looked like it might break skin. Addison accepted his aggressive onslaught with practiced ease. He was apparently used to a hungry lover, and I was no better than my Fletch.

What was it about Addison that made me want to both attack and protect? I supposed it was his fragile beauty—the bewildering androgyny of one so stunning and yet tall and strong. Beneath his clothes, he was indeed thin but also muscled, without a trace of fat to hide the lean curvature of his chest, stomach, and hips. I longed to devour and hold, destroy and cherish.

Fletch's voice interrupted my tempestuous musings. He leaned up above Addison on his elbows. "Have you had sex with a man before?"

Addison chewed his lower lip to hide what might have been a large grin.

Fletch used his thumb to free the captured flesh. "And did you enjoy it?"

A nod, followed by a tug that brought Fletch's lips back to his.

Fletch kissed down Addison's chest. When his eventual destination became apparent, Addison reached for me. He held gently to my face and pulled me close so that we could kiss. One of his hands found my breast and teased at my nipple until I moaned against his throat—long and low so that he could feel the vibration.

He gasped against my lips. I didn't have to look down to know Fletch had taken him in his mouth. Addison's eyes fluttered shut, but he didn't let go of me. Like a reflex, his fingertips massaged my scalp as Fletch worked his magic.

When Addison made another of his noises, I eyed my husband. He looked absolutely decadent with his mouth on Addison's cock and one hand between his legs—lower. He was opening him up, and God, if Addison's stuttered breaths were any indication, our human greatly enjoyed it.

Then, suddenly, Addison reached his hands out to both of us and lifted his head from the pillow. He tugged on Fletch's hair until he stopped everything. I'm sure my husband's stomach dropped in dread like mine as Addison started to sign.

"Why does it feel …" His fingers hesitated. "More?"

I held my hands up between us. "Our saliva is like a drug. We only gave you a taste last night."

Sweaty and debauched as he was, the furrow of his brow was almost comical. "A drug?"

"The only effect is increased sexual sensation," I signed.

He nodded and chewed his lip again before Fletch went back to work, and Addison's head fell with a heavy *thunk* against the pillows.

Within minutes, Addison clawed at Fletch's shoulders, and Fletch had to put one hand on the young man's hip to keep him from bucking off the bed. I would have thought him completely unaware of his surroundings if not for his two fingers, deep inside of me. He had more talent in those two digits than most men had in their entire bodies.

My husband sat up but twisted his fingers around Addison's free hand to calm him. "Lube, my love?"

Barely coherent, I floated on sensation but managed to nod and reach for the small table by our bed, filled with all sorts of sexual accouterments. While Fletch prepared himself, I brushed Addison's hair with my fingers and rubbed our noses together. I still carried with me that mysterious dichotomy of wanting to both fuck this beguiling creature but also cuddle him gently to my breast.

My husband was a man of great strength, which he proved when he picked Addison up and shifted him where he wanted. Addison smiled at being manhandled—something a person of his height was surely not accustomed to. Fletch knelt in the middle of the bed and pulled a kneeling Addison flush against his body, Addison's back to Fletch's front. They rocked together like that, Fletch's hand on

Addison's dick, before my husband leaned our human forward a bit—which was when Addison held out his hands.

"Condoms?" he signed.

I leaned up and touched his cheek. "We're dead."

He blinked his large eyes at this, and I think he might have looked sad.

There was little time for mourning, though, as Fletch pulled Addison back against his chest and slowly entered his body. In response, Addison melted against him, his head flopped on Fletch's shoulder, mouth wide. My husband thrust twice before wrapping Addison in a tight embrace, one hand on his stomach and the other at the base of his neck. He would leave bruises, I was sure of it.

Somewhere in his immaculate haze, Addison had the resolve to reach out for me. He pulled me close and kissed me. He sucked my lip into his mouth and bit.

"Ride him, my dear Ivy," Fletch panted. I'd rarely heard my husband sound so wrecked.

Kneeling above them both, I stared down into Addison's half-open eyes. My hips fit perfectly in his hands. I brought the tip of his hot flesh against my entrance and slowly lowered myself down. Addison trembled at the feel of me, overwrought with pleasure. He clung harder and harder to my hips and rested his open mouth against my collarbone.

We moved as one, rubbing and fucking against each other. I moaned at the stretch of him inside me and gripped his shoulders tight. This wouldn't last—it couldn't. It was so, so much, especially for Addison. He moaned against my flesh.

I caught Fletch's gaze over Addison's shoulder. We bit down on opposite sides of the young man's neck at the same time, and

Addison shuddered in our embrace. His blood tasted of youthful innocence.

When he came, it seemed a surprise to him. It was certainly a surprise to my husband, who stopped drinking and stiffened at the feel of Addison's muscles clenching around him. A single thrust later, and Fletch finished with a cry, a drop of blood on his chin. I licked at the open wound on Addison's neck but soon found myself tossed onto my back with Addison's head between my legs.

Despite the spend that surely lingered, Addison sucked my clit into his mouth. I arched off the bed and dug my hands into his hair. No matter that he couldn't hear his name from my lips; I said it anyway, again and again. He did not hear it, but he certainly felt my orgasm. With one of his hands on my stomach —surely reading my breath—a wave of pleasure crashed into me so hard that I saw stars. My lips tingled on the precipice of numb.

Addison wilted and rested his face against my upper thigh. My dearest Fletch landed at my side and kissed me, caressed me, adored me. A few minutes later, I thought Addison might have fallen asleep—until he snuck his way between my husband and I and sighed with contentment as we wrapped him in our arms.

He lifted his hands to sign. "I thought you said you wouldn't kill me."

Fletch laughed and sucked on the teeth marks that adorned the side of Addison's neck like precious jewels.

"You make noise during," I signed. "Did you know?"

He nodded.

I took his chin in my hand. "I can't wait to hear your voice."

If Addison wanted an explanation, we didn't give it.

Together, Fletch and I performed our ritual. Addison allowed himself to be moved from one side to the other as we dripped our immortal blood into his ears. I said the words in Latin and, in my blood, drew a cross on his forehead. God listened to the damned, too.

Fletch pulled the blankets up over the three of us. I planted soft kisses along Addison's cheeks. Before he fell asleep, I signed, "Things will be different and yet familiar in the morning."

A SUDDEN JOLT ROUSED ME. I pushed the veil of my blonde hair out of the way and reached my hand out to find an empty space. Sensing my distress, Fletch's eyes opened, and he leaned up on one elbow. In the dimness of our room, protected from the sun by heavy curtains, I recognized the pale glow of Addison's bare back. He sat up between us, blankets tangled around his waist.

He jumped when I touched him. I tucked rouge hair behind his ear so I could see his face—and it was painted white. His eyes, large already, were now big as the moon.

"Addison?" I said.

He sucked in air that quickly turned to a sob. Dried blood still coated his ears, although the cross on his forehead had worn off in the night.

"Again," he signed.

"Addison," I said.

He turned to Fletch and poked him in the chest.

Fletch said his name and grinned.

He covered his face with his hands as his sobs shook the bed.

Once Addison had calmed enough to actually move, I

wrapped him in one of Fletch's robes. In the kitchen, I made him breakfast. He tilted his head and listened, smiling, as the bacon sizzled.

Fletch was never far. Almost constantly, he lingered at Addison's side. He touched the young man and kissed his head, his shoulder … anywhere really. His hand played with the shaggy hair on the back of Addison's head as Addison simply sat and listened. I suspect my husband felt the same as I—that unfamiliar need to protect something precious—especially when Fletch left to get a wet cloth. He cleaned the dried blood from Addison's ears and even checked the bite marks on his neck, mostly healed already thanks to the unexplainable magic that surrounded us like a friendly ghost.

Addison barely touched his food. He took three bites before signing, "It's so loud," and wandering off to the living room.

We followed, of course.

He thumbed through our albums, pulled out the Debussy from the night before, and handed it to me before sitting on the floor in front of a speaker. Fletch joined him as I worked the turntable. They sat together, folded with Addison's back to Fletch's front, just like the night before. Cuddling, they rested on the floor as I put the album on the turntable and set it to play.

When the first quiet notes of Debussy's "Clair de Lune" tiptoed into our apartment, Addison grinned. I sat in front of him and watched the changes in his face—first wonder, followed by something like pain, then to joy. His eyes filled with tears as the music developed and built.

Once the song finished, he signed, "I didn't remember it feeling so good."

I nodded. "There are so many new things for you to hear out there."

He grabbed my hand and squeezed—hard—before signing, "Are you abandoning me?"

I glanced over his shoulder at Fletch.

We always had before. Every time we performed another so-called miracle, we usually left our lovers to live new lives. No matter how much good we did, we were monsters paying for past sins, and there was no need to infringe upon light with our damned darkness. But the way Addison stared at me, as if he raged against the mere notion of departure ...

"We will not leave you," Fletch whispered.

Addison leaned back against him and curled his arms up to hold tight to my husband's head.

I didn't know if I had the strength to watch this young thing grow old. I would not damn him, not like us, but I saw no future in which I could watch him waste away and die without losing my sanity. The mere thought of his soft skin wrinkling twisted my stomach as though something beloved had already died.

"Ivy."

The unfamiliar sound of his voice broke my dark reverie.

"Ivy." He said the word slowly as though tasting it. Like his sweat-soaked moans, his voice was deep and resonant, surprising for a man with such elfish features.

I reached forward and squeezed his hand. "My darling."

No, we would not leave him. The eventual pain was worth the present joy. I wrapped them both in my arms and thought not of what might one day be but of what was: the feel of Addison's warm body against mine and the tickle of his hair against my face. One more miracle and not the last—but certainly the one I would never forget.

# FIFTY-FIFTY

## KIKI DELOVELY

I blame technology. How else does a modern day vampire stalk their prey? It sounds like the setup for a bad joke (and I kind of wish it was) but I swear it's the truth. I actually met a vampire through a dating app. It could've gone either way, but we both swiped right on each other. And then she swooped in.

*When and where?*

None of that "hey" bullshit. This one cut to the chase. I wasn't accustomed to such a brazen pursuit but I'll admit I wasn't mad at it.

She had her age set to 99 which I thought was cute and funny, perhaps even a way of warding off the same twenty-something baby dykes that I had no interest in. But no. I mean, maybe the latter as well but she was truly 99 years old. Basically, the vampire equivalent of a baby dyke.

*Meet me at the Lux. 10pm.* (My best attempt at coming off as cool and confident as her.)

I wasn't completely naïve. I told a friend where I was going. My ex, if I'm being honest, but you know how lesbians do—all our closest friends are our exes. Tasha came over and lazily draped herself across my bed, vetoing all my wardrobe choices, interrogating me on my latest date.

I held up a tight little black dress. "How about this one?"

"Too slutty for a first date."

"This one?" A longer light blue number.

"Not slutty enough."

I rolled my eyes and offered up my favorite red dress. The one that hugs the curves of my belly, hips, and ass but has enough coverage to look like I'm not trying too hard.

"Hey! You wore that on *our* first date!" This time I turned around and rolled my eyes in the direction of my overstuffed closet. I was reaching for more options when Tasha continued, "Just kidding. Wear the dress. It totally worked on me." There was something in her tone I couldn't quite place, but she moved on before I could give it too much thought. "Where'd you meet her?"

"Online."

This time the eye-rolling was all hers.

"And what do you know about her?"

She was like a dog with a bone.

"Next to nothing. Her profile is basically empty. Except for her 'Anthem'—some opera song or something."

"Which one?" She was never showy about it but Tasha was clearly more cultured than me.

"Ummm…some type of duet…about flowers maybe?"

"Lakmé. Sous le dôme épais." She chuckled at that but didn't bother to let me in on the joke. "What's her name?"

"Ale."

"A lay? I didn't ask what you were hoping to get out of the evening!" A good ribbing always has been Tasha's love language.

"No. Well, yes, that too, if the stars align. But I'm pretty sure her name is pronounced 'AH-lay'—accent on the first syllable."

"Well, here's hoping that your stars ah-lign." Laughing at her own joke. She always did find herself more hilarious than anyone else. "Just text me by midnight so I know you're not in a ditch somewhere. I don't trust people named Ale."

<hr>

Short for Alessandra as it turned out.

"But no one has called me that for many, many years." I

know it's cliché, but her Italian accent was so damn sexy I was hanging on every syllable.

Her mouth. There was something about it. I would try to focus on what she was saying, to give good eye contact, but my gaze kept being pulled toward her mouth—mesmerized by the formations of her lips, the slight trill of her tongue, the scintillation of her teeth....

"So you're originally from Italy?" As soon as I said it I realized how stupid it sounded but I didn't care. Anything to keep her talking.

"I came here from Italy, yes, but I was born in Egypt. Although I do not recall that time, it was so long ago now...." Ale's voice drifted off even as her mouth continued to move.

She was more striking than I had imagined she would be, possessing a certain magnetism that photos simply do not capture. An unfamiliar but not exactly unpleasant tingle of electricity buzzed just beneath the surface of my skin. It caused every last hair on my body to stand on end—an animalistic instinct I should've heeded. I was too preoccupied imagining her mouth on my neck.

I'm quite certain I was floating somewhere outside of my body when Ale shifted suddenly, drawing me back in.

"I am not a big fan of small talk. Or of this swill they pass off as a red. I have a fantastic bottle of Brunello di Montalcino back at my place that you can practically sink your teeth into."

It was equal parts invitation and assumption.

I usually let them buy me at least a second drink before going home with someone new. But seeing as though my first one had gone untouched minus an initial sip, and I couldn't focus on a damn thing she was saying anyway, I figured why not?

Famous last words, am I right?

She drove us just outside of the city and up the winding mountain roads. Between all the twists and turns combined with the haze that seemed to enshroud me all night, I wouldn't be able to find my way back if my life depended on it. All I know is that we kept gaining altitude because I distinctly recall my ears popping at one point.

Her home, though much smaller, reminded me of photos of European palaces that Tasha had once shown me, decorated elegantly with antiques older and in much better condition than any I had ever laid eyes on.

My hand instinctively reached out to touch one particularly gorgeous piece. "This is, um, real, isn't it?"

Ale smiled, almost condescendingly. "Yes. It is 2,000 years old."

"You've got so many beautiful things." I examined the chandelier above and then the rug below, followed by my scuffed kitten heels that suddenly seemed out of place.

"I am a collector," she began, stepping close enough for me to notice her cool breath against my flushed face, "of beautiful things."

Somehow the line came off as genuine. The nearness of her wasn't hurting either. I felt the heat of my blush under her touch as she stroked the side of my cheek, fingertips lingering lightly under my chin, slowly tilting my head upwards, leading my lips towards hers. What she did next surprised me. Barely brushing my lips with a light peck, Ale pulled back, examining my face with a serious expression and then she turned and walked away. In that moment time stilled and the heartbeat in my clit quickened. The seemingly innocent kiss was far more erotic than any passionate make-out I had been expecting. And it served to leave me wanting, watching helplessly as she crossed the room, pouring two glasses of the decanted wine.

I stood in place, my legs apparently no longer functional, feeling needy and slightly ridiculous. Fortunately she didn't seem to notice, offering me a glass upon her return.

"What do you taste?" The intensity in her eyes could've initiated the fall of Rome.

"Um…I don't know. It tastes…fruity, I guess?"

"Yes," she sighed, "but that is easy. What else?"

I took another sip and shrugged. Ale's scrutiny was making it difficult to concentrate.

"Close your eyes. Now put the glass directly under your nose. Inhale deeply." I did as instructed, I mean, how could I not? Her inflection was both dominating and sensual—a balance I find irresistible. But I'll admit to peeking when I heard a clinking noise. My glimpse revealed her placing a long, shallow box filled with tiny glass vials on the table. "I can hear you blinking."

Bossy *and* brusque. I kind of liked it. So I acquiesced and squeezed my eyelids shut again.

I felt her turn back towards me, moving closer. "What is this scent?"

"Chocolate."

"Now take the glass to your nose again. Two short sniffs, one long. Then sip."

"Oh, wow! I can taste the cocoa!"

She repeated the process several times.

"Dirt?"

"Yes, scorched earth."

"Licorice?"

"Star anise."

"Berries…no, cherries."

"Both."

"Mmmmmm…violets."

"Good."

Then a new clinking noise. One I knew well. The distinct sound of metal on metal. And I could smell it long before it neared my nose. "Ohhhh…leather." Unable to stifle my obvious arousal.

"Very good. So you are familiar with BDSM." Her assumptive habit becoming more apparent as she slid her palm down the inside of my elbow. "Safe, sane, or consensual?"

"Ummmm…are you asking me to choose just one? Isn't it supposed to be all of the above?" She cuffed one wrist, quickly followed by the other. "And I thought we had moved onto risk-aware consensual kink or personal responsabil—"

"Time is up. I choose for you. I will do my best to keep you safe. But do not count on me maintaining a sound state of mind." Ale jerked my arms together behind my back, locking them in place with the restraints. "And you can forget about giving a green light. All I see is red. And in my world red means I take what I want."

I won't lie. It got me wet. It shouldn't have. But it did.

"The notes of leather in this Brunello are exquisite but they remind me of death." She fed me a sip, catching a rogue drip with her tongue. "I prefer the taste of life." Her tongue making its way toward my ear, she continued in a whisper, "My cravings are for an even deeper red, something more viscous, metallic even…."

All night she had been dropping plenty of hints that I simply wasn't picking up. The buzz beneath my flesh felt almost shocking at this point and I began to tremble.

"You will think me ancient but I am quite young for my kind. Just shy of my first century." Only as she slowly and firmly dragged the flat of her tongue along my carotid artery did it begin to sink in. The realization. The pit in my stomach.

"And with us young ones…shall we say…restraint is not one of our virtues. It is…challenging," she struggled with the word, "to not simply drain you dry." The shaking took over my entire body, terrified and still (*still!*) wanting her with every last cell in my being. "You are very beautiful but also quite foolish, no?" It was more of an observation than a question. I knew enough not to answer.

"Open your eyes." I wasn't sure whether she meant physically or metaphorically so I went with the former. Ale stared at me with a violent hunger and I could hardly breathe. My chest jutting forward due to the bondage, I felt as if I were on display for her—another one of her pretty pieces of art.

I jumped as the silence was broken by the trilling of my phone. I had forgotten I set an alarm for just before midnight. "I, uh, have to text my friend Tasha," I chuckled nervously. "Otherwise she'll think you've left me in a ditch somewhere."

An instantaneous regret on my part, a flash of fury in her eyes. "I reserve the right to do exactly that."

Composing her calm once again, she fished my phone out of my purse, half-circled me, and forced my thumb up against the device's concave circle.

Damn technology. Not so secure if your hands are bound behind your back.

Ale quieted the alarm and I could just barely make out the message she typed to Tasha: *I am fine.*

She tossed my phone back into my purse, returning her

attention to me. "I have to be careful. I must take enough blood to leave me sated but not so much as to take your life."

"What, uh, would you say my odds are?" My poor attempt at humor didn't lighten the mood in the slightest.

"To survive the night? Perhaps fifty-fifty." I could tell from her tone that she, on the other hand, was far from kidding and it quickly quieted me into submission.

Eyes downcast, attempting to control my belabored breath, the next thing I noticed was my panties had gone missing, and I had been transported into another room. I didn't even have time to marvel at what a feat of strength it would've taken to lift me so effortlessly as if I were an empty handbag because the thought that I was about to be used as Ale's own personal blood bag clouded my mind. A moment later I was out of my head and back in my body as she strapped more leather across my ankles, thighs, hips, chest, and forehead. With one fluid motion, she had me strung up facing the floor, floating practically weightlessly from various chains, in awe of the sensation of it all instead of bothering to wonder why she had kept my legs together.

Ale slowed her movements purposefully so that I could catch a glimpse of the cock she was about to strap on. Having never seen one quite so long, I inhaled sharply. "Blood is not unlike a good wine in that it possesses distinct notes and layers, some more pleasing to a refined palette." I could hear the cruelty of her smile in her voice. "Personally, while I enjoy the taste of fear, I prefer for it to be equally mixed with pleasure, so trust that while this will certainly be painful, you will revel in the experience as well."

Then silence and I swear I heard a droplet from my slit hit the floor.

With more grace than a gazelle she leapt above me and

must've been supporting her own weight on the chains because all I felt was a slight rustle before the heavy fullness of her inside me. I moaned under her, momentarily forgetting that she fully intended to harm me. The mystery of both the size of her cock and the position of my legs was solved. The extra length served to squeeze between my thighs and accommodate the curve of my ass as she fucked me from behind. Even still, it was a lot to take, but between the rush of fear and thrill of unknown stimuli, I was more than ready.

Ale fucked me with a swiftness that was enough to leave me dizzy but as she sunk her canines into my left shoulder, my vertigo reached new levels. It felt tingly and also a bit like I was on the receiving end of a powerful suction straw used by a dentist.

My screams only intensified her frenzy and she fed harder, fucked more hungrily, working her way up towards my neck as she drank from each bite. She reached around and pinched my nipples hard as my tits swung freely mid-air, then slapped my clit softly but so quickly if I hadn't recognized the effect, I would've sworn her hand never left my pussy.

Her hands were everywhere at once and still only the weight of her cock on me, in me. Each thrust angled perfectly against my G-spot, forcing me to squirt several times in succession, and even when there was nothing left in me, Ale refused to stop, my orgasms bleeding one into the other, unending arousal and agony.

My eyes rolled back, my head spun, I wasn't sure if I would faint from lack of blood or from the exquisite, excessive torture. My vision was tunneled by grey pixels as Ale slammed into me one final time, my cry echoed off the walls, her snarl reverberated within my cells and then everything went black.

I WOKE to headlights blinding me. In a ditch. Nice touch.

All I could see was a silhouette but as soon as I was scooped up I recognized Tasha's scent. She was so warm and felt like home.

"How...how did you know?"

She settled me into her truck and wrapped a blanket around me. "You never miss an opportunity to use a contraction. Let alone the period. Seven exclamation marks, sure? But a period in a one sentence text? Never." She smiled at that then turned serious again. "With three simple words I knew that something was off. I linked your 'find my phone' account to mine a long time ago so I used it to track where you were at."

Maybe technology wasn't all that bad after all.

"I didn't realize you paid so much attention...." I was still feeling hazy. I shook my head a bit as if the movement would bring reality more into focus. Tasha's voice sounded as self-assured as ever, but I felt like I was sitting at the bottom of a pond, trying to make out the words through murky water.

"It's you who isn't detail oriented. Me? I notice everything. Especially when it comes to you." She gave me a stern look brimming with equal parts love and concern before half-circling the truck and jumping behind the wheel.

We drove for a few minutes in silence. I slid across the bank and she wrapped her arm around me.

"Are you...okay?"

I knew exactly what she was asking without having to ask it, and I immediately felt guilty that I had left her worrying so.

"Yes, yes, it was all consensual...well, I mean, not exactly but...um, it's hard to describe." How the hell was I going to explain that I thoroughly enjoyed the most horrific experience of my life? I gradually recounted my version of the evening. Knowing Tasha wouldn't let it slide, but also not wanting to burden her with the most gruesome bits, I edited quite liberally. I knew I'd have to share the full story one day with her, especially as I sensed the possibility of our spark being rekindled, but we had time. In the meantime I could just enjoy the relief of being safely snuggled up next to her warm body.

Even all these months later, knowing now what I *should've* known then, I still wouldn't change a thing, foolish as it may seem. But then again my hindsight has always been more like fifty-fifty.

# THE MARRIED WOMAN

CALYPSO KANE

She wasn't what he was.

When he listened he caught the placid drum of a heart, the steady rush of veins. In the room with her he even felt her heat, a balmy air that refused to stay trapped under her robe. He forced his lungs to breathe again and knew there was nothing under the robe but her. Straining, he convinced himself that he detected a whiff of last week's menses in the dark carpet between her legs.

She was waiting for something to approach. This she did standing by the cellar wall, her fingers grasping the sill of a squat window. Outside he saw the night where he'd been a second before. He had been out there, condensed into a serpent, staring through the grass at her. The moon was only half-present and there had been enough light to reveal her face at the glass without erasing the pane in a white glare.

Her eyes had thrown back the moon the way animals' do when confronted by a lantern.

He had made a habit of searching out those eyes and all other pertinent features of hers for some months. Thus far she had offered many pieces of her for viewing. He had seen her dress and undress, had seen her slip into the scented broth of her tub, had seen her splayed atop the sheets of her bed, bared in deference to the summer. These things he had first witnessed with his usual appetite.

He had had many women in his time.

Always beautiful, if inconsistently succulent. Always a treat, if only in the getting of them. Most lived. Some disappeared. In his greener nights he had drunk deeply and foolishly until he held only a sack of bones. He'd learned to temper himself and to always ruin the wound. Better to have the cattle think there was some cutthroat loose than see punctures in a thick artery, left unhealed by a conversion. But such meals were usually meant only to bleat and die. Not the type of food he played with. The woman he watched now, whispering into the night, had originally been in the latter category.

He had teased himself with the sight of her long enough to warrant it. But there had been more to see than skin. More than the round weight of a breast, more than the sweep of a hip, more than the coils of her hair. A woman could be pretty. A woman could be gorgeous. And, so very rarely, a woman could reach the sublimity that this one did, achieving a level of allure more synonymous with need than lust. Ordinarily, he might have had her the first night he saw such a thing as her. He had before.

He had changed them too. The sublime ones. The ones who would break the frozen block of his heart if he had to imagine them shriveling with age and rotting into the earth. Creatures like them were as rare as horrors like him. It was charity. Certainly it wasn't to keep them to himself. He left that to the hoarders. Supposedly there was some greedy leech living in Romania somewhere, snatching up damsels to dump in some silken corral, like those wealthy enough to gather up exotic pets for a personal zoo.

His own conversions he left to their own business. With advice, of course, explaining the hoaxes of sunlight and crosses, the truths tied with invitation, how garlic was surmountable if one remembered not to breathe, and so forth. But he was neither mentor nor babysitter. Never a lover for longer than a month. There was too much of the world and too much sweet flesh in it to bother with just a single partner.

But even to this tradition he barred the woman in the cellar.

She was smiling now. The action made a plump claret curl under her nose.

Through the window he could see the guest she had said, "Come in," to a moment earlier. He had heard her say it and, in line with the few laws that governed his species, took the invitation for himself. He'd slipped in through the window on the cellar's opposite side. Snake had become bat had become a shadow so thin it had oozed around the locked pane like oil. "Come in," she cooed again. "Come in, come here. It's alright."

The rabbit hopped readily to her. When she reached out her hand it did not run, but laid its head in her palm. She stroked its ear.

He bristled to see it. Just as he had bristled every time before.

Rabbits, squirrels, songbirds, lizards, deer, and even—most apropos—some farmer's stray lamb that had hobbled out of sight and mind of both the shepherd and sheepdog. Others came as well; cats, foxes, crows, and the odd wolf. These she would stroke and shoo. Favored species, he guessed. He had seen her make do with a bear rather than bring the former strays into her cellar. And if there were no bears, well.

That was what the men were for. From the valley on occasion. More often travelers. Not often enough to raise suspicion, mind, but enough for her needs. Her practice required her current chore's performance on the dirt of her cellar once a month. It seemed timed for a week after her own bleeding. He had happened upon her the first time last year while she was bringing that month's guest home. A fellow so bulky with muscle he seemed fat, bearded to the neck, no wedding band on his knuckle. He'd grinned like a cat the whole way to her door.

He'd heard her name for the first time:

"Thought you had a husband to worry about, Vivian."

"I do. But he isn't in the house."

Time would pass before he realized there was a dish of wedding rings she kept by her vanity. More time yet until he heard one of the rumors in the valley, that her husband was moneyed and enraptured enough to have bought her a ring for every day of the month. Certainly he was well off enough that he could build a grand home in the forest's privacy.

Vivian had named her husband. "Elian will be away for some time," she had said, opening her door. "Too long for me."

"What sort of man would leave a thing like you all alone?" asked the man as he pulled the door shut behind him, never seeing the shadow that had stopped at the threshold and stood, bodiless, glaring at his skull. Through the wall the shadow had heard, growing fainter, "Like leaving a steak out in front of a dog…"

Somewhere inside another door had opened. Hollow footsteps had plunked downstairs rather than up.

He had gone to the cellar window. The red smell of Vivian's guest was already floating out to him. He had crushed himself down into a wolf to observe her process. When it was done, she had lifted her head. The bright coins of her eyes had found his, as if always knowing she'd had an audience. Smiling, she had brought a heavy cut of her guest to the window. It was the thickest muscle of the man's arm.

"Here you are, love," she said as she opened the window. The muscle, fat and dripping, coated her hand in gleaming scarlet threads. "I'll have the rest out in the open soon, but first come, first served." Her hand had come out of the window. It had been colder that night and steam had risen from her gift. "Go on. It's yours."

It and everything else. If he'd dared to shed his pelt and take her by the wrist. Not to pull her out, for the frame was too small. No, she would have pulled back in shock and the tug, with his hand still manacled to her, would have been an invitation sans speech. He would have poured in then, would've had her on the carrion bed she had made for them, would have suckled every stain from her fingers, her teats, the secret split in her thighs—

Instead he had taken the flesh from her palm with gentle teeth. She had stroked his ruff, leaving blood and her own scent smeared in the fur. Later, he had still been there when she hauled the rest of the man's remains out to the back of her property. Wolves and foxes and crows and cats had appeared in a hungry swarm to pick them clean. And so his vigil had begun.

A vigil that would end once he was sure of what he had found out here in the wooded night.

A witch, clearly. But what breed?

Witches came in myriad flavors. There were those mistaken for witches simply by dint of knowing what herbs did and enjoying a little skip around a maypole. Others made wishes on crystals, hung up dry flowers, spoke to spirits who might be there or only in their heads. A few could play prophetess or exorcist, maybe toss some blessings and hexes around that actually had noticeable effect. But the ones worth worrying about, certain inhuman parties whispered, were a whole and separate kind unto themselves.

Here in the present, he watched her cradle the rabbit against her as if it were her own child. It was calm in her arms, staring up into the bright chasms of her eyes.

"Thank you. For all you have given, all you give tonight, and all you will give for the nights to follow." Her mouth printed a kiss on the rabbit's brow. "I love you."

At which point her hand snapped shut around the rabbit's neck. There was a muffled crack. When she knelt to begin painting the floor he could see her robe part over a leg. The dark V of her sex peeked out at him. He watched her go down on her knees, watched her crawl in the monthly circle. The rabbit's blood pricked his nose with the coarse tang animal gore always carried. It did not incite any appetite in him.

He'd drunk his fill before coming. His teeth would make no hasty mistake on account of thirst.

Seeing the way the robe hung from the smooth hills of the witch's hind end, he knew this was the night he'd make a far different mistake.

Still, he kept his peace until her chore was finished. The rabbit's blood became a crisper O than Vivian's finger-painting had managed. More precise symbols and sigils flared to scarlet life inside it, ditto the arcane angles of some bastardized star. These pulsed dimly in the earthen floor once before disappearing entirely. Vivian mulled the headless rabbit's pieces—stew or food for her four-legged neighbors?—and then smiled as she rolled one of its feet between her fingers.

"I don't know why they say these are lucky. The rabbit had all four feet and no fortune at all." Vivian lifted her head and nailed her eyes to his own. "Do you eat these or is it only human giblets for your sort?"

He nearly bit through his tongue. It was a bluff. Talking to the wall behind him, perhaps, or whatever spirit had eaten her drawing.

"It's taken you this long to come in, you tick. Will it take you another year to talk?"

"You talk to yourself," he ventured. "I couldn't be sure you addressed me."

Before he could decide against himself, he grew solid. The shadow peeled off the stonework and became the shape of a gentleman. He'd taken pains to piece the look together from modern aristocracy. There were a few wealthy sons and husbands missing beyond the valley in honor of this visit. The leather and gold hung better on him anyway.

Vivian regarded him with no change in expression. Her smile was a carving.

"Look at you dressed up so pretty. I hope I'm not keeping you from some better engagement." She flicked the rabbit's foot to the side. "If you're after one of those powdered debutantes there are cities waiting on the other side of the mountains."

"There are." He took a long step closer. "But I have no other stops in mind tonight."

"No?" She did not move.

Another step.

"No."

"Are you here to have your fortune told?"

Step.

"No."

"Maybe a spell to fix your cold knob?"

Step.

"It isn't cold tonight. I've enough blood in me to flood the valley."

"Then how about a name? You seem to be lacking there."

Step.

"Is Vivian your real name?"

"It might be."

"Then mine might be Victor." It had served well for over a decade.

"Victor meet Vivian," she said, offering her hand. She could only extend it so far—he was less than a foot from her. Heat rose from her crimson fingers.

"Vivian meet Victor," he said, meaning to lock his fist around her hand. He did so. Her hand crushed back as if her bones were iron. And they cooked. Holding too long might have left a tan in the shape of her grip. There were candles standing around the cellar. He wondered if the umber dancing in her eyes were their reflection or some deeper inferno crackling in her skull.

"Did you want to come upstairs, Victor?"

"Anywhere is fine for me, Vivian."

"Upstairs then."

She took him to the steps. Wanting to do something, he willed the candles to snuff out. The perfect blackness was pricked only by the thin moonlight from the windows.

"Thank you," Vivian's silhouette said before producing another light. He mistook it for a candle at first. Looking closer, he saw that a fire was balanced between her first and second fingers.

She led them up from the cellar, past the broad rooms of the first floor, and on up the second flight of stairs. Curiosity could not crane his head one way or the other to investigate the interior. He had spent too long spying through the windows for the rooms to hold any surprises. Including the bedroom. Nothing had changed from the last time he'd peered through its curtains, clinging to the exterior like an insect.

Vivian blew her handheld flame out. The lamps lit themselves in the same breath.

Tarnished gold gleamed while velvet and silk whispered to themselves. The bed was a colossal pond of fabric standing on an ornate rug. The design woven in its nap was a cousin to the one left in the cellar. He had yet to see Vivian bring a guest into this bed. Otherwise he might have introduced himself far earlier and with far more visceral aplomb.

What he had seen instead was Vivian seeing to her own needs. The afterimage of her performances remained branded on his eyelids, replaying themselves no matter what girl he nursed from in her stead. He thought back to the deft hands, circling her nipples to points, tenderizing her breasts into pink hills. Then she would turn herself, arching her buttocks into the air, planting her knees apart. And then she would use one of two methods.

Her own hand, practiced and quick.

Or a tool. Blackly polished, stiffly curved. Running clear oil over it made the shaft flare with tiny symbols. Once she grazed her thigh with its head, the thing crawled up of its own volition. It moved with her without her ever touching it.

Whichever she did, however she did herself, she would drop her mouth open in ecstasy and then—

Then he would have to sink his teeth into his own arm to keep silent. His free hand was put to work, keeping time with her pace.

More than once they had gasped their completion together.

Did she know?

As she turned back the sheets she met his gaze through a fall of hair. Her carved smile had been engraved to higher points on her cheeks.

"You seemed to enjoy seeing me use my little friend in bed. Did you want to meet him yourself?"

"I've considered it." Fashioning the exact details of his consideration, he flung the image into her mind. It succeeded in jolting her a moment. The blazing eyes widened. He allowed himself a flicker of pride. It really was an impressive vision.

He'd filtered it from a compilation of assorted daydreams he'd sampled in the last few months.

Vivian, on hands and knees, being filled from behind by her plaything. Meanwhile she was filled from the front by him. His hand was sunk in the snarl of her hair as the three of them rocked in tandem.

She regarded him across the bed with her expression smoothed back out.

"That is something to consider. But not something I'd consider until after you'd befriended him first."

Then he was struck by an intruding vision of his own. It fell into him like a hammer that nailed the image into his mind's eye for perhaps the next hundred years.

He saw himself howling, hands planted against the ceiling, back to the wall, as the dark base of Vivian's tool sunk to the hilt. It bounced him wildly on its tip. Meanwhile Vivian sprawled on the bed, skimmed through a narrow tome, and slipped apple wedges in her mouth.

The image slithered to the rear of his mind and made room for itself to leap back out at him at intervals forever after.

Vivian batted lashes like wings at him.

"Well? Are you," she gestured below his waist, "open to the experience?"

"I don't believe I am."

"Then he will just have to wait for another night." She regarded his belt. "If you can find yourself under all that supple cowhide, do peel yourself out." Vivian undid the sagging knot of her robe. The cloth fell around her ankles in a silken puddle. "I'll be waiting—," She was about to seat herself on a padded chair. He was already a bare shadow behind her, his raiment piled on the floor.

"No more waiting."

He had her up in his arms in one motion and flat on the bed in a second. When he retreated down to her thighs it was with a fevered scrambling he might have been ashamed of on another night. But she was here, she was under him, and the smell of her was so dense it was a taste. He opened her legs and was paralyzed for an instant by the nearness of that dewed flesh. His tongue grew from him in a long red trail.

When he took his first taste both of them shivered; he from the heat, her from the cold.

"Were you going to do anything down there, Victor?"

"Merely acclimating, Vivian."

So decided, he braced her thighs in both hands and ate. Presently a hand nested itself in his hair and gripped his scalp.

"I was," she breathed, "I was given to believe that your type was more endowed above the neck."

We are, he would have said were his mouth not full.

Instead he produced the rest of his tongue. Inch after inch after inch. Vivian's voice broke up into vowels and curses. He thought she might wrench his head off as neatly as the rabbit's. Another image fell into his mind. He couldn't tell if it was his own or sent from her.

His head, still conscious, removed from his body. She would take it down from a pillow on a shelf to tuck between her legs each night.

He almost spoiled his work with a laugh.

A damp tide misted his chin and filled his nose with the distinctly human aroma of climax.

Human, he reminded himself. Witches, however old or young, were all human at their base. He mulled her thighs. A love bite would fit nicely over this mole or that patch of goose-flesh. But suddenly she was out of his hands. Impossibly.

Just as impossibly she had flipped him on his back. He didn't have time for questions before her hand was on him. He had been growing hard since the second flight of stairs and now was erect nearly to the point of pain. He had no doubts about his longevity—such concerns for their kind were relegated to simply having enough blood to support arousal and he'd glutted himself enough to last a night and a half—but he had lapped at her until she was damp and loose for him. He had no plans to be wasted with a pumping hand.

But she did not seem to share such plans. Both her hands were at work, stroking, tickling, and otherwise operating him like an instrument she had memorized since birth. That she had not bothered to clean the rabbit's blood from her digits did nothing to help his focus. He made his first mess in half the time she'd made hers. It left him in a spray of red-streaked white which showed brightly on the black of the covers. Vivian frowned at this, lifted the soiled sheet, and dabbed most of the stain away on his leg.

"Will you need to rest? Maybe hang from a branch until the blood rushes down?"

"Not at all. But I could use a drink."

"The rabbit is still downstairs."

"No, nothing so robust. I was thinking of something lighter."

Decorum kept him from biting down when she let him nurse from one nipple, then the other. Caution kept him from it through the rest.

He played—or told himself he played—at kissing his way to her throat. His fangs had grazed the line of her artery before he found himself being cupped again. Her fingers had crackled with a telling energy that was worse than heat.

"No marks." Her thumb pressed distressingly against his base. "Can't have my husband asking questions."

"What husband is that? Elian? Abner? Lucien?"

"All the same. He has more names than there are stars. He'd hardly grudge me a few new ones." He paused at the change in her voice. When he pushed himself up he could meet her eyes. They did not see him. They were not eyes.

Set in her sockets were windows filled with the crackle of an endless fire. For only a moment the smell of her was usurped by the odors of charred bone and cooking human fat. She batted her thick lashes once. Her eyes returned. And she waited.

*Run,* her stare said. *Run if you're scared, little tick.*

She quite misread him. Her surprise flashed out at him when she felt him grow stiffer in her hand.

"I'll take great care, then."

He let a hand creep under her to goose.

She fired a tingling spark into his groin.

The inevitable came not long after. Vivian spread herself and Victor slid inside. They made a matching soundless noise, tensing at the canceling of warmth and cold. The moment passed and they went to work.

Once. Twice. Thrice. Again. Again.

Neither party seemed willing to pause or to maintain the same position. Backs changed places on the bed and they took turns with their heads thrown back in the air. A particular image sunk deep into him: the sight of Vivian above, her hair flying in a black arc as her head went back. Her neck stood out in a smooth column. It transfixed him more than the quiver of her breasts, the pliant weight of her in his lap and hands.

His jaws ached from thinking of it. With each climax he found it harder to think of anything else. When it became the only thought he had he began to rut in earnest. He had the blood of four healthy young dandies in his veins and all their unspent energy lacing it. Even with whatever mystic cheat Vivian was using to extend her stamina she began to slow, to focus on breath rather than gasps.

She sighed when he left her. The carven smile had turned lax at the edges. All of her seemed soft and placid. And her eyes were closed.

"That was nice," she announced.

"Only nice?" He spoke with only half a voice. There was a sheaf of hair over her neck. He coiled it around his knuckles and let it drop behind her shoulder. Her eyes stayed shut.

"Very nice," she allowed. "Don't take offense. Most things with a prick never get to use it when I bring them in."

"My thanks for making an exception." He spoke to her sternum, his lips moving against the bone, then the meat of her left breast. His mouth climbed.

"No marks."

"I heard." His tongue trailed over the length of her throat and dipped into her mouth. He wondered if she could taste herself. The kiss broke. "I won't leave a mark."

The converted never bore a mark. They were always licked away and smoothed to cool, inconspicuous flesh. As his teeth broke the skin he tried to inject a reassurance into her bloodstream. A vision of their future.

No more playing the villain of folktales, boxed away in the wilderness with only fodder and fauna for her world. They would fly to the plushest corners of the globe that the treetops and the anchor of her bloodied floor hid from her. Would she keep her magic? Maybe. Maybe not. It would not matter. Not after he shared his gifts through this single rite of pain. No acts of fealty in the cellar required. They would go on agelessly, unbound to anything but their own whims, making livestock and jesters of their former race.

And they would glut themselves on the cattle for the sake of remaking this supple night ad infinitum.

He had his teeth into her up to the gums before she could do more than open her eyes. Her blood rushed into him in a scalding tide. For just a moment he was paralyzed by the flavor of her, like drinking a hearth, a wildfire, a sun—

She could not turn her head well at this angle. But he could still meet her gaze.

Her smile had been carved into a rictus of glee.

Her eyes were fire.

By the time epiphany began to burn on his tongue Vivian's hand was clamped onto his head. The other dug like a pitchfork into his back. He might have screamed if his throat wasn't already an arid tube of ash.

"Thank you. For all you have given, all you give tonight, and all you will give for the nights to follow." She blew a kiss into the candle-spotted gloom. "I love you."

He gurgled weakly against her neck.

Her blood was a molten thing and it made kindling of all it found. The pain was briefer than he expected for incineration. What was worse was the sensation of crumbling. It was a brittle feeling. His bones and veins and the useless atrophied masses of old organs all dried as one. It might have taken a full minute for him to break apart naturally. But Vivian was kind.

Both of her hands snapped shut. Ash burst in grey clouds from her fists. The rest of the shape disintegrated in a cloud that was given no time to settle. Not before the rug beneath the bed sucked the mist of it down into the design of its nap.

Warmth rose up from the rug, through the bed, into her skin. She came a last time as the heat filled her in every way.

"I love you," she said as the candlelight flared into torches and boiled the wax. "No bride ever loved more."

The fires agreed in the crackling language only they and witches know. Then they were gone, leaving only the smoke in the air and the remains sinking into the rug. By morning even the ash was gone.

# SAVING TOBIAS

## JEFF MANN

(for Tiffany Trent)

Tobias Crockett has good taste in accommodations. The Tabard Inn is quaint and historic, full of antiques, paintings, and well-heeled sorts chattering over meals and cocktails. All a bit noisy for me, an undead introvert accustomed to the high, forested silence of West Virginia's Potomac Highlands, so I'm sitting as far away from people as possible, here in a dark corner of the parlor. The ceiling's low and dark-beamed, like the Cape Cod tavern where I used to hunt in the mid-seventies. Tonight's February-gusty, so the big fireplace is in use, flame-light flickering over glossy wood-paneled walls. The few table lamps are turned low, creating an atmosphere of dim intimacy. Perfect for sipping red wine and studying Tobias across the room.

His name befits him. *Tobias.* It's Hebrew for "God is good." God has been good to him indeed. So far. Handsome blond giant, wealthy, talented, powerful, he's as magnificent as Oedipus must have been a few hours before the truth, before the kingly fool thrust the pin of his mother's brooch, his wife's brooch, into his eyes. The truth can do that, certainly. Put out the eyes, splinter the soul, castrate, eviscerate, shatter. The truth is what I bring tonight.

I've had my sights on Tobias for several years now. But with immortality to enjoy, why rush the consummation of a passion? Back during his country-music days, he was one of few men who brought out the bottom in me. His bulk and rough-rebel persona were the reasons, I think. I would examine the images on his CD covers—blond goatee, blue eyes, pouty lips, cowboy hat—and wish he were on top of me thrusting away. When I attended his concerts with my country-boy lover Matt, who's an enthusiast of all things Nashville, I'd watch Tobias swagger the stage, finger his guitar, gift us with that resonant baritone and those macho bad-boy lyrics, and imagine him pushing me over a sawhorse and ramming me with the yee-haw vigor of the Virginia farm boy he used to be. It would be a heady pleasure to be filled up by a man that burly, that much bigger than I. I might even let him come inside me before I turned on him and put him in his place.

But Tobias has, alas, put music behind him for politics. That's his fatal misstep, his *hamartia*, as Aristotle put it when analyzing *Oedipus*. That's what he's doing in DC tonight: using the good looks and charisma that made him a country-music superstar to network with Republican hangers-on and syco-phants. A long way from his Wytheville roots, his glamorous years in Nashville. Now he's a member of Virginia's General Assembly, a busy senator moving back and forth between Rich-mond and Washington, a power broker planning the move from state to national politics. The five middle-aged men sitting with him and guffawing by the fire are probably congressmen. All quite wealthy, judging by the cut of their business suits. And all right-wingers, no doubt of that.

My handsome Tobias should have stuck to songwriting. If he had, the fantasies I entertained about him wouldn't have shifted so radically and moved into the sphere of practical planning. I wouldn't be here tonight, only yards away, admiring his face and body, sipping this cabernet, readying the scourge.

What a fine specimen he is. He leans back in his leather-upholstered chair, drinking beer, grinning at some colleague's joke. His eyes are as blue as the photos on his CD's. He has a full head of curly blond hair, and his goatee is golden brown and closely trimmed, bespeaking carefully controlled wildness. His lips are very full, the lower one so thick it contributes to the surly look he's known for in the press, a pout made all the more dramatic-dark by the rare gleam of his arrogant smiles. The jeans and muscle-shirts of his Nashville days have been replaced by slick politico suits, though he has yet to relinquish his cowboy hats and boots, just to retain the good-ole-boy image that appeals to so many of his conservative constituents. Expert at studying clothed male physiques and discerning how those forms might look stripped bare, I can make out the wide shoulders, thick chest, and beer belly of a well-fed ex-athlete. At his age, mid-forties, the bulk's as much fat as it is muscle, a proportion that has always appealed to me, bear aficionado that I am. Big as he is, he'll keep me snug and warm tonight, after our official meeting.

My kind—Scots Highlanders, mountain men—we love to tell stories. I order a second glass of wine from a lean young waiter with hairy forearms and an angular Mediterranean face shadowed with beard—a muskily aromatic boy who, due to my plans for Tobias, will be spared my sharp attentions tonight—and I think about those whose stories brought me here. Karen, Charlotte, sweet little Chet: three of my handsome senator's ill-fated constituents. Vivid narrative often makes for the most convincing political advice. Once Tobias retires for the night, we'll begin that summit discussion.

As if on cue, Tobias checks his watch, orders a bourbon nightcap, knocks it back, and says goodnight to his little crew of sartorial vipers. It's approaching midnight, and he has early morning meetings, he explains. No distant human ear could pick out his words over the chatter of the parlor, but I can. I can smell him too. As he passes me, heading for his room, he leaves a lingering scent of spicy aftershave, and the sweat-smell of a big man whose deodorant gave out by late afternoon. I lick my lips. Beneath the table, I nudge my hardening cock with the back of my thumb. He will, without a doubt, taste as fine as he smells.

I have had several hundred years to learn the subtleties of strategy, and so I wait for a bit once Tobias leaves. After what will happen to him tonight, I don't want anyone remembering me as a suspicious character who directly followed him out. Instead, I finish my wine slowly. I think of Karen walking into the barn, Chet standing by the creek, Charlotte gasping in the hospital bed. I study the waiter, whose shirt is open one flirtatious button too many to be truly professional, and I make out, in the cleft his open collar makes, the black chest hair I've tasted on so many Middle-Eastern, Italian, and Greek men. Perhaps, upon my next trip to DC, I will have to sample him, though carefully and abstemiously, considering his frail build. With a man as hefty as Tobias, my appetites will have significantly wider range.

It is time. Leaving my asocial nook, I stand by the fire to take in the heat and finish that last sip of wine. Cold as I am, cold since 1730, I gravitate to fireplaces, to any flame, those restless substitutes for the sunlight I am denied. Matt, sweet husbear, pants away summer afternoons stripped to the waist, chopping oak to fill the woodshed, and by the time I rise with dusk, he is richly rank and tastes of sweat-salt all over. With those hard-won cords of wood, he keeps the hearths hot all winter in our snow-swathed Mount Storm farmhouse. Every night, as hard wind rattles the panes, he fixes us hot Scotch toddies, strips us both and pulls me into bed to curl with him beneath the quilts. He wraps his big arms around me, presses his hot, hairy chest and belly against mine and sighs, head lolling dreamily, as I carefully and blissfully feed on him. Sweet boy, he has never entirely reconciled himself to what happens when my rages and my hungers go untrammeled, but he certainly understands my need for erotic and culinary variety, and, as grief-stricken as he's been lately—sobbing on my shoulder every night for a week—I think he understands the necessity of this mission I'm on tonight. The nation, after all, stands in need of improvement.

Outside the Tabard, thickening snowflakes scurry down N Street like swarms of white flies. In order to visit Tobias with complete discretion, I must indulge in a little shape-shifting. That's the ability that Matt has always most envied in me, ever since he found out what I really was, a wintry night much like this one, down by Kanawha Falls. My paranormal powers delight him, especially when I gently pluck his adorable, furry mass into my claws, spread my wings, and give him a ride up to the top of Spruce Knob to take in the summer stars.

So, were there onlookers—and there are not—they might see, striding into tonight's dark DC alley, a tall man dressed in a long black Western duster, sporting unruly, grey-streaked hair and a silver beard. They might see, flying out of the alley, an unnaturally large, hoary-backed, black-winged bat, a bat that methodically hovers by window after window of the Tabard Inn, front and back, looking for ingress, some escape from the cold. To those hypothetical witnesses, the size of the bat would be odd enough; odder still, its presence in midwinter, when it should be hibernating.

Here is Tobias, in a top-floor room in the back of the inn.

He's chosen it for its spacious privacy, its relative isolation, desires that conveniently dovetail with my intentions tonight. I perch on the sill, swaying in the cold wind, hungry darkness on the edge of the light, savoring the warmth so soon to come. He's pulled off his blazer and tie, unbuttoned his dress shirt a few notches, and rolled up his sleeves. The light of a single lamp glints along his forearm fur. He sits at the desk, big fingers working over his laptop. He uncaps a bottle of Scotch, fills a water glass with its amber, slugs it down, and sets out his clothes for tomorrow's meetings.

And then Tobias strips for me. Not that he knows he has an audience. He stands, tugs his shirt over his head, and tosses it on the couch. He pulls off one cowboy boot, then, hopping around, pulls off the other. He unzips his charcoal-gray slacks, shucks them and his boxers down his thick, hairy thighs. For a few seconds, as if aware he has an admirer, he stands naked in front of an ornately framed antique mirror. His back to the window in which I peer, he grins at himself, knowing his power. He grins and lifts his glass to his own reflection. The world is his. His charm knows no limits. Tonight, he sleeps only five blocks from the White House, but in the future, perhaps…

Tobias is built just as my careful study of him in the parlor led me to believe. In the mirror's depths loom his huge football player's shoulders, his chunky pecs, his solid, muscled arms. Only a little blond hair around his nipples and over his sternum, to my disappointment, though there's a decent thatch across his tastily broad, gone-to-seed beer belly, honey-blond fur the color of broom sedge that whispers over abandoned pastures back in Appalachia. His back, turned to me, is wide and muscled; his ass is beefy, smooth, curvaceous, and very pale. It will feel like volcanic velvet beneath my cheek. He's the perfect combination of occasional weight-lifting—my guess is his ego demands that he stay in some kind of shape—and regular gastronomic indulgence—a poor boy who grows up to live high on the hog just can't forego good food and drink.

Ripe, ripe, mature, ripe. Other than the sad sparseness of his chest hair, he's exactly my type.

The proud gentleman from Virginia gulps the last of the glass and steps into the bathroom, beyond the line of my sight. There's the rush and splash of the shower; wafts of steam curl around the frame of the bathroom door.

Time to focus. My membranous darkness and silvery fur dissolve. As glowing chartreuse mist, I hover about the window, find a slight opening between brick and frame—these old buildings are always blessed with expedient little gaps—and enter. Time for Tobias' surprise.

By the time tonight's lover has finished his shower, I'm naked too, cozy coverlet pulled up to my belly, propped up on thick pillows, hands behind my head. If he were gay, he might perhaps—if he were into leatherbears instead of twinks—enjoy the sight of me, my thick beard, my hairy chest and armpits, my tattoos. But he's straight—a nasty homophobe, in fact—and besides, it takes him a few seconds to notice, in the low light, the silent stranger awaiting him. Oblivious, he fumbles about for his robe in a closet at the other end of the large room, pulls it on, belts it, pours himself another shot of Scotch, and then turns toward the bed.

If I were in his shoes—well, in his situation, I should say, since he's barefoot—I might drop the glass in shock. He doesn't. He simply gasps. He tightens his grip on his drink and, born fighter, starts assessing. You can tell from his song lyrics that he was quite the redneck bar-brawler in his day. He's bigger than I am, he figures out fast. I'm naked, I have no weapons in sight. His initial second of fear metamorphoses almost instantly into anger.

Tobias backs up a step and says, low, intense, "Who the fuck are *you*?"

I smile. I stare into his wide blue eyes and start feeling for a purchase in his thoughts. He shakes his head and takes another step back.

"Bad manners, Senator Crockett. Aren't you going to offer me a drink?" I arch luxuriously against the flannel sheet, run my fingers through my silver chest hair, and keep smiling. "I prefer single malt, but I'll settle for that blended you have there."

Two more steps back, then three to the left, and he's put the Scotch on a dresser and pulled a gun out of his suitcase. *That does it*, he thinks. *Checkmate. I was born to take control.*

"I asked you a question. Who the hell are you? And why the *fuck* are you here?" Tobias levels the gun at me. I level my glance at him. I take in that heaving chest, the heartbeat speeding up with adrenalin, the soap-scent of his crotch. I would have preferred him unwashed when I took him. I like to carry a man's dense musk in my beard after we part.

Our eyes lock. I continue to dig. Sensing an intrusion he's never encountered before, he shakes his head again and again, trying to dislodge me. Big man, big will. It's like arm-wrestling. But he's only had forty-some years to gather his strength. I've had centuries.

"Put down the gun, Tobias," I say quietly. "I know you're an avid gun-toter, but those days are over. Put down the gun."

He shakes his head. His big hand begins a fine trembling.

It's intoxicating when they fight me. It makes overpowering them all the more thrilling. Forcing strength and beauty to submit: that's a quest worth the dedication of many lifetimes.

I rummage through his brain, trying to find it, the place from which to rule. Rare is the human whose will I can't subdue. Like wrapping my hand around an uncut diamond, like holding a man's heart-lump in my grasp and squeezing ever so tenderly. The fulcrum with which Archimedes suggested we might move the world.

Here. Here, I think. I press down. Tobias blinks, staggers back, lowering the gun.

"Why don't you put down that gun and fetch me a Scotch?" I'm stroking my beard, smiling at this latest in several centuries of triumphs. And, just when I think my fingers have sunk deep enough to encircle, enslave, his will flexes—an abrupt expansion, a hardening, like the sudden strain of an athlete's biceps. His eyes grow wide, and to my amazement, he shakes me off. He raises the gun, pointing it at my face.

"You tell me who the hell you are, you bastard, and what you want, or I'll blow your head off."

"So you're one of those," I say, sitting up. "You really are remarkable. In all these years, I've met only a handful of men who could do what you just did. Warriors and heroes, every one of them. A magnificent will to match a magnificent body."

"Get the fuck out of my bed, asshole." Tobias waves the gun. "And do it slow, or I'll shoot."

"Yes," I say. "Gladly." I obey. I stand in front of him naked, a mere yard's distance between us.

"What the hell?" Tobias stares down at my erection.

"This is what beauty inspires," I say. "Your fault entirely."

"What are you? Some kind of fucking—?"

That's all he gets out before I leap. I'm on him before he can lift his eyes or draw another breath. In a split-second, his grip's broken, his gun's on the carpet at his feet, and my hands are wrapped around the pulsing trunk of his neck.

"How—?" he gasps, before I dig my thumbs into the flesh over his windpipe and cut off his breath. His big hands claw at mine. His robe falls open as we sway and circle. "Jesus," he croaks. His eyes bulge and water. His face reddens. He's very, very strong; even robbed of air, he weakens very slowly. It takes more time and effort than I ever would have expected to force him backwards, step by straining step, to the bed's edge, to force him down and then back onto the sheets.

"And I was trying to make this meeting as cordial as possible," I say, lying on top of him, his nakedness so warm beneath mine, so moist with terror's sweat. "But of course you're a fighter. I should have known you'd opt for troublesome."

All that blood, pounding in his neck as he bucks beneath me. "You're only making me harder," I say, wrapping my legs around his to subdue his panicked kicks. He's been too proud to try to summon aid, but finally now his fear overcomes that pride. Too late, too little breath left. His cries for help are no more than frantic wheezes. I gaze into his eyes, studying the rapid flickering of his long lashes as he pries futilely at my fingers.

"Please," he says, such a small whisper from such a large man.

"We're not done yet," I say. I kiss his full lips, lightly, then strike his temple with my right knuckles—one sharp rap to the skull, as if his head were a door. He grunts. His blue eyes close. Beneath me, he goes limp.

I leave him there, slumped across the bed. For a few minutes I stand by the door, listening. Silence in the hall, no one roused by the brief struggle. Fetching his abandoned Scotch, I stand by the window, watching the snow sifting down outside. When I'm certain there will be no interruptions, I light a candle, place it on a side-table, and search among his belongings for what's needed next.

---

TOBIAS IS READY NOW. Many hours yet till dawn, so I can take my time, I can savor the Scotch, stretch out in this big bed beside him, relish the sight of him sprawled unconscious on his back—hairy, handsome, and entirely helpless. He's naked now in the candlelight, sleeping his next-to-last sleep. I tousle his blond curls, rub his bearded chin, run a hand over his broad breast. Such a splendor; such an evil. Such a pity that I must erase one in order to erase the other.

With the terrycloth belt of his robe, I've tied his big wrists together in the small of his back. Not snug-tight, the way I like to rope up my sweet lover Matt, but hurtful-tight. Tobias' politics require it. With a leather belt found in his suitcase, I've bound his arms behind him so tightly his elbows almost touch; I want his big muscles contorted, his joints racked. With another leather belt I've cinched his ankles together. To stop his speech, I've tied two dirty white gym socks together at the toes, stuffed his mouth with the fat, foot-sour knot, and secured the ends behind his head. He's exceptionally beautiful this way. The world will be less one loveliness tomorrow.

Tobias shifts beside me, coming awake. Bending over him, I lap his chin. His eyes flicker open, blurry blue. He groans, rolling onto his side. His eyes wander, fall on me, focus. He grits his teeth around the gag, growls deep in his throat, and tries to rise. He fails. His muscles strain. Awareness of his thoroughly powerless position fills his eyes. Truly delicious, such frantic surprise. The trammeled thrashing and stifled shouting begin.

"Keep still, Tobias. You'll hurt yourself," I say, but it's too late. Wide as the bed is, his struggles are so violent that he rolls off the edge, landing on the floor with a thump and a grunt.

I slip off the bed to fetch him. He lies stunned, on his side, knees drawn up in a fetal curl, fists clenched against the small of his back. When his struggles recommence, as do his muffled shouts, I stand astride him, then lift a foot and press it hard against the side of his face.

"Be quiet and keep still, or I'll crush your skull."

He obeys immediately.

"You're going to do what you're told?"

Tobias hesitates a second, then nods. How it must pain him, that reluctant recognition of superior strength.

"Good boy." I bend, heaving him upright. He sways there on bound feet, glaring down at me, panting into the cloth stuffing his mouth, then loses his balance and topples into my arms. I catch him, lifting him beneath shoulders and knees. I can feel him stiffen with shock as I carry him to the window.

"Look. It's still snowing," I say, gazing out into the restless sheets of white, then down at him, folded up in my arms as if he were my son. I smile. "You're wondering how a man so much smaller can pick you up?"

He sucks in air through his nose and nods. Shudders course through him.

"I have a secret," I say, "and some stories to tell."

I carry my captive to the bed, gently lower him onto it, and slip onto the sheets beside him. I gaze down at him, at that well-muscled bulk trussed up tight and panting in candlelight. He stares up at me, eyes moist with terror. I love it when they want to sob but their masculine sense of shame won't allow them. Their eyes grow wet at the edges like a farm pond's ice giving way with spring thaw.

"Take a look at you now," I say, dragging a finger over the delicate pink flesh of his gagged lips. "The Virginia senator has nothing to say?"

Tobias shakes his head slowly. How badly he wants to look away or close his eyes, but he can't. Never in all his most agonizing nightmares could he have imagined himself so powerless.

His shuddering is even more violent now that we're in bed together. Plus the building's old, the room's drafty, snow's swarming the windowpanes.

"Are you cold?"

Tobias nods. "Poor boy," I sigh. Stretching out on my back beside him, I pull the covers over us, lean back on the pillows heaped against the headboard, and say, "Put your head on my chest." Bound as tightly as he is, it takes a little squirming on his part, a little nudging on mine, till the weight of his big head rests over my heart.

"Isn't this sweet?" I sigh, wrapping an arm around him. "You feel so good against me. Comfortable?"

Tobias shakes his head emphatically. Behind the sock-knot a grunted "Huh uh."

Chuckling, I play with the hair fringing his nipples. He stiffens against me; jagged trembling runs through him.

"You hate this, don't you? My touching you?"

A slow nod. More trembling.

"Good. Would you like to know why I'm here? Other than to do this?" I tug at his belly-hair now, squeeze the thick muscles of his shoulders and arms, the thick meat of his chest. "Other than to pay homage to your considerable might?"

"Ummm mmm," he mumbles into the socks, breathing heavily through his nose. I pull him closer, sip my Scotch, and stroke his head of golden curls.

"Let me begin with this," I say. Even after these several centuries, I can't keep the sorrow from my voice, stern as I might want to sound tonight. "In 1730, my lover Angus and I were caught making love, attacked by a gang of men like you. Men who thought their God hated us. Angus died. He was stabbed to death. I was saved for another life."

Tobias emits a low, long groan. His shaking grows more violent.

"Do you understand? This is why I am stronger and faster than you could ever be, why my skin is so chilly against you."

Tobias shakes his head. He gives a small sob.

"You're still shivering. Are you still cold? I am as well. Here, let me hold you closer." Rolling him onto his side, I curl up against him, his broad back to my chest. My left arm pillows his head, my right arm I wrap around him.

"Better. Ah, you're so, so warm," I say, caressing his beefy chest beneath the blanket. "Tobias, do you remember that hateful amendment you helped pass? The one outlawing same-sex marriages in Virginia? The one insuring that 'any contracts between same-sex couples that might approximate marriage would be illegal'? I think that was the wording. Tonight really began there. And with three people with whose fates I'm familiar. I wish you could have known them. Perhaps then you and I would never have met."

I rest my palm against his breastbone. His heart drums madly beneath my hand. I nuzzle his nape, smell the blood coursing beneath his thin, fragile skin, and lick my lips.

"There was Charlotte, a bar-buddy of my lover Matt's. She was driving home one night when a drunk driver hit her head-on. Her lover Grace was barred from her hospital room. Thanks to your amendment, Grace was not considered family. So Charlotte died alone. Can you imagine that?"

Another choked sob. A gag-muffled "No," a shaking of the head.

"Then there was Karen, Matt's friend from college years ago. Her ex-husband swore to identify her as a lesbian in court if she fought him for custody of their two sons. She hanged herself in her barn. That's the kind of world your laws help create, Tobias. Can you see that?"

"No, no." Muffled, but louder.

"And sweet little Chet, Matt's cousin. Just sixteen years old. Thanks to your adept political maneuvering and all your fundamentalist friends, his high school wouldn't allow a gay-straight alliance. No sympathy from his parents, who told him he was a damned-to-hell monster. The boy drowned himself in Peak Creek last week. My lover's been weeping on and off ever since."

As I whisper in Tobias' ear, I press my hand over his brow, and inside his skull I cause them to appear, the consequences of his demagogical bluster: the bloated body hung off creaking rafters, the pale limbs splayed in gray water, the woman sobbing in a hospital waiting room. Beneath my palm, the images cascade through his brain, on and on, on and on, the pain, the deaths, the fear he's helped create.

Enough. I lift my hand from his forehead, and the stream of stories stops. "They were my kin. Now do you see why I'm here?"

This time a nod. This time a sock-muted "Yes." This time an unchecked stream of silent tears I wipe from his cheeks with my thumb.

"Good." For a full minute I stroke his streaming cheeks, tasting the salt, the remorse, the appetizer of brine. Suddenly, roughly, I roll him onto his belly, climb on top of him, and clamp one hand over his gagged mouth.

"What a Christian," I say, stroking the fuzzy crevice between his buttocks. Tobias gasps beneath my grip; his broad shoulders heave.

"Here's your salvation," I say, spitting into my palm, then moistening us both. "Here's your forgiveness." I burrow a wet fingertip into him, and his muscles spasm against me. Manly beauty has always inspired in me an urge to possess, dominate, punish, and control. But the combination of beauty and hatefulness that Tobias embodies sparks in me a sadism no human can long survive.

Were I to give him the benefit of the doubt, I might assume that these sobs wracking him are born of guilt in the face of the destruction I've shown him, the misery he's helped create. I suspect, however, that what's really evoking his tears is the certainty of what's about to come, as well as the bodily pain I'm causing as I roughly push one finger in. Men I respect, men like my lover Matt, I take slowly, solicitously. Tobias, well, I'm using very little spit and very little patience.

"Sweet country boy, sweet virile Virginia virgin. You're so

tight and sweet and soft inside," I sigh, wedging a wet second finger in. He jerks and whines. Sobs shake him like winter rattling the windowpane.

"If you were fat and old and homely, like most of your right-wing colleagues, you'd be spared this," I say, pulling out my fingers only to nudge my moistened cock against his tightness. "This is what comes of being so proud and handsome," I say, pushing into him an inch.

Now he goes wild beneath me, screaming against my hand, tugging on his bonds, thrashing and bucking. I love such resistance. It only highlights my own supernatural strength. Wrapping an arm around his torso, I let him flail and shout for a minute or two before shoving my cock's entire length into him and simultaneously burying my fangs in his sweaty neck.

I pump into Tobias, Tobias' blood pumps into me. Contrapuntal rhythm. Ass full, mouth full. Spilling not a drop, I gulp down his strength, his will, his youth, his manhood; my gray hair, beard, and chest pelt slowly blacken in answer. Beneath my hand, he keeps screaming for a while. Beneath my weight, he keeps thrashing for a while. Then, as the tide of his blood recedes, the screams slow, dwindling to barely audible pleas, and the struggles slacken.

Practice allows me perfect timing: I retract my fangs just before he passes out but well after he's too weak to put up any further fight. He simply lies there now, wheezing beneath me with each cock-thrust, bound hands fumbling at nothing, brushing my belly hair as I ride him hard. Occasionally, in response to a particularly savage slamming, he manages a muffled groan. This is a judicial ecstasy I've been long yearning for, so, as much as I would enjoy prolonging this, I'm soon done.

Wrapping an arm around his throat, I shove into him one last time, shudder, grunt, explode.

I wake with a start. Sated, I've been happily drowsing on top of him. It is, I sense, about four hours before daybreak. The candle has burnt low. Snow still fills the windowpanes with busy, silent static.

I roll off Tobias and lie beside him. His bonds and gag are still in place; he's still breathing, still conscious. Eyelashes fluttering, slowly he shifts his stare from the sheet to my face. In the candlelight, his cheeks gleam with tears. I kiss his gold-brown goatee and his bloodied neck. I press my lips to his big ass, lap the smooth, pale skin there, the red marks my fingernails left, then spread his cheeks and push my tongue inside him to harvest violation's crimson ooze. What might he have been without evangelical poison in him, the Christians' vicious piety?

He's perfectly still as I untie his elbows, hands, and feet. When I prop him up into a sitting position, he slumps against me. When I heft him with eldritch ease into my arms, huge man that he is, his head falls against my face, his arms bounce loosely.

"It's time to end this, Tobias," I whisper. Around the knot of the sock-gag, he takes a deep breath. Exhaling slowly, he nods acquiescence against my beard.

The bathroom is even colder than the bedroom. It's spacious, with a marble sink covered with the tentacles of potted plants, a window of glass bricks against which the thickening snow bats. The shower is simply a tiled corner without a curtain, with a big floor-drain down which I might later rinse any scarlet stains my hunger misses.

Carefully I shift docile Tobias from my arms to the floor, turn the water on, adjust its temperature, then drag him into the streaming wet warmth. On the floor I sit cross-legged with him in my arms, his heavy linebacker's body cradled in my lap. I nuzzle his gagged mouth, then loosen the socks, let the silencing circle of knotted cloth fall around his neck, and kiss him tenderly on the lips. I caress his rapidly moistening curls, his nipples, his fading heartbeat. His head sags against my shoulder. He hasn't strength enough to groan.

Warm water sluices through my shaggy dark hair, running through my beard to drip over his face. It runs down his thick torso, his hairy belly, and mats up his pubes. I cup his flaccid cock in my hand. "Warm enough?"

His lips move silently. Another long draught and he'll be done.

"I'm Derek Maclaine," I say, apropos of nothing.

"You are so beautiful," I sigh, rocking him in my arms. "You were so strong. You could have been so good, so true. Why did you listen to them? What a warrior you could have made. What a brother-in-arms. I would have been proud to love you."

Lifting his limp right hand from the tiles, I hold it in mine. When I squeeze it, with what life he has left he returns the pressure.

I gaze down into Tobias' glazed blue eyes for a long time. "It's all right," I say, smoothing curls off his brow. "Sweet boy."

He smiles up at me sleepily. He lifts his free hand to touch the barbed wire inked into my upper arm, then, with a visible effort, reaches up to brush my tangled black hair and beard before his fingers droop and his hand drops exhausted into his lap.

"Here You are," he whispers in disbelief, words so weak even I can barely discern them. "It's You. You. Oh, Lord, oh, Jesus, I been waiting for You."

Together we listen to the snow-wind beyond the walls, holding hands in the steamy rush of the shower. Prisoners of necessity, we are both late for different destinations, and it is nearly dawn, nearly time to part, but let us sit here for a while yet, pressed together in this warm womb hemmed in by winter. I will stay with Tobias till he closes his eyes, till his hand releases mine, till, soon, soon, he needs me no longer.

# MERCY

---

## MARÍA DUENDÍ

C an I ask you a favor?"

I looked up at the man behind me. I had often thought about his jugular, painted across the side of his neck, curving under his beard. I had been watching it for a week as he sat at the other end of the table. And his hands. And the broadness of his shoulders.

We were in a co-working space, a room that anyone could come to, twenty-four hours a day, seven days a week, and work on individual projects—freelancers, mostly. And oh, how boring my freelancing was! I was good enough at it, though, that it cost me nearly nothing of my productivity to look at the people around me. There was the woman in the Cleopatra wig who edited portraits of people's pets on a slick laptop. There was also the large man whose fingers flew across his tiny keyboard and who spoke softly into a headset to his kids. They lived with their mother in Australia, and he liked to catch them after school.

None of them were potential victims. I hunted in a different way.

The man behind me was older than me in appearance—although I was probably older than him when his first ancestors came to America. His veins throbbed in a painfully sweet rhythm, lighting him up in shades of red.

He was blushing as I turned around. If I was still human, I would have blushed too—a collar of pink and red around my neck.

"Can I ask you a favor?" His voice sounded like that of someone who had given up smoking years ago, but still retained a raspiness to their voice.

I raised my eyebrows, gesturing for him to continue. I

fiddled a bit with my hair, down to my tailbone when not in a bun, to make me look less still, more human.

He looked like someone who had never tripped over his words in his life, certainly not over a pretty pale girl in a drab gray t-shirt and jeans for want of washing due to a lack of laundry money. "A, er, couple of my files are about to go dark and I need to save them. Do you—"

"Flash drive?" I guessed.

He grinned confidently. "Yeah."

I rifled through my bag—mouthwash, toothpicks, perfumes both alluring and refreshing, that stayed true to their scent since I excreted few pheromones now.

I found the flash drive—black, utilitarian—and handed it to him.

"Thanks," he said, barely registering the flash drive in his hand. He put out his other hand. "I'm Cal. What's your name?"

*Ah,* I thought. *Here we go.* Nearly three hundred and seventy years, and it always started the same. I liked it—the sameness, the rhythm. I liked it especially with him, now that he had dropped the blushing routine and was more direct.

But then, there was the matter of my actual name.

"Paysh," I said quickly.

"Hm," he replied. "Is that short for something?"

I sighed and rolled my eyes inwardly. This was the same too. The young men who I consumed were especially interested in my name. "Patience," they'd say, as I ripped off their clothes. "Don't seem too patient right now, do you?" The feel of my teeth against the most sensitive parts of their bodies often stopped the joke.

I said my name very quickly, attempting to brook no comments.

"Patience," he repeated. "Old-fashioned."

I smiled. He had no idea. I was born during a time when parents thought they could imbue a virtue into a child by giving the baby its name. I doubt it worked for many. It certainly didn't for me. I had no patience for chores, for minding my brothers and sisters, for waiting till marriage to feel a hand up my skirt. And that's where the trouble started, really, and how I became acquainted with the Horned One and his mercy.

"So, Paysh," he said, and I noticed he took a moment to relish it. "What are you working on?"

I rolled my eyes for real this time. "I'm part of a community—you know, Sevensies?"

"Oh yeah," he replied. "Odd jobs."

"Mhmm." I tilted the screen towards him and his chin practically rested on my shoulder. The heat of his blood was making me dizzy.

"Accounting," he said, and chuckled. "Very exciting."

"What did you think I was doing then?" I said, laughing too. The accent of my former life, Yorkshire with a dash of flat American, revealed itself.

"Oh, I don't know. Escort service?" I put my hand to my mouth to stifle my laughter, and his head knocked against my shoulder.

"So what do you do over there?"

"I grade EFL students' papers from China," he replied. "It's just easier to be up for their questions or complaints."

"Oh," I said. "Do you teach?"

He shook his head. "I used to but—" He grew quiet. "I need to get back to it. There's probably a virtual line of them."

I nodded. "Nice to meet you, Cal." He smiled in response.

The next night, I arrived to my part of the table to find a

coffee cup waiting for me. I put my computer down and sniffed it, an aroma thick and rich rising from it. The liquid was a dark brown, almost black, with a single marshmallow in the center.

Cal spotted me and walked briskly over to me. He raised his eyebrows as if to ask if I liked it. I took a long swallow and its heat made my body throb.

Thick and rich, hot and sweet. Just like the blood I imagined dribbling down Cal's neck.

"So," he asked, watching my neck as I drank, "do you like it?"

I moaned with pleasure, amplifying it more than I normally would have so he could hear.

He chuckled. "Yes," he said. "I think you do."

"Thanks," I said, and unpacked my laptop. "Where'd you get it?"

He smiled widely. "There's this place a few blocks away. Ange Noir?" He waited a beat to give me a chance to respond.

I shook my head, as I'm sure he expected me to do. Even in the twenty-first century, courtship is a dance. My victims were never a part of such a waltz, and it had been a long time since I had had such an attractive partner as Cal.

"It's nice. Dark, candles. Sometimes they have live music." *Sounds vampy*, I thought. I raised an eyebrow. Cal might know more about me than I thought. Whatever, it wasn't illegal to be a vampire, not anymore. It was just dangerous for the innocents that crossed paths with the unscrupulous.

Unscrupulous like me.

"Are you asking me out?" I asked, a smile playing on my lips.

"Yeah," he said, and stood still. He didn't fiddle with his fingers or shift his weight from one foot to the other. He just waited, but his eyes filled with doubt when I didn't respond. "Let me guess," he said. "You don't 'do' dates."

It wasn't that I didn't "do" dates. I did do them, in a way.

As my friend Sonia had put it, "You hunt drunk freshmen who have strayed from the University and lost their car keys in the snow."

Lost, sometimes. Many times, stolen. I didn't need unnatural stealth or quickness, just my skills as a pickpocket learned in the narrow streets of Boston a long time ago.

"Oh my god," I'd say, in the flattest American accent I could conjure, adding a girlish high pitch to my voice. "Did you lose your car keys?"

He'd nod. "I parked somewhere—" he'd look around at the dead end I lived in, tapered like a spider's web, vibrating with the noise of laughter and music coming from the local bars.

He hadn't parked anywhere near it.

"Well," I'd say. "Do you need help? Order a cab, maybe?"

"Yeah. yeah," he'd say, continue to pat his pockets while stealing glances at me.

"You can call from my place?" I'd say, and grin.

He'd shake his head. "I don't want to bother you. And I have a cell—" He'd slip his hand in his pocket. "Shit," he'd say. "I lost my phone too."

"Come on," I'd say, placing a gentle but firm hold on his wrist and pulling him towards my apartment. "I left my phone upstairs."

It didn't take too long to get their clothes off. They'd squint at me, as if that would stop the spinning, and say something like, "God, you're really hot. Damn."

I'd come closer, my breath heavy from want of blood—what he thought was want of his body.

"You too," I'd breathe, and kiss him.

He'd grunt and take off his clothes—a button-down under

his sweater and khakis seemed to be the uniform for young men who lost their car keys.

Their bodies were almost the same—hair or not, attempts at carving pecs that had been quickly abandoned, the start of a beer belly protruding under the skin.

Down I would go, my clothes still on while I swallowed his cock. I loved this part. My lips were sensitive from the desire to drink blood, and I found immense pleasure from moving up and down his rod with my mouth.

I would stop after a few minutes, knowing that these college boys were always ready to come with as little stimulation as the wink of an eye. I would invite him to take off my clothes, which he would do clumsily. I didn't wear anything with buttons or hooks because of that.

Removing my shirt was always a cause of wonder on the part of the young man. "Holy shit," he'd say. "They, like, defy gravity." Or something similar. They were quite perfect, as I was told week after week, dark nipples embossed on my white breasts. I'd take a hand and place it on one of my tits. His mouth quickly followed. I would moan, just a little, until I was almost as turned on as him. The rest of me, however, was focused on food.

When I couldn't resist any more—the lust for blood and the lust for a hard cock thrusting inside me—I made him lie down on the bed and mounted him. Many of my vampire friends my age had had problems with lubrication, but I never had. I was always sopping when it came to this part of the hunt.

I kept the pace, my hips undulating as I took him in my entrance. I'd moan, I'd screech, and I'd paw at him. Part of it was true. I enjoyed sex and nowadays it was only when I was hunting that I had any of it. I had other things on my mind when I wasn't hunting, like putting money together to survive. I'd slow down so he could catch his breath. "Man," he'd say. "Wait till I tell the other guys. Wow."

It was almost like a cue. "Too bad," I'd say, panting, "you won't get a chance." I bared my fangs but they barely registered to whoever was under me. I'd keep fucking him, until I could tell he was about to come. And then I would strike.

His moans would become screams as I pierced his skin. I kept taking him inside me, milking his dick while I milked his blood.

Finally, he would come, in time with the last drops of blood that stained my mouth. A fine orgasm. It was the least I could give him in exchange for my sustenance.

I guess it was a dance, one that was not as deeply intriguing than the one I was currently engaged in. It had been decades since I had met someone who seemed worthy of being a true lover—magnetic, confident. Cal seemed to be all of these things.

"So," Cal asked, bringing me back from my thoughts. "What do you think?"

I looked into his eyes, and gave a small shrug of my shoulders. "I can make an exception," I said.

THAT DAY, as the sky went from dark to blue, I dreamt about Cal. In the dream, he held himself over me, his glasses off and revealing a pair of playful black eyes. He settled his knees between my legs and I breathed his weight in, his skin scorching mine.

He ran a finger down the middle of me, throat to navel. I felt like he had total control of my body, and he could move it any way he wanted.

His large hands ran down my curves, teasing the sides of my breasts, outlining my pubis without coming near my clit. His dick grew hard as it lay near my hot opening.

He ran his hands down my body again, firmer, this time coming closer to my nipples, inching towards my clit. He used his nails, feathery at first but then sharper. I nearly cried out from the pressure building in my bud—and he hadn't even kissed me or touched the spots I desperately wanted him to.

"Please!" I moaned.

"What?" he asked innocently. "What do you need?" His face hovered over mine—those delicious looking lips that I wouldn't mind sucking until they could give me no more. He thrust at me, his dick right above my hole.

I panted. He was too big for me to turn over, even if that was what he was expecting. My body was built more for slyness than strength. I could talk my way out of anything, but not get out of something using brute force.

He gave a little sound of sympathy, and raked a fingernail down my nipple. My back arched, wanting more.

He smiled, and kissed me deeply. I held onto his tongue with my fangs, wringing out more than a few drops of his honey-laced blood.

He rolled me over on my belly.

I woke up with my hand buried deep in my snatch, stroking my clit furiously. Images from the dream came to mind, other scenarios that hadn't happened yet filled me like I wanted, so very badly, for him to fill me.

I came with a loud howl, and I hoped that I hadn't disturbed the other vampires in the boarding house. I got up and removed my t-shirt, plucking at my nipples to remember the sensation of the orgasm I had just had. I took a shower and picked out my clothing for the night. I picked a long-sleeved brown silk shirt with a neckline that nearly came to the navel. I made it more decent with strings of beads across my chest. A pair of black linen pants came on next, the material so thin that you could feel my ass under it and know that I wasn't wearing so much as a thong.

I drove to the place Cal had told me about, Ange Noir, and I was disappointed when I came in. It was even vampier than I thought. Red velvet, candles inside smoke-blacked holders. A vampire stood on the tiny stage in the back and sang songs from "the old country."

The waitress, human, came to take my order. There was no alcohol served and I wasn't hungry for blood, so I settled for another hot chocolate. And I waited.

I waited three hours, near closing time, and Cal did not show up.

The manager of the house, a black vampire with blonde slicked back hair, came to my table.

"I sense that you are unsatisfied, pilgrim girl."

I rolled my eyes. There were those vampires who made it a hobby to guess the period of time during which someone had turned. It was a parlor trick, like being able to predict some-one's drink at a party.

"I was waiting for someone," I said. I tried to swallow the lump in my throat.

He nodded. "I see. I see. A companion."

I shrugged and buttoned the last button on my coat, leaving without speaking further.

I came to the co-working space ready to feel humiliated, a

sensation that was unfamiliar and very uncomfortable. I had grown so angry at the thought of what had happened that I had nearly stolen another phone and fed again, even though I still had days to go before I had to feed.

But he didn't show up. Not the next day, or the next. My anger soon gave over to concern, but I had no email, no phone number to reach him at. All I had was the sensation of wanting to cry, and being unable to.

Cleopatra Wig summoned me on the third day. She minced no words when she found a spot in a corner, obscured by empty bookshelves.

"Cancer," she said. "Terminal." She removed an e-cigarette from a pouch at her side and pulled.

I started to say something about whether she should be vaping in the co-working space, but stopped myself. All that I needed to care about, to know, was in this woman's head.

The air smelled like crème brûlée after she vaped. "Ah," she breathed.

"It's not true," I insisted. "We saw him a few days ago. He looked fine."

I'd once had a lover whose brother had been healthy, a mountain climber—and then, from one day to the next, he had dried up like a corn husk from cancer. It could be, and my heart pounded harder than it should have.

"H-how do you know?"

"I heard him talking to his wife." She let the last word drift, waited for my response. I nearly scoffed. I had left a line of grieving widows in my wake. It mattered nothing to me.

"Did she say when, or—"

"Testing," replied Cleopatra Wig, as if putting herself in the role of diviner. "That's probably why he is away."

I nodded. "Okay," I said, standing up, my shoulders seeming to drag farther towards the floor than a few minutes before. There was an ache in my body, as if I had been parted down the middle. Cal's and my jokes seemed to stop. That's what I was worried about.

He came back on the fifth day. I didn't notice him coming in because I had an angry new client on my hands. Apparently, there had been some huge mistakes in their reports, and they were threatening to leave a bad review if I didn't fix them ASAP. I wasn't one of those vampires who had a hoard of money in a French chateau. I was more the mouse being trod underfoot, always hustling for another source of money.

I looked up to focus my eyes and there he was. He was drawn into himself, and his polo shirt was too big. He seemed to be without the vigor that I had sensed in him just a few days before.

He didn't carry a computer bag, or an umbrella to shield him from the rain outside. It seemed like he didn't intend to stay long.

Our eyes met, and he came over to my side of the table. "Hey," he said, and tapped my left hand before taking it into his own. "I need to talk to you."

I let him hold my hand as we walked out of the building, under the green awning. The rain pelted it with drops.

"You should know that I have cancer," he said, as if he had rehearsed it many times before, as if he had given the speech a hundred times already.

"I know," I piped up.

"Who told you?"

"Cleopatra Wig," I said, uselessly jerking my head in the direction of the co-working space.

"That was none of her fucking business," he seethed. I stepped back before his ire.

I tried to calm him down. "She said she heard you talking to your *wife*." I smirked.

He laughed, the coals in his eyes dying down. "Oh," he said. "My sister. Yeah, she's made my death her latest project."

I folded my arms and waited for him to continue. I fought the temptation to rock back and forth on my heels.

Cal broke the awkward pause, finally. "I need to ask you something."

*Something new. A turn in the waltz.*

I nodded distractedly. Inside, my computer admonished me with its large square eye of a monitor, and the client's numbers danced on it.

"You see, these treatments are...terrible," he said. "Agony. Like something is eating you from the inside out. I can't even taste food right."

I nodded again, imagining the blank stars on my Sevensies profile.

"I'm supposed to do them until I die," he said. "Supposedly they're better than the alternative: the living envy the dead when they're not being treated with the chemicals they've been giving me."

"I'm sorry," I said, while I did calculations in my head.

"Don't be," he said gently. "I-I think you can help me."

I shook my head and laughed, although I knew what was coming. "Try your luck," I said, my voice suddenly high-pitched.

My stomach sank with a heaviness like a bowling ball before he said it.

"I want you to kill me."

I pursed my lips. "I'm not a hospice," I said. There were some services set up like that, for those who didn't have the stomach for doing themselves in. The vampires wore latex gloves and pat assurances, smiling sweetly before taking a bite.

His eyes twinkled and he looked into my eyes. He smiled for the first time during our entire exchange.

"No," he said, "I think you'll be more *fun*." I smiled uneasily and we began to walk together.

I started to doubt the plan as his black SUV came into view. I stopped walking. "I can't do this," I said.

He turned around. "Why?"

I shrugged. "It's not what I do." The Horned One knew how many screams I had plowed through to orgasm, with no feeling but hunger and the satisfaction of survival.

"So... you don't fuck?" he asked.

"Of course I do," I replied.

He ran his tongue along his teeth just long enough to tantalize me. "And you don't feed?" He bit back a snicker. I couldn't see his jugular in the moonlight, but remembered the way it pulsated against his collar under the fluorescent lights of the co-working space.

"I don't..." Do nice things, is what I wanted to say. To keep living, you had to walk forward, let cries for help fall to each side of you—the beggars, the young vampires looking for guidance. They all had to fall away. Satisfied with my reasoning, I turned around and walked away.

"What about mercy, then?" he asked.

I stopped, but didn't turn around. "Mercy and survival don't mix," I snapped.

*Mercy.* That's why the Horned One said he saved me from the fire that I had been thrown into by the elders in our village after being caught with the chaplain. Afterward, the Horned One had set me down in a forest nearby, in a shed.

Then he did his work. He put his mouth to my neck and revealed a pair of fangs that I couldn't see, only feel. I grunted softly and tries to get my weakened body to move, but his hand held me down. My lungs felt solid now, like alabaster.

A chill settled over me, but I was alive. I looked up at my savior—a man properly dressed with a tall hat and buckled shoes, with coal-black hair and eyes that burned red.

I understood. The Horned One may give at times, but he always took. Fully aware of what was happening now, I started to unlace my bodice, guiding him towards me.

He stroked my cheek. "No, Patience," he said. "For mercy."

My life, as it was, had been made from mercy, and now it seemed like I was being called to show mercy like the Horned One had. I didn't relish the idea. I enjoyed bloodplay during my trysts with lovers decades and centuries ago, but they did not end in being drained.

It wasn't a tryst that he wanted, anyway. It seemed to be more serious, more passionate, what he wanted. His eyes were alive with the depth of the things he was carrying.

*Maybe I could change his mind,* I thought, and then shook my head. I should care about him just as the Horned One did about me, in the end. A small act of goodness in a sea of wrong. The person didn't matter.

I turned around and he came towards me. "Fucking. Feeding. Mercy," he said. He put a hand to my cheek. He put his mouth over mine, grabbing the back of my neck with one hand and letting the other roam over my breasts. I moaned rhythmically as he placed his knee between my legs and he ground it into my pussy. I used my free hand to feel his package. It was promising, very promising—

Suddenly, he stopped. He stepped away and raised his eyebrows. "See?" he walked around the car to open the door on the passenger side. Thoroughly convinced, I stepped into the car.

He had wanted to go to his place, but I insisted on mine. He cited reasons—disposal, cleanup—all the things to consider that his sister had come up with from the Internet.

"Don't worry about all that," I assured him. There were plenty of disposal options in a boarding house full of vampires. My preferred method was the incinerator, the largeness of which was emphasized to me when I had first toured the house.

He thought about this when I told him. "Hmm," he said. "Well, I guess she can't account for everything." He laughed, and it made me foolishly happy. Then he stopped. "But what about you, what about any connection to me—"

It was my turn to laugh. "Oh." I said, lightly. "I'll be long gone before morning." I took a deep breath. The stock of frat boys was running low, and it wasn't going to be long before people saw the patterns between lost cars, a dead end, and a boarding house full of vampires.

We soon came upon the squat, five story building that was my boarding house, made up of drab, faded brick and crumbling mortar. It was crowned with lights that were meant to repel more than attract, and a door painted a subtle shade of slate.

Cal turned to me as if to say, "Is that it?" before stopping and parking the car. Before he opened the passenger door, he leaned over and kissed me. Shivers of dread and arousal ran up my spine. Something told me I would not survive the night—my heart, or my body.

"Cheery," Cal quipped, when we came through the door of my room. The walls were exposed brick, and nothing hung on them, except for a slip or two of Italian silk I was able to steal from the house of a former lover. The floor was knee deep in clothing tangled around itself—mostly clothing I had discarded to decide on an outfit to meet Cal at Ange Noir. Other than a surprisingly clean (but useless to me) bathroom, my room was my entire living space, but it was *my* space, and I could control it however I wished—it, or whoever was in it.

Cal got onto the bed and raised an eyebrow. "This? Really?" he asked. He patted it. "I have a real mattress," he said. "Covered in plastic for tonight but still." He sighed. He looked up at me. "I mean, don't you have anything to absorb the mess?" He didn't hesitate over "mess," even though we both knew "mess" meant "him."

I scooted over next to him so that we were side by side. "I'm very clean about it," I said, and disgusted myself by how I sounded—as if I had done it before, as if it meant nothing.

It meant too much to someone who spent her weekends hunting drunk college boys.

I felt heavy and repulsive. Time to get on with it. I jumped onto his lap, brushing my breasts against his mouth. He groaned in surprise and started to knead them through my shirt, but moved his face away when I thrust my tongue out and tried to kiss him.

"No," he said gently, and put his hands on my waist. He looked up at me and our eyes met. "Can we take it slow? For me?"

I squeezed his hands. "Sure," I replied. "It's your funeral."

I started to laugh, but stopped when I saw the earnestness on his face. He frowned.

Cal moved me off his lap and onto the bed on my back. He lay down looked me over, leaning on his elbow. "Jesus, Paysh. You're beautiful." I looked into his eyes. They weren't lazy, like the young inebriated men I was used to. Cal was more alive than he thought he was, and he made me shiver. He traced circles on the skin above my sternum. He stroked my belly button, exposed by my shirt.

He pulled my shirt over my head. The cold air made my nipples hard and ready for his warm mouth, but he moved to my pants instead, easing them off of my hips, revealing a black thong underneath. He hooked one finger around the waistband, and pulled the underwear down. He removed it inch and inch down my legs, and gently pulled it over my feet. His hand wandered slowly up my thigh and rested right over my mound. I squirmed and tried to lower my clit over his hand to grind down against it.

He looked up at me, thoughtful, opening his mouth and closing it as he hesitated. "Taste me," he said.

I sat up, his fingers closer to my bud, but I was too distracted by his request to notice. "What?"

"A nip. So that I know."

I smiled. "So you're bound to change your mind."

He pulled his body up so that his face was level with mine. "I didn't say that," he said, and shook his head. "I want to know."

I knew what he wanted. He wanted to try on the pain, like an overcoat. Imagine what it would be like to be bitten without dying. I had had lovers like that, back when I had found one worthy of me—they wanted the pain without death. They liked it, hungered for it, fed me the very blood from their wounds when it dripped down their chests.

My breathing quickened. *This*, I thought, I could do easily, and gladly.

"I've been thinking about those lips of yours since we met," I said, huskily. I unsheathed my fangs and brought him closer.

It started off as a normal kiss, like the one we had shared in the car, but it wasn't long before I was unable to resist nipping at his lower lip. I punctured the thin skin with just the lightest pressure from my fangs, and he inhaled sharply.

I sucked at those marvelous lips that I had imagined kissing me from my ankles to my scalp. Cal groaned in submission. His body was trembling with delight and fear.

I put my hands on his chest and removed his polo shirt. His blood dripped onto his bare torso and then onto the comforter on my bed.

This wasn't going to be clean. This was going to be messy. Very, very messy.

He put his hand over mine. "Slow," he said, through gritted teeth, but I was swallowed by bloodlust and the desire to have his cock inside me. I reached into his underwear and stroked him.

He sighed. "Oh, *fuck it*," he whispered, and moved over me. I let go of his lip and guided him into my entrance. He pumped his hips immediately, and I quickened the pace of my own to match him. He asked me to taste various parts of his body, like the skin beneath his nipples. I shook my head when he asked me to bite his shoulder. It was too close to the jugular I had salivated over at the co-working space.

"Okay," he said, and suckled at my breasts instead. I moaned loudly in rhythm with his thrusts. It had been so long, the young men I fucked and killed were as skillful as blunt instruments when it came to my pussy—

The thought of them suddenly made my skin crawl.

The blood continued to trickle over me, onto the bed and the sheets. They would have to go in the incinerator, as well as the mattress.

As well as him.

I shook my head to get the thoughts out of my head. I felt like screaming.

"Do you want me to stop?" Cal replied, panting.

"No, no," I replied, "No." I grabbed onto his ass and forced him deeper inside me.

"Oh no," he said. "Not like that—" He cried out as he came. He sighed as if it had not lasted long enough, as if he hadn't made his last bout of lovemaking epic enough, cherishable.

"It was amazing," I breathed. I wished so much that such a lover did not want to die.

He sat up and brought his thighs up to his face. His shoulders suddenly shook with aching sobs.

I put my hand on his arm. "Cal," I said, finding myself concerned. "What—"

"I don't want to go," he said, and sat up. "This—and so much more. I don't want to go."

I looked away. "I could make you one of me—of us," I said, and regretted it immediately. One night of amazing sex did not predict the success of a decade—or thirty—together.

"No," was his reply. "I don't want that heaviness I see in you. I don't want to disgust myself when I look at myself in the morning."

I considered this. "It's not disgust," I said softly.

"Guilt?"

I shook my head. "Regret," I said. "That I cut so many young men's lives off at the bloom and salted the ground around them." I was shocked at myself. These were words I hadn't expected, or wanted. They came from a well of poisoned water at the pit of my stomach that had started to overflow.

I tried to lighten up my voice, make my accent flatter and younger, just like I did with the college boys. "Want another go?" I asked, putting my hand on his thigh.

He brushed me aside. "It's time."

"Now?"

"When, Paysh?" he snapped. "Dawn is almost here."

I nodded to myself. "Where do you want me to—"

"Here."

"Okay." I fluffed the pillows like a chambermaid. Cal moved towards the middle of the bed. I crouched over him, the saliva pooling in my mouth just as it would with any victim.

He looked over at me. "Paysh," he murmured. "Why are your eyes closed? Why are they—"

I was watching myself be fed upon by the Horned One, the moment playing itself out on the back of my eyelids. I saw the very breath enter my body again.

I opened my eyes.

My fangs severed his jugular vein in one snap, and I sucked greedily at the wound.

Cal cried out in pain, and when his body had caught up to his brain to discover what I was doing to it, he started to fight. His arms pounded at my back, his fingers tried to grasp what little fat there was on my body. But it was too late. I was so hungry that I couldn't breathe. I was blind with lust for his blood, and deaf to any shouts.

He died like anyone else, except he didn't have the dumb,

cowlike look of my other victims. I had cut him off at the bottom of the stem, and the last expression on his face held no forgiveness. So much for mercy.

I looked out the window from the edge of the bed. Dawn was coming indeed, and I would have a lot of explaining to do. The blood all over my room and the nasty mess of it, not neat like we were supposed to keep our kills, would be quickly sniffed out by the vampires in the boarding house. I would be kicked out for certain, and have no home. My rating on Sevensies would maybe be high enough to sell children's caricatures for five dollars each. I would be destitute.

I could go somewhere else, as I had always done. The cities blurred in my head, the streets I had trod to survive. *Survive.*

Three hundred and seventy years had not worn me down, but this night had. I was very tired. Perhaps the treatments in his body were making me so. I lay my body over Cal's, hoping to doze with the window wide open. I would see a fragile slice of the dawn I hadn't seen in nearly four centuries.

I hoped the Horned One would be there, wherever I was going. I hoped he wore his tall hat and buckled shoes. Maybe we could talk about mercy. Maybe we would talk about whether it was worth saving or destroying a life in an attempt at redemption. I wondered if the Horned One felt as though it was as failed an attempt for him as it was for me.

# WE SAIL BY NIGHT

## GUSTAVO BONDONI

The Captain was restless. I'd heard her stirring even in the afternoon, before the sun was all the way down as I stood guard beside her door.

"Careful," I told Higgins when he came to deliver her meal. "Something's on her mind."

He nodded but didn't pause. He pushed a sailor, one of the men from the *Marlin*, a ship out of Manchester which we'd boarded days before, ahead of him like a talisman. The captive didn't resist. He just stumbled and muttered, and I smelled the rum fumes that rolled off of him in waves.

As soon as the other man was across the threshold, Higgins closed the door and rushed away.

I steeled myself for what I knew was coming. Rustling, then the sounds of a man being driven to an ecstasy beyond human endurance. Then the screams and the begging for his life.

I shuddered at my post. Why was it that none of them ever sounded drunk when the time came for them to die?

Night fell over the water and the blood-red sky turned black. My shift would be over soon, and I could breathe easier.

The door opened a crack, and I froze.

"Come inside." The words were the dark whisper of velvet rustling in the dark.

"Yes ma'am." I wondered if I might be better served by throwing myself over the railing. The tender mercies of the sharks seemed almost preferable to what I'd just heard. But I sighed and entered. I'd been taking my chances since joining her crew. The considerable rewards outweighing—if only barely—the risks.

She stood in the glow of a single candle, completely naked. I swallowed and wondered whether my time had finally come.

Sometimes, when food was scarce or a meal failed to satisfy, she would take one of the crew. Not often, but I'd seen it happen.

Captain Sylvana smiled. She knew exactly what I was thinking. "No, no, Mr. Jarry. You're much too valuable to feed on." She prodded the lifeless man on the floor, skin pallid white, throat torn open. "Besides, there are plenty of his shipmates left if it comes to that."

I couldn't move. The door, pushed by the wind, had closed behind me. I was completely in her power. She knew it, and moved closer to the candle, letting the light display her soft curves and white skin broken only by the triangle of deadly black between her legs.

Sylvana's generous breasts were covered with blood, her legs shone with sweat and the emissions from the frantic lovemaking. Hers? His? It was impossible to tell in the flickering dimness.

Her hair was as dark as night, framing delicate features marred—or made more irresistible, depending on one's view— by ripe lips.

From where I was standing, I would not have been able to resist for a single second. She smiled again, watching my member grow under my pantaloons. I was powerless to move my hands or to keep myself from swelling.

She laughed. "That's not why I brought you in here, Jarry."

The spell broke and fear returned. Healthy self-preservation overcame the lust that I couldn't control. Just the sight of her, not even in full light, made men lose their minds. The problem was that they always lost their lives in the process.

She dressed quickly and I started shaking, realizing how close I'd come to… something. The rumors in the crew said that she could kill you at that exact moment of supreme pleasure.

They said she gave that privilege to members of the crew that she took, as a way to court their forgiveness for the need to kill them. I'd never heard it happen: the dying screams had always been agonized, the sounds of men in unimaginable pain.

"We have a target tonight."

I nodded. I didn't know how she knew there was a ship nearby, but she was never wrong.

"A rich man and his wives."

"Wives?" I asked. "Is he an Arabian?"

"No. He's a European like you and me. In fact, I've known him for many, many years."

I looked at her face. She looked to be twenty, at most. The twenty of an upper class woman who spent her days under a parasol, not the twenty of a country lass with three or four children who toiled under the sun.

And yet, I'd spoken to men who'd served with her for almost that long.

"Who will board?"

"A small party this time. You and Phillips will take the wives. Higgins will choose one or two men to bring the treasure. I'll take care of the Baron myself."

"And the crew?" I spoke without thinking. Sylvana didn't like to be interrupted. But this time, she let it pass.

"Don't worry about that."

---

OF COURSE I DID WORRY. We might have an infallible captain, but boarding a ship in the middle of the night without a plan for dealing with the men aboard seemed like a good way to thin out the crew.

I also worried that she'd sent me in to deal with the wives. Everyone on board knew that I had been married, had had a daughter of my own before consumption had taken them both. I would threaten women, but I wouldn't beat them or... anything else.

Fortunately, there was a lot to do. The night was dark, so the only reason we found the ship was because Sylvana had taken the helm. She guided our vessel on a straight course with an eerie confidence, only turning once. Minutes later, as if by magic, we appeared alongside a cargo ship with all its sails deployed even in the dark night.

"Hoist the colors," I told the men at the mainmast. The flag, shining blood red in the middle of the night as though it had its own source of light, soon appeared.

We dropped planks between the ships. I had my knife in hand, expecting the crew to swarm over and attempt to repel us, but nothing stirred on deck or rigging. The ship appeared deserted.

"The wives will be in the bow," Sylvana told me.

I shrugged and crossed the makeshift bridge. I didn't have much to fear from a ghost ship; my soul already belonged to something far more monstrous.

The ship was as empty as it looked. We stopped to light a lamp, something most boarding parties usually forewent in the interest of stealth.

The stairs leading below decks creaked. Everything smelled of mold and rotting wood. How did this ship remain afloat? Who was steering? We made our way forward. The light of the torch illuminated scurrying creatures. Ship's rats bold as brass, grudgingly giving way to the fire, not the men who bore it.

"That must be it," I said, gesturing to the door.

Phillips was a stout man who sweated profusely in even the best of circumstances, but much more when, as now, he was afraid. "Do you think the crew's in there, Jar?"

"I'm not sure there's a crew. Captain said she knew the skipper of this boat from a long time ago. I'm thinking a long time ago might be something like three hundred years. Anyway, they sent us to deal with the women. We won't be facing anything too frightening."

"I hope you're right, mate."

The hold we were traversing ended abruptly at a wooden wall which cut off the prow of the ship—I would say fifteen yards worth of vessel—from the rest. A door, just as rickety and rotting as the rest of the ship, was centered in the wall, slightly ajar. Welcome light spilled out from behind it, a warm, yellow glow.

I pulled the door open to reveal an unexpected room.

"That looks like a French whorehouse," Phillips sniggered. And despite my anxiety about what we'd find here, what I might have to do to get the women to comply to our commands, I found myself chuckling along.

"Come on." I stepped inside. The large, well-lit area had been partitioned with cloth curtains that hung from the roof, staggered maze-like to leave thin passages between them. Carpets and cushions covered every inch of the floor, but none of the wives were visible.

I pushed one of the curtains aside. A long niche between two partitions ended at the outer hull. A woman lay on a pile of pillows nestled against the wall. Acrid smoke—not tobacco—curled in the air above her head. She was dressed in gauze that left even less to the imagination than had the captain's nakedness. Red curls tumbling down the front of her chest offered the only concession to modesty. Green eyes stared at me: empty, hungry.

"Come with me," I said.

Her eyes blinked slowly and she let out a sound, part hiss, part keening. I heard the rustling of curtains and realized that more partitions had fallen away to reveal three other women. One was a lovely pillar of ebony as pure as the Moorish night. Another was pale as the northern mountain flowers. The third was less striking in skin tone, but seemed to have been built of all the curves that men dreamt of.

None of them wore much more than the redhead, and all three walked towards me with strides that called my role as their captor into question.

I took a step forward. All my promises, to myself, my dead wife and daughter, and even to captain Sylvana, flew out of my head in the face of such raw, wanton beauty.

I was extremely surprised to realize that Phillips was edging back, slowly moving towards the door. "Their eyes," he whispered.

It took me a long moment to realize what he was referring to. Distracted by more obvious charms, I hadn't studied the eyes of any of the women before me. Now I checked and knew I was lost: six red irises returned my gaze. A red that no living person could ever achieve. The red of the Captain's eyes when she was hungry for blood and the pleasures of the flesh.

*Run away!* my mind, or perhaps the instinct that every human had within, screamed. I tried, but it was no use. My body, of its own volition took a step… forward, into the arms of the pale elfin wife.

I could have taken satisfaction in knowing that Phillips, who'd always preferred cabin boys to having his way with any women we might capture on out travels, threw himself into the arms of the dark girl and the curvaceous one, his preferences overcome just as easily as mine. But I didn't stop to revel in the fact.

What I actually felt was jealousy that the other two women had chosen him in my place.

But that was short-lived. A soft kiss on the base of my neck told me that the redhead, forgotten as I watched the approach of her companions, had joined us. A cream-colored hand reached around to undo the upper button of my shirt and my intellect made a last attempt to tell me what was going to happen: I lie with the women, for an hour, maybe two if they were feeling particularly hungry for the energy of human lust. Then I would die, begging for mercy, drained of blood and discarded like a piece of spoiled meat. I needed to run, now.

As if she could read my mind, the little blond woman chose that moment to brush up against the front of my tunic and slip a hand down the front of my belly. In the instant it took her fingers to get past my belt, even before her fingers closed around my cock—I always wore my belt tight on raids to keep it from becoming a distraction—I was already at half mast.

Thoughts of flight—had they actually existed?—were banished and I fumbled with the leather and the metal of the strap around my waist, desperately lowering my breeches.

Soft nibbles around my neck which, I knew, would later become the deep bites from which my life's blood would flow reminded me that I was pressed between two of the loveliest creatures I'd ever seen. I turned my head to kiss the woman behind me, and my half-mast became a throbbing urgency.

Something sharp, a fang, caressed my manhood. It was a magical touch, strong enough for me to feel the ivory of the tooth, but not enough to hurt me, to draw blood. Pleasure flowed across my whole body. I felt the tip of the blond woman's tongue darting this way and that before she took me in her mouth.

I was expecting her mouth to be warm, like those of the whores that managed to take my money when I was on drunken shore leave. It wasn't. It was the temperature of a spring day, and I wondered how I ever thought that warm flesh could be seductive. I thought I would burst—never had I felt such a perfect caress.

"Are you going to let her have all the fun?" the redhead's voice whispered in my ear. "Are you going to stand there and do nothing?"

It was the call of the siren, impossible to resist. I tore myself from the blonde and took the other woman in my arms. She allowed herself to collapse, laughing, onto a pile of cushions behind her, pulling me along. I ripped the gauze away and thrust myself into her. There was almost no resistance; her flesh swallowed me whole, and she gasped in unholy pleasure. I saw her fangs, fully extended, and felt a thrill of fear—Sylvana only showed us her fangs when she was furious… and when Sylvana was angry, men died.

The terror added urgency to my lovemaking. I pounded into her as hard as I could, feeling the agony of pleasure rise to a fever pitch. I wanted my release to come at that moment. It couldn't be long, not feeling that way.

But even as I pushed, the blonde laughed softly. She'd taken the other woman's place beside my ear. "No, no. You'll come when we decide you will. Not a moment sooner. And you have a lot to do before we allow you that."

She ran her fingers through my hair and then, without

warning, grabbed hold of my locks and pulled me away. Despite my desperation, I obeyed, submissive, and allowed her to drop me onto my back.

I looked into her red eyes. The little blonde's angelic features suddenly changed. She smiled a smile that held all the cruelty of the devil, all the wickedness of a pagan goddess. It was the cruelty of a cat. She would end my existence as soon as she tired of playing with me. But while she felt like playing, I would be hers. Impossibly, my cock grew even harder in the power of that gaze, and as she ran her tongue over the extended fangs, the skin of my member felt so tight that I was certain it would split. The pain was excruciating, and I had to look away.

Phillips was taking the curvaceous woman from behind while the beautiful Moor pressed herself into his face.

But I had little occasion to watch them very long. A hand on my pulsing flesh wrenched my attention back to the woman who controlled me. Hypnotized, I watched her squat, legs splaying open as she lowered herself with excruciating slowness onto my swollen erection. The redhead, I realized, was holding it up like a mainmast, grinning madly.

"Hurry… please," I moaned.

But the blonde just leered at me. She descended slowly and brushed my tip with her open, wet, lips. Desperate, I tried to push myself as far inside her as I could. A tiny slip of a woman like that, I would break her in half.

But the redhead must have had the strength of ten men. She held me down with one hand, without showing any sign of strain, just a slight widening of that bloodthirsty smile. The image of cats playing with a mouse grew ever stronger.

But no mouse ever yearned to be consumed by a cat that way I did. I strained against the iron grip while my eyes were glued to the tiny opening and the soft yellow fuzz perched on the point of my swollen member.

When I thought I could bear it no more, the little angel let out a loud animal noise, half snarl and half scream, and let herself fall. This time, the resistance as she wrestled me into her made me gasp. Pain mingled with pleasure and I roared back at her.

She began rocking back and forth, her tight confines tearing at my flesh. I had never experienced a pleasure so intense, a woman so wet and slick but, by the same token, the screams passing my lips bore witness to the agony she was subjecting me to.

My view of the beauty causing me such intense emotion was blurred by a patch of crimson as the second woman, all but forgotten, pushed her open vagina into my face, lips spread and bearing testimony to the fact that she'd just been fucked.

"Give me pleasure, little man," she said, "and perhaps I will allow you some in return."

I put my hands on her buttocks, squeezing with all the strength of my desperation, and put my tongue between her legs, pressing hard. She moaned.

I pressed my index finger through the ring of her anus. Then the middle finger, pushing them as far as they would fit, hoping to hurt her as much as her companion was hurting me, hoping to share the pleasure and pain together.

"Good," she breathed. "Make me feel alive. Harder!"

I almost faltered. Suddenly I was awake to the fact that the perfect woman sliding over my manhood and sending waves of intense sensation across the very core of my being was cool as a night breeze, that the cavern I was exploring in my tongue, though wet and fragrant, held none of the warmth of a true woman.

That single offhand remark almost broke the spell, but the blonde chose that moment, exactly that moment, as if she could tell what I was thinking, to suddenly push me even deeper inside. I felt the uncontrollable rush and knew that I would soon spend myself deep within her body. I thrust like a madman, feeling the sudden buildup, knowing that no power, whether heavenly or demonic, could stop it now.

We came together, that unholy creature and I. She screamed like a pig at slaughter, I like a dying lion. Unconsciously, I bit down on the redhead in my mouth, and she, too, shuddered and yelped in release—even though my teeth couldn't have caused her anything but the most awful hurt.

When she finished, she pushed me away, a spent force, and I looked over at my companion.

Our triple climax sent the group beside us, the two women using Phillips for their pleasure, into a frenzy. Phillips was lying atop the dark woman now while she used her legs to push him as deep as possible while the other one sodomized him with a finger.

Phillips moaned as he bounced maniacally up and down. Red streaks appeared on his back from fingernails that raked his skin.

Suddenly, the only sound was that of Phillips' pleasure. The ebony goddess had stopped moaning and her legs suddenly went slack.

But the quiet lasted only a moment. The sounds of pleasure gave way to a sudden growl of hunger and the curvaceous brown-haired woman pulled her hand away from Phillips exposed anus and threw herself on his back, desperately running her tongue over the blood from the deep scratches on his back.

The blonde and the redhead were just a heartbeat behind. With a hiss, they joined the others in tearing gobbets from his back and shoulders.

I watched, mesmerized, free yet unable to run, held by something I couldn't fathom. I'd always imagined that Sylvana —surely these women were of Silvana's kind—fed carefully, almost fastidiously; certainly, the corpses we took from her rooms were never mutilated in any way except for the broken skin of the neck. But these women tore the flesh open to reach the bubbling crimson treasure that flowed in Phillips body.

The man himself seemed not to notice. He kept pumping into the woman beneath him, moaning with the pleasure of a sailor in a brothel. She alternated between gasps of pleasure and bouts of feeding.

Something wet and warm sprayed onto my face and I absently wiped at it with my sleeve. Only when it came away crimson did the glamour finally collapse.

Panic replaced lust. I had to run, my life depended on that. I concentrated, straining. It was like pulling on a stubborn rope… and until it snapped I didn't know if I would be strong enough to budge it. When the spell lost its power, I ran without looking back to see if anything followed, without making any attempt to retrieve my lamp or the lost pantaloons. I simply ran, slamming the door behind me.

The hold was dark as Davy Jones' heart, but I knew I just had to keep going straight to reach the stairs leading aft.

My foot caught against an exposed rib, and I tumbled head over heels into the bilge water. I got up unhurt, but the fall had destroyed my sense of direction. I walked to where the opening should have been and encountered the curved wall of the hold.

I forced my terror aside. I had been at sea for the better part of fifteen years. I should have been able to find the back of any vessel, from dinghy to man-o-war, without hesitation.

Slowly, my senses returned. The direction of movement and the swaying of the vessel became my guide, and I turned, unerringly into the darkness. I would soon be out of this hold and into the night.

Something rustled in the darkness behind me, and the self-imposed control disappeared. I ran in the direction opposite the noise, ignoring the objects that came out of the dark to strike me from all sides. Rats clambered over my feet, and up my legs every time I stopped for breath. I stomped on one, feeling the satisfying crunch of tiny breaking bones.

But it was hopeless. I'd lost my bearings again, and the noise was getting closer. I ran in the opposite direction and slammed into the hull.

A grip like iron shackles closed around my wrist, and my will to fly subsided. I would have gone anywhere the owner of those fingers led me—even into the charnel house where Phillips, whose screams I could still hear, was being consumed.

A sudden light blinded me, the yellow of a lamp, and I looked into eyes of the deepest red.

"Hello, Jarry," Sylvana said. "You seem to have lost your clothes."

"Captain, I'm… I'm glad to see you." Relief flooded into my body as I realized that I would not die that night, or at least not yet.

"Yes," she replied, her eyes looking down to where my spent member had leapt back to attention under her influence, "I can see that. But it will have to wait." She shook her head sadly. "I thought that you might be able to hold out. But if not you, then certainly Phillips. He should have been immune. He has no use for women."

I swallowed. "Those women certainly found a use for him."

"It's too bad," she said. "I'd hoped you would be able to hold off until I was finished."

"What will you do with them?"

"I was planning to kill them all, but since they have Phillips… they'll be busy for a while. They are powerful enough in their own way. By leaving them to finish their meal, we can leave without risk and scuttle the ship with our cannon from a safe distance."

I was unsurprised by the cold-bloodedness of the proposition. I knew firsthand just how cold-blooded her kind was and shook as I remembered the feel of that cold flesh against me. Wet, slick, perfect… but not warm the way a woman should be.

We returned to our ship, and I dressed before returning to help with the final unloading of the other vessel. As we cast away, the Captain approached me. She handed me a leather pouch with something heavy inside.

"I want you to hold this with you until dawn. Then I want you to remove the contents of the pouch and put them in the sun. There will be some ashes remaining. You should sweep those into the sea." She held my gaze. "Will you do that for me?"

"Yes, Captain." I would have obeyed even if she'd told me to throw myself overboard. "May I ask what it is?"

"It's a memento from an old friend," she replied and walked away.

I managed to keep the temptation of looking into the bag at bay for only a few minutes. Long before dawn painted the east, I had undone the leather thongs keeping the mouth of the bag sealed.

Inside was a head. A human head, or at least mostly human: two long fangs that no true human had ever sported lay on the remains of the bottom tooth.

The features, the whole head, seemed to have been removed from a corpse long dead and leaf to dry somewhere. Desiccated skin flaked off in my hand and sunken matt-toned eyes stared back at nothing.

Somehow, I sensed there was still life in this ancient piece of parchment-like flesh, that if it was reunited with its body and given time, it would heal, take life and form. I didn't know what it would look like when it did, but I suspected that the man would be young and beautiful, and that he would have red eyes.

I also realized that this, not the perfect skin and creamy flesh, was the reality. I stared at it long and hard, and watched the daylight burn it away. I concentrated intently, trying to burn the memory into my mind.

Because I knew that the time would soon come when Sylvana would call me into her bedchamber. Maybe if I remembered what she really was, I'd be able to resist.

But even as I swept the ashes of the consumed remains into the sea, I knew that, even if I lived forever, I would never be able to resist Sylvana's charms.

All I could really hope for was to die as the pleasure came over me. Heaven knew there are many, many worse ways to die.

# ONE GOOD TURN

## RHIDIAN BRENIG JONES

A nd now, gentlemen," said Professor Discombe, squaring his papers on the table, "to the last item on our agenda. The collection of Sir Ambrose Lynn. Mr. Marsh, if you please."

Throats were cleared and expectant glances exchanged as the college bursar wound the wires of his spectacles around his ears. Glancing briefly at his ledger, he said, "Thank you, professor. As you requested, I have reviewed our financial position. It remains far from healthy. To be brief, the college will not be able to bear the cost of installing electric lighting *and* offer for the de Chaulmes journals. It must be one or the other."

There was a short silence.

"Surely there can be no question," growled Dr. Hatfield, our specialist in the mythos of the Scandinavian lands. "It is imperative that we offer for de Chaulmes. Be damned to electric light. Gas serves us well enough."

Noisy muttering broke out all around, which the Professor quelled by rapping an impatient pencil against his water glass. Into the hush that followed, Dr. Wilson dripped his honeyed tones.

"One assumes, of course, that the volumes are worth the outlay? You are assured of their authenticity?"

The Professor bristled, reddening. "A collector of Sir Ambrose's eminence is hardly likely to possess them otherwise. There can be no doubting it."

"I beg your pardon," Wilson said, silkily unfazed. "I do not question your judgement in the matter of their authenticity. But will their contents bring a fuller understanding of the arcane? I suggest only that your own unquestioned expertise lies in the magic of the Orient, not of the Romance lands." He studied his fingernails. "Unfortunate, wouldn't you agree, if we found ourselves having bought a pig in a poke."

"*A pig in a poke?*"

"My dear sir, Jérôme de Chaulmes was a child of France and wrote in Occitan, the accurate translation of which is, I suggest, outwith your skill and mine. Before we rush to empty our scanty purses, should his journals not be assessed by a scholar fluent in that language, so that we may be certain of their worth to the college?"

"Certainly they should. Which is why I shall be asking Dr. Callard to visit Sir Ambrose at Mount Martin."

Every eye swivelled to me, and I colored in my turn. As the youngest scholar, not yet six months in post, I had felt constrained from entering the fray, and I startled at hearing the professor's words, especially as he had made no mention of this to me.

"Dr. Callard?" said Dr. Mason-Morgan, the Americas specialist. He frowned at me through his antique quizzing glass, an affectation I always found absurd.

"One doesn't doubt our young colleague's *linguistic* competence," Wilson continued, "but does he have the knowledge and experience to judge outside his own field?" He gave a tight smile. "De Chaulmes is about more than bloodsuckers. Or so one would hope."

*Bloodsuckers.* I felt my anger rise, and turned in my seat to meet the man's supercilious stare, but before I could respond the Professor said, "Dr. Wilson, you will kindly refer to Dr. Callard's studies with the respect that they merit."

"Of course. My apologies."

But he had scored a hit and my feathers were ruffled. As a specialist in deep hermetic magic, Wilson did not consider the vampire a fitting study for a college of such academic distinction, poor as that college might be; indeed it was dismissed by many as being suitable only for a vulgarian public, hungry for salacious yellow journalism and dubious potboiler novels. My scholarship was tainted by association, and snobs such as Wilson lost no opportunity for reminding me of the fact.

Professor Discombe dipped his pen into the inkwell. "So, gentlemen, are we agreed that we should bid for the journals, if persuaded by Dr. Callard's report of their value to us? Yes? All in favor? Excellent. That concludes the meeting. Dr. Callard, a moment with you in my office, please."

"I'M SORRY ABOUT THAT, Ben. Insufferable rudeness."

"Think nothing of it, professor. I believe Dr. Wilson relishes being the burr under the saddle."

"Even so." He picked up the bronze boline that he used for cutting pages, to the anguished consternation of Dr. Stephenson, our scholar of Celtic witchcraft, and ran a finger over its wicked curved blade. "I shall send a telegram to Sir Ambrose to advise him of your visit. I should warn you that he is a wily fox, much given to playing games. He likes to toy with people. Old and frail he may be, but you must take care with him." He laid down the boline with a sigh. "There is more. I find this distasteful in the extreme, but it must be said. Sir Ambrose is a lifelong bachelor. Immune to the charms of the fair sex, if you follow my meaning."

"Ah."

"Yes. He is of that sort."

"Surely you can't think…"

"He might. You're a good-looking young fellow and I should not wish you to be shocked or alarmed if he should…"

"Make advances."

The professor's lip curled in disgust. "Or make the securing of the volumes contingent on your response to such advances. We want de Chaulmes but not at the cost of insult to you."

"Have no worry on that score. I have encountered men of Sir Ambrose's inclinations before and come to no harm."

I had, however, come across their sweating bellies. Come into their mouths. Come, crying out my pleasure, into the deep recesses of their bowels. But never once since taking up my post at college. My lust for men was fierce and constant and unslaked, but it was outweighed by my desire for advancement. I intended to make my mark in the annals of scholars of the occult, and even a suspicion of my desire for congress with my own sex would bring my burgeoning career to a swift and unhappy end.

"Even so, Ben, I begin to doubt the wisdom of asking you to visit Mount Martin."

"There is no one else at college able to read Occitan. Rest assured, Professor, I shall examine the journals, form my judgment and return here unmolested. Believe me, if I can tolerate Dr. Wilson's digs, any remarks by Sir Ambrose will be water off a duck's back."

---

"The grave beckons, Dr. Callard. But, of course, you know this. You would hardly be here otherwise."

I felt the discomfiture natural in an Englishman made party

to such a bald statement, and fell back on a few awkward words of repudiation.

Sir Ambrose waved a thin hand, then let it drop to his lap. "Death awaits us all." He smiled, revealing over-sized ocher teeth. "Although one hopes, in the case of charming young men such as you, many years hence." The smile reshaped into a breathless grimace of pain. Gesturing to the sideboard he said, "The tantalus is unlocked. Perhaps you would be so good as to add five drops of tincture to a glass of brandy. From the brown bottle."

His color, never good, had worsened; his lips had taken on a bluish tinge. Nervously I asked, "Should I summon the attendant?"

"George will only fuss to no purpose. The tincture, if you please."

I did as he asked, counting the drops carefully, then set the glass on the table at his elbow. Sensible that he might not wish me to observe his taking the draught, I walked to a window and looked out. Spring had yet to brighten the year. The extensive grounds of Mount Martin slept, only the lawns and a stand of speckled laurel showing dull green, and in the several stone urns on the terrace the elongated daffodil buds were still tightly wrapped in their papery spathes. A dreary outlook, God knew, but given the choice, I would have stridden out into the cold to empty my lungs of the miasma of illness that hung so heavily in the room. Besides, I should have liked to take a closer look at the statues that stood here and there on low plinths. I gazed at the nearest, a muscular hero, posed contrapposto, and wondered whether they were what they purported to be, or simply modern copies of the Hellenistic genius of old. Looking farther, I spied no fleeing nymph, no helmeted Athene, no stern matron: every figure was male. The old baronet clearly shared my preference for the masculine form.

A phlegmy cough brought me back to myself, and I returned to my chair. The medicine had tinted his cheeks with a flush of pink, and the glance he gave me was not devoid of a certain sly knowingness. I felt my neck grow hot.

"To business, then." Interlacing his fingers, he said, "I incline to candor, Dr. Callard, so let me be frank. Your college is only one of many that are eager to secure my collection, but I've not yet come to a decision about which will benefit."

Here was a hook on which he hoped to catch me, but I had no intention of wriggling on it. "I appreciate your plain speaking, sir, and I shall endeavor to do likewise. Jubilee College is not wealthy. We cannot compete with the likes of Trinity or St John's. The price of the whole collection is beyond our means, but we've sufficient funds to bid for certain items."

"Candor, Dr. Callard, candor. You refer to the de Chaulmes journals."

"I do."

He nodded, then pushed himself to a more upright position. Pointing to a pretty lacquered cabinet, he said, "You will find a box on the shelf."

The box, of burred walnut, was fashioned in the shape of a miniature cupboard, two ebony knobs on its doors. I brought it out, then looked to him for further instruction.

"The journals are inside. I need hardly ask you to handle them with care."

My pulse galloping, I placed the box on a table and opened its little doors. Inside were four stout books, sixteenth-century quarto in dimension, their covers fine Sokoto goat leather of an ox-blood hue. There were no spine labels. Gingerly I slid one out and laid it on a cushioned book support. I lifted the cover.

The fine vellum page was written completely through in a spiky, cramped hand, the tiny letters much faded. I touched it with a reverent fingertip and turned the page. The verso held an illustration of the Sephirotic Tree, beautifully colored, each emanation outlined in dull gold. Another page held a drawing of Michael the Archangel, a fiery sword in his hand. Yet another seemed to be a receipt for protection against the succubus. Oh God, what further marvels might be contained within these pages, what mysteries of the arcane uncovered! How much might be revealed to my own scholarship by these, the diaries of Jérôme de Chaulmes, the greatest occultist of his or, arguably, any age. Lost in wonder, I did not at first take in what Sir Ambrose was saying.

"I beg your pardon, sir?"

"Dr. Callard, I have spent the greater part of my life in amassing a collection of writings on the supernatural that would rival any in Europe, if not the world. De Chaulmes is, of course, its finest jewel, but there are other treasures. It may be that my fine Legnanese *Clavicule of Solomon* rivals it. At the closing of my life, it would grieve me to think of my collection broken up and scattered to the four winds. No indeed; it must pass from me entire."

Any argument I might have tried died in the face of this uncompromising declaration. This was no toying for amusement; he meant what he said. I bit back my savage disappointment and cast a longing glance at a minutely detailed sketch of a handsome Knight of Cups.

He went on, "I have no family, Dr. Callard, no loved ones to whom I could leave my fortune. Money means nothing to me.

There are no pockets in a shroud, after all. So, I shall not sell my collection. I intend to donate it, free of charge or encumbrance, to the worthiest recipient."

I stared in astonishment. "Free of charge?"

"Free of charge. At least..." He considered me, rheumy old eyes half-lidded. "One good turn deserves another, does it not? How would it be if I offered my collection to Jubilee College in return for a small kindness from you? From you personally, you understand."

*Oh, hell and damnation!* My face must have fallen at the thought of those veined hands skittering over my cock. The horror of that wrinkled maw mewling and gnawing at my lips. His ancient member flopped out from a balding groin, awaiting my attention...

As if he had read my mind, he gave another of his ocher smiles. "A small task only, which, I suspect, you would not find unduly onerous."

If truth be told, I would have let him have his way with me if that was the price to be paid for securing de Chaulmes, but I was mightily relieved to know that this didn't seem to be what was required. "A task, sir?"

"Yes. Many years ago, when I was a young man, I made a promise to a friend, the nature of which need not concern you. To my lasting shame, I have not kept that promise, although I swore that I would." He picked up his glass, swirled the mixture that remained, then swallowed the rest. "My life is drawing fast to its close, Dr. Callard, but the promise remains. Now that age and infirmity confine me to this house, I must entrust its fulfilling to another. To you. Will you undertake this task for me, so that I do not die forsworn?"

The shake in his voice moved me. I had no idea what this

task might comprise, but I answered without hesitation. "I will. What is it that you want me to do?"

"Only take a letter. Take a letter to my friend and put it into his hand."

Surprised, feeling not a little disappointed by the banality of the request, I said, "Is that all, sir?"

"Take the letter, Dr. Callard, and put it into his hand. That is all."

Why could he not send it by post? I didn't like to ask. Perhaps, I thought with a surge of excitement, his friend lived abroad. Did he fear the letter becoming lost on a lengthy journey to far flung parts, to Russia, perhaps? Malaya? Bechuanaland?

"And whither am I to deliver the letter, sir?"

"To Yorkshire."

---

SOMEWHAT STIFF AFTER MY JOURNEY, I clambered from the trap, the last of a series of conveyances that had carried me on the journey from London. The city of York had been a mediaeval splendor and I regretted that I had had no time to explore its magnificent Minster, or walk its ancient walls; I determined to return one day to do so. The miles to my final destination had crossed wild and beautiful moorland, although Jim, the dour old rustic who drove the trap, had received my appreciative remarks with no more than a mumble around his pipe.

"This is Haddingham Hall?" A fine William and Anne house lay at the end of a short drive and I took a moment to admire the elegance of its plain lines; I have never been one for frills and furbelows.

"'Appen."

"I shouldn't be above a quarter of an hour. Please wait to take me to the inn."

Another grunt.

As I had done a hundred times during my journey, I checked my breast pocket for the letter. Reassured that it had not somehow fallen out on to the floor of the trap, the gravelled drive or otherwise vanished into thin air, I tugged the bell.

"Good afternoon. My name is Callard. I believe I am expected."

"Yes, sir." The servant nodded and stepped aside to allow me entrance to a spacious hall. He took my card and relieved me of my hat and coat then led me across checkered marble to a set of double doors. Opening them, he said, "If you wait in the drawing room, sir, I'll inform the master of your arrival."

An elegantly furnished room, if not quite to my taste. Its high ceiling elaborately plastered, its walls moiré silk of an apricot shade, luxuriously upholstered sofas and chairs grouped around small tables. But my attention was captured by a picture above the mantelpiece. In rich and glowing oils, it depicted the figure of Saint Sebastian, his naked body bound to a tree and stuck all over with arrows. Rivulets of blood ran from each gash, yet he showed none of the agony that such wounds would inflict. His arched throat, the cords standing rigid, the abandoned expression on his beautiful face all seemed to convey rather a dark, ungodly pleasure. I had seen such expressions on the faces of men at the moment of sexual climax, and I felt my cock begin to grow heavy on my thigh.

"Dr. Callard? Ah, forgive me, I made you jump."

I hadn't heard anyone come in and my embarrassment was compounded by the realization that not only might he have been watching me as I stood absorbed by the painting, but also that he was startlingly good-looking.

"Not at all. I was…" I straightened my shoulders and started again. "Good afternoon. I have a message for Mr. Andreas van Althuis, which I am instructed to deliver in person."

"I am he."

*What?* Sir Ambrose had given me to understand that the letter was for a friend of his youth, a youth that must have blossomed and faded some sixty years earlier. This man could not have been above thirty. Perhaps he was a grandson, or some other family member who shared the name. Feeling even more of a damned fool than ever, I ventured, "Is there perhaps another Mr. van Althuis?"

"No, there is not."

Dumbfounded, I studied him. Tall, sparely built, dark-haired and with eyes so black that I could not discern the margin of pupil and iris. A remarkable face, reminiscent of a Velázquez nobleman, pale, proud, remote.

"May I?"

Short of calling the man a liar, what else could I do? Still irresolute, I drew out the envelope and gave it into his outstretched hand.

The seal broke with a crack and he drew out a single sheet. As he read, his expression softened. A small smile hovered on his lips, which broadened as he refolded the letter. I felt its warmth as if the sun had suddenly broken through lowering cloud and, despite my misgivings, I could only smile in return. He tucked the letter into his own pocket and as he did so, a faint scent drifted from him, musky, a note of the feral animal about it. Calamus? Some unknown exotic herb? Whatever it was, I found it oddly agreeable.

"Thank you, Dr. Callard. This is most welcome. I have waited for it for some time. But see what a neglectful host I am! Please, do sit. May I offer you tea? You must be tired after your journey."

"Thank you, but the man is waiting to take me to the village. I've a room at the Bell for the night."

"The Bell? Dear me, I won't hear of it! You must stay here, of course."

"I couldn't possibly impose—"

"No imposition, I assure you. Quite the reverse. Remote as we are here, visitors are rare. I seldom have the opportunity to pass an agreeable evening with a gentleman of education and refinement."

Surely it would be more comfortable to spend the night here than it would be at the inn, struggling to make conversation with old Jim and his tongue-tied compatriots? I was puzzled by van Althuis's youth, but the man had a gracious manner, and, I suspected, possessed a sharp intellect, in addition to handsome looks. Yet I hesitated, although I didn't know why. "I've promised to send a telegram to Sir Ambrose telling him that I've delivered the letter. I must visit the village post office, so—"

"One of my servants can do that for you."

To make any further protest would be discourteous. "Yes… if you're sure, then yes, I should be delighted to stay."

"Excellent. Some tea, and then you must rest before dinner."

---

A GOOD WASH, clean collar, and fresh drawers had had to do. Van Althuis had dismissed my embarrassment at having no evening clothes with a wave of his hand, a gesture that brought

Sir Ambrose to mind, although the two could hardly have been more different. The smile that warmed me again over the dinner table was dazzlingly white, the teeth tight, square and masculine. I disliked the U shape of some fellows' teeth: too womanish, as unattractive in a man as fat hips. There was nothing feminine about van Althuis. Slender he might have been, but he was slim as a rapier is slim, or a whip. I had taken only one glass of an excellent red Bordeaux, but when I found myself picturing the shape of his cock, I wondered whether I might not be a little drunk.

"Please, do eat. I have little appetite."

I'd had no food since I'd breakfasted on a currant bun at King's Cross, so I set to with a will. The lamb was tender and well-flavored with mint, and the almond tart that followed delicious. As I ate, he crumbled a piece of bread and listened intently when I elaborated on the circumstances that had brought me to his house.

He said, "So he is near the end?"

I patted my lips with my napkin. "I fear he is."

"I see."

Because he had raised the subject I thought it not inappropriate to turn to the matter that had perplexed me since my arrival. "Forgive my impertinence, but I expected to meet a gentleman of more mature years, but…" I trailed off, struggling to find the right words to express my curiosity with some degree of delicacy.

"I am younger than you expected."

"Well, yes. Sir Ambrose spoke of a friend of his youth, whereas—"

"Can an older man not maintain a friendship with a younger? I imagine that you have friends of all ages. Is that not so? Tell me," he continued, before I could press him further, "tell me something of yourself."

How neatly he had avoided answering! "What would you like to know?"

"Ambrose tells me in his letter that you are a junior scholar at Jubilee College. What is your field of study?"

I wondered what else had been contained in the letter. Certainly, he did not seem inclined to enlighten me. "I study the vampire."

"The vampire? How very interesting. And your study encompasses...?"

"Its history, its nature. Legends abound, but I am attempting to establish what lies behind the legends. They persist in many countries, and go back thousands of years. Ancient Mesopotamia had them, as did west Africa. Welsh folklore tells of a vampire *chair* that gnaws the sitter's backside, if you can believe it! Can there have existed some...being that gave rise to this multitude of legends? That is what I hope to discover." Warming to my subject, I said, "It may be that de Chaulmes will reveal something unknown to current scholarship. I did not have the opportunity to delve into the journals beyond a few pages, but I hope that a more leisurely reading... well, who knows."

"Who knows indeed? Dear Ambrose, as closed with his treasures as an oyster with its pearl. But the bargain you struck with him might provide you with the answers you seek."

"One hopes so. I long to decipher the journals."

"I'm sure. But what else can you tell me of yourself, Benedict —I may call you Benedict?"

"Of course."

"Then I am Andreas." He inclined his head. "Are you a married man? Do you have a family?"

Wishing to divert his interest from my private life, I answered lightly, "A poor scholar's stipend hardly extends to the keeping of a wife. My parents died when I was a boy. I have one sister, Irene, living in Canada."

"So, quite alone in the world. As am I." His dark gaze lingered, dropping from my eyes to my mouth. If the picture of Saint Sebastian suggested his proclivities, his lazy smile now confirmed them. I felt a flash of heat in my groin. I hadn't been with a man for so long and never with one of such… promise. "I've arranged for coffee to be served in the library. I have a modest collection of *objets de vertu* which might interest you, if you would care to see them?"

"Most certainly. Thank you."

---

AFTER A CURSORY EXAMINATION of the contents of the bookshelves—an eclectic collection that demanded further study— I followed him from the library into a small anteroom leading off. I suppose I should have expected it; certainly, it came as no surprise. The painting on the facing wall was of grief-stricken Apollo, holding the body of dead Hyacinthus close to his chest, but it was a long, glass-topped table that caught my interest. It held dozens of ancient artefacts: winged phalluses in lead and bronze; a pottery figure of lecherous Priapus, his gigantic penis as long as he was tall; a shallow bowl of fine workmanship, its interior showing a bearded erastes and a youthful eromenos locked in sexual congress. I was taken aback, not by the objects themselves—as an accredited scholar I had been given entry to certain restricted rooms in museums in Naples and Florence—but by their open display. Thunderheads of excitement building, I finished my coffee and moved farther along to examine a glorious marble head.

"Antinous?"

"Yes. A sixteenth century copy. The marvelous youth. Can you imagine the beauty that so enraptured an emperor? He must have been breathtaking."

I touched a stony curl of hair. "If the sculptor didn't exaggerate."

Andreas came to stand so close behind me that I again caught the scent of his body. Stronger then, redolent of… *Christ, what was it?* Looking over my shoulder, he said, "I think the likeness must be faithful to the original. Hadrian adored him. He made him a god."

I swallowed hard. "I wonder what happened. The circumstances that led to his drowning."

"Who knows?" He drew nearer still. "Do you remember the story of Tithonus?"

I did, of course, but lust had emptied my mind of everything but trembling anticipation. I was in his house; I could not make the first move. How would he do it? Would he touch me? Rest his hand on my shoulder? Slide his arms around my waist and kiss me?

"A prince of Troy, a mortal. So handsome that the goddess of the dawn loved him. Fearful that he would be taken from her by death, she implored the gods to grant him eternal life. They did so, but foolish Eos had neglected to ask for eternal youth."

"Yes, I remember." His purr poured like warm honey through my veins, a luscious flow to my testicles and cock.

"Year by year Tithonus aged, his beauty decaying even as his life extended. And Eos shut the old man away so that she could no longer hear his feeble croaking, his begging for death."

The rich fluid had filled me to overflowing. I felt it seep from the slit of my erection and run down to soak into the cleft of my buttocks. His breath stirred the hair at the back of my neck, and it took all my will not to turn and crush my mouth to his.

"Think, Benedict. Antinous. Hyacinthus. Tithonus. Robbed of their glory by death or by the terrible changes wrought by age. Would you not wish to have your youth preserved, forever unchanged?"

I was so inflamed, so charged with desire for him that I could hardly form the words. "Who would not?"

"Many would not. Ambrose did not."

"Sir Ambrose…?"

"Given the chance, he refused. Many times he refused me, although he loved me as I loved him. But at the hour he finally abandoned me, he made a promise. He swore to find me a companion, one to fill the place at my side that he would not, and at this late hour he has sent you to me. Will you ease my loneliness, beautiful Benedict?"

Drugged as I was by his nearness, by my need for him, his words made no sense. Slowly I turned in the circle of his arms. The fathomless dark of his pupils was lit red from within, as if a flame glowed in the depths. He lowered his arms and gripped my hips and I felt the press of his iron length against mine. A moan broke from me, and his lips parted in response.

For a second, shock held me frozen. My eyes starting from my head, I staggered back, my hands flailing for the edge of the table. As white as if chipped from the marble of Antinous's cheek, twin fangs were revealed, long and slightly curved inward, sharp as thorns.

"Ah, Benedict, Benedict. With all your learning, after all your studies, you did not know me."

"No, oh, God—"

"There's nothing to fear. Nothing at all."

*"Stay away from me! Stay away!"*

"I offered Ambrose life, Benedict, as I now offer you. Ten times the span of a man's life with beauty, strength, vigor unfailing. And pleasure. Pleasure that you will never find in the embrace of a man of your kind. Pleasure beyond your imagining. But know this: there is a price to be paid. We live long, but we are not immortal. We die. And for us there can be no life in the hereafter, for we will have surrendered our souls."

I gave a whisper of denial but even in the extremity of my fear, my cock remained hard, harder than it had ever been in my life. The glistening fangs seemed to mesmerize me, and the thought of their bite, of their sinking into my flesh, rather than filling me with horror, sent such a bolt of desire through me that my bones became molten. He brought his face nearer and licked my throat. His tongue was the scouring rasp of a cat. A great cat. I gasped as I felt the first caress of his fangs, the points scratching lightly to graze the skin under the curve of my jaw.

"Come now." The vampire took my hand and, as if in a waking dream, I walked with him out of the library to the hall. There I paused as fear momentarily assailed me, but it passed as suddenly as it had come, and I gripped his hand more tightly as we ascended the stairs.

I LAY NAKED on his bed, whilst he, likewise bare, stood to one side. He fixed his unwavering gaze on my body, and the purity of his lust made my cock lift on my belly. I had had many men, taken them into me, or penetrated them in turn, but even before he laid hands on me, I knew that this would be a union like no other. Something primal had awoken in my heart or my entrails, I could not tell which, a famished hunger that only his bite would satisfy. His bite and his cock. The pounding of my heart slowed to a pulsing throb of desire. I opened my thighs and heard his hiss of approval.

In the wavering glow of the candlelight he touched both points of his fangs with the tip of that panther tongue. "You weep for me, Benedict. Your need for me drips from you, as mine does for you." He touched a finger to the crown of his own rigid cock and spread its wetness over my lips. The scent was strong, distilled in that fluid. "You lick like a wolf cub at its dam. But be sure. To take my seed and give me your blood will tie us in an irrevocable bond. And I must hurt you, my love, but you will need to bear the pain once only, the first time I take you. Once only. Are you willing for this?"

For a second, the mists lifted from my mind and I was able to think clearly. What awaited me back in the halls of Jubilee College? The gratification of my fellows, delighted at having secured the journals, but their praise would be fleeting and my triumph soon forgotten. What would follow, once the excitement had passed? A return to my studies. Arid years of research, hunched over my books. A solitary life, enlivened by an occasional furtive coupling, always looking over my shoulder. And when my looks had faded, when my youth and strength were all spent, a lonely death. No. That was not for me. I looked into the burning dark of Andreas's eyes. What need had I of de Chaulmes, of other dry volumes? The answers I sought would be found in his embrace.

"I am willing."

At my words his cock clenched, the great shaft lifting. I brought my knees up and tucked my hands under to hold my buttocks apart. To reveal the gateway to a strange new life. His black eyes on the opening, he ran a fang over the inside of his wrist. Blood oozed from the wound and fell in fast drops to my testicles, trickling lower to mingle with the fluid of my arousal. He spread the warm wet around the ring of my anus, using its slickness to ease the movement of his fingers as he worked me, massaging and stretching to loosen the muscular ring. He hovered over me, his cock probing and sliding in scarlet until he found my center. Steadily he pressed, and I opened to the crown of his cock. There was discomfort, as there always is, but such pain is merely a welcome forerunner of the bliss to come. With one sobbing moan I surrendered and he entered me fully, and I cried out at the impaling.

Hot and thick and hard as stone, his cock reached deep. Every nerve in my flesh flared alight with sensation at each slow thrust. In and out, in and out, moving in the age-old rhythm of two males joined. I held him, my arms tight around his back as he moved, the bone of his pelvis thudding against the under-curve of my buttocks. It was not enough. I arched my throat and turned my head to the side. For the other piercing. For his bite.

His smile revealed every inch of those terrible fangs. But he didn't bite. Instead, he cupped my face and held it steady. "Bene-dict…" And deep in my entrails I felt such monstrous pain that a shriek burst from me. Maddened, terrified, I screamed and fought to push him from me, but he had me pinned. Murmuring my name again, he withdrew and the long slide out caused such agony that I thought I must surely die of it. He sat back on his heels, his cock in his hand, and I gave a cry as I perceived the cause of my suffering.

The head of his cock was thickly covered with fine spikes or spines, stiff pins dripping blood.

More blood ran from me and he swooped down and fastened his mouth to suckle greedily at the ravaged hole. A long while he lapped, little growls of pleasure escaping him, and, by degrees, the torture inside me lessened. Lessened, then faded to nothing under his suckling and his spittle and the slide of his rough tongue in and out of my body. I let my head fall back to the pillow. Pain had weakened my cock, but lightning flashes of pleasure flickered as he took it into his mouth, drawing it between the twin barbs of his fangs until it stiffened again, and my testicles drew up tight to my body.

"Once only, my Benedict. The pain is over for you now."

Smooth then, as smooth and wet and silky as mine, he slid his cock back into my bloody hole and pressed his lips to my throat. The bite came with no warning, a ferocious puncturing, deep into my flesh. My blood spurted into his mouth and he snarled and as he again drank deeply, deeply. His prick swelled inside me, as if each long swallow filled it further, hardening it to an impossible degree. He lifted his face away, his lips and fangs shining wet, and thrust his shaft in to its uttermost extent. It was enough. Semen boiled from the depths of me in a blinding intensity of pleasure, and in the same moment I felt the gush of his seed, warm and plentiful, replenishing what he had taken, giving me new life.

WE DO NOT REMAIN in one place for long—several months at most. For the moment, we are in Kraków. Our apartment off Floriańska Street is small, but supremely well-appointed; I tease Andreas that none of my researches had revealed the vampire's love of luxury! We have found others of our kind here, and yet more in the smaller town of Tarnów, some fifty miles to the east. The line of the vampire must be perpetuated and so they join with us in our hunts for men to turn—beautiful young men at the zenith of their flowering. There is one such who assists in an apothecary's shop in the square, shy, softly-spoken Fabian; we will have him soon. He will lie between us and one will pierce while the other watches, for we take it turn and turn about.

At idle moments, lying next to my lover, my thoughts turn to my old life and I wonder whether any of the scholars of Jubilee College remember young Dr. Callard, who secured the entire collection of Sir Ambrose Lynn, and who disappeared in such mysterious circumstances. I smile to myself as I imagine their perturbation. Andreas senses me smile, and turns his dark eyes on me. I feel the sting as my fangs emerge, and he smiles in return.

# PERMANENT POSITION

EMILY L. BYRNE

*R*un, my mind sings. *Run.* And I do. I am almost flying now, my heart thudding against my ribs like a rabbit pursued by hounds. My bare feet pound against the dirt as I do my best to outstrip whatever it is that hunts me.

*Bare?* I glance down at a frothy lace confection of a nightgown, at my pale naked feet twinkling below me in the darkness. *Why am I wearing this...thing?* The thought jars me awake just ahead of the phantom grasp of my pursuer.

Just ahead of the alarm as well. I sit up, heart still pounding as I turn off the loud buzzer. When I look down, my nipples are still hard under my thin t-shirt and I can smell a rusty dampness between my legs. Cursing, I scramble into the shower, grab a tampon, a coffee and a snack. Grateful that my roommates are out at their jobs, I relish the quiet as I get dressed, then haul my carcass out to catch the bus.

I stare out the window at the twilight, looking at city streets without seeing them, and let my imagination run wild. I imagine myself the star of every Gothic-romance I've ever read until the bus stops in front of a big red brick building with high arched windows. Two large stone pots filled with scraggly brown leaves and twisted stems stand on either side of the doorway. Not for the first time, I wonder what it was before it died.

I'd also wonder why they don't shell out for landscaping, but then, I've been inside. I know the answer to that already. Genteel decay doesn't begin to cover it. Once through the doors, I have to stop and blink for a while to adjust to the dimness and the dust. There are ancient red velvet curtains and musty old Persian carpets and dark, dark wood everywhere, and I love it more than words can tell. I'm sure it must be haunted or something; I wonder if this temp gig will last long enough tor me to to find out.

I don't see Therese until I almost bump into her. Not that I mind that part. She and her brother Gerard are the best part about working here. Besides the atmosphere and the pay, of course, which warms my little temp's heart more with every paycheck I anticipate. I don't even ask why it's higher than usual.

"Hello, Magda," Therese purrs down at me, not bothering to step back. She's about five inches taller than me and round and curvy in all the right places. Her big black eyes come into focus as my eyes adjust to the dimness and she flashes a bright white grin down at me. She takes a deep breath and her pale white cleavage heaves just below my chin.

I am trying not to make an idiot of myself, so I search my thoughts for something workplace appropriate and neutral. Or at least something that isn't Therese's boobs. I love hearing her say my name. In her deep voice with its indefinable accent, "Magda" becomes an exotic Eastern European beauty with cheekbones to die for and yards of black hair. My imagination runs away with me. *Of course, I do look just like that, except for the cheekbones. And the hair. Well, all right, I look like that in my dreams, at least.*

Therese moves slowly away from me as her brother, Gerard, comes into the hallway. "Hello Magda. We've got some fun stuff for you tonight." He smiles reassuringly, teeth dazzling in the gloom. He is long and lean in contrast to Therese's abundant curves. They both have the same melting eyes, pale skin and black hair that looks more like raven's wings than raven's wings, if you know what I mean. Their hands are pretty similar too, all long fingers and slightly tapered nails. Just the right size to fit into all kinds of inappropriate-for-the-workplace things.

In contrast, Richard Samuels, their fulltime employee, is more than a little creepy. He has eyes that kind of slide away before they really catch yours and his footsteps make no noise, even when they should. I follow Gerard into the next room and Samuels wanders up behind us. When I glance back, he's standing a bit too close, eyes half closed, mouth twisted into a weird hungry smile.

I flinch away and Gerard notices. "Didn't you say that you wanted to get started on the billing, Richard? I'll be in to talk to you about it in a few minutes," Gerard's voice has just the right authoritative ring to it and Samuels dutifully trots off without a backward glance. I hope the office lights are too dim for Gerard to notice my small sigh of relief. I wouldn't want him thinking that I don't play well with others.

They keep the lights low and work at night because he and Therese are both light sensitive. I'm finally getting used to it. A little bit, anyway. Soon, like their general gorgeousness, I'll just take it in stride. I tell myself that when he leads me over to his computer. His hand rests lightly on my shoulder. All of a sudden, I want that frothy lace horror I was wearing in my dream. I wonder if he'd like taking it off.

But then he breaks the mood by taking his hand away and standing tantalizingly out of reach as he tells me what he wants me to do. I'm having trouble concentrating. The room is getting hotter. Maybe it's just the dark red velvet of the curtains drowning out the last of the setting sun's watery light. Maybe it's the rise and fall of Gerard's voice as he speaks to me. Maybe it's my recurring fantasies about what I'd like to do with him.

I reach up and unbutton the top two buttons on my blouse but he doesn't seem to notice and it doesn't cool me off at all. The room spins slowly around me and instead of listening to the wonder of invoices, I find myself imagining the touch of his lips, the feel of those long fingers on my skin. Perhaps even daring to lay a hand on his crotch and feel him harden at my touch.

"You're confusing her, brother dear." Therese slinks in to sit on the edge of the desk, as close to me as she can get. I turn my chair a little so my leg touches hers ever so slightly, just enough to send shivers up my spine. I am getting wet listening to them banter back and forth above me, soaking my tampon until I wonder if I'll leak out a small sea of molten fluid when I stand up. I contemplate throwing myself at both of them. But what would I do if they turned me down? How humiliating would that be? *Coward* says the little voice inside my head.

Therese leans forward to point out something on the screen and I can see down the front of her dress. Round breasts glow like alabaster against the soft dark blue of her dress and I long to bury myself in her cleavage. She reaches out and I feel her white fingers caress my face. I turn to kiss them. *Wait, that's not what's happening. She's reaching out to get a paper from Gerard. Damn, Magda, get a grip.* I drown in her eyes anyway and come up gasping.

My fingers play with the next button on my blouse. "Are you too warm?" Gerard purrs solicitously and from somewhere a cold breeze startles my flesh from its daydreams. Goosebumps run down my arms and my nipples leap erect. I gasp aloud at the sudden chill.

"Too much, I think." Therese stands up, her fingers now

gently stroking the goosebumps from my bare arm. I chew my lip in a frenzied effort at self-control. I should go get a glass of water, take a break, do something, anything so I don't make a fool of myself. Not here, not in front of them.

With a huge effort, I make myself say, "I'm fine, really. Well, I should probably get started on this stuff." They both smile down at me and for an instant, I remember my dream and my body braces for flight. Then the moment passes, leaving nothing but my pounding heart behind as they glide like panthers from the room. Therese gives me what I interpret as a smoldering gaze over one shoulder and my lips part in a soft pant.

The door shuts behind them and I am left alone in Gerard's office with its ancient wood furniture and red velvet curtains and…a giant stack of invoices. When I look down, I can see rivulets of sweat running down between my breasts. *Are you showing enough boob there, Magda?* The voice of my common sense is shrill and annoying, but I ignore it in favor of wishing that I had worn my good lace bra today instead of my sad nylon one.

I don't rebutton my shirt, but I do make myself work for a while, trying to make myself pretend that the growing wetness between my legs isn't there. I firmly squelch my new fantasy of being chased through the woods by both of them. Or better yet, being caught. It works for a while. Or so I try to pretend.

Then I give up and begin typing with one hand as I unzip my boring khaki skirt with the other. I stick my hand inside my waistband and touch myself. My fingers swim upstream to my clit and I imagine they are Therese's tongue, circling, stroking, then darting inside me. Heat washes up my thighs and I quiver against my own touch. I abandon the keyboard to stroke my nipples through my shirt and bra, first one then the other, pinched into points with my, no, her, free hand. My clit hardens beneath my fingers, her tongue, skin slick with my own juices, with her imagined softness. Her phantom fingers slip inside me and I ride the wave, cresting it with a soft moan, legs shaking against Gerard's chair.

I hear the click of the door before I open my eyes. In an instant, I am looking doggedly at the screen, both hands resting on the keyboard. Casually, I reach back and zip up my skirt. But when I look around, there's no one there.

Dinnertime rolls around eventually and I go and eat my sandwich in the backyard. It's an old garden about the size of a postage stamp, all overgrown with old rose bushes and morning glories. I can pretend that I'm Sleeping Beauty while I sit on the old iron bench and remember what summer looks like. Samuels glances out the door at me, faded eyes sliding all around me, but he doesn't come outside.

I'm overjoyed when he disappears back inside. There's something creepy about his weird gaze shifting and wandering but never quite coming to rest. If it wasn't for the pay and the chance to lust after hotties like Therese and Gerard, I'd tell my agency that I wanted to be pulled from this job.

Not that I remember that thought once I'm back inside.

I close the door behind me and notice Therese through the open door of her office. She's talking to someone, perhaps an actual client. They don't seem to have all that many of those, possibly because of the evening hours. Or maybe it's that silly slogan: Forever Insurance Insures You Forever. I mean, who needs insurance *forever*? Other than vampires or something? Lifetime total is usually enough for most people.

Therese leans forward toward her computer screen, talking

with her hands all the while and looking earnest. Definitely a client. I wander back to Gerard's office in time to find him sitting at his desk. He gives me a sleepy grin and stands up to usher me back to his chair. The way he hangs over me when I sit down almost make me wonder if he can smell whatever wet warmth I may have left on his chair earlier and I squirm against the upholstery at the thought.

I wonder what would happen if I turned around and unzipped his fly to take his dick in my mouth. In my mind, it's just the right size and he groans at the touch of my tongue. I rock my head back and forth, then pull away to lick my way slowly down to his balls. His breath quickens into short gasps as I embrace him with my mouth once more. He clutches my shoulders in an effort not to ram himself down my throat. I can feel him shake with desire and I smile a little. I just love polite boys.

He reaches down to grab one of my hands and pull it up to his mouth. I can feel his mouth on my fingers, then his tongue on my wrist: distracting, but not unpleasantly so. I work harder until I can taste his salty tang and as he comes in my mouth, I feel his surprisingly sharp teeth sinking into my wrist.

I groan in startled desire, panting as I release his dick to watch him drink from me. His tongue on my skin sends a spark straight down to my clit and I spread my legs, straining against the chair. I rub my free hand between my legs until I forget where I am and come in waves.

When I wake from my sexy daydream, Gerard is gone and I've got nothing better to look at than the computer screen. I remind myself sternly that there was no way Gerard was going to be doing the temp at work, not with the door open, anyway.

The voice of my common sense takes over despite the imagined slight ache of jaw and wrist.

I type listlessly until it's time to go home. Therese is done with her client and she and Gerard are talking softly to each other in her office when I say good night. They stop talking to smile at me as Samuels holds the door open for me to leave. I wonder if he lives upstairs. He's always there when I get there and there when I leave. I look up at the curtained windows of the second floor where I have yet to venture. They look deserted but my flesh crawls a little as my eyes meet their glassy blank stares.

My dreams are more intense tonight. This time, I worry that something seriously awful will happen if I get caught and I run faster than ever. But despite how fast I flee, something grabs my ankle and I fall, tumbling not to the ground, but into the wakefulness of a sunny afternoon and my empty bed. The last thing I remember seeing in my dream is the curtained windows of the second floor of Forever Insurance as I run past them, pursued by whatever it is. Terrific. I hate it when my subconscious works overtime.

The memory of the second floor windows fills my brain until I need to know what's up there. I decide to take the proverbial bull by the horns or any other available body part and check it out on my next dinner break. Once I knew there were no dead bodies or whatever up there, I'd get over this whole thing and the dreams will stop. I hope.

Samuels, the groovy ghoulie, is the only one at the office when I show up. "Therese and Gerard are meeting with clients downtown," he informs me in a voice like a damp fog. His bulbous, colorless eyes gaze just past me until I get impatient and slightly queasy. I flee to Gerard's office and my very safe invoices. *Joy.*

Samuels wanders past the open door on his way to his own office down the hall and soon, I hear him pounding away on his ancient keyboard. As long as he's busy when I take my break, this is probably my best chance for checking out the dreaded second floor. I just need to know that I'm overreacting, then I can make it all go away. Tomorrow is my day off and I'll go have lunch with some friends, maybe catch a matinee or something. Get back to normal, whatever that is.

I do remember being normal. That was that time when I wasn't having weird dreams about things chasing me and could enter invoices for hours at a time without even once thinking of fucking my bosses. Back then, I wasn't looking at little cuts on my wrist and wondering where they came from. It's not like anything actually happened yesterday so I really don't have a clue. I rub them a little and they fade under the pressure, disappearing into my skin like they were never there. Bizarre.

I wait a reasonable amount of time before I head out into the hall. I poke my nose around the door of Samuel's office and wave the universal signal for "see you later." He bares his teeth at me, whoops, no, that was a smile. Sort of. He goes on talking on the phone, so I move as quietly as I can to the big staircase. It has dark wood banisters that curl at the ends and it's very dark up at the top.

I hesitate and give myself a pep talk. *All right, just go up, look around, then back down,* I tell myself. I'm shivering a little on the first step and a lot more on the third. By the time I get to the seventh I know this wasn't a good idea. But on step ten, I know I might as well go all the way up. Five steps more and I'm on the landing. There's a little light coming in from somewhere, but not much.

The air is really still up here, like it's anticipating something, and it's a lot cooler than downstairs. There's a short hallway to my right and I walk down it, swearing to myself that I'll just peek into that open door on my left. Then I'll go back downstairs. Just one little look...the room is almost empty, except for the three long wooden boxes on the floor and the hurricane lamp on the table above them.

I make myself open the nearest box. I have to know. They aren't sealed or anything but the dirt inside doesn't tell me much. Maybe they're into gardening. Sure, and they keep boxes on the second floor, in the dark, far away from the garden. Or maybe, they're...*What?* My little inner voice demands. *Blood-sucking fiends from Transylvania?* Outside in daylight, I would have laughed. Up here in the dark, crouched over an open box of dirt that's big enough to stash a human in, I start shivering.

I close the box as quietly as I can and stand up very slowly. Only a few steps and I'll be down the stairs and out the front door. Then, all I have to do is call the agency tomorrow and tell them things haven't worked out. I don't see Therese in the doorway until I bump into her. "Hello, Magda. I see that I don't need to chase you this time." Her eyes are black pools and I fall into them, drowning until I would crawl over broken glass to get to her. Or let her chase me through my dreams until she catches me.

She kisses me with lips so cold they burn mine and a tongue that freezes the inside of my mouth. I kiss her back, trying to warm her with my breath, my desire. We move slowly down the hallway to another room, her hands busily unbuttoning my shirt. Tonight, I wore my good bra, the red lace one with the snap in front. Not that it matters. She has both shirt and bra off in moments. Her cold lips pull away from mine and drop to my breast. She takes my nipple in her mouth and I harden at her touch until my skin is almost numb.

I don't feel her teeth sink in, not at first. But then I realize that she is drinking from me, draining me of something I didn't know I had. Something I hope that I don't want. She unbuttons my skirt and it falls to the floor. My underpants follow with an expert tug. She pushes me backward onto the bed, an antique four-poster with curtains. *Black velvet, natch* the analytical portion of my brain notes, as my eyes adjust slightly to the glow of the single candle.

Therese releases my breast and looks up to meet my eyes at the thought. I whimper as I watch her lick my blood from her lips and she smiles knowingly and slides down between my legs. Her icy caress finds my clit and strokes it, first with fingers, then tongue and I shiver and shake with longing and desire. She tugs the tampon out of me and I close my eyes as she licks it like a lollipop before tossing it aside.

Then her tongue and icy fingers are inside me, drinking me, draining me, savoring me. I am cold and hot and all the points in between. I come, bucking wildly against the glacier of her mouth, and she drinks from me like a goblet.

One moment, it's just us on the bed, with me writhing against the persistent pressure of Therese's fingers and teeth, then Gerard's there with us. His pale skin glows against the velvet of the curtains as he climbs in naked. Therese lifts her face and bares her fangs at him, my blood staining the pale glow of her chin. "Share and share alike, sister dear," he responds as he kisses me and I know they've done this before. For an instant, I wonder what happened to the others: are they dead or what?

Then I find myself on all fours, my face buried between Therese's suddenly very naked thighs. I lick fiercely because right now I want to be the one they keep, the one they share between them and tell all their secrets to. I want them to want me like I want them: desperately, all barriers gone. Therese is very dry against my tongue, but I hear her breath hiss against her fangs, feel her body stiffen slightly.

Gerard slides up behind me, his fingers guiding himself inside me until he fills me with his biting cold. Therese pulls my hand up to her mouth and sucks fiercely on my wrist as he rides me, my groans muffled in her flesh. I try not to get too distracted, my tongue still coaxing her clit, begging her to lose herself in me. Gerard sinks his teeth into my shoulder and I whimper at the momentary pain. I want to surrender but my instinct for survival is too strong and I struggle, fighting against losing myself utterly.

Therese releases my wrist and slides down between my arms to kiss me. "Gently, little one. We will not hurt you. Much." Her voice purrs on the word and I relax into her arms as Gerard shifts position so his fingers can stoke their way up between my thighs. He is still inside me when I come again, howling against Therese's neck. As one, they drop their mouths onto my neck and begin to feed. My body shivers in arousal, in terror, in frantic desire, until I pass out.

When I come back around, I'm at Gerard's computer, fully dressed and very tired. It's the end of my shift. I notice that the stack of invoices is gone from the basket and I feel as empty as it is at the sight. Are they out of work for me? What if they don't want me back? The office is very quiet as I log out and get my jacket and there's no one around to ask if they have work for me to do next week. I crawl home, depressed and exhausted.

I don't remember why I'm so tired or sore, at least not at first. But I don't have any dreams that night. Bob from the agency calls in the morning and says that Forever Insurance loves my work, but they don't have anything for me just now. He tells me about some other gig and I answer like a robot until I can get off the phone.

Then I curl up around the big empty space inside me and cry. I wonder what used to fill it. My fingers find my wrist and I massage a sore spot, dully surprised that it hurts at all. I get up to look at myself in the mirror and I look like I haven't slept for days. Bats could nest in the dark caves of my eye sockets. I wonder what Therese and Gerard would have seen in me, if they could see anything in me at all.

The imagined touch of their hands thrills me for a moment, and I close my eyes, then open them and make myself head for the fridge. It wasn't real, none of it. I just have to get over them. I'm insanely hungry this morning, for whatever reason, and I make myself a huge lunch.

It's only after I've eaten and I go back to get my ice cream from the freezer that something starts to click. Something about the way that the cold freezes my fingers makes me realize that I'm supposed to remember last night as an elaborate fantasy. But what if it wasn't?

I stagger against the fridge door as it hits me: I got used. A little blood, a little sex and then I got put away like yesterday's news. The thought hangs there in my head until I get good and pissed. *Who the hell do they think they are?* I wanted them to keep me, maybe even make me one of them, but what do they do instead but try to glamour it all right out of my head.

I make some preparations. That night I will myself to sleep, thinking of nothing but my dream until I find myself back on the road. Nothing pursues me because no one knows I'm here yet. I lean against a tree in the dark, waiting, and I pull my tampon out so that my blood runs freely down my legs. They will come, called to me by its rusty scent. My fingers toy with the small crucifix around my neck, then stroke the rough wood of the stake that I dream into being in my outstretched hand. They need a new employee at Forever Insurance. I just hope they can see that before I have to hurt them. Much.

# SLEEP PARALYSIS

## ELLA G. HOARE

I'm asleep, or on the cusp of sleep. I can't move my arms or legs. I try to wiggle my fingers or toes. No response. My eyes are closed, I think, but I can see him. I see his eyes gleaming red in the darkness—or is it the battery light on the smoke detector? Am I seeing double?

I think I fall into a deeper sleep, but not for long. I still can't move. His eyes are closer. I see the smoke detector light further away, behind him. I know it's him. This has happened before. I'm too numb to feel dread or desire. My heart beats sluggishly, not quite paralyzed like the rest of me.

"Wake up!" part of my brain screams, tries to rouse me. My body doesn't respond. I try to move, try to take a deeper breath, but the paralysis continues.

A cool finger on my cheek. His finger. The contrast feels good. I was too hot, but I didn't realize it until now. I think I sigh. Maybe. I wish I could shift positions. I try and fail.

His eyes are close to my face. I can smell his grave stench. I wish my smell receptors were as unresponsive as my limbs. He is close enough that the outline of his high aquiline nose is clear, and the ivory incisors stand out. He's hungry. He wouldn't be here if his appetite didn't bring him.

"Get up!" My brain screams again, more urgent and just as ignored by my body. I lazily wonder if he is keeping me in this state, if he has the power to command my body to act against its best interest. I've never felt sleep paralysis for such an extended period while I've been awake.

He slides the blanket down. I would blush if I could. I'm not wearing anything. It was too hot for pajamas, or even a tank top. I regret that now. I'm going to be found dead and naked, one of my worst fears. It's not enough to get adrenaline coursing through my veins.

A metallic click. I see his hands moving near his gut. He's unfastening his belt. Fabric rustling. I watch fascinated by his fluid movement as he removes his clothes. It's not that interesting, I tell myself. Even in the darkness I'm reminded of an alabaster statue. His flesh is hard, impenetrable. Not human. He didn't do this before. He didn't remove his clothes or take his time. He drank and left. I don't want this. I don't want to feel his cold body pressing against me.

"You don't remember much, do you? If you didn't want this, your blood wouldn't call to me," he whispers in my ear. "You want this. You pretend to be a good girl, but I know what you want. You want to surrender to me. Your blood is begging me for this. Why do you think your body yields while your brain protests?"

Is he right? Do I want this? Do I want him to push my legs wide open to make room for him? Do I want to be wrapped in his arms, feel those icy lips planting rows of kisses from the hollow between my breasts to the hollow of my throat? Do I want that fetid breath perfuming my body? I tremble. It's involuntary but it's a movement I made on my own.

I wrack my brain, trying to remember. When was the last time? It was like a dream. Last week, or two weeks ago? It must have been longer. I remember the tapping, tapping wings beating against my window. I ignored it for many nights, or so it seemed in that long-ago or not-so-long-ago dream.

When did I fling open the window, push out the screen that I found bent and destroyed among the shrubs? I pushed it out with such force that I couldn't simply put it back in place. There he was, red eyes claiming victory. Standing no more than a foot in front of me. Why did I let him in?

"That was only the first time in this room. Think harder," he was taunting me, knowing how hard it was to think of anything but what was happening now.

Was I drifting away again? A glimpse of him in a shop or café. It was a late blustery winter evening, not quite sunset but so dreary it could have been midnight if there wasn't so much traffic. It was a shop, or rather, a bookstore. I was looking for a book that would satisfy my need for something different.

"This might interest you." A red volume. One of the Loeb Latin books, in Latin on one page and English on the facing page. Ovid's *Metamorphoses*.

"I don't know about that," I said.

"You like old things. You will enjoy it." The glimmer in his eye. What did he know about what I liked to read?

I took the book. I didn't want to seem rude. I paid for it and then I went to the café. That's why I was confused. I knew he was watching me from another table. I was flattered but scared. I'm not the kind of person who interests others. I'm plain and round in all the wrong places. Not a leggy supermodel. I'm no longer young, much closer to middle age.

"Young is relative," he cuts in on my ruminations. "You are starting to remember. You don't remember the thoughts you had, or you don't want to admit to having them."

I would shake my head if I could. I'd protest. I was a nice woman, not the kind that—

"Fantasizes about being raped and tormented by an immortal? You are quite, quite mistaken. You are exactly that kind of woman. I'll prove it."

He crawls on the bed and towers over me. His knees press against my shoulders. My lips wrap around what he offers. Is that of my own volition? I can't tell. My fingers and toes remain limp. He fills my mouth, penetrates my throat. His fingers twine my hair until his hand palms my head. He could crush my skull if he wanted to. He pushes my head against his crotch. I don't gag like I've done whenever I've done this with other men. Other men let me control how deep I went, I was on my knees or on top when I pleasured them.

"You see, you remember doing it with others. You weren't even married. What would your parents have said if they had known?"

My parents liked Jake. We were engaged, and I couldn't imagine being with anyone else… but then he went to Iraq during Desert Storm and he came back in a coffin draped with the American flag.

"Your mind is wandering, and I don't like it!" He withdrew long enough to slap me. My cheek burned as if he had branded me. "Let's try this again."

I am chastened. I try to focus on thoroughly waking up. If I gagged it would be a response. It would force me to awaken from this nightmare. But maybe it wasn't a nightmare. Maybe I would wake up and find that I was very aroused. Was he right?

He grunts as he works. My jaw and throat ache. They aren't used to anything of that size doing this. He moves in and out, in and out so fast that I wouldn't be able to keep up on my own, if I was awake and in control. Is he a man? What is he? A monster. A monster who knows my most sinister desires. A monster who is breaking me down with every forceful thrust.

He pulls out and I feel empty. The rush of fresh air fills my lungs. Is that a deep, refreshing breath? Am I gasping, gulping in the oxygen? I can't tell. I'm confused in this limbo state between sleep and waking. I'm tired of not knowing. For a minute I even thought I was with Jake.

He turns me on my belly. It's unnerving how my limbs flop

heavily. Now I'm uncomfortable. My arm is wedged beneath my body. I try to shrug my shoulder. Still no response. Maybe I'm already dead except my brain.

I know what he's going to do. I've only done it this way once before. It was so long ago, when my then-boyfriend, Dave, convinced me to try it. I didn't want to admit I liked it back then. I wasn't supposed to like it. I was supposed to be a good girl. Doggy-style was the realm of naughty girls.

"Of course you like it. You like it rough. You want to hurt for me. You want me to taste your tears. I could whip or cane you and you'd beg for more. If I'm feeling generous, you'll live long enough to experience that. It's hard to believe you didn't bother looking for a local kink group to satisfy so much pent-up desire. Tonight, I have other plans and I prefer to keep you in this doll-like state. You do feel like one of those sex dolls you used to imagine being when you were younger, don't you?"

I hated that even those wild imaginings of my virginal self weren't hidden from him. He could see the image of a younger me in the Gothic Lolita dresses I never had the nerve to buy or wear anywhere. "The problem with mortals are they always leave the best fantasies unfulfilled."

Was he right? I still couldn't move. I ought to be able to move now. It's been too long. He shoved my legs towards my torso until I was kneeling, a deep child's pose bow. My head was buried in the pillow and I figured I'd suffocate before he noticed. He planted himself behind me. His fingers delved, probed. I could hear how wet I was, feeling him spreading my juices all over my vulva. My body was betraying me. Every minute I couldn't move or speak I knew was another minute closer to never wanting him to stop what he was doing or leave.

"Don't hate yourself. Spending eternity hating what you are isn't healthy."

I hated that he could read my thoughts. A little privacy, please? He laughs, rich and deep. I thought it echoed off the walls, but maybe that's in my head.

He pushed those soaking wet fingers in my mouth. My juices were sweet. "I knew you'd like a taste," he said. Maybe he was lying. I wanted to shake my head, object. He was smug. He couldn't know.

"Your blood doesn't lie." He leaned over me, his face near my ear. "And your body certainly isn't lying."

I wanted to shake him off, tell him he was wrong, but I knew I was his sex doll. Just a slight movement, a finger or toe, I begged my sleeping body. It ignored me. At this angle penetration was deep and even a little painful. I might have cried if I could. Instead, I was groaning, as if he was pushing the air out of me. He had a firm hold on my hips, digging his icy fingers into my flesh. There will be fingerprint bruises later, his mark. Even if they disappeared I'd know where they claimed me forever.

He gathered my hair and pulled. I thought he would tear my hair out. He was savage, growling and bending me backwards like I was a bow. I saw his teeth, the gaping mouth, only a moment before his teeth pierced my throat and the connection was complete.

My pulse beat, he sucked, his tongue lapped at the wound, my blood spurted and strengthened him. In return he fucked me with greater ferocity. I was his prey and as he drank I knew my blood was begging him, cajoling him to use me, harder, faster, take more and more of my life. Millions and millions of cries for him to use me for eternity. I was drowning, floating, not caring if I couldn't move, relishing the paralysis, the sensation of weightlessness and being filled and emptied all at once.

Don't stop. Don't stop. Don't stop. Keep drinking. Keep fucking.

He stopped. "There's still a hole I haven't used," he said. "I can't let you go without enjoying it."

I told Dave that was one thing I'd never do. I think that's one of the reasons we broke up. But now, there isn't any other choice and he is forcing me to see that maybe I wouldn't mind it. Maybe it wouldn't be so bad as I imagined. Maybe it would be like the fantasies that I kept pushing out of my head whenever they crept up.

I felt the tip of his cock, it pushed ever so slightly. His finger was rubbing my clit and I wanted to move my hips back and forth. Why did it feel so good? Why this quandary? But I couldn't move. It was torture. Still, I felt him pushing into me. It was relentless. I felt my body yielding, opening wider and wider. I knew he was tearing the sensitive skin and somehow, I reveled knowing that when I woke up I'd still feel that.

His teeth pierced my throat again. I felt whole knowing that my blood and discomfort were savored by him. I could hear my blood calling for him. I wish I was more ashamed of myself for having such dark passion, a desire to die from his kiss.

How long did it last? How long did I feel the length of his cock sliding in and out of my ass? How long were those teeth buried in that artery? I was glad for the paralysis that kept me from jerking away, breaking that connection, tearing my throat wide open.

He is spent. I am spent. I am a discarded ragdoll, still unable to move, shift, settle deeper into sleep. He rolls me to my side, my head pressed against his cold chest. I should hear a heart-beat. I don't even hear the pulse of my blood rushing in my ear.

I feel a twitch. It's almost a tickle in my foot. It grows. I feel like an earthquake is shaking my body. I don't know whether to be scared or if this is a full body orgasm and I'm releasing all the desire that I've built up over the years, especially tonight, desiring him even though I didn't think I wanted him. Not this much. Not as much as I want him. A tear escapes my eye. It runs a path over my nose and cools at the tip. I wish I could swipe it away, but that would take too much energy. My body is so heavy now.

I'm cold and thirsty. He moves me ever so slightly, tilts my head up to receive a kiss. His kiss is metallic, what juices flood my mouth? I am so cold, growing colder and colder. I don't know if I'll wake up or sleep. Either way I remain the vampire's whore.

# FOR AS LONG AS YOU NEED ME

---

## DELILAH NIGHT

elicity pursued her newest prey. Sam hadn't done anything wrong, yet. But if Felicity had learned anything in two hundred years, it was that with men, it was almost always *yet*. All she had to do was wait for him to fail her test.

So she followed Sam, and waited for him to slip up.

Testing men and finding them undeserving was her hobby. She would stalk her target for two weeks—the same duration as her marriage. If they did nothing wrong, they could live. If they didn't…well, that's what she was there for.

*Why wouldn't he give her a reason to kill him?*

He was helping a woman with her groceries. Surely he'd make a pass at her? He didn't. He called his mother. He always said please and thank you. He called women "miss" and "ma'am." He tipped shoeshine boys and newspaper boys. He was irritatingly *good*.

Her husband Adam had been her first vigilante murder in her chosen role of protector of women. After decades of death and debauchery with couples about to marry or just married, she had wanted to start over—to be good. She'd chosen to become a mail order bride to a man who'd seemed charming in his letters. Two weeks after the wedding he'd tried to hit her for not preparing his dinner the way he liked it (in truth she barely knew how to cook and had said so in her letters). She'd sunk her fangs into Adam's neck in retaliation. She'd changed his shirt, burning the bloody one, and had raced for the doctor, pretending that he'd keeled over during dinner. She'd pretended to keen at his funeral.

Her husband's brother, Paul, arrived and took possession the land she'd inherited through marriage. He'd pointed out that, as a woman, she had no legal right to own land in Kansas. He'd offered to keep her on "out of Christian charity" if she'd sleep with him. Her last act before leaving town was to kill her brother-in-law, too. His terror had been even sweeter than her husband's.

Be good or be eaten. They always failed, and her belly would fill with hot, rich liquid.

Sam didn't fail the first week. Or the second. By the rules of her game, she should move on. Instead, she persisted in watching him—three weeks, four weeks—daring him to slip up.

Felicity was following Sam down a darkened street when a car backfired. Sam shrank down, covering his head, and let out a cry. Without thinking, Felicity shot forward, wondering what had happened.

"Are you okay?" she asked him.

Sam didn't respond as he rocked back and forth, his hands still covering his head, his eyes distressingly blank.

"Sam?"

Nothing. Had his experiences in the war done this to him?

Felicity had enjoyed the Second World War. Women had gone to work in factories to support the war effort. Fascinated by women doing "men's work," she had joined them. Work was a feast. Some women were brazen, approaching each other for carnal friendship while their husbands were away. Others quietly signalled their availability with a scarf tied just so—a secret code amongst the women. There was no shortage of partners or blood. Her monster had quieted, sated by seduction and the sweet blood of her lovers.

Then the war had ended. Men flooded their way back into America. Women were told their services were no longer needed, that they were taking jobs away from the men. Felicity, and the women she worked with were fired en masse. Her three favorite lovers broke things off with her because their husbands had returned. Even the widows now seemed to absorb the guilt they'd denied during the war years for "unnatural acts" with another woman.

She shook herself back to the present moment.

"Sam?" she asked again.

Sam didn't move.

The dark creature inside of her urged her to rip out his throat and gulp the hot blood. He was frozen in fear, and it would be sweet and velvety as it coursed down her throat. The small bit of her soul not yet corrupted told her to take him home, and for once she didn't give in to her inner demon.

How many honeymoons had she destroyed? She'd devoured countless brides before climbing into their marital bed and waking their grooms from slumber. They'd spilled their seed over her wicked tongue, the last moment of pleasure in their lives. So much to atone for.

Felicity picked Sam up, and took him to his tiny apartment. The irony that she was carrying him the way a husband was supposed to carry his bride didn't escape her. She'd been changed just after accepting her beloved's proposal, and there had been no wedding for her.

There'd been no Thomas, either. Not long after she'd been turned, she'd escaped her creator, and followed the only cogent thought in her head—a mental picture of her fiancé. Instead of finding refuge, her new instincts drove her to gorge herself on his blood. Her first victim, the first of thousands.

Sam shook in her arms the whole way. Felicity dug his keys out of his pocket, and let them inside. She placed him on the couch and knelt between his legs.

"Sam?" She snapped her fingers in front of his face. "Sam!"

His eyes focused on her, his pupils still too large, too blank.

Felicity did something that would normally repulse her. She kissed him.

Sam's lips were as tense as his whole body. But as Felicity brushed them with her own, they softened. Her tongue flicked out and traced them, and his lips parted. She slipped her tongue into his mouth. Suddenly he was kissing her back. She gasped when his arms banded about her, holding her as if she might disappear.

A flame of lust ignited within her. She couldn't remember the last time she'd sheathed a man's cock between her thighs. In the months since the end of the war, she hadn't touched a woman, either. She still might drink Sam dry, but the wetness flooding her silky panties meant her inner succubus needed to come out and play first.

"Sam," she whispered.

"I don't care that you're not real," he said, and kissed her again. It was a kiss full of need. He pulled her into his lap. "Make the bad go away."

"Undo my dress," she said.

His hands nimbly undid the yellow buttons marching up her back and she helped him push the dress down. He opened her bra, freeing her breasts. She straddled him as he suckled at one breast, while his hand worked her other nipple. Felicity moaned and let her hips roll against him, pressing her core to the bulge in his pants.

"I need more," he whispered.

"Take more," she encouraged.

He opened the teeth of her garters, and pulled her girdle over her head, leaving her in her panties and stockings. He moved them so that he was lying atop her, her legs spread wide.

"Do whatever you want. It's your fantasy," Felicity said, feeding his notion that she was a hallucination.

Sam reached between them, his finger tracing the seam between her legs.

"You're so wet," Sam groaned.

"For you," Felicity whispered. She told herself she was playing a role, but deep down she knew it was true. She was eager for him.

He brushed the cotton to the side and slid a finger into her as he continued to kiss her like she was oxygen and he was a drowning man. She revelled in the difference between the touch of her female lovers and this man's thick, rough fingers. He traced a path from her hole to her clit, setting her on fire. She arched beneath him, wanting more, needing more. Sam fingered her, making her gasp as his thumb circled her clit, then dragged over it, using the rough skin to make her writhe beneath him.

Her orgasm was like experiencing a bomb's explosion first hand. She'd known that if she lengthened the time between her feedings that sex could be more intense, but she'd never gone without food or orgasms for so long since her change.

"That's right darling," Sam crooned. "Come for me."

A second finger joined the first, seeking, stroking the part of her that sent her wild. His teeth grazed her neck.

"I want you inside me," Felicity hissed.

Sam slid her panties from her body and replaced his fingers with his tongue. Felicity felt successive concussive explosions as her body jerked in ecstasy. Her tongue caught on a fang and she tasted the chilly sludge of her own blood. She craved the taste of his neck as his cock was buried deep in her.

"Inside me!" Felicity demanded.

Sam chuckled. He stood and removed his shirt. Scars marred the smoothness of the right side of his chest.

"What happened?"

He looked down and closed his eyes. "I wish the scars were gone." He opened them and glanced down hopefully.

"Damn. They have to ruin even this," he muttered.

Felicity knew what it was to regret your scars. The one on the left side of her abdomen was a reminder of the day she'd decided to redeem herself. She'd murdered a bride, and adorned herself in the gown and veil. Felicity had been crying at the sight of her reflection, aware of how far she'd fallen. The groom came in to find her standing over his cold bride, dressed in the stolen finery. He pulled a gun on Felicity, and she learned that gun wounds hurt, but did not kill her. She hadn't killed him, escaping past him with her preternatural speed to den in a cave while she slowly healed, gnawing on whatever wildlife wasn't smart enough to know her scent meant death.

Felicity took Sam's hands and placed them at his belt. "Never worry about them, lover. I want to see all of you, have all of you."

He hesitated, so Felicity took hold of him through his pants. "Don't you want to be inside of me? I'm so wet for you."

Sam swallowed, and Felicity watched the bob of his Adam's apple. His hand trembled, but he undid his belt and removed his trousers and boxers.

Felicity had heard from the other women at the factory that there were men who came back from the war *changed*. Some turned mean, others drew into themselves. Still others were harmed in ways beyond understanding. She mused that Sam's change was no more wanted than hers had been. She understood why the sound of a car backfiring could sound like gun fire, or an explosion, and could traumatize the soldier it had injured.

Felicity still couldn't tolerate entering her home state of Georgia. She'd never traced the line of descendants her siblings must have left behind. She couldn't bear the idea of watching them from afar, never part of her own family again. What had her family thought after she'd disappeared? That she'd run away with her creator? That she'd been abducted by whatever had killed her fiancé? When the crazed madness following her creation had lifted, she'd been as relieved to learn that her family had not been among her victims as she was devastated that Thomas had.

An unbidden thought wound its way through her mind— maybe Sam could understand her in a way no one else ever had.

Sam froze, and she worried her woolgathering had taken too long, had ruined the mood.

"Come here, lover," she purred.

She'd forgotten was it was like to have a male body cover hers. The weight, the heft of that big frame and strong muscles pinning her to the sofa was a change from the soft, lithe bodies of her female lovers. The coarse hairs on his leg caused her to writhe against him.

"Come for me, princess," Sam whispered, sliding his hand between them, slipping two fingers inside her, crooking them to find her most sensitive spot. His fingers stroked while his thumb circled her clit and his tongue plundered her mouth.

Heat built inside Felicity until it felt like she could burst into flames like the vampires in motion pictures. Her hands dug into Sam's back, the blood red nails scoring his pale skin. She could scent the beads of blood her scratches had caused. Sam seemed insensible to anything but her and her pleasure, unaware of the predator's instincts he was stirring. Intoxicated by his fingers and the blood she could almost taste in the air, the world ceased to exist before exploding outward like a thousand suns going supernova.

"Yes. Yes, give it to me," Sam murmured in her ear, leaving his soft vulnerable throat exposed.

"Inside me!" Felicity wailed.

Sam was hard and eager. He pressed against her opening, and she swore as she stretched to accommodate him. There had been only fingers and the occasional toy made of ivory or glass for so long, her body had forgotten what it was like to sheathe a flesh and blood cock.

"It's all right," Sam soothed, his thumb returning to her clit. "I'll go slow."

"No," she replied. "Hard. Fast. All of it."

Sam's eyes met hers. Offering him a closed lipped smile to hide her now full sized fangs, she nodded. He took hold of her hips and was inside her in one long thrust where pain and pleasure waltzed together. He paused once inside her, letting her feel his length and girth.

"You're the best fantasy I've ever had," he whispered.

Felicity tweaked his nipples in response, and he cursed.

Sam moved inside her, and Felicity undulated her hips, matching him thrust for thrust. Theirs was no sweet lovemaking—it shifted and became need crashing into need.

Felicity turned her head and saw the long column of Sam's neck, and the blueish glow of the blood pulsing beneath his skin. Felicity's lips parted in anticipation.

"Sam," she breathed.

"Goddess," he groaned.

She couldn't hold back anymore. As the orgasm built

between her thighs, she grabbed the back of Sam's head and yanked him to her lips.

"So good, so wet, so *fuck—yes!*" Sam cried out as her fangs sank into his artery.

Blood coursed over her lips. The adrenaline of sex made his blood savory and filling in a way that fear-based blood never was. The hunger she'd built up overpowered her and she sucked and swallowed as her hips met his in a frenzied mating.

This time the orgasm washed red across her vision. Red like the lipstick smeared across both their faces. Red like the stripes on the flag soldiers like him had carried into battle. Red like the blood filling her mouth, soothing her hunger.

Sam convulsed above her as he came, cursing a blue streak.

Somewhat regretfully, she let go of Sam's neck, licking the wounds to promote healing. She could feel his hot blood flushing through her body, sating her hunger.

"You're a good man, Sam," she whispered, unsure of whether he'd heard her or not before he fell into a deep sleep.

For the first time, she gave a male victim the gift of his life.

That should have been the end of Sam's story. But Felicity found she wasn't so easily freed from his allure. A few days later, she stalked him as he walked to work. A week later, after stalking a rapist and finding his blood lacking, she broke into Sam's apartment and was pleased to find him sleeping in the nude. She slithered out of her clothes and climbed into bed with him.

"It's you," he breathed when her kiss woke him, and pulled her to him.

Felicity blinked rapidly, and was shocked to find tears falling onto her cheeks. The idea of Sam as a long-term partner flitted through her mind and she dismissed it as the nonsensical musings of a lonely vampire. Then again, if she wasn't alone, maybe she wouldn't need her test?

In the lead up to the passage of the nineteenth amendment, there had been threats of violence against the suffragettes. While they chanted, Felicity prowled through the men who jeered the suffragettes, picking out her targets. They'd all failed her test immediately.

During the Great Depression, Felicity had targeted rich men who owned grocer's markets. How many of them would make women trade their bodies to feed their children? They never made more than three days of her test. Then she emptied their fat wallets and left their money on the tables of the women they'd hurt.

But the blood was never as satisfying as it was when a man was foolish enough to think *her* a potential victim. They weren't tested—they were dinner.

But now? She would hunt, attacking those who would hurt women, only to find their blood less filling than Sam's. So she'd go to Sam's apartment. He was always grateful for his "dream girl" to show up. She embodied his fantasies and he unknowingly donated to her sustenance. She could never stop hunting abusers and users—she owed it to every vulnerable woman she'd hurt—but she felt drawn to Sam like a moth to a flame.

With Sam, she luxuriated in the boozy taste of blood thickened with arousal as it pumped through the large vein in the thigh. Luxuriated in the sounds he made when he came, first from Felicity's tongue and then from her pussy and fangs. Luxuriated in feeling sated without wanting to drain the bag of flesh dry as a punishment.

When Sam asked her name one night, she was shocked to hear herself give her real name.

"Felicity," he'd whispered before burying his face between her thighs.

She toyed with revealing herself as a living—well, living adjacent—person, and not the personification of his sexual fantasies. Maybe he'd want to stay with her forever. Could she turn him? She never had done so before. Would he stay with her after she aided him through his early years as a vampire? Could they help each other find a way through their pain?

"We don't need to have sex if you don't want to," Sam said one night.

"I—what?"

"You can just take the blood," he said.

Felicity blinked stupidly. "What?" she repeated.

"You heard me," he said quietly.

"You know?"

"Fantasy girls don't leave bruises on the neck."

She was dumbfounded. "And you're okay with it?"

"You've been my salvation for nearly a year. It's like you know when the shadows are encroaching, and you protect me from the nightmares. When you're here, you soothe me. And you've never thought less of me for needing to be soothed. Why wouldn't I want to share my blood? It's a small price to pay, especially if you'll be around more."

The monster inside Felicity had quieted every time she was with Sam. The lucidity and sanity that came from being near him was a welcome respite.

Felicity kissed Sam. "For as long as you need me."

Once again, she pictured him as a vampire, and thought *and as long as I need you.*

# LAWFUL EVIL

ERIN HORÁKOVÁ

## Inns of Chancery, 1843

While Jasper Warren sometimes pretended to revere the luminaries of the legal profession in which he was as yet but a novice, he was not wholly proof against all traces of genuine awe. Mister Vernon Durand, esquire, who now sat before Jasper and behind a great partner desk that had never accommodated any partner, was a grand old snake of Chancery. He had a charmed gaze and a smooth voice which held lumps of jargon suspended in it like dabs of unwhisked flour left standing in a shoddily-stirred gravy. Jasper had long known *of* him, of course—who in the business had not? And in knowing something of Durand, Jasper had come to respect his cunning as a rising predator respected a monster in its prime.

For all his fawning professional courtesy, Jasper held himself at a distance from other men and made his judgments from that perspective. His respect was a fine evaluation of others' power and abilities, and of their capacity to work upon the world (and to do him injury thereby). Jasper had developed in his childhood a habit of calculating wariness that had ever served him well, when little else had. He sat before Durand (man of affairs, a superbly controlled and enviably successful vision of what Jasper himself might be in time, if he worked like the devil and was lucky besides) and said that it really was a pleasure and an honour he'd looked not for to be called here today. What could he do for Mister Durand?

"It is not everyone," Durand said slowly, interlacing his fingers, "who is truly—suited, to the law. Do not you find that, Mister Warren?"

Jasper suppressed a snort, thinking of Timothy. He and Timothy Belmont, a boy a few years his junior, had come up together as clerks in the same firm. Despite their humble origins, due to gruelling work, exceptional ability and good fortune, both were now set to enter into the ranks of articled attorneys. But Jasper knew Timothy wouldn't be happy in it, and that unlike himself, Timothy *needed* to be happy to get on. "I've thought the very thing 'ere now, sir. Why, it's as though you see into my mind."

Jasper only meant it as a habitual piece of flattery—a conversational nothing, such as he dealt in every day. But the temperature of the room seemed to drop a degree after he'd said it, and Jasper added, "if you'll pardon the expression, sir," while thinking *now what about that don't he like?*

"Not at all, young Warren." Mr. Durand said, in a tone that bent curiously inward, somehow. "Pray, be candid. I wish to conduct our business in an open and exact manner." He inclined his great head with judicious gravity and, for the moment, said no more.

Jasper thought Durand's manner of wielding silence to accumulate power to himself a very neat trick indeed. He wished he were so positioned as to employ it. His carefully-constructed, unimpeachably unassuming persona (which provided him with a great deal of protection, in a field that had little use for anyone not born middle-class) was incompatible with such silences as Durand's, which made all the power in the room roll to one side like marbles accumulating in the lowest corner of an uneven old floor.

"I feel I may confidentially say to you," Mr. Durand continued after this pause, "that I suspect you've *quite* the legal disposition."

Jasper's heart beat a little faster. Durand couldn't be offering him some form of clerkship with *him*, could he? Durand couldn't have an eye to bringing him on? So far as Jasper knew, Durand hadn't heirs, and to inherit his practice would be something indeed. Word might have reached Durand of Jasper's particular abilities—why not? Few men were as good as he was at what he did: Jasper knew it. Why, if he were Durand's heir he might be any man's equal. He might be Timothy's better at last, and then they'd see, wouldn't they?

"Oh yes," Durand countermanded Jasper's modest denial, "I see a great deal of potential in you." He held out his hand, presumably for Jasper to shake.

"Oh *thank* you, sir," Jasper said, standing and advancing a step towards the desk.

Suddenly Mr. Durand was excessively close. Jasper blinked, surprised, and opened his mouth to say something—perhaps to remark on his potential benefactor's extraordinary speed. Once more Mr. Durand inclined his grave head, and then Jasper, somehow unable to move, to jerk away, felt a searing, screaming pain the like of which he'd never known.

"Jesus fucking Christ that shitting hurts," Jasper hissed, all pretences dropped. He struggled, but Durand's grip was made of iron, inhuman-strong. "What the *bloody*—"

Mr. Durand raised a mouth that, to the still-immobile Jasper's horror, dripped red. "Precisely, Mr Warren."

———

WHEN TIMOTHY OPENED the door to his rooms—reluctantly, for he'd asked who was calling (at this hour!) and gotten an honest answer, which gave him neither pleasure nor an understanding of what his visitor could want of him—Jasper sprang in like an unleashed Jack-in-the-Box, pressing the door shut behind him with one long hand and then rubbing the pair of them together before him as he whirled on Timothy.

When Timothy had been young, he'd thought Jasper had no such thing as a smile about him. Over the years, however, Timothy *had* seen Jasper muster a few sly grins. Now he positively beamed, his smile mirroring the white scarf tied securely about his neck.

"Why, Mister Belmont," Jasper crooned, advancing on Timothy in a way that made Timothy take a step back. "What a positive delight it is to see you looking so well."

"To what do I owe the—" Timothy largely succeeded in keeping his voice uninflected at this point, though he found Jasper's rigid professional front and unctuous put-on civility absolutely maddening, "*honour*, Mister Warren?"

Jasper's smile twitched, and he gave a short, falling laugh that seemed to Timothy acutely false. "Aha. Won't it please you to call me Jasper, Mister Belmont? Now, don't make me beg you yet again."

"Very well," Timothy said shortly, "Jasper. I confess, I had not expected to see you this evening—"

"Well, as it happens I've something particular to say to you," Jasper exclaimed, clapping his hands together. "Now Mister Belmont, do you notice anything different about me?" He accompanied his question with a gestural flourish that took in his whole body in a manner Timothy found oddly lewd, despite there being no easily-named element of suggestion in it. The turn of his wrist, especially, struck Timothy as actionable.

"Not in particular, no," Timothy said coolly and automatically, even as he seriously examined the man before him.

"Why, nothing at all?" Jasper said, as though egging him on, leaning in a little—presumably to allow Timothy a better view of the prospect.

Timothy frowned in thought. He could discern no definable change, and he didn't want to play this stupid game with Jasper. (Especially not after midnight, when they'd work in the morning.) And yet—*wasn't* something amiss? Something tugged at Timothy strongly, like an important commission he'd forgotten. His eye compared every aspect of Jasper against the well-known inventory stored up in his mind, and while not an element diverged from Timothy's expectations, the whole was on a tilt. He looked up at Jasper, eyes narrowing in a silent inquiry.

"Can't you guess?" Jasper asked. A hollow-dimpled grin settled on his cadaverous face, as though he were a merry goblin.

"I ask you plainly, why are you here?" Timothy snapped, disturbed and trying to cover over it with brusqueness.

Jasper sighed, as though Timothy's incivility really did disappoint him. "Oh Mister Belmont," he shook his head, tsking, "is that any way to behave towards one who has ever and always esteemed you? No, it won't do." He turned a strange, fierce eye on Timothy. In the light from the candle Timothy held, it seemed to gleam red. "Why not invite me to sit down, eh?"

Timothy felt, under the influence of Jasper's gaze, as though the rushing river of time churned slower, and gave way to a lazy stream. "I—" he began, confused. He stopped. Tried once more. "I—"

"Yes, Master Belmont?" Jasper asked, breathless, his whole body canted towards Timothy as though Jasper lived in expectation of his reply.

A bead of wax ran down the candle Timothy held and

trickled onto his hand. It ought to have hurt—to have made him cry out and drop the candlestick. Yet Timothy hardly felt it: a little drop of warmth that cooled, a wax that turned from liquid to cream on his skin.

"Yes," Timothy said, "yes, of course, I—Jasper, won't you sit down?" Timothy extended a languid hand to gesture at the somewhat-shoddy sofa, feeling tired but curiously free of any urge to sleep.

To Timothy's surprise Jasper took that gesturing hand, holding it in his own. Timothy frowned.

"It's warm," Timothy said. His thoughts were slow and sluggish, as though it were a hot day. As though he were swimming in a pond, and the air around him was that heavy, murky water. "Your hands are never warm. Ever since I first shook hands with you, they've always been so very cold, Jasper."

Jasper's smile grew small and subtle. "Bad circulation," he said. "I caught a nasty disease in the charitable establishment I was housed in as a boy, an' its remnants 've been with me ever since. Such things went around, there. Educating us all together amounted to a perfected method of transmitting contagion. I expect they hoped we'd die off a bit and decrease the numbers. I've never told you this, have I, Belmont?" Jasper looked away. "Suppose I never felt I could, before."

"Why not?" Timothy asked plaintively (forgetting in his distraction that Jasper had not actually explained his present freedom from the sad effects of his old malady). Timothy couldn't understand why Jasper should think him an unfit confidant. He was sympathetic, as far as people went. He was nice, wasn't he? (Jasper *never* thought him nice.) And Timothy knew he of all people understood what it was to be uncared for, and at too tender an age. Hadn't he worked his youth away in the same office Jasper had?

"You are sweet, Belmont," Jasper murmured. "I've ample proof of it. You just ain't always sweet to me. An' if I'd told you, you wouldn't have cared."

It didn't bother Timothy that Jasper knew what Timothy thought but forbore to say—that Jasper implied knowledge of things he'd no business knowing. Jasper's last assertion did bother Timothy, however, and by the softening of Jasper's bitter gaze, Timothy it must have shown.

"Come sit by me," Jasper said, changing the subject and drawing Timothy down with him to the sofa. "Why don't it ever occur to you to invite me to call *you* Timothy, hm?"

Timothy's breath caught. He looked at Jasper: the prominent bones of his face, his snow-pale skin, the drawing, coal-smoulder brightness in the very depths of his eyes. 'Why' seemed far off.

"Why not do it now, Belmont?" Jasper purred the suggestion.

"You'll only demur," Timothy said. "You're always doing that sort of rubbish, and you never mean it."

Jasper gave a sharp laugh. "But I won't this time," Jasper assured him. When Timothy had done it, Jasper said "Well, Timothy." He then paused, closed his eyes and said the word again, as though it were a thing too good.

Jasper opened his eyes once more, refocusing on the slightly younger man. "Now try and tell me," he said, "what is that made you frown a moment ago. What struck you amiss? What did you see when you looked at me, Tim?" He lingered on the name despite technically abridging it, pulling it out and slapping it luxuriantly back into his mouth like a child making the most of a piece of soft toffee.

Timothy diligently described Jasper's particulars, tip to toe, and noted how, while there was no alteration in them as such, still something felt awry. Some unknown, perhaps even sinister power swirled about Jasper.

"If even you can't see it, with all your wit and knowing me as you do, why, no one will," Jasper mused, rubbing his chin. "And think of you paying me such attention. You see, I've had something of a change of fortune since last we spoke. A very great lawyer in the city has taken me on." He drummed his fingers on his thigh.

"Not just anyone can do what I do, Tim—oh, no. It takes a certain," he mused, selecting the word with an air of self-indulgence, "constitution. One might add to that, an appetite for the work. My new partner thought me fit for it, and now you might say I'm another sort of attorney all together." His smile was sharp. "A minute distinction, perhaps, given that about the only difference between one type of attorney and another lies in the amount of blood they drink."

"Congratulations, Jasper." Timothy gave him a sleepy smile. "Is your fortune really made, then?"

"Oh, forever and then some," Jasper said, immensely pleased with himself. "Now suppose you congratulate me a little more warmly?"

"Jasper?" Timothy asked, blinking in confusion.

"Don't be shy," Jasper said, looping a finger underneath Timothy's modish cravat and pulling Timothy towards him by it. "You've no cause to be."

Softly, slowly, Jasper pressed his lips to Timothy's. Timothy drew in a shuddering gasp, and Jasper breathed into his mouth.

"Ain't this pleasant?" Jasper murmured, encouraging, planting another chaste kiss on Timothy's lower lip. "Oh, isn't it just," he sighed, daring to dart his tongue into Timothy's mouth. He pulled Timothy up onto his lap and gave him a squeeze, coaxing Timothy's arms around him.

Timothy lost himself in the intoxication of it all: the pooling warmth of kiss after kiss. He breathed Jasper's name, and Jasper gave a small moan.

"That's it, Timothy," he cajoled, pulling back to rub his nose against Timothy's, "just like that. Are you liking it?"

Timothy nodded, and Jasper swallowed hard, reaching out to touch his hair.

Feeling bold, Timothy pushed his tongue into the older man's mouth. Jasper made a startled noise that tapered off into a groan. Timothy was only vaguely embarrassed at the way his erection strained against his trousers, pushing against Jasper's torso. Timothy slid his tongue over Jasper's teeth, intent on exploring him thoroughly. Even through his stupor, Timothy frowned at discovering one of Jasper's teeth longer than it had any business being. He tested his tongue on the tip and found it sharp.

Jasper hissed and pushed Timothy back, holding Timothy's shoulders with both hands. And yet for all he'd put a stop to Timothy's explorations, Jasper panted, looking flushed and excited. Timothy observed that while during his earlier examination Jasper's mouth had looked as it always did, it now unmistakably contained long fangs—whiter than the rest of his teeth, as though they were new-grown. A drop of blood besmirched the upper-left specimen, smearing when Jasper went to lick the fang clean with his tongue. Timothy touched the tip of his own tongue with his index finger. It came away red.

"You'll have to be careful of them, sweetling," Jasper said, crooking a finger to summon Timothy back to him. "I expect they make themselves felt when I become excited."

What Jasper now was, Timothy knew. There was no point in saying it. Feeling sharper and more aware, though not yet questioning the daze he'd been in, Timothy shook his head. "This isn't you, Jasper." He touched his fingers to his lips, as if wondering at what those lips had been at but a moment ago. "You've never done anything like this with me before, never hinted at any wish to. It's this change, this disease making you come to me—it's no natural desire."

"What I feel for you," Jasper said (maintaining his calm with an effort, if Timothy were to judge by his expression), "what I've *long* felt for you, is the most natural thing in the world. Why, it makes more sense than the bulk of it. For that matter, the change suits me pretty well. This is only what I always have been, underneath it all—apparently it don't take, if you don't already have an inclination that way. Now if you *would* come *back*, Timothy."

His gaze compelled his prey. Jasper had always been uncannily good at getting people, Timothy not excepted, to go along with his plans. This more than natural augmentation of his abilities felt altogether unfair. At least Timothy thought as much before Jasper started caressing his neck. The soft brushes and strokes of Jasper's long fingers gave way to feather-light kisses, which in turn gave rise to suckling, pulling ones that made Timothy's pulse speed up and his breath come in pants.

"You'll leave bruises," Timothy said muzzily, pouting.

"Won't I just?" Jasper said with quiet rapture. His hands

divested Timothy of his frock coat and waistcoat, but he left Timothy's trousers and shirt as they were (albeit loosened at the neck). He stoked and petted Timothy over his clothes, making Timothy squirm with desire he didn't voice.

Jasper shook his head. "Now I won't do what you're thinking of, much as I'd like to," he murmured. "But isn't this delicious as anything? I just want a little sip of you. I bet you're milk with the cream left in. I bet you're sweet cider and Christmas punch."

The suggestion of Jasper's consuming him rung alarm bells in Timothy's sluggish mind.

"You've always been hungry," Timothy said slowly, coming 'round to himself. His lingering distraction made him honest, and he knew Jasper's ambition of old. "You never can get full. Underneath your façade, you *love* it when the law lets you revenge yourself upon your betters. I can hardly believe that anyone, even another damned creature like yourself, was so stupid as to hand you tools to do it better."

Jasper grinned at him, very hard.

"But now," he countered Timothy, "I can be so pleasant in how I go about meeting my needs. I always took care to be pleasant, and now I'm even more so."

When Timothy tried to wrench his gaze away from Jasper's, Jasper collected both Timothy's hands in one large palm. His fingers skated over the throbbing pulse-point in Timothy's wrist, and he gripped Timothy's chin with his free hand.

"You will let me have a taste, won't you Timothy?" Jasper asked politely. Dragged down by a stronger exercise of mesmeric power than Jasper had hitherto attempted, Timothy nodded, but the realisation that the hands on him were probably so lovely and warm because Jasper had *eaten before he came* sent a much-needed bolt of revulsion and terror through him.

"Who," Timothy said through his teeth, "did you murder before coming, Jasper? Or don't you know?"

"*Damn* you," Jasper hissed, dropping Timothy's chin. Timothy's resistance had deflated Jasper, and damaged his glamour by upsetting him. With that ripped away, the full danger of Timothy's position suddenly struck him. Jasper seemed not gentle and alluring, but dynamic and predatory. Timothy sprang away and Jasper rose to his full, imposing height.

"You know it would be a treat for once, it *really* would, not to have to work myself down to the bone to see anything I want done set in motion."

Jasper turned his back on Timothy, pacing the room and sweeping a hand through his short hair.

"All I wanted was a few kisses from my sweetheart—a few caresses, and the barest drop of 'im. Was that *so much* to ask?" Jasper berated the ceiling, as if begging an answer of God. "People *like* being drunk from, Timothy." He whipped his head around to glare at Timothy when the younger man scoffed. "Oh, it does hurt at first—and how. But *then*," he gave a wicked, fangy grin, "it becomes a most interesting experience. And if you thought too much on what was so *different* about my kisses, why I'd distract you, or fuddle your memory a little. And now you've gone and ruined it. I can't—" he made an elaborate hand gesture, "*fuddle* this fight. And I've not even had so much as a taste of you!"

"*Why*," Jasper whirled on Timothy, fangs prominent and eyes blazing, "are you always against me, Belmont?"

Timothy observed him, stunned. "How could such intimacies ever be amenable when I wasn't given any choice in the matter? Now *who did you eat?*"

"*No one.* In this entire godforsaken town, no one does *anything* but live off others, often at great expense to 'em, an' often to the point of killing 'em. Yet you think I'm some unique threat to the populace, or some still-greater parasite. I wonder if you'd come on quite so strong if I had a well-bred accent, like the one you've broken your tongue to, or finer still, like 'my betters'." Jasper's sneered. "Is it even my way, to suck 'em quite dry, do you think?"

Timothy grudgingly had to admit that Jasper was all premeditation, all craft. Outright murder wasn't like him, if only because it was the wrong sort of crime. Jasper rarely needed to transgress the law, exactly, to expose and work upon its inequalities and frailties, and to thus accomplish what he wanted with it.

"My new firm," Jasper said tightly, "doesn't conduct business that way, besides. A complete extraction's out of the question —too messy."

Timothy winced. Jasper's semi-ironic usage of terms of art was always painful; at present, it was excruciating.

"My sire's 'generation,' as it were, was obliterated in villages on the continent at the turn of the century. Now he keeps his head down. Our condition is something of a liability. The more notice you attract, the more at risk you are. There ain't much truth to that daylight business, but all the same, if bodies go missing, bobbies have questions. I'm to leave 'em be, after the fact. It don't take much to tide me over."

"And so you're what," Timothy asked, "your 'sire's' steward?"

"It's a complex world, nowadays. It's my sort of world. He needed a good factor—new blood, as it were. I had to sign a contract, even." Jasper sighed, bracing his hands on either side of the window. "At least I can send mother a substantial cut of my earnings."

Timothy's head was spinning, and he tried for a worldly, lofty tone to help him regain command over the situation. (It had been a spectacularly draining evening in that regard.) "This is all very interesting, I'm sure—"

Jasper made a noise expressive of an incandescent rage. He wrenched a chunk of Timothy's window-trim off in frustration, seemingly unaware of his altered might and the damage to the woodwork alike.

"Nothing," he seethed, "is ever good enough for you, is it Belmont? No attainment or trick I can bring to bear earns me a grain of your precious respect. Not even being turned into an unnatural creature of the night makes you bat one pretty eye. *You*, who relish anything fantastic and unusual. When *I* do it, why, you've seen vampires before."

Timothy was too stunned to quite take any of this in properly. Jasper's incredulous laugh came out all wrong, sounding a little like a sob. "You still think I'm dirt, and as I see you always will, you might as well just stake me now and make it true. Here." At last Jasper noticed the piece of wood he was holding. He threw it to the ground before Timothy. "If you can stoop to conquer, why, as ever, I'm yours."

Jasper slumped to the ground on his knees, wretched and furious, heaving breath Timothy supposed he no longer in truth required. Perhaps it was a habit. Or histrionics.

"Did you get a cheap-seat for Richard III when it played last month?" Timothy asked wryly, without quite realising how breathtakingly rude he was being. "I expect so."

"*Fuck* you, Belmont," Jasper said with feeling.

Timothy's eyes widened at his language.

"An' I wish I had done, too," Jasper added mulishly, taking in Timothy's expression.

Timothy let that one pass, and with it a long moment as he considered all he'd just heard, the night in general, and the longer course of their accquaintence. "I wouldn't say I am precisely—unaffected, by your change of state."

Jasper drawled insincere thanks.

"*Or*," Timothy continued, "that I am unmoved by your evident feelings. They've revealed you to me as never before. You are a more complex man than I ever credited you with being. There is a good deal more bound up in you, for good and ill, than ever I knew."

Jasper arched an eyebrow at him, looking wary in the face of compliments: an article he'd never had from this shop before, and thus did not know whether to trust.

Timothy slapped a small fist against his palm, finding the words. "Look, Jasper—you must come frankly before people. I see very well why you do not, in the normal course of things, but at a certain point you must sufficiently respect the individual you wish to—"

"Pardon, are you attempting to tell me that I don't respect you?" Jasper pressed his palm hard against his chest, over his heart; it looked almost painful. "Why, who do you think I respect in all the world, then? There's no one with such native keenness as you 'ave, and no one alive with such a terrible power to hurt me."

"You've never respected me enough to trust me," Timothy responded. "You try and dupe me, as you try and dupe everyone. Don't you see that the way to love me is to win my favour, forthrightly, and try your chances?" He advanced towards

Jasper, compelled again, but this time by internal rather than external forces. He extended a hand to Jasper's cool cheek. Held it there.

Jasper's eyes flared wide, and now he seemed the mesmerised prey. He stood motionless.

"You're always trying to best me," Timothy said in a tone just above a whisper. He swallowed, and his voice gained strength. "Well I've been overmastered before now, and so have you, I see. It may have left you with the impression that that's what power is—that that's what *life* is—but it left me with a distinct idea of the limitations of the sort of behaviour the world so often understands as strength. Of how shallow and pathetic such strength is, at its dead heart. It's left me with no taste for bullying, or for letting myself be thus abused. You'd do better to be frank and yourself with me: to show me, honestly as you can, who you are and what you want." He moved his hand from Jasper's face, and pretended not to notice the way Jasper leaned after it just slightly, on instinct. He knew Jasper was probably ashamed of that, though Timothy found it touching.

"It ain't pretty," Jasper said bluntly. "What I feel. It is not calculated to win you."

"You are of necessity," Timothy reminded him, "not the most objective judge of that. If you cared less, you'd see me better in that regard."

Jasper sucked in a cheek. Released it. "Let's get the pleasant bits out of the way—if you can call my sodomitical leanings pleasant. I'd like to protect you, for sometimes you do need it. Though not so often, perhaps, as I think."

Timothy was glad he'd admitted as much, for he hardly thought himself helpless and hopeless. Jasper continued.

"I want to help you find out what it is you're supposed to do

—for it ain't this, I'll wager—and to aid you in it, for you're a treasure the world don't realise it's got. I'd like to be by you, as often and as long as I can, and as for *looking* at you—I don't know how you'll take it, but I've never been able to keep my eyes away from you. My very palms sweat when you're around —or they did, before the change in me removed the danger. That ain't polite, but it's true. I've tried to keep it from your notice, but I expect you're too observant not to have observed. And where I looked, I ached to touch. Lord, how I've always wanted to touch."

Jasper wet his lips, staring intently at Timothy, who felt his face heating under the flattering onslaught, the waves of Jasper's want—more effectively ensnaring that his mesmerism, for it was so specifically fitted to its target, and this glamour was true.

"Why, just the curl of your hair—lord, to wrap it 'round my finger 'n let it loose after 'while, like a pressed-down spring. I'd lick you heel to crown if I had half a chance. I'd do anything *you'd* a mind to: I guarantee there ain't a thing I've not thought of doing to you a hundred times, so whatever you'd fancy could hardly be outside my purview."

Jasper sucked in a deep breath, his narrow chest expanding with it. Timothy watched, entranced. "And that includes the meaner things people can do to one another. For I always 'ave resented your easy way with the world, your quickness, and most of all, how you weren't mine. I've wanted to rake your poor back with my nails when I was angry, to hurt you in return for some cruel, indifferent word. It ain't attractive, how much I love you. It ain't proper, how deeply I need you to give a little of it back. I never could move on, and while I could live without you it'd rot me inside. Oh I'd look all right, going about the streets, but I'd be like a cucumber with a firm skin and a soft, sloppy core. A man is supposed to be independent," Jasper shook his head, giving Timothy's damaged window a sarcastic grin. "but there never could be anyone but you for me."

"Oh," Jasper laughed, as if the thought suddenly came to him. "An' I'd do about anything to keep you from marrying. I blackened your name with that girl you fancied. Told her horrifying, infinitely repeatable things about you and our guvnor's housemaid. Now what do you think of that?"

"*What?*" Timothy started, blindsided, for he'd never had any notion what had put the girl off.

"Oh, yes," Jasper said with bitter conviviality. "For I was never likely to get what I wanted—an 'ouse somewhere with you, where we might grow to such an age as would impress later 'istorians. Given that there were to be no late nights of conversation, no queer suppers of whatever we found in the market that looked likely, no reading to you when you were ill, no talk of bringing up a needful child such as you and I had once been together, and no coming back from theatre in a hired carriage with your head on my shoulder, with you falling asleep, for it was past midnight and you'd drunk until your cheeks were rose-pink—well given *that*, why not spoil *your* chances, eh?"

"Is that the worst of it?" Timothy demanded, pacing back and forth.

"I don't know if you'd call that the worst," Jasper mused, "for the moment my new station came upon me, I thought, of course, of the all-unknowing partner of my fate—that is to say, yourself—and how he might come to share in my good fortune."

"Jasper!" Timothy pronounced like a curse.

"Mm," Jasper hummed. "Yes, I thought, *some might not see sweet Timothy Belmont as 'aving a great potential for the vampiric arts. But I know 'im better.* You're like me." He levelled his gaze directly at Timothy. "You're more like me than you ever will admit. If I'm greedy for your affection, you're desperate for everyone's. It's worse with you, for you want to charm an' influence people and be *liked* for it—if you could you'd be a shadow, in every room with so much as a flicker of light in it, at every creature's back. So it came to me that after a while, if I accustomed you to taking my fangs," he licked them obscenely; Timothy shuddered, "you might be willing—eager, even—to take a little more. You might want a life beyond this one, such as only I could offer you."

"I want nothing of the kind," Timothy said firmly.

Jasper closed his eyes, as if listening to a far off strain of music. He opened them again. "My little liar," he pronounced with tenderness.

Timothy slumped upon the couch, propping his elbow on the arm of the sofa and his head in his hand. Jasper lurched up from the floor and came over to join him, perching primly on the other end, with miles of upholstery between them.

"I told you you wouldn't like it," Jasper said with a kind of satisfaction, like a man enjoying savagely digging into the infected wound he knew he'd die of.

"It was awful," Timothy said frankly. "It was more awful than I could have expected. But it was the truth, such as no one's ever given me. I expect that every heart has its mean corners, and strains of savage violence. Once, Jasper, when you'd worked me to a state of rash anger with you, I fantasised about killing you."

Idly, Timothy slid his fingers up Jasper's arm, which Jasper had slung over the back of the couch so that it framed the empty space between them. Jasper held firm under the touch—didn't shiver. Trying to be brave, Timothy supposed. And succeeding —credit where it was due.

"I pictured shoving my letter opener through you. No," he shook his head, "no, *into* you, Jasper. Twisting in the hot, heavy point and pushing, until you quivered around it. Until you gasped for breath. Pulling it out and then shoving it home again. And again, and again. Positively destroying you with it."

Timothy met Jasper's wide eyes. "I think that if you have been dishonest with me, I have, at times, been as dishonest with myself, and you thereby."

He glanced at Jasper's lap and couldn't quite suppress a smirk.

"Where were we," he murmured, climbing back onto that receptive platform, pressing against Jasper's renewed erection with a soft rock of his hips. "So you want to talk to me all night, do you?" Timothy asked politely, biting Jasper's lip to catch the answering 'uh huh.'

"And to keep me," Timothy whispered into Jasper's ear, licking it. "And to take me to the theatre—"

"Damned right I do," Jasper rasped. "Now, how do you come by this present boldness? Not that I'm complaining."

"I'm fairly ready in a crisis. This is one. I must admit the situation is not such as I ever expected to encounter. But I feel I owe your love some trial of the prospect, and I find I owe myself some exploration of my own feelings for you. They are not slight or simple. I *want* you," Timothy said, ducking his head against Jasper's neck to murmur it into his collarbone. "Not just because you've toyed with me tonight, but because I've done so longer than I ever saw it. I hated your dishonesty and discretion because I wanted so much more from you than that. If I wanted everyone's approval, I wanted yours most."

Jasper clutched the small of Timothy's back, pitching up his hips so his erection slid against Timothy's again-stirring cock. "Is that so?"

"Yes, Jasper," Timothy said, so starkly as to banish even Jasper's ready suspicion. "Now get back on the floor, if you would. You were terrible to me, molesting me without so much as a by-you-leave. I want payment in kind."

Jasper's eyes were wide and dark, the pupils waxing fat like moons. He practically slithered out from under Timothy, urging the other man to turn and settle and unbuttoning Timothy's fall-front trousers with an eager hand. "Was this what you wanted, then?" Jasper asked, cocking an eyebrow up at Timothy, who nodded.

"Y-yes," Timothy said, trying for sternness.

"What, even with these?" Jasper said mildly, his tone half a tease, running his tongue over his fangs again.

"You'll be careful," Timothy assured him. "You're a careful man, aren't you, Jasper?"

"Oh, infinitely," Jasper assured him, rubbing his hands together in glee. Jasper took his time, urging Timothy's trousers down around his knees. He breathed an appreciative sigh over Timothy, now clad in just a shirt.

The breath of air made Timothy twitch, and made his virile member jerk as though it really were a discrete member of some bodily society Timothy himself was but the trustee of.

Jasper made a thick sound, eyeing the cock before him like a sweet, and proceeded to lacquer sloppy kisses all over Timothy's thighs.

"You're so soft," he pronounced with a pleased sigh.

"I'm softer here," Timothy said, palming his cock and giving it a couple authoritative strokes, until it plumped and firmed in his hand.

Jasper watched him as though he couldn't have moved if the room had caught fire.

"Well, Jasper?" Timothy asked, pushing the tip of it against Jasper's lips.

Jasper gave the very crown a delicate kiss, and Timothy shivered.

That coy introduction—"you've never done this before?" Timothy asked. Jasper shook his head, *no*, wholly unembarrassed—gave way to a more vigorous sweep of his tongue over Timothy's slit.

Timothy gasped. "Not so hard. At least—not yet. You know how even on your own, certain touches are far too much to bear initially, but then they're just exactly what you want when you're further along?"

Jasper popped the whole head of Timothy's cock into his mouth and nodded agreeably.

"Fuck," Timothy returned.

Jasper grinned (as best he could under the circumstances—he found his new vampiric accoutrements helped) and slid the first inch or so of Timothy's shaft into and out of his mouth, the head of Timothy's cock bouncing against the cold frame of Jasper's extended fangs, which pressed neatly against each other, like machine gears, and didn't risk catching Timothy at all. The very base of the head of Timothy's cock popped in and out of this ring, as though he were fucking a tight cunt, and Jasper's thin lips pressed against the edges of his teeth proper, cushioning Timothy from them.

"Fuck, fuck, fuck," Timothy breathed, squirming helplessly and throwing an arm over his eyes.

Jasper delicately slid Timothy out of his mouth, a glinting string of saliva dangling between them for an instant—Timothy peeked through his fingers at it, and thought that was disgusting, and that Jasper was working so hard to please him, and all the while the sight of it sent another pumping rush of blood through him. It pooled in his reddened cock, making it harder still.

"You're right about your being softer there," Jasper said, leaning back and taking Timothy's sack in his hand, weighing it as if it were a good to be bought at a market stall. Gently he rolled the testes, applying only the lightest pressure.

"Ah," Timothy cried, pushing himself further into Jasper's grasp.

Jasper laughed, what ought to have been a self-assured chuckle all taken over by manic glee. "You do seem to appreciate the fangs, my love. Does the danger entice you, do you think?"

"I don't think I'm in any danger from you," Timothy said heavily, "so long as I'm yours. And even if I weren't, you could only bring yourself to spite me viciously. Seriously harming me is beyond you—you'd have to unmake yourself to do it."

Jasper rolled his eyes, though his expression was warm. "Leave it to you to ruin a piece of lewd suggestion."

"It was filth you were after?" Timothy asked. "Oh, I beg your pardon. Jasper, *please* suck me off."

Jasper wrapped a hand around Timothy's cock, giving it a sound stroke. Timothy's own hands scrabbled for purchase against the couch cushions.

"That's nice," Jasper said, "keep that coming, why don't you?"

"Please," Timothy said even more sweetly as Jasper once again took the head of Timothy's manhood in, letting Timothy fuck his mouth shallowly with jerky thrusts of his hips. "Please,

Jasper—" Jasper touched his tongue again to the slit of Timothy's cock, and Timothy cried out.

It was endurably good, this time—he was ready for it. Jasper's hand was even and steady on his shaft. He mercilessly tongued the rim of Timothy's cockhead, the sweetly sensitive spot just beneath it, and the very tip, first with the flat of his tongue and then with the blade.

"Do it 'till I spend," Timothy babbled, shoving at Jasper's head, "oh take me, for god's sake, Jasper let me come in you, won't you let me? God you've such a mouth, I could fuck it all night, please, please Jas, I—I—"

Jasper slid off, earning a whine from Timothy. "You know, it does occur to me," he said cheerfully, "that vampires don't actually much need to breathe. Why, I might—" He demonstrated, slicking back his fangs with an apparent effort of will, rolling his lips fully over his teeth and carefully sliding Timothy to the back of his throat, flicking his tongue up against Timothy's shaft and sucking as hard as he could.

Timothy whimpered and tossed his head and beat tight fists against the sofa cushions. He pitched it down Jasper's throat with ugly growls, as though he were a pet dog gone feral.

Timothy fell back and draped limp on the couch. Jasper abandoned his cock with an immensely satisfying, smacking sound.

"Let me do it," he begged around his fangs, and Timothy nodded.

He cried sharply when Jasper's fangs sank into the flesh just above his hip, and indeed a fat tear rolled down his cheek at the sudden pain. But his cries turned to a low, lasting moan as Jasper started to draw, suckling at him with the avidity of a starving child. Timothy felt warm and providing, nurturing and giving. Immense, erotic satisfaction rose in him. It was unlike the orgasms he'd had from handling his own cock—more akin to the lush sensation of fingering his arse, shame-facedly imagining a handsome boy enjoying him thus.

"I'm going to come again for you," he murmured to Jasper, who he knew would want to be apprised of it.

Jasper looked up at him, worship in his eyes, his hand frantic and fast on his own cock, which he'd pulled out of his trousers.

"Go slow," Timothy said, "don't take too much. I want you to spend before you have to stop. I want you to make me peak, doing this."

Timothy bit his hand to muffle the wretched cry of his conclusion, and Jasper sobbed into his hip, pressing his face against Timothy's skin. White ejaculate, flecked with blood-pink, spilled out over Jasper's pale hand.

He reared back, shaking, and bestowed a last kiss on Timothy's cockhead while rubbing Timothy's bite-mark. Ever so carefully, Jasper let the tip of one fang graze the very tip of Timothy's cock, and licked the resultant drop of blood.

Timothy positively screamed into his bit hand, his strange, intumescent orgasm finishing on a ripped, jagged high. He fell forward onto Jasper, pinning him on the floor, kissing him with a frantic lassitude.

"Oh god," he gasped, "oh god, we can't do it every day, I'll want it too much, I'll die, I—"

"I couldn't handle it every day," Jasper laughed, struggling to his feet with Timothy in his arms, as though the other man weighed nothing. Jasper bore Timothy to the bed, throwing the both of them down on it and nuzzling at Timothy's neck, his face. They lay together gasping, for though Jasper didn't strictly need to gasp, he certainly felt like doing it.

# SUBMISSION IN SEVASTOPOL

## JORDAN MONROE

May I see you today, *gospozha?*"

This was it. The time she'd waited for. A tingling sensation arced up her spine and she strove to maintain her composure. Calmly, she held the phone to ear and replied, "Come straight from work. Be here in one hour. Bring a bottle to impress me. You will be generously rewarded."

There was a sharp intake of air on the other line. Clearly, his imagination was getting the better of him. "*Spasibo*, Mistress. I will do as instructed."

"See that you do." Before he could answer, she hung up and placed her cell phone on her cedar desk.

Nastasiya rose and stretched her limbs. The golden afternoon sunlight illuminated the papers littered on her desk with a glow, as though to remind her of what she'd worked for this past year. Her office contained centuries of information that today could incriminate anyone from the lowliest al Qaeda courier to the highest echelons of the Saudi royal family. She'd brought down courtiers in the gilded viper pit that had been the French court at Versailles, Catholic cardinals who'd forgotten their master during the religious conflicts of the 17th century, and high-ranking officers of the Third Reich.

Getting rid of them had been a delight.

She left her office and made her way up the grand staircase to her plush master suite. Upon entering her closet, she removed her chic black romper and reached for a sapphire blue satin robe, the hem reaching her mid-thigh. As she tied a simple knot at her hip to secure the robe, she went into her bathroom and surveyed her appearance.

*You don't look terrible for 600 years.*

Nastasiya brushed her ash blonde hair to one side and

quickly braided it, the end reaching the middle of her back. Her makeup hadn't smudged, so she reached for her perfume and spritzed a small amount of mist between her breasts. Finally, she rubbed unscented lotion between her legs, shuddering as she did so.

A metallic pang reverberated inside her skull. She slammed her eyes shut and gripped the sink, willing it to pass. She'd satisfy her craving soon.

She allowed herself several deep breaths. This was not the time to falter; this was the time to decisively act. There was a task at hand, one that could not wait any longer. Her clients needed that information before it arrived in Moscow.

Minutes passed and the pain subsided. Relaxing her shoulders, Nastasiya got into the required headspace. This was as much about her pleasure as it was about his. His acceptance of her control gave him freedom; for her, the utter joy of domination. The physical and mental turmoil was necessary for their release.

Her toes curled into the plush carpet and her hand snaked in front of her. With her other hand, she gently pulled the satin across one of her breasts, coaxing the nipple to a taut peak. *Give and receive, give and receive, give—*

The doorbell rang and she heaved a deep sigh. Nastasiya waited a beat, then made her way downstairs and opened the heavy oak door. "You're looking as fine as ever, pet. Come in and remove your shoes and socks. You will have no need for them."

Evgeny Bordyukov bent forward slightly, then followed her into the elegant townhouse. He shut the door behind him, placed both his leather briefcase and a slim black bag on the floor, and slipped off his loafers. She watched as he lifted each leg to peel off his black socks. After he stuffed them into his shoes, he turned to face her.

Nastasiya swiftly slapped his beautiful, bearded cheek. "Did I give you permission to look at me?"

Clutching the side of his face, Evgeny answered, "No, Mistress."

"And what happens when you take what is not granted?"

"Punishment, Mistress," he whispered.

"Do you wish to be punished, slave?"

He remained silent, mulling it over. Nastasiya was a patient woman and would have no qualms leaving him here in the foyer to think about his answer. This evening, however, she required urgency. She reached out and squeezed his testicles with a tight grip.

Evgeny's knees buckled and his face screwed with a mixture of pain and pleasure. His mouth gaped open, but his lips turned upward, while his eyes were shut, and he'd tossed his head back. *Oh yes, this will do nicely.*

"I'll not ask again, slave."

She squeezed a little harder and he panted, "Yes, Mistress!"

"Yes what?"

"Yes, I wish to be punished."

Nastasiya released his sac and gently stroked the tender area with one hand and his stricken cheek with the other. "Leave your belongings here. Go upstairs, pet. Kneel. You know your place."

Evgeny obeyed, as Nastasiya had expected he would. As he climbed the stairs, she allowed herself to watch the muscles of his ass ripple with each step. His nondescript charcoal grey suit fit him perfectly. Briefly, she mourned its imminent irrelevance.

When he was out of sight, she shook her head, picked up the

briefcase, and made her way to the study. With care, she lifted it on to her desk. Evgeny might have been her slave here, but he was a GRU officer in every other context, a sworn servant of the Kremlin. If he heard her, the evening would end a great deal messier than she wished.

Nastasiya caressed the supple leather, taking a moment to congratulate herself. It had taken her six arduous months to dominate Evgeny so completely. Up until tonight, he'd never brought his briefcase with him. Nastasiya knew he kept it in his office at the distribution center he used as cover, a place too risky and too full of tempting morsels for her to enter. Clearly, she earned both his body and his soul, and while the journey had been enjoyable, she had never lost sight of her goal.

The locks on the briefcase were brass and Nastasiya gently rubbed her thumbs over them. Each clasp had four numbers. She didn't have time to go through all the possibilities for the combination. The only solution available to her was to consider what sequence he would pick.

Evgeny was a steadfastly loyal man, but he was not one to recall random bits of information, least of all numbers. The combination to his briefcase, in which he ostensibly kept important documents to send to his superiors in Moscow, would be particular and personal. She bit her bottom lip, careful to not let her protruding fangs pierce her soft flesh, and tried the following combination:

0710 1952

She pushed the latches aside, and they released with a satisfactory click. Nastasiya released the breath she hadn't realized she'd been holding.

*Putin's birthday. Ever the obsequious one.*

Opening the briefcase, she struggled to contain herself. Right at the top of the stack of papers was a red folder marked "Secret." Ignoring the warning written in Cyrillic, she opened the folder and first saw a list of names. Flipping through the folder, she saw copies of emails, text messages, passports, and money transfers. Evidence of subversive activity in Ukrainian hacking communities that the Kremlin certainly would not appreciate. Nothing untoward nor harmful had occurred yet, but neither the GRU nor the FSB would care. Evgeny, distrustful of Ukraine's cybersecurity apparatus, would send this information to the Russian capital and within days, the people on this list would swiftly be ensconced in Siberia, or worse.

She ripped the folder from the briefcase, walked over to the fireplace, and picked up the lighter on the mantle. Nastasiya breathed a sigh of relief as she lit two of the corners and tossed it into the fireplace. The freedom fighters hadn't used the email addresses or phone numbers in the folder in months, and she'd instructed them to use cash or cryptocurrencies for their financial transactions. They would not be caught. Not any time soon, at least.

The pages were now a smoldering mess. Time for some amusement.

Nastasiya closed the briefcase on her desk and took it outside, placing it next to Evgeny's shoes. Finally, she could smile. Her actions might not remove the unwelcome occupying forces from Sevastopol, but they would shorten the GRU's reach long enough for her friends to cause trouble.

As she climbed the stairs, Nastasiya turned her attention to her charge. The possibilities were endless with Evgeny. No matter her demands, he would not merely acquiesce, but enthusiastically assent to her rough ministrations.

Turning away from her master suite, she opened the closed door to her sanctuary and let herself into the vast space. A mahogany dresser was against the far wall, with a small box of tissues on it. Drapes covered the windows and the tea lights along the mantle were lit, the small flames dancing and bathing the room in haunting warm light. Her medical table and St. Andrew's Cross were set to rights. There was of course a bed in the center, which was properly made up, the white sheets tucked in tightly. She noticed a suit hanging on the closet door knob, the trousers folded over and the scarlet tie draped over the lapels. Nastasiya found the sight oddly domestic. At last, her gaze settled on her subject.

Evgeny was kneeling in a corner, his back straight and defiant. His hands were clasped in front of his body, shielding his groin from view. She feasted her eyes on him, admiring his broad, hairy chest and thick thighs. Out there, the man contained in this body was eloquent, able to charm wealthy clients to part with both their money and their secrets. In here, he was meant to serve and bend to her will. She loved the paradox.

Nastasiya walked over to him and lifted his chin so he could meet her eyes. The look he gave her was one of adoration, as though the very act of gazing at her was a moment to treasure. She wanted to kiss his lips but held back. Instead, she stroked the dark stubble along his jaw.

"So many ways to play, my dear. What shall I do with you?"

He swallowed, the knob of his Adam's apple bobbing. "Whatever my mistress wishes." He lowered his head and kissed her palm.

Nastasiya inhaled sharply. The tender kiss shook her resolve, but only slightly. She turned away and opened one of the drawers. Her black silk scarf was right at the top and she grabbed it. Walking back to her charge, she twined it around her fingers.

"You know what I am about to do with this, yes?"

"Yes, Mistress."

"Please tell me what I'm about to do."

"You are going to blindfold me. I will not be able to look upon your face so as to be consumed with sensation."

Ever the loquacious man. "What is your safeword?"

"*Ovtsa*, Mistress."

"And why did you choose that word?"

"There is comfort in sometimes being a sheep. We all need a chance to follow and not be burdened with the responsibility of constantly leading."

"Good." She walked behind him and placed the silk over his eyes and the bridge of his nose. Nastasiya secured the scarf around his head tightly. "Is this uncomfortable?"

"No, Mistress."

She returned to stand in front of him and held up two fingers. "How many fingers do you see?"

"None, Mistress. I cannot see anything."

"Excellent. Hold out your hands."

Evgeny did as she instructed and she placed her hands in his. She pulled and he rose to his feet. Nastasiya led him to the cross and lifted one of his arms, wrapping the soft leather cuff around his wrist. He raised his other arm and she imprisoned the other wrist. After securing the clasp, she brushed her fingertips along the contours of his forearm. The dark hairs rose and his skin prickled. He sighed and leaned forward into the cross.

She stood back and took her time to survey his body. Long,

lean, and elegantly brutal, Evgeny had been a joy to bring to heel. This would be their last encounter, and she intended to savor it like an inmate savored his last meal.

Nastasiya went back to the drawers and pulled out her cat-o'-nine tails. The handle was thick and wrapped in supple black leather, while the tails were knotted rope. She knew just how the ends stung sensitive flesh, and she also knew that these brought particular pleasure to Evgeny. Walking back to the cross, she gave herself a couple of practice swings, making sure to make the tails whistle through the air.

Evgeny sucked his teeth and Nastasiya saw him clench his fists. The veins in his beautiful forearms protruded against his skin and her fangs descended automatically. The hunger was getting worse. She steeled herself and swung the instrument once more, catching the tied ends with her other hand.

"I haven't gagged you, pet. Do you know why?"

"I do not know why, Mistress, but I can guess."

She toyed with the frayed end of one of the knots. "And what is your guess?"

"You want to hear what happens to me and how I react to it."

"Correct. Relax, pet."

She struck him, the tails licking his upper thigh. Evgeny grunted but she didn't give him any more time to recover before flogging him again. The blows came quickly, and she watched with delight as his skin blossomed from pale to pink. She decorated his firm ass with stripes and reveled in his cries of pleasure-pain. Giving him time to catch his breath, she squatted to see between his legs. His sac was tucked up against his body and his erection stood tall and thick. She rewarded him with a gentle teasing stroke along the seam between his balls.

Evgeny's knees buckled and he shuddered. "Can you take more, pet?"

He panted and answered, "If it pleases you, Mistress."

Nastasiya closed her eyes and savored his statement. She scooted away from him, dropped the flogger, and walked back to the drawer. After making enough noise by rifling through her supplies, she picked up a small bottle of lubricant and a heavy butt plug. She smiled.

*He's more than ready.*

The time away from him had allowed his flesh to flush scarlet. Nastasiya placed the toys on the floor, walked over to her consenting prisoner, and rubbed the rounded cheeks and Evgeny pressed into her hands. With her thumbs, she rubbed the line between and pulled them apart. He groaned, and she gently massaged the muscles.

"What is your safeword?"

"O—O—*Ovtsa*, Mistress."

"You are free to use it."

"I know, but I don't want to use it now."

"Then let us continue."

Nastasiya picked up the bottle and coated her finger with the clear liquid. She spread his cheeks aside again and teased his opening. He quivered and she pushed inside, feeling the muscles settle around her finger. He released a long, primal moan as she flexed her finger and made tiny circles inside him. Looking up, she watched the veins dance underneath his skin as he clenched and unclenched his fists. Her fangs fell again, but this time she didn't pull them back.

When she'd had enough, Nastasiya removed her hand from his sensitive opening and picked up the plug. After covering the silvery knob with lube, she pried him open again and pressed the plug next to his skin.

Evgeny gasped.

"Is there something wrong?" she asked.

"No, Mistress. It's just cold."

Nastasiya smiled. "It'll quickly warm up. Relax."

She waited until he was once again settled in his bonds. When she was satisfied that he was comfortable, she pushed the plug past his boundary. He clenched his fists again, and she stopped herself from drooling when she saw the veins. Returning her gaze to his ass, she smiled with delight as the silver end shone in the candlelight.

Nastasiya stood and picked up the cat o' nine tails. She swung her arm hard and struck his ass sharply. The knotted ends hitting his muscles brought forth a wonderful percussive sound and she struck him again. He groaned, an ancient sound that would have brought her to her knees had she been a weaker being. Nastasiya rotated her wrist as she swung, the ropes connecting with different parts of his back.

Evgeny released a high-pitched cry, which gave Nastasiya pause. She stopped and dropped the tool.

"Is everything all right?"

He panted, and she watched beads of sweat drip down his striped back. Although she had a strong desire for it, Nastasiya did not lick the droplets. Doing so might overwhelm her, which was something she did not need. Not yet, at least.

"Everything is all right, Mistress."

"I am glad to hear it. You've taken enough punishment."

Nastasiya quickly removed her robe and pressed her body to his back, her breasts flattening against him. She stroked his front, pinching his nipples and running her fingers through his chest hair. His breathing slowed, and he relaxed more heavily in the cuffs. Inching her hands lower, she teased the coarse hairs on his belly and then at the root of his cock. Slowly, she circled each finger around the thick rod and gently pulled at him.

He flexed in her hand and thrust his hips forward. She stroked him and inhaled his salty, musky scent. Oh, but he was a joy to discipline and he took such pleasure in her treatment. With her other hand, she rubbed his back and the rounds of his ass, still warm from the beating. Evgeny moaned and bent his knees, and Nastasiya knew he'd had enough at the cross.

She let go and reached up to remove the cuffs and blindfold. When his arms were free, he let them hang by his sides.

"Lie down on the bed, pet. On your back."

He blinked his eyes open, then bent his head and she watched him walk over to the bed. His erection wobbled with each step. She nearly salivated at the thought of what she had in mind for him next. It would be an entirely new experience for him, but she had done this before and had been told it was extraordinary.

Evgeny climbed onto the bed, his swarthy complexion in stark contrast to the virginal white sheets. She went back over to the drawer and put her scarf away, trading it for a small medical bag. Another sharp tingle shot through her and she felt the liquid heat between her legs. She shut the drawer and stood at the foot of the bed.

"I want you to watch me and I do not wish to bind you. However, you are not to push me away. You must rely on your safe word. Do you understand?"

Evgeny nodded, his cock twitching slightly.

Nastasiya opened the bag and pulled out a thin stainless-steel rod. She displayed it to him.

"Do you know what this is?"

"I do not, Mistress."

"This is a sound. It goes inside you."

Evgeny chuckled. "Forgive me, Mistress, but something else is already inside me and feels far too good to be removed."

Nastasiya gave him a knowing glance, then lowered her torso to his, his chest hair tickling her nipples. "It goes inside somewhere else. Don't worry; I'll go slowly."

She watched his face, recognizing the confusion and then the surprise. His eyes grew wide and his neck tensed, yet his mouth remained inscrutable. To reward them both, she reached for one of his hands and placed it on her breast. Instantly, he stroked the taut peak and gently held the heavy round flesh. Nastasiya leaned forward and wove her fingers in his thick hair, urging him forward. Evgeny, needing no instruction, brushed her nipple with the tip of his tongue.

She exhaled and pressed into him. Evgeny closed his lips over her sensitive spot and drew upon it. Dutifully, he left her other breast alone, though Nastasiya imagined that was its one unique torture. A sharp, exquisite feeling shot through her: he'd pressed her nipple between his teeth. Hearing her moan, Evgeny held on to her, sucking as he bit. Before she lost all control, Nastasiya pulled his face away from her.

His eyes shone with unadulterated lust. Nastasiya slowed down her breathing, for she would need a steady hand. "Lie back, pet."

Evgeny relaxed into the pillows and let his arms hang by his sides. His legs splayed open and she knelt between them. Looking down, she caught a glimpse of the metal in his ass. She smiled and reached for his stiff cock.

He sighed as she stroked him, working him until he was

utterly inflexible. Nastasiya watched as sweat dripped from his brow and he chewed on his lower lip, clearly in the throes of sensation. With her other hand, she reached over to the thin steel rod and touched it to the swollen head of his cock.

Evgeny shuddered and arched into her hand. She circled the tip, catching the clear fluid and smearing it over his sensitive flesh. "Tell me again. What is your safe word?"

"*Ovtsa*, Mistress," he answered between pants.

"Good. Use it as needed. I'm going to put this inside you now. Are you ready?"

Kremlin officer though he was, she cared about his safety and pleasure. Nastasiya prided herself on maintaining a safe and consensual environment. Any slip in that mindset would spell disaster for her practice.

Evgeny nodded. She held his cock steady with her left hand firmly at his root. Nastasiya, ensuring her right arm wasn't shaking, held the sound over the small hole. The slick fluid gave the head a slight sheen, but she focused her energy on getting this right. His last experience on Earth should be a pleasurable one.

She was charitable, after all.

Slowly, she slid the rod into his cock. Evgeny groaned as the metal went into him, centimeter by centimeter. Nastasiya pulled it nearly out, then pressed it back in to him, giving him time to adjust. His hips began to shake, and she saw him gripping the sheets, his knuckles white.

"How does it feel, my dear?"

His chest rose and fell rapidly. "What, Mistress?"

Without stopping her movements, she said, "How does it feel to be doubly penetrated?"

Evgeny sank further into the pillows, tilting his hips further into her hands. "I cannot describe it, Mistress. It's—ah—it's exquisite."

By this time, she'd been pushing the rod deep into his cock. Nearly half of it was inside him. Nastasiya wondered if she should push it all the way into him, but since this was his first try, she thought better of it. Instead, she increased the pace.

"Do you like this faster tempo, pet?"

His eyes were closed, the small wrinkles at the corners creasing further on his face. Evgeny clenched his jaw and Nastasiya noticed the veins in his arms protruding again. It's too much, she thought.

"Pet, answer my question."

"God it feels so good I am trying to hold on please don't stop oh God—"

Nastasiya let go of the sound and his cock. He cried out; she had stopped him from falling off the edge. Evgeny moaned a little more and relaxed on the bed. When his breathing slowed, she carefully pulled the sound from his cock and placed it back in the bag. Next, she instructed him to lift his legs onto her shoulders. As he did so, she knelt up and reached down to remove the plug from his ass. She released him, left the bed, and wrapped the warm metal in tissue. The instruments would be cleaned later.

Nastasiya turned her attention back to her charge. Evgeny was still hard as steel but looked soothed. She crawled back onto the bed and mounted him. Without asking, she gripped his cock and teased her clit with it.

"Touch me, Evgeny."

Eagerly, he stroked her back, her sides, her ass, and finally her breasts. His thumbs circled her nipples, and as she rocked on him, he pinched them sharply, as she had long ago instructed him. She was slick with need and coated his cock with her arousal. When she couldn't take it any longer, she knelt a little higher, angled his cock, and slid down on him.

They sighed together as she settled. She undulated at an agonizingly lethargic pace, wanting to draw out this coupling. Evgeny had been assaulted with sensation, so she forced him to hold off his orgasm. She leaned forward and gripped the headboard, thrusting her breasts into his face.

"Suck," she commanded.

He lifted her breasts and pressed them to meet in the middle of her chest. Opening his mouth wide, he took both of her nipples between his lips and sucked greedily. Nastasiya groaned and fucked him harder, reaching down to hold his head to her. His response was to run his tongue over both nipples, which drove her further into a frenzy. She pushed herself from the headboard, pulled away from his lips, and lowered herself, pressing her chest to his. The soft hairs teased her nipples and she felt his large hands grip her ass.

Nastasiya rode him harder and harder until finally both of their needs became too urgent to ignore. She ground her hips deep into him as she moaned. The grip on her ass tightened and he buried his face into her neck. They came, clawing at each other and holding on with desperation.

With his cock still deep inside her, Nastasiya reached up and pulled Evgeny's hair to one side. He resisted a little, but she exposed his carotid. She drooled and lowered her lips to the thin skin. As his orgasm receded, she licked the skin. She felt his limbs go limp around her and she chose that moment to pierce him.

"Ouch! What? Mistress, I—"

Suddenly, everything around was tight. He squeezed her

arms to her sides and tried to wrestle her away. However, he didn't know she'd had centuries of this under her belt. The metallic liquid slid down her throat and his grip on her body weakened. His blood was thick and rich, full of nutrients, the rich diet of an officer posing as a wealthy wine merchant. She savored him, much as she savored every moment they'd shared.

The draining had taken mere minutes. Nastasiya peeled herself away from the body, her hunger more than satisfied. She rolled her shoulders and looked at the shocked, still face. To the empty room, she said, "You invade my country on your tyrant's whim. You turn my leaders with pretty words and prettier things. Your entire apparatus seeks only to destroy the will of my people. You, my dear pet, had this coming."

She found her robe and pulled it on, tying it loosely. Her friends from the shadows would come in due time to collect the body; ghouls would never turn away a free meal. When she returned, she could expect the room and the instruments to be spotless.

Nastasiya went downstairs to her front door and picked up the gift bag Evgeny had left. She pulled out the bottle and smiled. He'd brought a 2004 Montepulciano, an excellent and rare vintage, one she was eager to drink. She went into her study and closed the door behind her.

She placed the bottle on her desk where the briefcase had been. Picking up her phone, she scrolled through her contacts until she found the one marked "Sasha." Without tearing her gaze from the bottle, she dialed the number.

"Yes?" A gruff yet anxious male voice greeted her.

"It is finished." She hung up before he could answer.

# LET LOOSE YOUR LONGING

## ISKRA RYDER

You must be dating some kind of vampire," her friends joke, seeing the bruises on Ellie's throat, the times her ever-present scarf slips down to her shoulders. They have no idea that what they're saying is no more than the truth.

Margaret (never Maggie or Meg) is like a queen from some elfin realm, small and precise, and so powerful that Ellie thinks it radiates off her, an almost palpable glow. She's brilliant and beautiful: her current identity holds a double PhD and manages a career as a dancer around her postdoctoral studies in particle physics. Her eyes are luminous and brown, like some kind of expensive wood, her chin delicately pointed. Her body is compact and strong, a finely honed tool for her craft, and Ellie wants nothing more than to worship between her thighs.

Sometimes Margaret even lets her. It's like a dream for Ellie, being permitted to nuzzle her way up one whipcord-strong leg, to part those lovely thighs with her hands. She wonders if Margaret will allow it this time, wrapping her arms around herself against the chill, damp air.

They have a standing date every Tuesday afternoon at 6, and it's the highlight of Ellie's week. She leaves the office where she works as a paralegal and hurries uptown to Margaret's apartment. It's in a nice part of town, somewhere Ellie would like to live someday, when she's saved up enough from her job and the gifts Margaret likes to give her, maybe. Ellie gets to the building and lets herself in with the key she keeps in a special pocket of her wallet. It seems like it should be oversized and heavy with iron scrollwork, but it's an ordinary brass key, cut at the local hardware store. Then she climbs the two flights of stairs (much better-smelling than the stairwell of Ellie's own apartment building) to the floor where Margaret lives.

She knocks on the door out of politeness, then unlocks it

and goes inside, where the living room is dimly lit and beautifully appointed. No ordinary postdoc-cum-modern-dancer could afford furnishings so luxurious, but Margaret is anything but ordinary. Ellie's obsessive love aside, Margaret is something like four hundred years old, and acquisitive; she's amassed quite a collection of exactly the sort of thing she likes over the centuries. Her tastes run to the ornate, curls of gilded wood and padding of rich red velvet on the chairs, heavy frames around the paintings Margaret bought when the artists were unknowns.

Ellie settles herself into a chair that's worth at least triple her yearly income and takes off her scarf. Margaret likes to see the evidence of her handiwork, gazing avidly at the livid bruises and wetting her lips with the tip of her tongue. Folding her hands and admiring the original Dégas on the wall across from her, Ellie waits. It's not long before Margaret steps out of her bedroom, looking absolutely perfect and not at all like she just woke up. Ellie looks at her, and it's like she's dissolving into Margaret's dark eyes like a marshmallow into cocoa.

"Good morning," she says cheerfully.

Margaret lets out a breath that's almost a laugh. "Good morning," she says, running one hand through her hair. "How was work?"

"Fine," Ellie says. "You know how it is: lawyers, clients..." She trails off, not wanting to bother her with minutiae, and cuts right to the heart of the matter. "May I worship your body tonight?"

Tapping one finger picturesquely on her lower lip, Margaret contemplates the offer, while Ellie squirms in her seat and tries not to let her mouth water too obviously. "Yes, I think so," she says at last. "Come into my room."

Ellie hops to her feet and follows Margaret back into her inner sanctum, decorated in deep blues and gold, like a night sky. Margaret takes off her simple black dress, lifting it over her head and revealing the body that has featured in all of Ellie's best dreams for the past two years, then sits down on the edge of the bed, spreading her thighs and looking up expectantly at Ellie.

She drops to her knees and strokes the insides of Margaret's legs, caressing the soft skin, letting her mouth trail up to the folds between them, where Margaret is redolent of the ocean. Borrowed blood, Ellie's own blood, makes her inner lips plump and irresistible, a deep shade of purple-pink, and Ellie kisses and licks them, sucking them into her mouth until Margaret hisses and sinks an impatient hand into her hair, urging her ungently to get a move on.

Her clit stands proud, jutting out of its soft hood, and Ellie breathes on it, enjoying this little bit of power she holds, the way Margaret's muscles clench and twitch. Then she licks it firmly, just how Margaret likes, and again and again, a quick, insistent rhythm.

"More," Margaret demands, and Ellie obeys, sliding a fingertip into her depths, then another, matching her strokes to the flicks of her tongue. Margaret's hips rise off the bed, pressing against Ellie's face, and it's Ellie who moans, eyes closing, welcoming the pressure and the demand, redoubling her efforts.

Ellie coaxes her through her orgasm, a second, a third, before Margaret's hand in her hair pulls her face away and up. "Enough of that," Margaret says, barely breathing hard, even as her cunt pulses with aftershocks around Ellie's withdrawing fingers. "Come up here and take your shirt off."

She obeys; her throat is so bruised already that Margaret will shift her attentions to another location for the night. Ellie's lush curves fill out her modest black shirt, and her pale breasts have a tracery of blue veins that wake a hunger in Margaret's dark gaze; she squirms under its scrutiny, fearing the pain of the bite and longing for it at the same time.

Margaret's mouth curves into a smile; she knows what she's doing to Ellie. She's done it to countless people before, and will do it to countless more when Ellie is dead and gone, Ellie knows. But for now — for now, Ellie is the only one who gets to see her this way, to feel her like this, to revel in her bloodthirsty power.

"Where, do you think?" Margaret asks rhetorically, running a fingernail down from the last bruise she left, still mottled black and purple, along the upper curve of Ellie's left breast. "Here? Or... here?" Her nail flicks Ellie's nipple, startling a shaky gasp out of her. "Oh, you'd like that, wouldn't you?"

Ellie's only answer, well-trained, is a ragged breath. Margaret pinches her. "I want an answer in words this time," she says. "Would you like that?"

"Yes," Ellie says desperately. "No. I don't know."

"Hmm." Margaret leans down, her breath soft on Ellie's skin, and her tongue darts out, teasing Ellie's nipple into a harder nub. Ellie watches her move, her fangs dropping into position at the scent of Ellie's flesh, and shudders. The anticipation is almost too much to bear, but she loves it just the same. "Ah..."

"Oh!" Ellie cries out at the sharp sting of pain, just at the edge between pink areola and paler flesh, where Margaret's fangs sink in, sharper by far than knives.

Now it's Margaret's turn to breathe harshly, gasps catching in her throat as she drinks greedily, lips and tongue working as she sucks. It's only in the throes of her thirst that Margaret welcomes tenderness; Ellie strokes her thick, satiny hair as they both lose themselves in pleasure.

Ellie doesn't know what Margaret is experiencing (will never know, a thrall destined to die when her ripeness withers and loses its savor) but the mingled pain and pleasure coursing through Ellie's veins, centered not on her clit but on the fresh bite, is so exquisite that she can't imagine anything better. It echoes in her fading bruises, singing like quivering crystal, and she struggles to remain still instead of arching up and begging for more.

Margaret makes a delicious sound, half groan, and releases Ellie's breast, licking the blood from her lips. Ellie lies there, chest heaving in the aftermath, and watches her as she tucks an escaped strand of hair back behind her ear. Margaret's cheeks are already flushing, heat radiating off her in throbbing waves. Ellie herself is ashen, but she'll get over it in time.

"Thank you," she manages to say, pushing up on her elbows to show Margaret that she hasn't done too much damage.

"And thank you," Margaret says politely. Her fangs retract, making her look, for a moment, like she's nothing more than human.

Ellie sits the rest of the way up and pulls on her shirt, taking a moment to admire the deep purple bruising on her breast before it's covered in sensible black cotton. "I should go," she says. "It's late."

"Mmm. Probably," Margaret agrees. "It's raining, though."

Ellie knew that, distantly; she can remember the patter of raindrops against the windowpane, counterpoint to their ecstasy, but she wants to go home anyway. "I'm not made of brown sugar," she says lightly, thinking of a hot shower, or a bubble bath, maybe.

"No? You're sweet enough," Margaret returns, licking her lips showily.

Ellie laughs. "I'll stay, if you want me to." She'd do a lot of things, if Margaret wanted her to. Staying in her apartment for a few more hours is the least of it.

Margaret considers this. "Not if you want to go. I won't keep you."

A double meaning, it hits Ellie like a blow; none of this is for keeps. "I'll go. Will you kiss me goodbye?"

"Not this time." Margaret turns away. "Be well, Ellie."

"Thank you. You too." Ellie leaves, fogged enough not to pay any attention to the artfully decorated living room or the lavish hallway; only the door, the stairs, the outside door, the rain-soaked street, her way out.

Is this worth it? Ellie wonders, sometimes, and this is one of those times. She doesn't think she's exactly beautiful, but the online dating profile she hasn't bothered remembering the password to still gets a few hits a day. Maybe one of the people clicking on the awkward late-night selfie Ellie took three years ago would want to see her more than once a week, or want her to stay the night, or let her go down on them more often than not. That would be nice.

When the relationship is good, though, it's so, so good, better than anything Ellie's ever done or dreamed of doing. Just pure eye contact with Margaret gets her closer to climax than a thousand fumbling fingers, a hundred clumsy tongues. And the bite: well, nothing compares to the bite, the shooting pain-pleasure like a meteor, the sweet spreading warmth, the way it lasts and lasts.

Surely there are other vampires, though, and some of them might even live in this very city. Maybe there's someone else who would sink their fangs into her, someone who would meet Ellie's friends at a bar after dark and joke about something better than Bloody Marys.

But Ellie doesn't want anyone else, not if she's honest with herself. An ordinary relationship has lost any savor it once had, and the thought of giving herself to another vampire pulls and twists at her guts.

No. She doesn't want anyone but Margaret. If she wants more than Margaret is willing to give, well, having unfulfilled dreams hasn't killed anybody yet, and maybe — just maybe — Margaret will be able to bend a little. It must have happened at least once in the centuries Margaret has spent at the periphery of the daylight world, and if not, well, Ellie is pretty stubborn herself. Stranger things happen every day.

Ellie is close to halfway home, now; she recognizes the buildings in this area even if the street names are blurry from the rain and teardrops beading on her eyelashes. She's gone several more blocks, nearly drenched, watching nothing but the slick sidewalk in front of her feet, when something dark flickers in her peripheral vision. Hope flares in Ellie's heart, but she keeps walking, step by careful step.

The darkness grows, rises, and envelops Ellie, crushing her against the wet wall outside the convenience store. "I changed my mind," Margaret murmurs, and kisses her. And oh, oh, it's wonderful: Margaret's mouth devours hers, as though Ellie's lips and tongue are as sweet to her as her blood is. Margaret's hands pull her head down to deepen the kiss, and Ellie goes willingly, wrapping her arms around the small cool figure under the cover of darkness, letting Margaret's hot tongue and sharp teeth leave her wrecked.

After a long, long time, Margaret breaks the kiss and takes a step backwards. "I realized," she says, her voice composed, "that I missed you."

"I've only been gone for — what, ten minutes?" Ellie says, with an awkward half-laugh, as if she hasn't spent that ten or fifteen minutes wondering whether to continue this relationship at all, wishing for exactly this.

Margaret doesn't dignify the comment with a response. "I missed you," she repeats, with a certain emphasis on the words. "Do you know how long it's been since that happened?"

"A long time?"

"A very long time." Margaret purses her lips and gazes into the middle distance. "A few centuries, at least. I had a pink dress with pleats in the back — it doesn't matter." She waves her hand in an unusually graceless gesture, brushing the memory away. "Anyway, the point is, I wanted you to know."

"That you missed me," Ellie says. Shock and warmth build inside her, like there should be steam rising off of her wet skin with a sizzle like a cast-iron frying pan.

"Yes," Margaret says, shaping the word precisely. "That you matter."

Ellie blinks. "Thank you," she says finally. "That means a lot to me."

"I know," Margaret says matter-of-factly. "That's why I'm telling you." She goes up on her toes, graceful once again, and kisses Ellie almost softly. "I want to see you more often."

"Okay," Ellie says. "We can do that." There's a wild, bubbly sensation in her solar plexus, like she's about to get everything she's ever longed for. Just to be sure, she asks, "Do you need more blood?"

Margaret rolls her eyes. "If I did, I'd get another thrall," she says. "I don't want to use you up too quickly. You're more to me than that. I'd rather have you as a lover."

"Cool," Ellie says, knowing her smile is goofy, not caring at all. "But that doesn't mean you're going to stop biting me altogether, does it?"

At that, Margaret gives her a wicked grin and a quick, sharp nip to the throat, sending bolts of exquisite pleasure zinging through her. "Not that easily," she says.

"Oh," Ellie says, touching the bite mark with a fingertip. "Good."

"I'll see you soon," Margaret says, and vanishes, taking the darkness with her.

Ellie turns her face up to the rain and smiles.

# TAPEWORM TONGUE

## JENNIFER LORING

He brings the offering, and the angel sings.

There is always so much to do first. So much dust from the crumbling mortar to sweep away, and always more of it the next day. Pieces of the collapsing roof to haul out. The carcasses of the bats it has eaten to dispose of. Candles to light, their fragrance banishing the stink of animal droppings and decay. Broken windows to repair—the angel prefers red glass, but it isn't so easy to find unless he breaks into the stained glass shop in the business district. Sometimes he resorts to red cellophane, which looks enough like stained glass when the light is right. No one asks this of him, but it has now become habit born of hope.

He'd been in a fight, on the night that seems so long ago now, the victim of an attempted mugging; bleeding and dazed, he had walked down a dark side street until he heard the voice. Someone was singing in the old Catholic church deserted at least ten years. He stared at it for a few moments, then pulled the door open. The rusty padlock had been long since busted open.

Candles burned on the altar. He approached the immense and crucified Jesus, his bloodied hands outstretched as if to apologize for the boy he'd left lying in a pool of blood with his skull cracked open like a fresh egg. Not his own blood after all, he was relieved to discover. He'd gotten away with a few bruises and minor scratches. Yet he'd never felt such rage, and now he felt nothing, not even guilt. He should have called the police, he supposed, but there was an unquantifiable pleasure in taking justice into one's own hands. To become a vigilante, a hero of the night, even if he was the only one aware of his heroics.

A voice whispered above him in syllables he could not comprehend. Then a glorious melody surged up out of the darkness, and the blood from his hands ascended into the air, an eyedropper working in reverse as each red globule vanished within the mystery concealed in the ceiling's shadows. His cock became as hard as iron, the way it had when blood first began seeping out of his would-be mugger's head to form a dark pool on the concrete. He'd been waiting for that attack, he realized. Waiting for it his whole life. Opportunity had knocked at last. Had led him here, tonight, for some greater purpose.

And now he'd witnessed a miracle that confirmed he had chosen the correct action. He was doing what the law couldn't or wouldn't do. Something holy dwelled here, and he must determine how to give it appropriate thanks.

There was power in the blood, as the hymn went, one of the few that had stuck with him from childhood—that and "There Is a Fountain Filled with Blood"—because of its sheer morbidity. Maybe that had been the first sign of his future proclivities; it was hard to identify the exact point at which the circuitry in his brain began to malfunction. And here he was, in a church. The Jesus looking on would surely approve. After all, who knew better than he the power of blood? His entire religion was predicated on the spilling of it.

It started with small blood sacrifices, stray animals he drained in the forgotten graveyard behind the church. Feral cats, mostly—they were everywhere, vicious and flea-bitten. He set traps for them with cheap cans of tuna and slit their throats to allow blood to flow into the communion chalice. Then he offered it to the angel, and as it enchanted him with its voice, the blood rose toward the vaulted ceiling. It approved, and this delighted him.

But it deserved better. He thought of the street thug who had assaulted him and paid for it, and how many more there were like him. How no one, probably not even their worthless parents, would mourn their loss. He thought of all the lost children, runaways and drug addicts, who would do anything for a meal, some cash, and a place to stay. *Anything.* Despondency dampened one's higher cognitive functions, let the primitive lizard brain take over in its quest for basic survival. Not unlike the feral cats.

He often wondered later, as he kept coming back to lay his young offerings on the altar and watch the blood flow up instead of down, if they too became angels despite their earthly sins. The possibility agitated him. Thugs and punks all, who derived their sadistic pleasures from preying on others. When no more blood came out, he buried them in the ramshackle graveyard with the abandoned dead amid the tangle of roots and knee-high grasses. The moon's frozen white eye glared down at him as the angel's music drifted through the back door.

He sets tonight's offering, a girl prostitute no more than fifteen years old, on the altar. She doesn't know the diseases, drug addictions, and violence he has spared her, and in this spirit, he refrains from squeezing her small white breasts. The crimson light of sunset bleeds through the red glass-and-cellophane windows. A voice rises softly beyond the candlelight, soaring effortlessly to the high, barrel-vaulted ceiling and back down again. He props the mop against the front pew and sits beside it, eyes closed and a rapturous smile upon his lips.

It rustles its feathered wings, or perhaps the cloth of the priestly surplice he imagines it wears, though there's no logical reason why it should. He kneels down and, weeping, prays to the angel that it will always sing to him.

*Gloria, gloria, morte aeterna...*

He opens his eyes and scans the time-scarred faces on the

walls—primal oil-painted saints, the Blessed Virgin and her Son, all simplistically rendered as if on a cave wall by a child. High up in the corners and onto the ceiling are painted angels, dark-eyed and dark-haired, wings outstretched like a second pair of arms to enfold him in their warmth and carry him away. Strange, he thinks, how they aren't depicted in the typical Euro-American way, how they aren't blond and blue-eyed and apparently Swedish. It occurs to him that the angel who lurks here has perhaps been here all along. Maybe the church— maybe the whole city—sprang up around it, or the belief in it. The church is a century old at most, but the builders had known. *Someone* had known that something has always lived here.

It sings until light blooms in the stained glass windows, its voice fading as colors splash onto the wooden floor and stain the walls. He wonders if the sad Son wilting behind the altar, Lord of the angels, has actually seen them, or if they ever sing to him. Did he hear them as he languished on his cross? Had they too forsaken him as his father had, instructed to let him die?

What if he hadn't forgiven them?

He tucks the bucket and mop away in a closet at the front of the church. Once more, he glances back at the altar and smiles, his soul singing its song.

*Gloria, Gloria, morte aeterna...*

---

THE CITY IS SUSPICIOUS NOW; there have been four disappearances. He has seen reports on the news of a suspected serial killer. He lights more candles, especially on the altar, and kneels in prayer to ask its forgiveness.

The eaves creak. Wind swirls in from the broken windows and extinguishes each candle. A sign.

*They'll catch me if I take another.*

He listens. He hears nothing, not even the rustle of feathered wings. He is like the Jesus that hangs behind the altar, deserted in his time of greatest agony. He's jealous of the children. Fetid with sin. The idea that they've become what he most wants, that they dwell with it, has clouded his reasoning. He has the angel's song, yes, but might he also feel its sacred mouth upon him? Its touch?

Is that even enough?

*There is power in the blood.*

He kills another cat, this one ill with anemia and dying anyway. It's not the blood that's important this time but its vehicle for delivery. He strips off his clothes and rubs blood all over himself, then lies on the altar. The angel will have to descend to feed, and quickly; the liquid is already drying in the hot, stale air of a summer night, on his feverish skin. He quivers to think of it. His cock rises until pointing directly at the ceiling, inviting whatever lurks in the ceiling's opaque gloom. He slicks more blood there than anywhere else in silent desire. And waits.

He cannot make out its features at first, this three-dimensional shadow that floats toward him. He sees as it hovers inches from his face that it is not beautiful, not in human terms, and yet it is the most exquisite being upon which he has ever laid eyes. Naked, hairless except for the black tresses that dangle over its face, it reveals a small swelling between its thighs that could be a rudimentary mons pubis. There are no other primary or secondary sex characteristics with which to identify it. Its chest is as flat as a child's and without nipples. Its eyes are black scrying vessels in which he can see all that was and will be; he is dumbfounded by how small and ignorant he—humans—are. How much remains hidden to their primate brains. He moans before it even touches him.

And then it does.

From between its pallid lips, it unfolds like a Christmas banner a red tongue that seeks and probes as if with a mind distinct from the angel. It explores him slowly, a scientist logging the characteristics of a new species. The tongue twists around his biceps. Around his throat—he tenses, and it moves on. It collects the drying blood on its way downward, flaking it away with its pronged tip, then retracts, and he shivers. The angel examines him with an impersonal gaze. Its expression, a beguiling smirk, has not changed. If it knows how much he longs for it to caress him, then it is dedicated to his torture.

The tongue unfurls again, long enough to wrap around his cock several times. It applies expert pressure, pulses in a sensual rhythm, the drumbeat of life, in time with the heartbeat it can surely feel. The spiraled tongue glides up and down his shaft like a fist. He bends his knees and arches his back, reaching for the creature that remains just beyond arm's length. Desperate to feel its porcelain skin beneath his fingertips, certain that it's just as cold as ceramic. Refreshing, chilled waves emanate from it like air from an open cooler. He wants it to rub that pale mound against him and see if it's capable of the same pleasure, see if there is some opening through which he and it can unite. The pulses quicken. It has tapped into the primeval part of his brain, the part that craves sex as much as food and shelter. Maybe more, and isn't that where everything has gone wrong? The consequence of original sin. Sweat drips from him, pools under his neck, his back, and rolls from his fingertips onto the floor.

Like a ribbon spun back onto its spool, the tongue withdraws once again but finds a new home. The tentacle investigates the tender edges of his asshole, awakening his nerves in a shower of sparks. His balls and stomach tighten. It inches inside, nothing like a cock or even a finger, and he has enjoyed both. Thinner, wetter, longer, and infinitely flexible, it painlessly works into him, tickling the sensitive skin, coiling again to initiate the necessary friction and palpitating against his prostate. The rest of the angel does not touch him or itself. His eyes roll back. His hips thrust upward, an involuntary response like his moans—incoherent because words are meaningless to signify his pleasure. Nothing about the impending orgasm is familiar or normal; he's never had a full-body climax, never experienced this hypersensitive awareness of every part of him united with every other part on a mission of ecstasy. He twitches, a marionette connected to this magical red string, before shattering like a tsunami over a village. Come explodes from his swollen cock, needing no assistance from his hands. Numb and immobile with bliss, he watches each creamy rope arc onto his belly until, at last, he is empty.

The tongue recedes. He lies gasping as his senses slowly return. The angel stares at him; he thinks that he ought to have understood its true nature long before the appendage slinks past his lips, the creature itself maintaining physical distance, before it slides down his esophagus. He gags, but the penetration deepens into his stomach. Into his blood-rich small intestine. His guts spasm, trying to dislodge the intruder from its walls. The pulsing again, but this time each one brings only nauseating cramps and a warm trickle from between his legs that smells of pennies. Blood pushes the other way, too, through his stomach and up his throat until it spills out of his mouth. He spits it onto the weathered hardwood floor.

Something stirs on the ceiling.

Watching the angel extract its tapeworm tongue from his throat makes him retch again, and this time he tastes bile. That the creature's new pink flush is the result of his fluids coursing through its veins sickens him nearly as much. And yet…

*Communion.*

His is the body and the blood that has sustained it. They have merged in some profound and wondrous way. He chooses not to think of the many others who must have come before him in the years—decades, centuries—since the angels decided they must go into hiding. He couldn't blame them; even God hasn't made a personal appearance in thousands of years. Yet somehow, He is the only myth people still believe in.

A hand grasps each of his arms and lifts him toward the ceiling. It is dark here, too dark for light to reach, and as icy as the graves marked with crumbling stone monuments out back. Blood drizzles out of him and patters onto the altar as he rises.

Dozens of faces flicker about him like the votive candles below. They are as beautiful as he dreamed and as horrible as the one he has worshipped all these weeks. He had not expected so many, or even more than one. They smile with reddened lips, and feathery black wings caress his face. The wings are enough to hide them in the shadows of the ceiling; they are otherwise naked, too. Their dark hair obscures their bright, pallid faces.

*Cursum aeternum,* one sings, engulfing him in their holy song. He is afloat on the wings of angels and the golden melody pouring forth from their sacrosanct lips. *Gloria, gloria semper; sanctus, sanctus in excelsis.*

*Gloria semper,* he whispers. Tongues plunge into his eyes and ears, his nose and mouth, into his ass and the head of his cock. Heaven and Eden and Utopia, every mortal fantasy. He is sanctified as the angels make love to him in their unique and bloody way, bearing him aloft, drinking him into their paradise. Music echoes throughout the church and in his ears. It is all he can hear and all he ever wanted.

*Gloria, gloria, morte aeterna, cursum aeternum*

*Gloria, gloria semper*

*Sanctus, sanctus in excelsis ...*

He opens his eyes and unfolds his wings. He sings without thinking. They have heard passersby outside, the lost and forsaken seeking sanctuary. They are all hungry, and they crave a new keeper.

# CHOICES

## ANDRA DILL

In her experience, every human consulting the Tarot asked a question about love or money. Every concern, boiled down to its essence, involved one or the other. Why should a vampire be any different? Catalina opened a battered pine drawer and lifted out her personal deck, wrapped in ivory silk.

Strands of white and blue fairy lights cast a soft glow upon the worn cards. A gift from her mother forty-odd years ago given with the admonition, "If you won't listen to me, listen to the cards."

A northern breeze pushed against the tent wall behind Catalina, making the lights sway and jostling the blue and gold tie-dyed print hanging there. Two others, in shades of green and purple, adorned the once-beige walls to her right and left. All three prints together were large enough to hide most of the stains from oil leaks and the elements.

Cupped in her palm, the cards felt warm and comforting. Catalina rubbed her thumb over the top card. She thought of Jake and what he wanted—what she desired—then shuffled the deck.

With a soft swish, she lifted the first card, representing her past, from the deck. The Ace of Cups—joy, contentment, felicity. The card spoke true, she'd been content and happy, something she'd never expected.

For fifteen years, following the death of Mateo, her maker, she'd chosen to live a solitary, nomadic life moving from one traveling carnival to the next. The transience of carnival life suited her. For the most part, her fellow carnies were affable. The majority lived by the motto "leave us alone and we'll leave you alone" and Catalina heartily endorsed it. No one commented on her erratic hours and, though the crowds were thin lately, the carnival patrons provided her a reliable food source.

When Jake had hired on two years ago, her complacent life had been upended. The man had surprised and alarmed her with his persistence. He'd burrowed beneath her shields and, despite her insistence that she couldn't, made her fall in love.

The card reflected her past. Her contentment had ended when a long-forgotten, yellowed letter fell from the pages of a book of poems. Like the snake in the garden of Eden, the letter offered life-altering knowledge to Jake and temptation to Catalina.

Gently, she placed the past onto the table. She'd chosen a three-card spread to answer a simple question. But questions were seldom simple and the answers, well, everything was open to interpretation. She turned the second card, the present.

"Hmph, of course." The Ace of Swords—a card of great force. That would be Jake.

She glanced up at the twinkling blue lights. Jake, knowing she adored blue, had hung them before she'd woken for the day. An olive branch extended after last night's—how had he put it? —dust-up.

The knowledge he hadn't obtained from the letter he'd wheedled out of her. There were many advantages for a mortal bound to a vampire: long life, enhanced strength, accelerated healing. But the price was dear. Her consuming desire to bind him unnerved her. She'd hammered back her need, trying to make clear all the costs. He'd gotten on her last nerve with his cajoling and entreaties, waving off her patient explanations. In frustration, she'd burned both the troublesome letter and the poetry book.

The obstinate fool was probably already hatching another

campaign to bulldoze her yet again, if not tonight, tomorrow. She knew mules who were more tractable.

A vision whipped out from the past, of her maker's docile companion, Isobel, her body seizing, pink froth bubbling from her mouth, her vocal cords shredded from screaming. Catalina slammed a steel door on that particular memory.

Her throat tightened, and a fist of anxiety squeezed her slow-beating heart. She closed her eyes, not quite ready to learn what the future held. Sounds from the midway drifted through the crisp evening air, music from the rides battling it out with the booming calls of the carnival barkers.

Another sound separated from the background midway chorus. The rise and fall of conversation drawing near, potential customers and maybe a snack. Catalina's coal dark eyes snapped open and she turned the final card. A foolhardy golden-haired dandy strode towards the edge of a cliff while a small white dog yapped at his heels, the Fool. Optimists read the card as life's journey and new possibilities. Catalina knew better. Sometimes a fool was just a fool. But was she a fool to bind him or a fool to let him go?

Feet scuffled outside her tent. A guttural, low-rasped voice was answered by a high-pitched tinkling one. Catalina swept up her cards. Quickly wrapping the square of ivory around them before tucking the deck into the drawer. She retrieved a second, newer deck while the dithering continued near the white and gold beaded entrance. Impatient for them to make up their minds, she rapped the cards against the small table's surface.

More scuffling and a body knocked into the canvas, making the walls and beads waver. The fairy lights trembled from the jarring movement. Catalina pursed her lips and frowned.

A slender, white hand parted the beaded curtain. The

woman-child that entered looked like a sprite, with her flowing, silver blonde hair and long limbs. Close on her heels a dark scarecrow of a youth followed, his face thunderous. A second young man elbowed his way into the now crowded tent. Taller and broader than the first, the flaxen blond radiated arrogance. She felt a brief flash of relief. The card must have meant the immediate future and here was the Fool.

"Welcome," Catalina said.

The blond man surveyed the confined space. His mouth twisted into a derisive smirk. One pale brow arched as he looked from the lights to Catalina. His greedy gaze lingered over her wide mouth and plush lips then trailed down her throat. The smirk transformed to a leer when his eyes landed on her small cinnamon-brown breasts, plumped up by a red bustier.

"Nice digs," the Fool said.

"I, we…" the sprite sputtered, making a sweeping gesture to indicate her companions, "would like a reading." Her hand fluttered to rest over her belly.

"Of course. All together?" She fanned the cards out over the scarred table.

Crossing his arms, the scarecrow shook his shaggy head. "Waste of money." His bulldog expression mirrored one Catalina had seen countless times on Jake.

A pretty blush spread over the young woman's face. Her pink mouth opened and closed like a landed fish as she glared at the scowling youth. Catalina could tell her that trying to change that one's mind would be fruitless but she doubted the girl would listen.

The fool laughed. "Oh, come on. It's all good fun." He

pounded his friend on the back hard enough to pitch him forward, almost falling across the tabletop.

"Damn it, Justin, knock it off." Righting himself, he jabbed an elbow into his friend.

"Please have a seat." Catalina inclined her head towards the empty wooden chair. "Your gentlemen friends won't mind standing."

"What? No, I don't, I mean, I... Wouldn't it mess things up, having all of us in here? It would mess up the reading, right?"

"Oh, come on, Becky," protested Justin.

"Let's go." The dark-haired youth stepped forward, nudging Becky back. He glared at Justin. The feral gleam in his eyes turned him from a rail-thin scarecrow into a whip-lean wolf.

Catalina tapped a finger over her lips, tamping down a grin. The youth could have been Jake's younger self. Her Ace of Swords fooled most people with his laid-back attitude and good ol' boy charm. But when pushed, he'd get that same wild, ferocious glare just before he attacked. The man fought as viciously as a wolverine. She didn't doubt this boy was as protective of Becky.

Usually Jake's overprotective manner amused her. Her pulse quickened with irritation now, thinking of how he'd harried her for a sip of her blood so he could better protect her. Binding himself to her through her blood would make him stronger. It would also extend his life, which was something her selfish side desired. Damn that letter!

"Please." The fairy girl rested pale, slender fingers on his broad shoulder.

His face softened. The tense set of his shoulders slumped. Catalina was impressed. If only she could get Jake to give in so easily. He muttered while strong-arming the golden fool outside, ensuring Becky's privacy.

In the silence that followed, she focused on the young woman. One hand resting on her flat belly, the other curled into a fist on the pine table. Catalina heard the heartbeat within the girl's womb. Another thing that would be taken from Jake if she allowed the binding. He'd never father a child and, for reasons she didn't want to examine too closely, that made her want to weep.

Catalina opened herself to listen to the cards. "Ask your question, child."

Normally, she had little interest in what the cards told her customers. Becky's darkling appeared as the Page of Wands. Catalina chided herself for being so pleased when the Sun, a card of marital happiness and contentment, appeared. After all, someone should get a happily ever after.

At the entryway, the sprite ambushed her with a hug. Nonplussed, Catalina extricated herself and passed the girl over into the waiting arms of her lover.

Justin's reading didn't go as he'd anticipated, though the cards of profit and fortune answered his call. She sent him off with a pat on the back. He teetered away with his friends. Licking her lips as she watched him go, she'd taken a bit more in payment than his coin.

Aware of the man behind her, a bone-deep pleasure suffused Catalina.

"Enjoy your snack?"

His snappish baritone reminded her she was put out with him. He was an unassuming man, three or four inches taller than Catalina, rangy build, with light caramel hair that perpetually needed a trim, and midnight blue eyes. His sun-darkened arms ensnared her, hauling her back to snug the length of her spine and plump ass against his work-hardened body.

"Now, Jake, don't pout. You know arrogance is my favorite flavor."

The scent of gear grease tamed by soap and Old Spice aftershave enveloped her. He'd taken the time to shave before coming to her. The corners of her mouth twitched, threatening to curve into a smile. She melted against him. Maybe the offering of fairy lights signaled an end to his campaign. Catalina hoped so. If she couldn't make him see reason… She wasn't ready to let him go.

Dipping his hand into her bodice, Jake strummed his callused fingers over her nipple. "I taste better than that college boy." He lifted the heavy fall of her sable-brown hair, pressing kisses along the length of her throat.

If he kept this up, she might forgive him. "Shouldn't you be at the Himalaya?"

"Mack pulled me to work on a gear problem with the carousel. Got it done before he thought I would so I'm free."

Cool air skimmed the back of her thighs as he rucked up her skirt. His hand slid beneath her lace panties, caressing the globe of her ass. "Come back to the trailer with me?" He punctuated his words with a squeeze.

She rested her head in the curve of his neck. Reaching back, she threaded her fingers through his hair, playing with the silky strands of caramel. He really needed a haircut. She dug her fingers into the overgrown locks and yanked. "Are you going to piss me off again?"

"Most likely. I'd say you could gag me but I think you'd like it better if I kept my mouth busy worshiping you."

"I'm a fool." Twisting out of his hold, she stepped through

the swaying beads. Returning with a "be back soon" placard, she smacked him in the chest with it. "Put that up for me."

"Here? But the trailer—"

"Who knows how much time we have? Mack or, God forbid, Ed, might come looking for you. Let's see how well you can please me with that mouth of yours. Shall we?" Mack would tease them if he came by. Ed Warner, a burr in most everyone's side, could be a problem.

Jake hooked the sign onto a nail poking through the canvas. Unclipping the inner flap with an urgent jerk, he hustled her back inside. The heavy tarp dropped, blocking the entrance. It wouldn't prevent anyone from entering if they really wanted but it would keep out polite society.

Catalina shoved the table aside, the legs scratching up a layer of dust from the hard-packed earth. Jake dropped to his knees before her.

Hiking up her skirt, she whispered, "Use your teeth."

A grin reminiscent of the Cheshire cat spread across his tanned face. Jake never took his eyes from hers as he leaned forward. His teeth grazed her skin, raising goosebumps. Catching the red lace between his teeth, he tugged the material down. He administered barely-there licks and feathery kisses as the lace scraped over hip and thigh, making her squirm.

Once past her knees, the fabric slipped to the ground, trapping her ankles. Jake eased her onto the wooden seat. He tickled the insides of her knees before pushing them wide. She edged forward, canting her pelvis.

"So beautiful." Jake stroked his thumbs over her labia. The look of a hungry predator affixed to his features.

Catalina watched him bend close and nose her pussy. Warm puffs of breath across her intimate flesh sent shivers up her spine. A whimper escaped her lips as he cleaved her folds with his tongue. Using the flat of his tongue, he teased her with slow swipes. Her muscles contracted, little twitches directing her hips to sway, following the heat of his mouth. Just as her body melted into the pleasing cadence, Jake switched, delivering fast, pointed licks directly over her swollen clitoris. Her back arched, head lolling backwards as he ramped her up to the precipice.

She mewled in protest when he abandoned her needy clit. Turning his attention to her hip crease, he licked and nipped over the pulse point there. Catalina raked her nails across his scalp. A wild thought flashed through her mind to demand he take out his pocketknife, score her flesh, and drink from her, all her good intentions be damned.

"Jake."

He glanced up, a hunger in his eyes that undid her. His dark lashes shuttered down. He covered her pussy again with his hot mouth and resumed teasing with languid, broad strokes. He suckled her lips. Drawing one into his mouth and setting the edge of his teeth against the tender flesh. The implied threat made the walls of her channel spasm. Alternating between cruelly slow-paced swipes that ignored her clitoris and rapid, pinpoint lashes over the distended nub soon had her writhing and panting.

Clasping his head, she held on for dear life. He slipped two fingers into her slick channel and pumped. Her hips rocked, grinding her pussy against his devastating ministrations.

The small tent felt like a furnace to her now. Heat coiled tight in her belly. The muscles in her thighs were tense and shaking. Jake hummed, the vibration ratcheting her up further. He pressed his digits firmly against the front wall of her vagina and concentrated his attention on her pulsing clit. Catalina cried out. Her body convulsed, hot-wired nerves sparking and muscles clenching with each wave of pleasure. Jake lapped up her juices. She curled over him like a lethargic, sun-drenched cat.

Wind rustled the tent walls. The colorful hangings bobbed, gently tapping against the canvas. She shifted, trying to bring her thighs together but Jake refused to give way. She sighed in mock exasperation.

Half listening to the sounds outside, she stroked his temple and his clean-shaven jaw. Touching him, smelling him, drinking in his angular features, relishing the quiet sound of his breathing, it made her ache. Catalina wished she could freeze this moment.

"I know you're worried that if you die, my death will painful."

And just like that the moment shattered.

"I should have gagged you," she groused.

His roughened hands untangled her panties from her ankles. When she held out her hand for them, he kissed her inner thigh and pocketed them. Shifting his weight to rest on his heels, he propped his chin on her knee. Catalina rolled her eyes. The man was impossible.

"I get it. I'll become addicted to your blood, dependent upon it." His thumb strummed the hollow of her ankle. "But if it keeps me by your side for a century or more it's worth it. I know you want this as much as I do."

She shook her head, as much to negate him as to ward off the suffocating crush of memories. Her maker's bound servant, Isobel, writhing in out-of-her mind pain after his assassination. Frantic to save her friend, Catalina had tried to force-feed the woman her vampiric blood. But she'd vomited it back up.

Catalina had tracked down a witch and begged her for help, only to be told no magic could sever the bond. Breaking Isobel's neck had been a nightmare and a mercy.

"I know what you went through with Isobel. I do listen." His hand glided up and down her calf. "But Cat, one day I'm going to die whether I'm bound to you or not."

Catalina jerked as if stung by a hornet. She wouldn't be responsible for him dying. It would tear her to pieces but she needed to move on, leave, and let him lead a normal life.

"If we could find an ancient, I'd take the risk of being turned."

"Jake, I've told you, very few survive."

When she started to rise, he caught hold of her upper arms. "I'm not Isobel."

Of course he wasn't Isobel. Mateo's highly prized companion had been a sweet, compliant, respectful woman. Any other vampire would have broken Jake's neck long ago. Where was he going with this?

"What's that supposed mean?"

"I know she was a tribute. I know she had no choice about the binding. But I do. Stop being so stubborn, give us both what we want."

The temptation to bind him pulsed through her veins. Breaking his grip, she crossed her arms, hugging herself tight. "You will be tied to me completely. Jake, you don't understand what you'll be giving up. How many times do I—"

"Catalina, I've made my mind up."

With a growl, she stood. "Well, I'm not binding you."

Jake shot up and wrapped his arms around her, pulling her against his chest. His erection pressing into her belly. "Don't think to run from me, love. I'll hunt you down."

She barked out a laugh. "You are the most arrogant, frustrating man. Hunt me down? I'm a vampire. I'll drain you dry, boy."

"No, you won't." He twined his fingers through the long dark strands of her hair and nuzzled her neck. "What did the cards say?"

"That you were a fool."

Abruptly, Catalina twisted, looking to the closed flap.

"What?"

"I hear a woman… I think she's…" she took two steps forward.

"Scott! No!" A woman's shrill cry propelled them both through the doorway.

Near the magician's tent, not fifty feet away, two men squared off. The shouting woman tugged on the arm of a burly man with a generous spare tire around his waist. The other, over six feet and well-muscled, bounced on the balls of his feet, Ed Warner.

"Hey! Hey!" Jake shouted, sprinting forward.

Catalina kept pace alongside him. She didn't have much hope for the younger man unless he could take a punch well. Whatever had started the altercation, Ed, an angry man always looking for a fight, wouldn't back down.

Scott pushed the woman away. She shrieked, landing hard on the trodden grass path.

Jake slowed, holding his palms up and making a "whoa" gesture. "Let's all settle down."

His words were barely out of his mouth when Ed swung. The younger man absorbed the punch and threw one of his own. The two hammered at each other. Then with a war cry, Scott lunged forward, steel glinted in his right hand.

"He has a blade," Catalina called out.

He plowed into Ed, and the two fell to the ground. Arms and legs thrashed, the knife flashed, slicing flesh, grunts and bellows erupting from both men. Blood perfumed the air. Jake waded in, trying to get a hold on Scott and haul him back.

The woman, up now, kicked out at Ed, connecting once with his shoulder. Then the men rolled and her next kick landed on Scott's back. Ed's bloody fist battered at his opponent's head. The younger man jabbed his blade, Ed's howl of pain rent the night. The woman kicked again. This time Jake took the blow.

The commotion brought others, carnies and townies alike.

Another pained grunt and Catalina scented Jake's blood. *No!* She grabbed a jean-clad leg and yanked. Ed skidded back, fists and booted feet still thrashing, landing a few more blows. Panic choked her, she needed to get to Jake. Taking hold of Ed's belt, she dragged him away.

The woman spun and kept kicking the now-free Ed. Two men Catalina didn't recognize snatched the furious woman back.

Looking across to Jake, she saw he had an arm cinched around Scott's throat. His hand clamped around the man's wrist, wrestling for control of the switchblade. Mack and a stranger were running to help. Panic gave way to rage as she drew in the sharp tang of Jake's blood.

Heaving Ed at Carlos, the magician, and another carnie, she ran for Jake.

"Stay down, Ed. You're bleeding like a stuck pig," Carlos said.

Ready to tear Scott's arm off, if need be, she shoved past others who'd come too late. She saw Jake hunched over, pressing his arm against his chest. His blue jeans were splattered with blood. The knife lay at his feet. There was so much blood, too much of it Jake's.

Mack and the stranger held Scott pinned to the ground. Swamped by blind fury thinking how Jake could have been killed by this fool, Catalina altered her trajectory.

Jake straightened, calling out. "Catalina. I'm okay."

Spinning to him, she saw blood smeared across his face, a thin stream coming from his nose. "Okay?" she hissed out the words.

"I just need to get back to our trailer. Get cleaned up."

"Get cleaned up?" She stalked to him. "Get cleaned up?"

"Catalina." Still holding his injured arm tight to his body, he gripped her arm, turning her away from the others. "Steady. Your eyes are blood-red and your fangs are out. Let's get back to our trailer." He wrapped his good arm around her waist. "Come on."

She ran her tongue over her teeth. *Damn.* Her control should be better than that. She wrapped her arm around his waist. "Lean on me. How bad is your leg?"

"My leg?" He looked down and grimaced. "I think most of that's Ed's blood and maybe the other guy's. I'm okay, Cat. He sliced my arm. Hurts like hell. The guy head-butted me." He winced. "Bloody nose but don't think it's broke. Got popped in the ribs by someone. That side's a little tender."

"That's an interesting definition of okay."

As they passed behind the fun house, Catalina heard people laughing and shouting. Buzzers, bells, and dings rang out from various games. None of it was as loud as Jake's words clamoring through her mind—'I'm not Isobel, one day I'm going to die, I've made up my mind.'

Sweet Isobel would never have considered arguing with any

vampire. She'd never demanded anything, never stood toe-to-toe with Mateo. Jake aggravated her to no end, but she admired his passion, his absolute certainty. No, he wasn't like Isobel and if he planned on surviving a century or more with her, he'd need every ounce of his resolve.

Mortals were too fragile. She could lose him so easily: a car accident, another fight, an accident working on the carnival's equipment. Even with her blood, death would claim him eventually. She wanted as much time with him as possible. She couldn't let him go.

By the time they arrived at his silver bullet-shaped trailer he was leaning heavily against her, half his shirt saturated with iron rich blood. Nostrils flaring, Catalina held open the door and helped brace him as he climbed the drop-down stairs. He turned on the lights, took a few steps, and collapsed onto the kitchen bench.

*He's made up his mind, well, so have I.*

"Can you get your shirt off or do you need help?"

"A little help, I think."

Standing between his splayed legs, she ripped his shirt open. Buttons flew, pinging away to land on the aged linoleum. He shrugged his good arm out first and she peeled the sticky fabric off his injured arm. The knife wound didn't look too deep, though it was six inches or so long. She wasn't a doctor, didn't know if it would need stitches…

"My blood will heal that quickly." She held his surprised gaze, waiting.

"What do you need me to say to make this easier for you, Cat?"

"Easier? Hmph. I've made up my mind, Jake. There's no going back. Are you listening?"

"I heard everything you said, Catalina. I'm not going into this blind. It's my choice."

"I know." Catalina shook her head and smiled. "Just don't gloat."

Jake returned her smile. "I won't."

"Liar."

He reached up and, wrapping his hand around the back of her neck, pulled her down for a hard, fast kiss. "I chose you, Cat. I chose us. Okay?"

"Okay." Eager to give into temptation, Catalina bit her wrist. She let her blood flow over the laceration then held her wrist up to his mouth. "Drink."

His mouth latched onto the offering. She watched the bob of his throat as he swallowed. His teeth and tongue rasped against her skin. Each strong pull zinging straight to her womb. When her body healed the gash she'd inflicted, Jake kissed her pulse point.

"Stay there, I'll get a washcloth."

"You aren't going to lick all this prime blood off me?" Jake grinned and gave her a wink.

"Dried blood tastes flat. It'll do in a pinch but"— she mock-shuddered— "I prefer fresh."

She retrieved a cloth and ran water in the tiny sink. When the temperature edged to lukewarm, she filled a bowl halfway. She moved back to him, setting the bowl on the table, and began wiping his face gently.

"Too full from that popinjay?"

"What?" She paused, the wet cloth hovering inches from his skin. Her brows scrunched together.

"That blond fool with arrogant flavor."

She sniffed and roughly scrubbed his neck.

"Give me that." He extended his injured arm then huffed in surprise. "It's sealing up." He opened and closed his fist, pumped his arms a few times. "Hardly hurts. Wow." He ran his fingers over the slash.

"Stop poking at it." She dragged her fingernail down his chest, scraping over his flat nipple.

Blue eyes sparkling with mischief, he caught hold of her hand and kissed her palm. "Turn around, Cat."

"Why?"

"Turn around, please."

Exhaling loudly, she did as he asked.

Jake unlaced her bustier. "Feed from me, love."

"I don't need to be naked to do that." When he had the laces loose, she began undoing the busk.

He palmed her breasts, fondling them. "I like naked."

"Hmmm, then these need to go." Reaching back, she scratched at his jeans.

Between slow, hungry kisses, shoes were kicked off and clothing carelessly dropped to the floor. She laughed when Jake picked her up. With her legs wrapped around his hips, he rushed them the short distance to their bed. They tumbled down in a tangle of limbs. Catalina scrambled about until she perched atop Jake's thighs.

She encircled his engorged cock with her hand, her thumb and fingers unable to touch. Stroking him from root to tip, she spoke softly, "Mine."

He pumped up into her clasp. "Yours."

Sliding down his legs, she bent low and tasted him. Her tongue swirled around the corona. Jake pumped up again and she drew him in deep. Her tongue laved the pulsing vein running along the underside of his cock. His blood called to her.

But drawing from that vein would snuff out all her plans. She swallowed a spurt of spicy pre-come. Mouth gliding up and down his length, her tongue teased him as her hand stroked his base. Catalina took her time.

His pulse ratcheted up, his breathing grew ragged. She released his cock with a wet pop. Angling her head, she found his pounding femoral. Jake wove his fingers through her dark hair, massaging her scalp. Her fangs pierced skin and vein. A rush of salty, rich blood flooded her mouth and she drank. After taking only a few swallows, she licked the puncture, sealing it tight.

With a sinuous twist, Catalina skimmed up his body. The crisp, pale golden hair on his thighs, belly, and chest lightly abraded her nipples. She kissed him, grinding her mound against his erection. He clutched her ass, squeezing, lifting, angling her.

"Ah. Ah. Ah," she chided him then bit his lower lip, licking at the droplets of blood. "What's the magic word?" She rolled her hips against him.

"Damned woman."

Her deep, throaty laugh rumbled through the trailer.

"Please."

"That's it." She rose, tilting her pelvis. His cock split her slick folds. Another roll of her hips and his glans notched into her channel. She sank down slowly, enjoying the way he stretched her, filled her. The walls of her vagina spasmed, eliciting a muttered oath from Jake.

He offered up his hands and she interlaced her fingers with his. Braced now, she set a fast pace, riding him. Her ass slapped against his thighs, her small breasts bouncing. The bed protested with creaks and squeaks. Catalina watched him. His eyes trained on her breasts. She snorted and his gaze zipped up to meet hers. He licked his lips and grinned.

Releasing her grip on his hands, she canted forward, dangling her breasts close to Jake. She planted her hands on the mattress. A breath later he lifted, clamping his mouth onto her breast. Her rhythm slowed but didn't falter. He suckled her, his tongue lashing her peaked nipple. His hips arched up to thrust as she sank low. The confined space was redolent with their combined musk and his sweat. Jake moved to her other breast. He nipped the underneath, then bit down on her nipple. Her vagina contracted, and Catalina gasped.

"Let me, Cat." He bit down again, staring into her dilated pupils. "Can you reach my jeans?"

Catalina's head whipped sideways to scan the floor. She found the blue jeans, the cuff tantalizingly close.

Jake held her hips as she dangled off the bed to snatch up the blood-stained jeans. She retrieved his pocket knife and opened it. He kept the blade sharp and it didn't take much pressure to score her breast.

She reseated herself and dropped back down, hands braced on the bed. Jake's hot mouth sealed over the cut. Their hips thrusting in unison, they regained their momentum. Jake's lungs heaved, nostrils flaring. The sound of his heartbeat making her think of the purr of a racing engine. Each little tug as he drank created tidal waves in her cunt. Her body bowed as she climaxed. Jake's hands dug into her ass, pulling her tight against him. He pumped hard and fast into her, still suckling at her breast. Only relinquishing his hold when, crying out, he spilled into her.

He rolled her, thrusting a few more times before collapsing in a heap, blanketing her. She stroked his back. His flanks heaved as he caught his breath. Catalina loved feeling his weight, pressing her down into the mattress. His head resting on her breast. She sighed, content.

"Where did the Fool come up?"

"What?"

"In your Tarot reading."

"Future."

"New possibilities, new beginnings, faith in the future."

Catalina shook her head, rolling her eyes. "You would think that."

He laughed. "I can imagine how you interpreted it."

"Sometimes a fool is just a fool."

Propping himself up on his forearm, he kissed her. "I get to be your fool for a very long time."

"I can live with that."


WHEN NOT DAYDREAMING about plot lines and characters, Andra practices yoga, reads voraciously, writes, rewrites, and then writes some more. She lets her friends talk her into all kinds of nonsense and loves road trips. Follow her on Twitter @aedill

# THE PRISONER

## BILL DAVIDSON

Even after the bomb, Sergeant Linda Haddon's nightmares were not of pain and burning, nor of Gunny Wilson kneeling in the sand front of her, swearing as he tried to stop the bleeding. Not even of the wheel of the upturned Land Rover, turning and turning, sending oily spirals of smoke into the hard, blue sky.

Her nightmares remained the same as always; a small grey stone, arcing through cold, drizzly air. She would wake, sweating and doped up in a foreign hospital, still anchored to that fucking stone.

Ten weeks later, she flew back to England, the plates holding her leg together setting the detectors off. Linda registered her mother's shock as she limped through arrivals.

In the car, Linda asked, "How's Elsa?"

Her mother glanced at her, the side without the livid line curving from temple to chin. Linda had always known she was pretty, taking it for granted. Now, only her right side was pretty.

"You mean, where is Elsa? She's mad at you, of course. But she's at work."

"Really?"

"There's this new group, helping people like her get into employment. She works at their café."

"Not paid work?"

"She's a waitress!"

"Doesn't she get it all wrong?"

"No. She wants you to be proud of her."

Linda kept her face averted, hiding her eyes. "I'm always proud of her."

When Linda walked into her Mother's house, Elsa was there —her sister at first sight like any other twenty-five-year-old.

Short, voluptuous and dark haired, with large eyes and full lips; they were obviously twins.

Elsa's stern expression disappeared within a second of Linda limping into the room. She stroked her face and cried for a long time. Then she started asking questions, like would Linda ever be beautiful again?

Weeks of painful physiotherapy later, she got a call from a Sergeant Dick Burns, saying his boss, Colonel Jones, wanted to meet. But first would she mind meeting with a counsellor? Just a few questions.

When the time to meet the Colonel came, she dressed in her uniform but, looking in the mirror, she saw, not a soldier, but an invalid.

A black Lexus drew up outside and she walked out to meet Burns, a big and capable-looking soldier. Handsome, in a dark, tough-guy sort of way. She noticed how he checked her out, not bothering to hide it. Then she was climbing into the back of the car, shaking hands with the colonel, the man tall and slim, but not young. She was wondering, what was going on—a full colonel, the oldest serving soldier she had ever met, meeting with a broken NCO in the rear of a Lexus.

The car started moving and the colonel smiled, asking how she was progressing.

"Physio is happy, sir."

"What do you see yourself doing next?"

"I don't know, to be honest. The thought of leaving the military…" she waved it away.

"That's what this is about, Linda. I'd like to recruit you."

"I'll never be fit for active duty, sir."

"This is guard duty. We don't need a sprinter, we need a

strong mind. Courage." He leaned forward. "Ability to keep a secret."

While she thought about this, he added, "I know about what you did, in the desert. But don't worry. We need someone who is willing to pull the trigger."

She was trying to stay relaxed, thinking about the resources this man had, the lengths he had gone to.

"I was worried, though, that you might have a death wish."

Not the first time she had heard this. The truth, as far as she knew it, was that she didn't wish to die, but if it happened then it wasn't really such a bad thing.

"That was what the shrink was for?"

"That's it. Her opinion, no death wish, but some deep-seated guilt. Thought you took those crazy risks because you were searching for redemption. Trying to atone for something."

Linda shook herself, a physical movement. "What would I be guarding?"

"You find that out if you get to the facility. The army has kept this completely secret for seventy years, not even a rumor." He lifted a sheet of printed paper.

"I've already signed the Official Secrets Act."

"You'd be making a pact with *us*. If you ever tell what we're guarding, you won't be prosecuted."

He paused, and Linda knew he wanted her to ask what would happen. She asked.

"You'll be killed. Your mother will be killed, as will Elsa."

As he said this he smiled, like he was giving her good news.

"And you expect me to sign? You're crazy. Sir."

"Can you imagine betraying a vital military secret."

She didn't have to think. "No."

"You've done things most people wouldn't contemplate,

Linda. It comes down to this. If you don't break the secret, then your family is not at risk. We only recruit people with families."

He placed the form on the seat between them, with a gold fountain pen. She caught the driver, Dick Burns, looking at her in the rear-view. He winked.

---

LINDA DROVE through the garrison town of Amesbury, catching the sign for Merehill. She steered along a narrow country road and finally here was the hill itself, rising remarkably steeply to her right. She stopped at a gate house, flipping her ID for an armed soldier.

"Been expecting you, Sarge. Go through to the big house."

She parked outside an actual country house and the colonel was coming out to meet her with another man, a short officer, heavily muscled.

"Linda! This is Captain Bob Calder. Bob will show you to your quarters then we'll visit the facility.

Thirty minutes later, Linda was following the two men, limping along a narrow-gauge railway track, which eventually swung toward a pair of huge doors set into the almost sheer face of the hill.

Calder swiped a card and the blast doors, two serious feet of steel and concrete, creaked open. They entered a sort of air lock, then went through another set of doors into a cavernous hall, filled with heavy racks, some of which held surface-to-air missiles.

Linda frowned. "Rapiers? That's it?"

Calder shook his head. "Wanted to show you this first, our

official reason for existing. The next bunker is why we're really here."

The colonel seemed amused. "Think you might know what our secret is?"

Linda thought, hell with it. "An alien."

Calder and the colonel exchanged looks and turned to walk back outside. Linda spoke to their backs, saying, maybe a UFO.

They followed the base of the hill to another entrance and Linda's heart was suddenly racing, painful in her throat. This time, as the outer doors closed behind her, she felt eyes on her, and ducked, struggling with an inexplicable bubble of panic.

There was nothing there. Just an empty space and the two men looking at her.

The Colonel. "When I started, thirty years ago, they briefed me first. It didn't help one bit. Now, we let you experience it, then talk."

As they walked through the next set of doors, the hair rose all over Linda's body. She was in a similar space as before, only with armed soldiers and men in a lab coats, surrounding something like a circular squash court. The Perspex wall of the court, she saw, was inches thick. Inside, there was a white marble statue.

Only, it wasn't a statue. It was a naked man, white, hard like marble and incredibly still. It wore manacles attached to hawsers snaking to the ceiling and around its neck was a heavy circlet.

Linda realized that her name was being called and forced herself to attend. "Sir!"

Calder hefted a short, high tech shotgun and asked if she was ready. Soldiers were taking up positions at slits in the Perspex.

Calder, more firmly, "Are you ready, Sergeant Haddon?"

"Sir!"

"Then let's meet Mr. Harvey."

She wasn't ready, and for the first time in her life she was truly terrified. But she followed through a door into the chamber.

She whispered, "What is it?"

"What do you think?"

Linda shook her head. "Can't say."

The colonel nodded. "Quite right. We don't use that word in here."

She stared. If she was to call this a man, he was a slim and sharp-featured one, hairless and lightly muscled, with his sex dangling obscenely between his legs. She put her hand to her mouth.

"I'm going to be sick."

---

LINDA SAT at the briefing room table with Calder and Colonel Jones, trying to stop shaking.

The colonel said, "We're a discrete unit. Thirty-two military. Fifteen scientists. Work two weeks on, two weeks off."

Calder. "The pattern of my life for ten years."

She said. "Mr. Harvey." Trying it out in her mouth.

Calder nodded. "At first they called it the prisoner. Then somebody came up with Harvey. Good name as any."

"It's… a vampire."

"Yes."

"I couldn't say that word, in there."

"Don't even think it in there."

"You've kept this secret, since…"

"1943."

"Why not destroy it?"

The Colonel raised a hand. "Bob?"

Calder placed a small box on the table. Using tweezers, he picked out a curved object, around two inches long.

"Not like the films, is it? More like a cobra fang, but harder."

"You pulled its teeth out?"

"In '62, they pulled both. The second tooth is ash, after they exposed it to sunlight. It grew others."

Now Calder put a section cut through a human skull on the table. The colonel pointed. "See how it's been cut to show this fold?"

Linda nodded, touching her own face, just above the incisor.

"We've all got them. We are, all of us, predesigned to be vampires. This fold is an undeveloped fang."

Linda wanted to laugh. She bit down, but some got out anyway.

The colonel smiled, indulgent. "If the fang is part of us, so is everything else. Maybe we can use that, trigger the bits we want."

"Like strength?"

"Like *immortality*."

---

THE NEXT MORNING, inside the airlock, she told Calder, "I feel like someone's drawing a bead on me."

"We're fairly sure it's telepathic."

Fairly sure. "We don't seem to know very much. Sir."

Calder gave her a flat look. "We know it's failing."

The door opened and there it was, on the other side of the

Perspex. She nodded to the soldiers on duty, one of them the big guy from the Lexus, Dick Burns. Again, he openly checked her breasts, came back to her face, and grinned. She held his gaze for a moment, then turned to Calder.

"What, dying?"

"It hasn't moved for years. It's never spoken, not one word."

"Don't you feed it?"

"It won't drink from a container."

Linda had to steady herself, as she made herself look at it. Its eyes were almost closed, nothing behind them. It stood, legs slightly apart so that its testicles and penis hung down.

"Has it ever got loose?"

"Killed some soldiers in the early days. It was in a real mess and they didn't know how fast or strong it was. All they knew was that it had no business existing. This was in the Blitz. Basically, it got blown up."

"You think it's dormant now? Safe?"

Calder shook his head. "I think it's waiting. For us to forget how unsafe it is."

Over the next weeks, Linda learned procedures. At night, she thought about Dick Burns, imagining herself pushing him to the floor and climbing on top of him. But she had never got involved with anyone in the service, and wasn't going to start now.

Two weeks later, she was back in the normal world, spending time with Elsa, shopping and watching her serve at the café. Merehill and Harvey seemed like a dream, something that couldn't be real. One day found them at Elsa's dressing table, Elsa smearing foundation over the lumpy scar. Linda watched her sister frowning as she worked, her own small scar showing at her temple. Hardly noticeable now.

Her first day back, Dick walked behind her in a corridor and let his hand brush her ass, then walked on for a couple of steps before turning, cocking his head to look at her unscarred cheek.

"You're still fucking gorgeous, Haddow. This side, anyway. We could have some fun, if you fancied it."

She felt the heat rise shockingly, her nipples tingling, and surprised herself and him, taking his hand and pressing it between her legs, where she was already wet. His eyes were wide, staring into hers, disconcerted. Good.

She pushed his fingers deeper and stepped her legs apart, massaging his cock with her other hand, feeling him hardening under the stiff fabric.

She leaned in to whisper, "I'll let you know."

She had just stepped back when a door opened behind her, Calder calling out, "George needs a sample of skin."

Ten minutes later, she was walking into the chamber with Dick and the scientist, George, a short skinny man with wispy hair and a nose that whistled when he breathed. Dick bumped against her before moving into position on George's other side. She was still uncomfortably wet, and shaky, astonished at her own behavior.

She sighted along the barrel of the gun as George moved in, and suddenly saw that Harvey's eyes were open. He was *looking* at her. Unmistakably, right at her. She tried to move, but the message wasn't getting through.

Harvey said, "I could be your redemption."

All hell broke loose. George screamed, and she was shouting, "Abort! Abort! You!" This to George. "Behind me."

Dick, panic in his voice. "Back! Moving to the door."

Once outside, George stammered, "It sp-p-p-poke!"

Linda nodded, not trusting her voice, because Harvey was still looking at her. Calder asked, "What did it say?"

George shook his head. "It spoke to Linda." Then, "Oh Jesus, it's still looking at her!"

Linda was hearing them as if from far away. The creature stood as before, obscenely naked, except that it was staring at her. Dimly, she heard Dick saying, "Tell her to move, get out of its sight."

Calder. "Why don't you tell her?"

"Can't. Not with its eyes on her."

It was almost a minute later that Calder spoke, his voice shaky. "Linda."

"What?"

"Stop looking at it."

For a few seconds, it seemed like she couldn't, but then she turned and her bad leg collapsed. She leaned against a wall and Dick stepped forward, but stopped short of putting a hand on her, the hand that had been between her legs, minutes earlier. His face was anguished. "I can't bring myself to touch you."

She pushed off, heading shakily for the exit.

---

THE MUSTER ROOM WAS FULL, Calder sounding winded as he told how Harvey had reverted to dormant once Linda left. Linda herself was staring into her coffee.

The Colonel asked, "You heard it speak? Yet nobody caught the words."

Linda shook her head with the others. I could be your redemption. A stone, turning lazily in the air.

"It spoke to *you*, though, Linda?"

"Sir."

Dick. "I couldn't make myself speak to her. Like she was…" He looked like he might be sick. "…dirty with him."

The colonel seemed excited, trying not to show it. "It's coming to a head."

He turned to Linda. "Can you go back in? This is remarkable, truly. The first time he has communicated. Ever."

George was concentrating. "Five words. First word was I."

---

HARVEY STOOD AS BEFORE, as Linda limped into the chamber, shaking visibly. This time, ten guns were pointed at him. At a sign from the colonel, she opened her mouth to speak, finding she couldn't. Finally, she managed, "You spoke to me."

He looked at her. Even though she had steeled herself, she felt the floor tip and had to look away as the air thinned and chilled. Someone's gun was tapping hard against Perspex.

Harvey said, "All these years, you never dropped your guard. You even burned the squabs."

His words seemed to slide around her head, but that last word, squabs, *hurt*.

"If I don't feed soon, I will cease."

She glanced at the Colonel, looking for direction, but he looked away, so did Dick. She took a gulping breath.

"You think we're going to feed someone to you?"

"Yes."

She was struggling, wanting out of there. He just stood there, his eyes boring into her, his obscene sex between his legs.

The colonel called out, addressing neither Harvey nor Linda. "How soon?"

Harvey acted as though nothing had been said, until she repeated the question.

"Days. But I don't have to kill."

Suddenly an image appeared in her head and she couldn't stand it anymore. She turned and ran.

---

IN THE MUSTER ROOM, the colonel was saying it wasn't up for debate, he wasn't going to have anyone kidnapped. George said, "Then we need a volunteer."

When everyone looked at him, he said, "It won't kill you."

Calder, angry. "You believe that?"

"It's not in its interest."

Calder. "I couldn't."

Dick. "I'd eat my gun first."

Linda didn't raise her head. "I think I might be able to do it. If he's tied down."

There was no back slapping. It seemed that nobody could even look at her. Eventually, the colonel asked, "You sure?"

"How the fuck could I be sure?" She was shocked at the anger in her voice. Speaking like that to an officer.

Everybody seemed uncomfortable after that, as though something terrible had been shared. Only she knew about the image that had jumped into her head before she had to get out of there. The one where she was in his arms, letting him feed.

---

HARVEY SAID, "THIS WON'T ANSWER."

Linda looked at the creature, bound tighter than ever. "What?"

"You will die."

She swallowed hard. "Why?"

"You will pull away and die. I must hold you, so you will submit."

This was too close to the vision. Still, she turned to the colonel, her voice harsh and shaky. "Loosen him."

"Linda…"

"Before I lose my nerve! Sir."

She could hear whispered voices, an angry exchange, then people yelling. Dick was shouting, don't you get it? He's in our heads! Still, the hawsers slackened and fell away.

Harvey's eyes were on her as his arms dropped and it was really going to happen. She had never seen him move, but he was moving now, making the air in the chamber stir, as though it wanted to slide away from him. She couldn't shout, even though she tried to scream.

The vampire was so close she could feel the sharp cold coming off him. She couldn't move, yet no part of her could stay still; her skin crawled to be away, her hair rippled to escape.

He put his hand up, almost touching her and outside the chamber there was a strange strangled noise. The hand…

Touched her skin. She looked into his eyes and no longer wanted to look away. She wanted that touch. He was holding her now, as a lover might. She wanted to tilt her head to show the vein, bulging, thrumming with blood. But she waited, submissive, letting him bend her head to the side and show his teeth, holding the moment before sinking into her. Outside, there was a collective sigh, and she was staring into his eyes even though her own were closed. The teeth were pinpricks, then ice-white agony, and she felt her blood, like it was still part of her even once it was inside him.

She opened her eyes to see Dick Burns, no longer sighting along his gun. He was pressed against the Perspex, mouth slack but breathing hard. Beside him, another soldier seemed lost in some dream.

Somebody, maybe Calder, kept saying, "Oh Jesus, oh Jesus."

She closed her eyes again, and pulled Harvey closer.

SHE CAME TO IN BED, with someone knocking. Then her door opened, and George peeked in, hesitant. He had always seemed shy, but his manner, as he stepped into her room with eyes cast down, went beyond that.

"How are you?"

"Exhausted."

"You seem fine, physically. Far as I can see, you've lost some blood and that's it. Not even a reaction round the entry points."

She put her hand to her neck.

"Harvey?"

"Different. Not pure white. Some other stuff that you can't put a name to."

"You're a doctor. You're meant to put names to it."

"May I… examine you?"

Something about the way he asked, deferential, eyes still not meeting hers, made her pause before nodding.

His hands shook as he took her pulse, and checked her blood pressure. When he took the stethoscope from his bag, Linda started to take her shirt off, but he stalled her, sounding almost panicked.

"No! Just lean forward."

She didn't. She sat back and looked at him. "I'm the only woman on this whole base."

"You've just noticed?"

"Were there ever others?"

He shook his head, no.

"That must have been deliberate."

George looked away, then finally met her eye. "The colonel wanted to see what happened."

"Maybe, what? Perk him up?" She put her hand to her scar. "I'm not exactly Kate Moss."

He blew out a shaky breath. "I've been thinking about what he said to you, that first time."

She made herself stay calm. "What about it?"

"You heard it perfectly, didn't you?"

When she didn't answer he said, "That was something, what you did in there."

She shrugged, and he continued. "Not all of the men are handling it."

"What have they got to handle?"

"Seeing you *submit*."

Linda just stared at him as his color deepened. "I've got to be honest, it stirred feelings in everyone. Some of the guys are just being dumb soldiers."

"I'm a soldier."

The colonel took her off normal duties, but she wanted to see Harvey, telling herself she was curious to see what her blood had done. When she limped into the bunker, the following day, Dick was there but he looked quickly away, pretending he hadn't noticed her.

She nodded to Calder, but he turned his back. Everywhere she looked, people were turning away.

"Linda!" George was hurrying across, smiling, the colonel by his side.

"I wanted to see for myself."

Even the colonel seemed strangely stiff. "Quite right."

Harvey remained as still as before but wasn't so white, and even had dark stubbly hair. He was wearing the heavy collar and fatigues, but the manacles lay on the floor.

"Wow. What's with the cuffs?"

The Colonel shrugged. "Just slipped off. We put them back on and it let them drop again." Then, an excited undertone in his voice, "You think it might respond if you spoke to it?"

"Now?"

"Why not?"

She stepped to the Perspex and, instantly, he looked at her. She took a step back.

She gathered herself. "Who are you? Really."

"My name is Mr. Harvey."

The colonel, excited, whispered, "I knew it! Where from? When? How did he become… that?"

Harvey waited until she asked and said, "Ireland, near Dublin. In 795."

George. "Shit, we were a thousand years out!"

"How did it happen?"

He seemed happy to answer, and she was finding it easier to talk to him. "Catherine made me to be her mate. We were together, until a German bomb blew us apart."

Linda had to suppress a sudden pang on jealousy. "And Catherine?"

"Destroyed in the blast."

"You are sure?"

"Certain."

"What were you doing in London, during a bombing raid."

"We did as we pleased. Until…" He pointed to his surroundings, "…*this*."

His sudden rage took the air from her lungs, so she could hardly stand. It was George who moved to support her.

---

IT BECAME EASIER, till she was living only for the moment when he looked at her. She even stopped dreaming about the stone.

Mostly, the men ignored her, although she sometimes caught them looking at her, trying to hide it. She'd been on tour with horny soldiers many times, but the hunger in their eyes was a whole other level.

One day, she limped into the rec room and heard Calder mutter, "Here's Harvey's ho."

She flushed with sudden anger and, acting on an impulse she couldn't understand, she stepped right up to him, pressed herself to him and pulled her collar aside, turning her head to offer him her neck.

His eyes danced, as though he couldn't get them to stay on her and, when she looked around the room, everybody was staring at the floor. She turned and walked quickly away.

Later, Harvey said, "Come in here. With me."

"I can't."

"If your colonel wants more information, you must come in."

Her heart fluttering with excitement, she glanced at Dick, the ranking NCO, but he looked away and Linda simply pressed the door release and walked in. She breathed deeply, air that had touched his skin.

"Are you telepathic?"

"Somewhat. But I must be invited in. If you ask, I can show you."

"Show me. Come in."

For a dizzying moment, she couldn't tell which thoughts were his and which were hers.

"Do you see me?" The whispering was inside her head.

She answered out loud. "I see you."

"Push me away."

"No."

"Do it."

She waited, putting it off, then closed her eyes and pushed, the terrible sense of loss almost making her weep.

He spoke out loud. "Now. I can't enter, unless you invite me."

***

THE COLONEL WAS FURIOUS, asking what the hell was she thinking, but that changed when she told him what she had discovered, and he came with her the following day, when she entered the chamber to ask his questions.

"Can you link to others of your kind?"

"Under this hill, I can't even tell if it's night or day."

"Are there many of you?"

"There were less than a hundred, when I was blown up."

"Is it difficult to replicate?"

"No, but why would we? All we require is a partner. I could make as many as I wished, had I the blood."

"At the moment?"

"Your blood was a shower in the desert. I am weakening already. If I attempted, it would be a mere squab."

That blunt, everyday sort of word, again, vile in his mouth.

"What is that?"

"If I was to drain you to death, without offering my own blood, you would wake as an abomination."

"Not a creature like you?"

"A squab looks similar, but it is hideous. Its mind is a twisted thing, with only a thoughtless drive to kill. It lives for a few nights, then dies."

"It makes others of its kind?"

"Like an incontinent rat. It becomes a plague."

"Have you seen one?"

"I destroyed it. Otherwise, in a month, there would be a hundred thousand."

"You make it sound… apocalyptic."

"Unstoppable."

"But it has never happened?

"Not for thousands of years. This island would be emptied within a month."

In bed that night, she tried to quest for him, invite him to come to her. But he was under the hill. A knock at the door and here was George, coming again to sit on her bed.

"Nobody is asking why."

"Why what?"

"Squabs. The human race has an in-built destruct mechanism. For God's sake, why? We are designed for both immortality and self-annihilation."

She ignored the question. "The blood I gave him wasn't enough."

When George shook his head, Linda grabbed his hand,

making him flinch. "You'll tell the colonel? He needs more, George."

Two days later, she submitted to him again, this time gladly, pressing herself to him. The pain was so sweet, and the feeling of her blood in his veins a stronger and more intimate bond. She sent her thoughts to his, telling him she loved him.

Around the chamber, the men stood holding their guns loosely, with expressions of open arousal and yearning. Even ecstasy.

———

DAYS LATER, Linda motioned to Dick to open the chamber door, but he shook his head and looked away. Then, almost as though the action had nothing to do with him, he pressed the button.

She could feel Harvey's eyes as she walked in, glanced round and there was George, pressed against the Perspex.

"The colonel won't be pleased I'm here."

"He won't send you away."

"How do you know?"

"*Listen* to him, Linda."

She stepped closer, letting her breath fall on him.

In her head, she said, "I love you. What should I do?"

In her head, he replied, "Show me."

"How?"

"Bring me something to show the depth of your love. Put it in my hand."

She thought about that, then she unbuttoned her shirt and he came to her. She closed her eyes when the pain came, and she felt him slide into her vein. She could feel his sex this time, hard and high against her belly and ground herself to it.

THE COLONEL WAS STANDING in her room, pale and furious. "Did I not issue you with a direct order?"

"I'm sorry, sir."

He shook, under poor control. *Listen* to him.

"See if this is any clearer. You are relieved of normal duties. I personally will sanction any further entry into that facility. Is there anything you do not understand?"

"No, sir."

And there wasn't. She had listened to him, to the oldest serving soldier she knew, and heard, greed, desire, and his need for her. She remembered how he had said it, her first day here. *Immortality.* He was an old man who didn't want to die.

Minutes later, George was there, and his eyes were wet.

"He permitted me to hear. How you are going to show him how you love him? The stone?"

She stared at him. Somehow her innermost self, the deep guilt she had carried her entire life, had leached out, into the air of the camp. She should have been horrified, but she shrugged. "The stone is just a stone. One I threw when I was seven."

Then she said, "Nobody knows about what I did. Not even my sister, who I hit with it." She pointed to her temple, where Elsa's scar was.

"He knows."

"Then he knows if I'd fetched help, she would have been fine. But I ran, hid in my room. Everybody thought she had fallen, lay there unconscious till it was too late."

"Did you hate her?"

"My twin? I always loved her, but I was jealous because she

was the smart one." She pushed her fist into her chest as her eyes teared up. "She's my *core*."

He leaned in, eyes greedy. "What will you give him?"

She shook her head and he stood and, shyly, kissed her cheek.

"I might not dare do that ever again. The colonel made a terrible mistake bringing you here, you know. It's as if you just being here has helped Harvey open a door. A trapdoor, and we've all fallen though."

IT WAS dark when Linda made the agonizing walk to the bunker, glad of the darkness hiding the severity of her limp. Inside, she made a big effort to walk steadily, but still saw Dick straighten up in shock.

She hit the button and limped into the chamber, her leg dragging. Harvey was smiling as she held shaking her fist out, closed over something, and dropped three dark and bloody screws into his open palm.

Swaying, dangerously close to a faint, she asked, "Is it enough?"

"It is good."

This time, when he bit her, the pain was worse even than the agony of digging the screws out of her own thigh bone. She could feel something venomous scalding its way to her heart, which faltered and stopped. Then started again, crashing against her ribs as it pumped to the tips of her fingers and the inside of her eyes. Pain was all there was, there was room for nothing else, until suddenly his blood was in her mouth and she gagged, swallowing.

He whispered, "The scientist knows what to do."

---

LINDA DREAMED she was running along a dark and twisting path, just ahead of something terrifying, but when she woke everything was white and still. She was lying in a brightly lit room with cotton over her face, and there were two people nearby.

She tuned into the breathing of the men, the beat of their hearts, and for a while became lost in it. One of the men was George, she could all but taste him.

The other man? She sent out her senses and felt fear coming from him, delicious, in jagged waves. Dick Burns.

Dick whispered, "You feel that?"

"Feel what?"

"It's gotten colder."

"You're just spooked. Sitting here on ghost watch."

"It's not a ghost we're watching for, is it?"

Linda was enjoying their fear, surprised to find it was solid and real, like a color she had never seen before. And it was *sexy*. She felt her hands, crossed over her chest, and sent her thoughts into her index finger, wanting to lift it a fraction.

"Fuck! I think she moved!"

"Stop waving that bloody gun around."

"Hit the alarm!"

"We'll look like idiots."

"Hit the fucking thing."

Linda sat up and when she looked at Dick he ducked as though she'd shot at him. His gun came up, but Linda was so fast, tossing the gun away and falling on him as though he had no strength with which to oppose her.

The big man thrashed and screamed, a trapped animal, and she felt herself quiver, felt her fangs slide from her face. She paused, looking at him as she held him, helpless.

She bent to whisper, "We could have some fun, Dick. If you fancy it."

She tore his neck terribly and gulping him down, feeling his life spurting, pouring down her throat and filling her, his terror filling her too, a hot sexual thrill. Then, all too soon, he was just old meat.

The scientist huddled, staring at her with huge eyes. She looked down at herself, naked and bloody, shocked to see that the skin across her chest had torn in the struggle, hanging in a ragged flap.

She pulled, and it came away like soggy card. Then she was ripping at herself, shredding her old, scarred skin away, sloughing it like a snake as the blood of the soldier went roaring, sparkling through her veins.

Finally, feeling like she had shed a filthy coat of sodden wool, she held her arms high, her smooth and bone-white skin glowing.

George knelt in supplication, his eyes travelling over her, terror and desperation coming off him in waves.

The erotic pulse of his fear made her groan aloud, and she stepped her legs apart, feeling herself unfurling and opening. Keeping his eyes on hers, he crawled, inching forward, till his breath was on her.

When she rolled her hips, he pressed himself in, moaning as he began to lap. She shifted, delicious waves running the length of her body, then took hold of his head and ground his face deep into her.

She knew that, if she chose, she could crush his skull like an overripe melon. She increased the pressure, thinking she might just do that, thinking too that everything was different, she could open herself, impossibly wide, drive him deep into the wetness between her legs. She felt him struggle and choke as the scalding waves broke, and dropped him.

At first, she though him dead, but he coughed and rolled onto his side, whimpering. Then he pulled himself to his feet, and bowed, holding out a bag of her clothes.

She spoke, noticing the strangeness of a voice without breath. "Is it night?"

"Yes."

She ignored the clothes. "Come, then."

"There's something to do. *He* told me."

George bent over the soldier, getting himself bloody as he removed the head. He stood, breathing heavily. "To stop him from becoming… you know."

The night was velvet to her perfect skin and she felt so light that she could fly, so strong she could tear the train tracks from the ground. George was a wheezing old engine by her side.

There were more soldiers than she had ever seen in the bunker before, all armed. Their terror and shock when they saw her, blood smeared and naked, was another scorching, erotic pulse. Soldiers shot at her, but she dodged around the curve of the Perspex. The colonel was shouting, for God's sake keep her away from the door control.

And it seemed that they could do that, there were so many of them. Harvey stood naked again, smiling, his penis curved hard against his belly.

It was George, pulled behind the line of soldiers, who pressed the door release. Calder shot him, but too late.

Some of the soldiers died quickly, but Harvey kept most

alive, including Calder and the colonel, destroying their guns and driving them into his prison. The Perspex wall of the chamber was already so daubed with blood that it could hardly be seen through and the soldiers pressed themselves back against it, trying to hide behind each other in their terror.

The vampires circled each other, naked and bloody. Linda glanced at the colonel, Calder, holding their eyes, then smiled as she turned to Harvey, pushing up her breasts in offering. He came to her then, and they caressed and shared blood, taking their time in front of soldiers who stood powerless, fear and arousal coming from them like a high song.

He squeezed her breasts, so hard that she would have caught her breath, if she breathed. He tore them with his teeth, splattering blood.

She understood. They could not truly be hurt.

She pushed away and walked slowly, swivel-hipped towards the soldiers, who milled and pulled aside. She smiled at them, pressed her hands to the bloody wall and stepped her legs apart as she pushed her ass out. Harvey grasped her hips and slid his impossibly erect penis along the crack, playing, not yet entering. Then he thrust himself, incredibly deep inside her, suddenly pumping her hard and fast, making her cry out.

She let him fuck her like that, then twisted, pushing him away, and they wrestled. He threw her bodily into the melee of soldiers, sheep trying to run, and followed on, thrusting himself into her again with shocking force. She writhed, finding she could grasp and squeeze him tight inside herself.

Calder was screaming suddenly, and Linda turned her head to see that Harvey had reached out and caught him and was holding him above her, gashing him to let his life blood pump across them both.

She laughed as he beat into her, speeding, urgent as the fabric of reality seemed to shred and fall away, so she imagined her fingers as talons, sinking through his rib cage, imagined his penis engorged and impossibly enormous, the gap between her legs massive, so that her stomach and chest bulged with each of his thrusts, bones cracking and tissue ripping. She tore at him, then bent backwards and squeezed her own breasts, screaming at him.

Reality was wafer thin, she could see that now, other possibilities opening to one such as she, a wild and wicked thing, a monster with massive breasts and gigantic wings that drove them crashing from wall to ceiling and into a boiling, purple sky.

Screaming, writhing, she felt him spill, electricity running through acid in her belly and they fell, spinning and tumbling to earth.

---

THE RAGE that Harvey had built over the years was written in carnage. He killed horribly, playing vile games with his captors, eventually leaving only the colonel.

The colonel turned to Linda.

"If you have anything left of the soldier you were, don't set this monster loose on the world."

Harvey laughed, delighted. "Don't you get it, yet? *You* will be the monster. I told you plainly what would happen, but you were so greedy to live you could not destroy me. The ones you love the best, think of them now."

He grinned and turned to Linda, wanting her to share the moment, it seemed. "Everyone on this island will die horribly."

Linda did not smile back, and the vampire took a long, long time, killing the colonel, finally draining him, deliberately so he would become a squab.

He dropped the body. "Is it day or night?"

She checked a corpse's watch. "It will be dark in an hour."

"You will never see the sun again, my love. A glimpse would turn us both to ash."

She looked around at the carnage. "Will it always be like this?"

"I think you shall be crueler than me. There is something hard at the core of you."

"Like a stone?"

"Like a stone. You have shed your old skin, darling Linda, but it takes time to shed your old self entirely."

They waited, and after Linda checked the time she led them, still naked and bloody, into the airlock. Harvey's eagerness lit his eyes as he carried the body of the colonel, weightless under his arm.

The big doors lumbered closed behind her and she took a long second, having to steel herself, before pressing the release button, watching the lights flash to warn the outer doors were about to open. She turned to put her hand to his face and for the first time his doubt showed.

"What have you done?"

"Do you recall the first words you spoke to me?" *I could be your redemption.*

When she was sure that he did recall, she told him, "You were right."

The vampires turned as the massive doors opened, letting in the searing light of morning.

# WHEN LIFE CLOSES A DOOR

## MARY TREPANIER

When the first band was done, I went up to the bar, holding my place on the brass rail with one hand. A boy in a plaid flannel shirt and black t-shirt leaned past, long dark hair swinging, to cut ahead of me into the bartender's notice.

"Hey!" I said. "I was in line!"

He stood back from the rail. "I didn't see you." He was only lying a bit; he hadn't seen a girl, only a body. Not subtly, he checked me out. He had a long bony nose and thick eyebrows. He was quite tall. "Buy you a beer to apologize?"

We traded introductions. Andrew had moved to Seattle with his college best friend to start a band. "What's your band's name?" I asked.

He wadded up his long face. "You don't want to know. Besides, we broke up."

"I'm sorry."

"We were pretty awful. I've been practicing with some other guys on and off."

"What about your friend?"

He looked down the bar, with its mirror like a window to a backward world: grunge scene types, most in black leather jackets, flannel and ripped jeans. The edges of the beveled mirror were a pretty color, like spring leaves. I wore a black leather jacket myself, on the back the sigil for air copied from a witchbook of my sister's.

"My friend is traveling now," he said. "I think he's in Europe."

I dropped the subject.

We met again in the park one early evening, when I was drawing trees in charcoal for school. After three years of college in Oregon, I'd moved north, enrolling at the Art Institute to keep my parents happy. Some time later, after we went to bed, I showed Andrew my portfolio: naturalistic drawings in charcoal and pencil, fantasy trees and windows in ink. I drew crooked trees in almost-darkness with hands like witches', windows all reflection, panes of mirrors reflecting mirrors, a path to a world that wasn't this.

"I should get you to draw me a window," he said. "A permanent window. So I can always find you." I couldn't decide if that was romantic or creepy. I let it pass. He was making me coffee, which was good in a boy.

---

I MISS THE PROMISE. I miss feeling life malleable to my will, as if in my hands I could twist the fabric of the universe. As if I were a goddess.

I had that for an hour, for half a day. We took chances. It's caught up with me—a lot of my health problems started then.

---

HE NEVER MADE a date for a meal. "I don't like eating with people," he said. "I'm allergic to a lot." He drank black coffee, water, and any kind of alcohol; that was all I saw him consume. We spent most dates in bed. He could have sex ten times a day— I liked that, though my libido didn't keep up.

After some nudging, he took me to his loft—one room of a set pieced together from drywall, in a larger industrial space. A toilet sat behind a curtain, a freestanding shower in a corner. A couple roommates stood propped in the hallway, smoking, as we came in. He waved at them vaguely and led me to his room.

It wasn't much more than a closet. It had no windows, and

when he turned off the overhead it was pitch-dark till he lit candles. They lay in saucers on a steamer trunk; the room held just that and a bed, ropes tied to its frame.

"Do you like being tied up?" he asked. We'd talked about BDSM in general terms.

"I've only tried it once. I couldn't take it seriously."

"I think I can get you to take it seriously."

We negotiated. Then he tied me down prone and blind-folded me. I was a lot more nervous than I thought I'd be. "Do I need a safeword?"

"If you want one. I'm not going to damage you. I like you." A pause. He must have realized how ominous that sounded. "We can use red, yellow and green if you like. Do you know how those work?"

I nodded.

He used a flogger, soft, then harder; he got a good rhythm going, and just when I thought I couldn't take more he laid off. "You have good pain tolerance." Then, something liquid and hot, hot, hot pooled in the small of my back. I cried out. Candlewax. Then ice on my labia and anus. I squirmed against the ropes.

"Do you want something?" he asked, with a laugh in his voice. I whispered. "Say it louder."

"I want sex."

"This isn't sex? Be specific."

"I want you to fuck me!"

"I want you to beg."

It made me embarrassed. It made me hot. Only perfect assurance on his part could have pulled it off. "Please, please, please fuck me. Please."

"All right. Since you begged." He took me from behind. At

the peak of the climax I blacked out, for a moment, and came to, still coming, crying out.

He untied me. I lay in the crook of his arm, sweaty, still throbbing. "That was amazing."

"You're a bit of a sub, Tess," he said.

"I guess. I don't think of myself like that."

"We all have a bit in us."

"What about you?"

"I don't switch for girls."

"For girls?" I eyed him with interest. "You like boys? I can work with that."

"A long story. I'll tell you sometime. You want some scotch? There's some in the kitchen." He pulled on his boxers and wandered out.

After that, he started biting me. He loved to bring the blood to the surface, so just a few drops shone in candlelight, then lick them off my skin. We'd traded test results, which said it was safe, but it squicked me. And I liked it. And it squicked me that I liked it.

"It's just blood play. Plenty of people do it."

"I've never met any of them."

He grinned. "I'm not introducing you to the others."

We didn't talk much. I didn't care. In Oregon, I'd had a perfectly nice boyfriend—courteous, gentle, sharing, and passive-aggressive. I'd come to the big city, and I wanted to be bad.

One evening, after dinner at my place—I ate, Andrew didn't —I pushed back my plate and said, "So how 'bout tonight I do you?"

"You want me to sub?" He raised one overgrown eyebrow. I had threatened to tweeze them, but it was only a threat. I liked everything about him, from his gangly height to his big nose to his almost-monobrow.

"I'd like to taste your blood."

Full stop. His eyes were black as a coal chute. "I don't think that's a good idea."

"Why not? Did you have a bad experience?"

"You could say that."

I let it go, but I couldn't help circling back. The next week, I insisted. In bed at my apartment, I sat propped on one elbow over him.

"What's your problem? I want this. At least tell me why you don't. You call me your girlfriend. It's like you don't trust me."

He looked up at me, biting his lip. "What if I told you I was a vampire?"

"I'd laugh at you. There's no such thing. Not in real life."

He blinked, and met my eyes. "Are you sure?" He sat up, pulling the sheet up over his knees. "You, with your witch sister. Are you sure?"

I stared at him. He was insane.

"Okay, I don't like doing this, but some of the superhuman shit is true. I don't want to break your stuff, so I should show you outside. Can you wait till later? It's not good if I'm seen."

We waited till 3 a.m., when even my neighborhood was asleep. Then he ran up the side of my building.

I stood staring upward, till he leapt back down.

Inside, I made tea in the kitchen. "So do you go around murdering people? Because I'm not okay with that."

"No. The easiest thing around here is to go up to the National Forest and kill deer. If I run flat-out, I can get there and back in a night."

"You seem okay with daylight."

"It's not good for me. It's like I'm allergic. I do better at night." It's true, he was incredibly sluggish during the day. I'd thought it was just from tending bar at night. He worked at a popular hole in the wall near the bigger place where we'd met.

"And the stake thing?"

He shrugged. "No one's ever tried to kill me. I think we're just really hard to kill. If you stake someone through their heart, that wound doesn't heal."

"Can't you catch something from drinking deer blood? Trichinosis or something?"

"Through my friend I met a doctor who's, well, in the club." A vampire, he meant. He looked down, at his hands—big hands, big knuckles, hairy. If you'd been casting a film, you'd have made him a werewolf. He looked pale, but so does everyone in Seattle.

A piece fell into place for me. "Your friend who's traveling. He made you a vampire, didn't he?" He looked at me helplessly.

"How long ago did he leave?"

"Ten years." He'd made it sound like a few months. Your perspective must change if you have all the time in the world. "You subbed to him." Shutting his eyes, he nodded. "You miss him, a lot." Another nod.

I hugged him, because he needed it. My heart broke a little for him.

---

IF YOU TRY IT, everything's realer than real. Colors are supersaturated—daylight is too intense. Sounds don't hurt; they just feel like it.

You run like you run in dreams, faster than any Olympian.

Sex is the best sex you'll ever have, and you can do it three days at a time. We got each other's rhythm. He liked me tied down and vulnerable. I came when he told me to. He loved that.

I had a hard time going to school, though.

---

"So you really want to do this?"

I nodded.

"This won't turn you, just give you the taste." He frowned. "Look, though, for real, take responsibility here. Everyone is different. You could go over the line right away. Any time is a risk, if small."

"I'll risk it." I didn't see the downside of vampirism. Sure, you had to move around a lot, and lie. It had a bad reputation. But I wanted to try. I figured I'd be safe, once.

We were in my bedroom, now more like his: blackout curtains and candles, all burning. He laid his head back over the pillow, exposing his long neck. "Bite as hard as you want."

I took the tendon of his neck between my teeth, and sucked and bit. "Harder." It was hard work, to do what he did so easily. I made a bruise, finally, blood starting to go dark under the skin. "Use your teeth." I was a little horrified. "Just keep going. I can take the pain." I bit, into resilient living flesh, rubbery. His skin smelled of sweat, faintly earthy, spicy, human-smelling. "Harder." I bit, sucking, biting, tearing, forgetting there was a being there: eating.

At last I got enough to taste. Iron and salt, but really, it tasted like very little.

Then for a half-hour I was like him.

I looked into the black, black eyes. I could see his history; I could see the boy who'd made him a vampire.

I could see murder. "You killed someone."

"I did. Jeff made me do that. I'm never going to do it again."

I felt him hunting, full animal mode, sensing the fear of a victim who knew what was happening, which the deer didn't. I'd begun to understand his sexual sadism: evoking fear that is lust, evoking submission. Now up through me welled his blood-lust, his desire to kill. Up from the stomach, from the body: Kill.

I saw a woman with black eyes. She spoke Spanish. "Where were you?"

"Mexico. Jeff knew some people."

"Not very nice people."

"No."

He bit far harder than I had, hacked with his teeth into her jugular vein. The impact went through me, and his satisfaction, his teeth deep in the chunk of flesh. Arterial blood jetted when his mouth released, on his clothes, hands, the concrete floor. He drew, like drinking and eating at once; sucking. Nursing. "Killing people is hot, isn't it?"

"Yes. But it's wrong." His shock pulsed through me: her closed eyes, the personhood gone from her body. Her hair, slightly coarse, curled on the floor, blotted red with blood, more blood closer to the scalp, dark puddles. His revulsion rose in my belly. "I've done what most people can only imagine, and all I can say is, don't. It's sick."

I made the Anne Rice argument, because it was there: "Aren't you more than human, like you're more than a deer? Life eats life. Why are humans special?"

"I'm more physically powerful than most humans. Does that really make me *more* than human?" He stared at me. "I never was a deer. I was a human. You felt how it felt, didn't you?" I nodded. "Would you want to be like that?"

I shook my head. No. It sickened me. He couldn't escape it.

"You can train yourself to be okay with it. But it's making yourself a psychopath. We were all human."

I felt a dip in energy, a hint of coming exhaustion. "Can I have more blood?"

"No. I want to see what it does to you. Wait a week."

"A week!"

"This isn't what you call safe. I told you that to begin with."

The following week I had to finish my term final, a series of woodblock prints. I needed to stay late at school, and I put Andrew off day to day. "For sure Thursday," I told him.

Ten p.m. Thursday, I had to give up. I called from a desk in a teacher's office. "I can't see you tonight."

"Really?"

"I have to work to pull this term out. I have to keep my grant." I'd tried hard to balance this new amazing thing against my schoolwork. I wasn't doing it well, and if I didn't concentrate now I was done. "It'll have to be this weekend."

Long pause. "Okay."

I missed him a lot as I worked. I thought about him, memories breaking over me in waves.

I was in love. I had been, really, since the beginning. I was trying to be careful. But in the end, I thought, *what's the point?*

When I saw him, though, we began off-rhythm. "Didja miss me?" He said it jokingly, but I took it straight.

"I did. Do you want to see my prints?" I spread them out on my scarred, white-painted kitchen table: a window, in greens, blacks, and browns. One branch hung outside the window frame, like a hand, beckoning.

"Would you make one for me?" he asked. "A window to come through?"

"If you like. You can't come visit me ordinarily?"

"Suppose something happens?"

"Like what?"

He met my eyes. "Like someone gets on to me. Like I have to escape."

"How would I make it work?"

"Witch it. Make it so, and believe it."

Everything had flowed easily up to that point, like a waterfall, beautiful and inevitable. But now I felt pushed. "Let me think about it."

Again, that night, he let me taste his blood. He'd been right; I'd taken a while to recover last time. It was if all the intensity of life I had available for two or three days had been used up in that half-hour, and the following two days were flat.

Tonight I took blood from his thigh, harder but easier to hide. "No, really, bite me."

I had to scrabble with my teeth. It felt wrong to do this to another living being, and just as before I quailed. "I'm okay with it," he said. "You saw how quickly I healed before." A week after I bit him, there was no mark on his neck.

The skin was thicker at his inner thigh, more rubbery, harder to break, and also hairy. His balls lay by my cheek, his cock partly tumescent.

"Harder," he said.

I chewed into him.

"There."

I licked the blood that finally came. "Bite me more, deeper. Suck." I worried at the wound and got more, nearly a mouthful.

I sat back, wiping my mouth. I'd made a sore on his leg, with torn skin, angry dark red. It looked horrible, like a disease.

I was thrown into a memory of sex with Jeff, which disoriented me. On a bed with black sheets, he received Jeff's thick cock, which hit Andrew's prostrate, wave after wave of intense pleasure. It put him further into sub space than I'd ever gone. The sensation poured through me.

Andrew smiled slowly. I felt overwhelmed, out of control. I couldn't tell if that pleased me. He undressed me, and fucked me anally, touching me at the same time. I came very hard, harder than I had before, but I held onto consciousness and rode it.

Then I lay curled up and he held me, kissing my hairline. "I love you," he said. "I didn't think I would love anyone again. It took me so long to get over him."

"I love you too." The heightened life was ebbing out of me, and I fell asleep.

The next morning was grey and flat. I woke before he did, got up, and made myself coffee.

Hunched over my kitchen table, I thought, *This is a mess. He has this power over me, and I don't totally trust it, or him.*

He'd killed people. He said just one, but he'd killed a woman. I guessed that he had sex with her. What made the difference between her and me? He loved me; he hadn't loved her. He said he'd never kill again. But he was still someone who'd killed a woman, a woman he'd had sex with. He could kill me.

He wanted me to turn, too. Oh, he was being good, but I knew he wanted it. Not for my sake, for his. He wanted a companion.

I loved him. But it would be trading real life for ... something else. It wasn't like a drug addiction. I could never get clean.

But was I being a coward? I was an atheist, an agnostic at

most. I didn't believe death was a gift. Maybe my desire not to go against the natural order was just superstition.

At breakfast—I made myself eggs—I asked, "Can vampires have children?"

He frowned over his coffee cup, which he held in two hands by his mouth, protectively. "What kind of question is that? No."

"Huh. I feel like shit this morning."

"Are you trying to pick a fight? Because I can leave."

The black eyes looked hurt, mostly. Suddenly I felt bad for him. Except for me, he was alone. Only I knew his secret, besides Jeff—wherever Jeff was. I got up, stood behind his chair, and hugged him.

For the holidays, my family planned to meet at my sister's house. "I gotta go," I told Andrew. "For at least three days."

"Okay." He didn't like it. He and I talked over coffee at a nearby shop, to the clink of heavy crockery—I'd planned that, so he couldn't end the conversation by grabbing me. Even before Jeff, he'd been on poor terms with his family. His father had left when he was two, and his mother sounded insane. "So how old are you really?" I asked him.

"Forty-one."

"You never had that thing where you want to get married and settle down? Have kids?"

"Sure. But I can't have kids."

"You could adopt."

"Oh, be real. 'Daddy's a vampire, that's why he can't come to your school conference.'"

"We could work around it." It was only after I said it that I realized I'd said "we."

"We'd be lying to the kid the whole time. Would you want

that?" I shook my head. "I got lied to a lot, as a kid. I don't want that."

I traveled south on the bus to my sister's Portland bungalow, all crayon colors: sunflower yellow, cobalt, crimson. The first night, in her front room, she laid a couple of quilts over me. "Dan's on kid duty. I can talk for a bit."

I told her about school; she told me about her work and her painting, her husband Dan's work, and their toddler's latest antics. I told her about Andrew. "Can I tell you something weird, Lizzy? You have to promise not to tell anyone. Even Dan. Cross your heart and hope to die."

That made her smile. "All right."

I told her about the vampire thing. She was willing to believe, provisionally. "I mean, in a lot of ways, he's perfect," I said. "He says all the right things. He means them."

"Well, set aside the bit about him being a vampire, and look at it that way. He's in his forties, he's a bartender, he doesn't want kids. You can't introduce him to anyone, or only, 'Here he is, bye now!' And if you go the vampire route—I just can't see that being good." She was a green witch and an herbalist; the natural order was all good with her.

"Would it matter if my husband were a bartender? Mom and Dad wouldn't care, really, as long as I was happy."

"Okay, but he's killed someone. Saying the right things may mean he's a good fake. A psychopath."

"If he were a psychopath, he wouldn't have told me about the killing."

"He didn't. You saw it."

I nodded slowly. "Still ... he doesn't feel like a psychopath. He's not empty. He's sad."

"Let me give you a reading." I'd hoped for that. Lighting a

couple of tapers in carved wooden holders, she got out her cherrywood Tarot box.

"I guess I have two things to ask," I said. "Should I stay with this guy, and should I become a vampire?"

She wrinkled her nose but said only, "I don't want to leave Dan with the baby too long—he's had a hard day. I'll do you two short ones."

I shuffled, and she laid out three cards: a woman in a lush landscape, below two cards from the suit of Cups. "There's a lot of good in this for you," she said, "a lot of sensuality. Maybe it's not the perfect love, but it's love. You're good for him as well." She pointed to the Queen of Cups. "So, staying with him—at least for now, I'd say yes."

I shuffled again. Should I become a vampire? The wind gusted outside, rattling the windowpanes. Fear rose in me. I had seen Andrew when he hadn't hunted lately—sluggish, skin clammy to the touch. My body didn't want to die.

Lizzy laid out the cards. The Seven of Swords led the reading. "It might work, it might not. It's not clear." She pointed below, to the Hermit and the Star, both reversed. "I will say Andrew's motives are suspicious. And he's frustrated he can't make you change. I don't think it's clear yet."

"What would make it clear?"

"Time." She folded the cards into their box. "You should sleep. Breakfast will be early."

In the morning I woke, in my mind the flavor of a dream: something wistful, something lost. The wind had been up all night, leaving bits of fir and maple in the yard. The street shone with reflected early pale-blue light; the grass lay furred with frost.

To live forever, to travel everywhere, be like a black wind in the night. But never to have children, never a permanent hearth, always to be the one outside the window, scratching at the glass.

But never to die. Oh, maybe by violence. But I could avoid that—I'd have the strength of a god.

Martin, in Oregon—we'd been good, but I knew I'd never marry him. Andrew felt more like marriage. And the sex ... Lizzy had made the sensuality sound optional. The sex was like the vampirism, like a train to the real world that lived under this one, like being in color after black and white. It didn't stop.

But sex could die. The summer I was 19, with Stephan—it was nice till we started fighting. Things would be permanent, with Andrew, beyond human marriage.

There was something hollow in him, too, like a boarded-over well, something to do with Jeff.

---

JANUARY HIT, hard cold. My course load was light. Andrew and I went to shows; I watched a rehearsal with his maybe-band.

It did not slow down, the sex: his hand grabbing my hair, his teeth on me, his cock. The taste of his blood said the world was lying—the skin overlaid on it wasn't real. We were meant to be gods, and we kept forgetting it.

"Tell me more about Jeff."

He sipped black coffee from thick-walled china, at the coffee shop. He wouldn't look me in the eye. "What do you want to know?"

"Everything."

He looked up at that. "You've seen the worst."

"But tell me."

They'd been friends in high school and got close the

freshman year of college. Then Jeff spent a year abroad, in Italy, and came back changed—sleek-haired, with a new motorcycle and new clothes.

"His musical taste had taken a turn for the worse, so I schooled him on that. But otherwise—ah, he was so cool! So much cooler than me. Being around him was the best thing." Jeff had a girlfriend at the time, but Andrew and Jeff spent much of their time together. "It's when I started drinking scotch. And smoking pot. Finally, I got him to tell me about Italy."

He closed his eyes, and I took his hand. It was cold. A smell of rot hovered around him. He hadn't eaten lately.

"First he fucked me, and I subbed to him. I was definitely the bottom. I needed it." Eyes still shut, head thrown back on the vinyl skin of the booth, hair a mess—I loved him a lot then. "Then he said, do you want this other thing?"

By then, Andrew had dropped out of college and was living in his mother's basement, with his stepfather threatening to throw him out. He had nothing but his music and Jeff. "I said yes."

"Have you ever regretted it?"

"After we split, yes." In his eyes I saw a wasteland. He pulled his hand back and looked away. "But I made peace with it."

"Where is he now?

"Somewhere in Europe. Come on, let's get out of here." I let him drag me home. I had enough for now.

Then he disappeared.

Two days with no conversation was unusual, a week unheard of. The back of my mind was all flashing red lights. It didn't seem smart to drop in at his apartment. But I didn't think he wanted to lose his job.

Toward the start of his shift, I sat down at the bar's far end.

The place lay nearly empty, pool table quiet, air free of cigarette smoke. Black eyes flicked toward me. "I have a break in an hour. I can talk then." I got out my drawing journal to keep people away.

The scent of a cigarette lit, fresh fire to paper, sweet tobacco —I turned to see Andrew beside me. "Draw me that window now," he said. "I need it."

"I can draw a window. But I don't know how to make an opening. I'm not a witch."

"You're a witch. I wouldn't be with you if you weren't." Propping his cigarette on the edge of the bar, he grabbed my head with both hands and kissed me, tongue fucking my mouth. Then he stepped back and studied my face, to see if the kiss had worked. I didn't like his scrutiny.

But I drew a window open to an autumn twilight with twisted skeletons of trees. Andrew leaned over, polishing a pint glass with a towel. "That'd work."

At his break, he took me to a back room by the stage: one wall mirrored, the others discolored with smoke. He locked the door, and we took one of two wooden benches.

A week ago, a van had delivered a large wooden crate to his loft. He opened it to find Jeff as near death as he'd ever seen him.

"I was tempted just to leave him." His voice came muffled. He'd curled into a ball, head on his knees, arms wrapped around himself. I put my arms around as much of him as I could.

He hadn't called because he didn't want Jeff to know about me. "I know the inside of his head, the fucker. The best thing he'd do is make you a vampire." Jeff had gotten into trouble. "He stole the wrong kill. If you turn a Sicilian Mafioso into a vampire, it doesn't make him a nice guy."

"What now?"

Andrew took a drag on his cigarette. "I don't know. He's all cheerful. He wants to come back to me, he wants to be part of my life, he's sorry it ever went bad."

In the room's brighter light, I noticed a bruise on his neck. I pushed myself away from him on the bench. "You've been having sex with him."

Andrew took another long drag, then met my eyes. "Yes."

Explosions went off in my head. "Did you use a condom?"

"Yes. I knew you'd want it."

Fear bit me. "So he knows about me."

"I said I was dating around." Breath sucked in, smoke came out. "He laughed at me. He thinks he has this hold on me."

I touched his shoulder. It was warm. He'd eaten recently. "He does have a hold on you."

"I couldn't just let him die." Black eyes stared into mine. "You have to see that."

A lock of his dark hair fell against his cheek. It kept confusing me, how beautiful he was. My body called out for his. But he'd betrayed me with a psychopath.

I drew back my hand. "I have to go."

"No!" He grabbed my wrist. More quietly, "No. Don't. Please."

I pulled my wrist away. Quietly, quickly, he said, "I owed it to him to revive him, but I can make him go away." He closed his eyes. "You have to understand. He's everything I don't want to be."

A knock on the door. Andrew's eyes flicked open.

Before he got up, the doorknob twisted. Then the wood of the door cracked. The doorknob mechanism pulled out, away from us, leaving a splintered hole. The door flew open.

What I hadn't reckoned on—I don't know why I was

surprised—Jeff was hot. Slender, English-looking, with dish-water blond hair, he had a long nose in a fey, pointed face and big blue-green eyes. Pallor suited him.

He smiled. So pretty, like hard candy in a jar.

Andrew sighed, as if he'd half-expected this, and stood. I popped up behind him. "I'm going to need you to pay for that," he said.

"Your bar can afford it," Jeff said. "The place is packed!" Through the door spilled a loud buzz of talk, glasses clinking, snips of a jukebox tune.

"Someone must've seen you, then."

"Glamourie." Jeff waved his hand vaguely. "I'm not stupid." He angled his head toward me, where I stood half-hidden. "And this is?"

"Tess."

"Enchanted." He shot me a sunny smile.

Andrew glowered. "Unless you want to pay for the door, we should go," he said. To both of us: "Go around back and wait. I'll get the rest of the night off."

I stared. Was it that easy? "Glamourie. I use it when I need to." As he passed Jeff, he grabbed his shirt collar, pulled him close and said, "Don't mess with her."

Jeff smiled as sweetly as a two-year-old.

In the alley behind the bar, the shine of street lights reflecting from puddles, Jeff inspected me—with pleasure, he made that clear. "I'm sure Andrew's said a lot of bad things about me. Don't believe everything you hear. I assume you're in on the secret?"

I said nothing.

He cleared his throat, an impatient sound. "So you're his girlfriend?"

I shrugged.

The occasional drops of rain came more quickly now. He folded his arms. He was only wearing a blazer. "I'm getting cold. I need to eat." I must have started. "Don't worry. I don't want to piss Andrew off."

Someone walked into the alley, and we turned to look. The coal of a cigarette lit Andrew's face, red. He came up and put his arm around me.

I realized I wasn't breaking up with him. I loved him. And he was my only protection against this shivering boy who could rip out a door handle with one hand.

"I made it okay," Andrew said. Jeff gave him the side-eye but said nothing.

That night, I understood how little Andrew used his power. What Andrew hid, Jeff used profligately. I think, too, Jeff was stronger. Perhaps it was like a muscle you had to exercise.

Jeff used a lot of glamourie on me—I must have spent half that time dissociated. Yet I think that, as much as he ever liked humans, Jeff liked me.

Back at Andrew's, in the main room with its pillows and door laid on cinder blocks for a table, Jeff created a party for us and the roommates. He laid out scotch, cocaine, and Belgian chocolate, which he insisted on feeding me. Andrew's face was crumpled, pissy, but he said nothing.

A slip of milky sweet; then I was sucking Jeff's fingers. Then he kissed me: thin lips, nimble tongue. He fingered my nipples through my t-shirt. Then he turned to Andrew's housemate, seated to his other side, and kissed her.

"Are you okay with this?" I whispered to Andrew, on my far side.

He shrugged. He seemed miserable, but over the next hour or so his heaviness lifted.

Despite the coke, the roommates fell away quickly, going to their rooms to sleep. Jeff went away for a bit, and we heard a girl's voice moaning. Then he returned. At Andrew's glare, he said, "Just sex."

Andrew put his fingertip to a smudge at the corner of Jeff's lip. "That's blood."

Jeff smiled. "I didn't *hurt* her."

It was still only midnight. He took us to a hotel bar. We drank cocktails before a gleaming wall of bottles. Then he took us to a room.

The city street lay far below, lights a strand of white and red baubles. Beside the king-sized bed, Jeff pulled Andrew's t-shirt over his head and kissed him. When he pulled away I saw blood on his lips.

Then he came to me, took me by the waist and drew me to him. He let go, and fingers brushed my nipples. I was weightless, as if the air were water. He fed me a mouthful of blood.

I'd never had so much before. Energy surged through me. My mouth opened in a silent scream. Jeff laughed. "I could make you," he said.

"No," Andrew said.

"Not yet," Jeff said.

He fucked both of us. There were no condoms. He watched Andrew fuck me, and the watching was like warm honey poured over us.

"Do her ass," he said, and Andrew did, touching my clit, and I blacked out and came to with them both tonguing me.

The energy thrilled through me, peaked and swung. I was

transported to fairyland, one of the wicked, laughing, dancing throng. I could rule the earth.

Jeff had me suck his cock; he had me suck blood from tiny cuts Andrew made in his cock. He ordered a bottle of Bordeaux, and I gasped when I saw its price, and Jeff laughed and poured a glass over me and they licked it off.

We stayed there two days. Jeff stepped out for a few hours both days, and each time for a bit I didn't question it.

Each time, before he came back, I began to come to.

"Fuck. My classes."

We stared out into grey Seattle rain. "You can make up the work," Andrew said.

"Do you think I've turned?"

He shrugged. "If not, you're awfully close." I scanned the black eyes. He took a deep breath. "Look, Tess. This is a slippery slope. You need to decide."

I was just about to speak when the door opened and Jeff walked in.

We ran like flying into a wet night. We ran faster than the rain. We stopped time, and the cars on the street were metal statues, and I laughed.

Deep in Rainier Valley—the closest Seattle had to a ghetto—we stopped in a dive bar, a place ordinarily I'd've been afraid to enter. The pretty barmaid disappeared with Jeff, and none of the patrons complained.

From the barstool next to mine, Andrew stroked my hair. I felt him tug at my energy. "Tess, sweetheart. You don't want Jeff to decide for you."

I didn't. But it felt so beautiful and so pleasurable, so right, to have this power. I wanted to keep it, as least for now. I wanted not to think.

Beaming, the barmaid swung open the door, Jeff following her. As she went behind the bar, her eyes glazed and she turned away. "Time to go," Jeff said.

I think Jeff thought I was under his spell. I think he wanted to implicate me.

He led us to a gravel lot beside a boarded-up building, gunmetal grey. We leapt the chain-link fence. "Have you ever done heroin?" he asked me. I shook my head.

In a tin-roofed corner, a figure lay curled in a sleeping bag. The smell hit me from across the lot. Jeff smiled at me and with a leap reached the sleeping bag. He pulled it off, tumbling its inhabitant to the gravel.

"What the fuck!?" A skinny white boy in a flannel shirt scrambled up, shaking violently. Jeff held the disgusting bag at arm's length. "What are you doing, man? Give me that back!"

Dropping the bag, Jeff stepped forward, with a quick glance gauging me. Then, lightning fast, he grabbed the kid's head under his arm. With his other hand, he yanked the kid's shoulder and broke his neck.

The snap of bone woke me. I screamed. The kid's blue eyes met mine. He was still alive.

Time stood frozen. Andrew's eyes locked on mine.

He grabbed my hand, and we ran.

Jeff had spent his energy; Andrew had husbanded his. We ran out of the city, circling, crossing running water, going through railway tunnels, into the National Forest. Toward the end, he carried me.

In a hollow among cedar roots, he fed me chunks of bloody deer flesh. "Now you have to decide." He helped me swim to the surface, and I looked at the view.

To be full of power, raw and deep; to see the hidden world. Sex for days. To be a god.

But blood, rot and always darkness. No children. If you used the glamourie, you fucked your karma. Maybe there was no karma—but I wasn't sure, and I didn't want to bet wrong. If you didn't use the glamourie, it was like contracting a nasty chronic disease.

Right away, we'd have to beat Jeff physically and kill him, negotiate a deal, or join him. There would be more Jeffs.

Forever was a long time. What would divorce look like, to vampires?

The rain dripped from the cedar to the ferns. I began to feel cold.

"I can't do this, Andrew," I said. "I love you, but I can't join the psychopaths."

He pulled me into his lap. I took in the spicy smell of him, the warmth of his skin. "It doesn't have to be like that. I'm not Jeff."

"If I join, I'll always have to deal with people like Jeff."

"But if you choose what you call real life—" he closed his eyes. "I'd have to persuade him I glamoured you to forget. And he'll be on me like glue. I'll never see you again."

I began to cry. A shower of rain echoed me.

"You haven't lived very long. You don't know how rare it is to meet someone you can be with. I'm forty-one, and I've only met two."

I laughed weakly. "You're a vampire, Andrew. That makes it harder."

"You loved it, these last few days."

"I did! Until the last part!"

He curled around me, and I sobbed. At last I wiped my face with my shirt. "I want real life."

He stood, in the green darkness under the cedar. "I'll get you home. But after this, you won't see me again. Oh, maybe on your deathbed. You'll be some withered husk, and I'll still be me."

"Don't make it harder!"

"I'm not the person to make you a vampire on your deathbed. I want you here and now. For forever. Unlike most people, I mean forever."

I cried. But I didn't change my mind.

We ran back in silence. Red fire seeped from the horizon as he kissed me goodbye.

---

I FINISHED the drawing of the window and framed it. Wherever I live, I find a corner to hang it. The day before my wedding, to a man I want to make a life with, I took it down. I meant to smash it and throw it away.

But I didn't.

Somewhere Andrew is waiting for me, half against his will, with the key to the world under the world, where the colors are brighter and darker.

Some days it takes all my strength not to stare at the drawing and will him back.

# PLAYS WELL WITH OTHERS

CECILIA DUVALLE

ulianna Webber, matriarch of the most powerful hive in Pacifica, put up her advert for a new convert just as the doctor informed me all medical intervention would cease on my behalf. My only hope at living was to become a drinker. It wouldn't be the *same* life, but I'd rather become one of *them* then give up on this world entirely.

I applied for the position immediately, along with another four-hundred dying souls, and was among ten she was interviewing in person. By law, each drinker was allowed to register one new transition every fifty years. It kept the overall drinker portion down by limiting their ability to procreate. And for Julianna Webber to have registered when she did was a miracle. I'd been through four interviews already, and you only get five chances before you're knocked off the registry's listings.

I had arrived at the same time as my competition. We were taken en masse to a locker room and instructed to shower and dress in bathrobes. I had hung back for the end of the line so I could be the last to be interviewed. We were led to a hallway overlooking a lovely garden and seated in one long row. An older man dressed in a Victorian Era butler's uniform took us off one at a time, leaving the rest of us to stew. I brought a book with me to keep me from fidgeting and got engrossed.

A gentle squeezing on my shoulder roused me from my story. The others had all gone.

The butler's lips twisted up in amusement as I stood up and shook myself from my stupor.

"The first portion of your interview will be in the library, sir." He led me through a series of corridors lined with precious artifacts and artwork.

I managed to keep up with him, but barely so. Maybe the doctors had been wrong about their prognosis. They had promised me a month to get my affairs in order, but the tightness in my lungs made me wonder about that. If things went well here, I would only need a week for the paperwork to go through.

The butler pushed a set of sturdy wooden doors open, stepped aside so I would be front and center at the door and announced, "Mr. Mercutio Kennedy, my mistress."

I don't know exactly what I was expecting, but this had not been it. I found myself at the entry to the most beautiful and ornate, honest-to-God-libraries I could ever have imagined. Having only read about them, I wasn't prepared for the sheer weight of it. The room was two stories high and ringed by books. And there was a smell—musty and alluring. My fingers itched to touch the books and to lose myself in all those delicious words.

Pacifica had saved many books surviving the War of Division, but the city of Seattle had sold their collection to fund more needed services shortly after the war was over. No new book had been printed since 2050, more than a quarter of a century before I was born, and all the old books had disappeared into private collections such as this. I'm sure I must have looked like a complete idiot, staring at all those beautiful old volumes, my jaw dangling open, and my mouth drooling with desire.

In that moment, I fell in love. I would do anything to become part of this hive if I had access to those shelves.

I was so enthralled by the library, I hadn't noticed the row of people seated at a long table until the doors shut with a decisive thunk behind me. A woman sat in the middle of the table with three men on either side of her. She was dressed in a stunning blue gown. It was a blue I've never seen in nature—rich, darker and lighter than cobalt at the same time and shimmering with a hit of something metallic.

The cut of the dress was simple yet alluring in an old-fashioned way—almost modest. While I had never seen a drawing or photo of Julianna Webber, there was no doubt this unpresuming, almost plain woman must be her. She sat in the center with three men on either side. They were dressed in matching robes of dewy blue-black satin, like a raven's wings in the sunlight. If I didn't know better, I would have described them as monks, except the fabric spoke of indulgence not self-flagellation.

One of the men seated next to the woman pointed to an oriental carpet in front of the table. I don't know if there was any mind-control in that moment, but I understood him easily. I stepped onto the carpet, stopping myself from checking under it for a trap door.

"Welcome, Mercutio. Is that what you like to be called?" the woman asked.

"Merk works, too. I assume you are Julianna Webber?"

She inclined her head. "Indeed. I prefer to call you Mercutio." She placed a hand on the forearm of the man to her right. "Don't you agree, Andreas?"

"To be sure. Tell us, Mercutio, do you know the origin of your name?"

"My mother adored Shakespeare. When she crossed over from the East, she could only bring a few things with her. One of them was a thick volume in tiny print of Shakespeare. The only book she ever owned." I threw a glance over at the shelves, wondering if they might have a complete set of the bard's work here.

"I fed off of Shakespeare once," Julianna said, running a fingernail across the top of the table almost absently.

"While he fucked me in the arse," Andreas said laughing. "Man, his cock was long and wide. I wish we'd changed him before he died. We thought he had a few more years to go, and were off raping and pillaging in France when he fell ill, poor bugger. What he could have done as an immortal."

Both sighed together contentedly, as if this was everyday talk.

"Seriously?" I blurted. "I find that hard to believe. Shakespeare?"

Andreas chuckled and tipped his head against Juliana's shoulder. "There is much about us that is hard for people like you to believe. But, you will, if you join us."

"But," Julianna broke in, "you are not here to listen to our reminiscences. You are here for us to decide if you would be a good fit for this hive. I'm sorry that you are facing the end of your naturally human life, Mercutio. There are so many things you will never do because of it, but if the choice is between complete death and partial death..." She held out her hands, palms up as if to say... *who's complaining?*

Not me. I eyed the books on the shelves. I could live here forever. It dawned on me then, that as a drinker, I could live long enough to read every book in the library.

Andreas clasped his hands together and leaned forward. "You have been on four other interviews. Why have you not joined any of these other hives? Why did you fail them?"

I put my hands behind my back to hide my clenched fists. "I didn't fail *them*. As you said, I'm here for us all to decide, together, whether or not I'm a fit here. The decision is not yours alone."

"Has anyone else offered you a placement?" Julianna asked.

"Three of the four."

"And you declined because?" Andreas asked.

"Their offers were not to my liking."

"With only a few weeks left to live, do you not feel desperate to have things settled?" asked a man at the right end of the table.

"I'd rather die than act out of desperation. Fifty years is a long time to indenture myself to anyone."

Andreas's smile was that of a father about to rebuke his toddler. "You will find that fifty years is not so much time in the long life of a vampire."

I cringed at the word. I preferred the local euphemisms: drinkers and bleeders. That way I could fool myself we were all human deep down. "I didn't click with any of the other hives."

"Let me tell you a few things about our little family. You've applied directly to me," Julianna said, "to serve me in any capacity that I desire. However, I am not a fan of reluctant behavior, so you will need to answer a series of questions from us all. Answer truthfully or not. We can tell if you're lying."

My knees went a little wobbly. I hadn't exactly lied on my application. I had merely stretched the truth a bit. If I believed it, maybe they would too.

"This group here is my immediate cell. All of these men pay homage to me and are my creations, as you will be should you decide to join us." She nodded to Andreas. "You've already heard from Andreas. He is my first, and my equal other—you must defer to him as you do me. In all things. Do you have a problem with that?"

Andreas' dark eyes smoldered in amusement. His tale of plugging Shakespeare's ass was still fresh in my mind. He was smaller than I by a good foot and a half. Surely, when I was one of them, I would end up the stronger?

"No problem."

"No problem, *Miss Julianna, Mistress, or Ma'am*." A dimple formed at the corner of her lips as she corrected me.

"No problem, Miss Julianna," I said, though I let a little sarcasm slip through. I wasn't her slave, not yet anyway.

"Oh, I like the way you rationalize, Mercutio," she said with a little laugh. "Let me continue with our introductions. George is in the middle, and his twin brother sits next to him." She paused with a slight tilt of her head, her eyes narrowing on me as I examined the two.

There was a definite resemblance, but Oscar looked old enough to be George's father. They each quirked an eyebrow at me as I studied them, and suddenly they were identical twins but for the extra age lines on Oscar's face.

"I see," I said. "George and Oscar were born together, raised together, but George… joined you earlier than Oscar. By fifteen or twenty years, perhaps?"

"Oh, he's a smart one," Oscar said, clapping his hands together in front of him. "I like him."

Further introductions came, and my head spun as I tried to memorize their names and faces in turn. At least I wouldn't be in an all male gang-bang *all* the time. Of the three hives that had offered me a position, two of them had been all-male. The third hive was a mix of male and females, but they were inarticulate and boring. Already, I could tell I would like it here. There was an energy, an aesthetic I found appealing. And the books.

"Now that you have met your closest companions here," Julianna said. "You must prove yourself a good fit intellectually and emotionally with the rest of us. If we all agree we like you, we will proceed to the physical examination."

Ah, so there would be that as well. I clenched and unclenched my fists, wrapping my hands around my forearms, breathed in slow to calm my nerves.

For the first time in months, a lightness of possibility flooded through me. Even more astounding, a flicker of desire followed close on its heels. Desire to be here. In this place.

The panel of seven asked about everything from my childhood to details of my disease. Did I like to read? *Yes, God yes.* Did I have children? *No.* Did I have any living family members? *Yes, but they support this.*

After an hour of exploring my life, the seven stood and gathered in a circle behind the table. They stood shoulder to shoulder, heads bowed toward each other, but not saying anything. I'd never watched a drinker do mind tricks before. It was creepy and fascinating at the same time. They were obviously talking about me. Making a life decision for me. Not being able to overhear them was annoying as hell.

The group broke up and everyone but Julianna and Andreas left. The two approached me. Julianna was much shorter than I, and she had to stand on her tiptoes to place both her hands on my cheeks and turned my head side to side. "Now for the physical."

Julianna's cool fingers slid down to my shoulders and she pushed my robe off. It pooled around my ankles. The room was warm, but I missed the luxuriant fabric against my skin.

Andreas circled around behind me and out of my vision.

"Good structure," Andreas said, his breath hot against my back. Though he was taller than Julianna, he was still a good ten inches shorter than me. His hands smoothed across my back and down to my ass, spreading me open. I clenched my jaw, my teeth clicking with the effort. "Tight, virginal ass, I would say."

Julianna's eyes narrowed on me, a cruel smile erupting on her lips.

"So, you lied on your registry questionnaire. Tell me about that."

"How… how can you tell?" I was told they couldn't read my mind without my permission.

"Your reaction to Andreas' touch."

"It's just…"

"On your application, you said *quite clearly* that you would be willing to join a hive where sexual relations with males and females were the norm. That you would be willing to top or bottom as required by the hive members."

"It wasn't exactly a lie. I fudged on the question about whether I'd enjoy sex with men. I haven't actually ever had sex with a male. I'm just pretty sure I would be fine with it should it ever happen."

"Are you, or are you not, willing to have sex with any of the men you met today?"

"All of them?" I asked, trying to understand the scope. At least none of them had physically repulsed me.

"All of them. Either all at once or one at a time, as per *their* whim. You will be the lowest of the pecking order for many years to come."

Andreas slid his hands along my buttocks again. Squeezing. Teasing. My cock twitched to life. I relaxed a little more as his hands reached around to spread over my chest and stomach.

"I think there's your answer," I said, looking down at my growing hard-on. "I have no experience, but that doesn't mean I'm not willing or capable."

Andreas pressed into my back, his cock hard against my ass.

I pointed at the books lining the walls. "Honestly? For this? I'll do just about anything."

Julianna laughed. "I see our love for books is a common passion. Now, let us go to a slightly more comfortable room."

I followed her, naked, through a door that had been merely a bookshelf moments before. Bookshelves as hidden doorways? What next, hidden passages and tunnels leading to dungeons?

"By the way, you will not have to fuck them all," Julianna said. "Joshua, for example serves me and respects the others, yet he can't get a hard on with another naked man within three feet of him. I need to see some assurance you will be happy here. There's nothing more tiresome than a morose vampire. You must prove you can play well with others."

We were now in a combination bedroom-dungeon, the room light and airy. A skylight let in ambient light without letting any damaging rays inside the room. A custom wood bed with rings and chains attached to its four posts took up much of one wall. Next to it stood a large cross with a wide center support. On the wall next to it, a variety of leather and metal devices were neatly arranged by size.

Various sofas, chairs, and other pieces of furniture formed a semicircle facing the bed and cross. The musky aroma of spent sex mingled with a bright citrus.

Julianna let loose her gown; the magical fabric fluttered to rest at her feet. She stepped out of it and lay back against one of three narrow chaise lounges—really a chair that allowed her to lean back and be supported, yet short enough that her pussy was easily reachable. She spread her legs open and placed her feet on the ground on either side. Her glistening pussy was open in invitation, so I didn't hesitate to kneel before her.

I placed my hands on the tops of her thighs, ran them down to her knees and looked up at her. "May I, ma'am?" I said.

"Very good, you remembered your manners, Mercutio," she said. "I take it eating pussy is not new for you?"

My cock responded before my mouth could formulate words. It bobbed against the chair as I leaned forward, spreading her lips with my thick thumbs. "Never had any quite like yours, ma'am." This was true, but she looked human, and her pussy smelled human. My cock responded to the sight and smell of her, growing and tightening in anticipation.

I lingered, licking, kissing, nibbling along, and skipped over her clit, giving the other side the same, slow attention. Julianna moaned lowly and shifted her hips upward, urging me for more. I grasped her knees with my hands and slid them up long and slow, my thumbs spreading her labia wide.

I placed the flat of my tongue against her clit and held it there, warm and flat, but immobile. Slowly, ever so slowly, I moved my tongue in the shape of the alphabet—an old but useful trick. I wanted her to get enough stimulation and yet keep her from orgasm. About the letter "m" she writhed under me, so I switched rhythm, slowing down to stop the impending tide.

She grabbed me by the back of my head, holding me against her. "Very good, yes…" she hissed, her hips jerking hard into my face. I lapped at her delicious juices, surprised at the sweetness. Before I could finish her off, though, she grasped my bald head and held me away from her.

"Now for the real test," she breathed. "Fuck me with that enormous hard cock of yours."

"With pleasure, ma'am." I didn't quite understand what she

meant by *real test*; after all fucking a woman was something I was pretty practiced at.

She spread her legs wide to accommodate me, thrusting her hips hungrily to take me all in. I pushed the tip of my cock into her. I slid in easily and soon adjusted to her low body temperature. It was as if I had been playing with ice.

"Now," she said, looking over my shoulder.

It was then I understood the test. *Shakespeare.* Julianna and Andreas were using me to reenact their time with the famous bard. Andreas had been standing to the side, totally out of my consciousness the entire time I was face fucking Julianna.

He spread my cheeks and lubed up my ass. I had to keep fucking Julianna even as Andreas knelt behind me, his thighs pressing into me, his hard cock dragging along my crack, back and forth with each of my thrusts into Julianna.

I waited for it. The pain. The violation. Whatever it was going to be. I'd never had more than a slim finger up my ass before, and that belonged to a doctor.

"Relax," Andreas said. "It will be better if you don't clench your ass together."

Julianna writhed under me, pushing up for movement.

Andreas slapped my ass, stinging; in that same moment, he spread my cheeks wide and plunged his cock into me. No fingers first. No warming up. The bastard just went for it.

The initial explosion was followed closely by something I had heard of but never believed would be true for me. Something exquisite. Andreas filled my ass up and clutched to my back and the three of us paused, immobile as our bodies adjusted. My asshole sucked in around his cock, adjusting to its slim girth as if it were the most natural thing in the world. The pressure on the inside as he hit deep sent ripples of excitement coursing through me.

Andreas pulled out completely, leaving me empty and devoid.

"No," I said, the urgency and hunger in my voice surprising me.

Andreas plunged back in, filling me up again. And, for that moment, I thought I could live the rest of my life with a cock inside my ass and be happy. How had I never known this? Why had I waited so long? What had I been afraid of?

Julianna laughed. "Oh, so there you have it. A cock up your ass and a smile on your face. Perfect."

We paused there, motionless for a moment. Then, Julianna breathed in and smiled, showing me her teeth for the first time. She raised an eyebrow, silently asking me permission.

"Yes, ma'am, please," I said.

She lifted her head and bit into my neck. The initial sting wasn't any worse than a needle for drawing blood. She suckled from me, taking a small taste.

"Good," she said. "You taste so good."

She dropped away to give Andreas room. His chest lay flat against my back as he took his turn. "God yes," he groaned. His tongue was warm against my neck, licking the bite closed. "He will do nicely."

"Now," Julianna said. "Now, let's get fucking."

It took us but a few moments to find a rhythm. Me thrusting deeply into Julianna, then Andreas plunging into me while I held myself inside Julianna. Andreas' fingers dug into my hips as he held onto me, mirroring my movements.

In spite of my dying state, I was able to keep it up until Andreas spent himself inside me.

"May I come inside you, ma'am?" I asked, not sure how much longer I could last.

"Not until I come."

I ploughed on, mystified by my ability to maintain an erection this long. I had honestly thought being on the receiving end would have had the opposite effect. As I continued to fuck Juliana, Andreas lay against my back, his arms clutched around my waist and his softening cock still filling my ass.

Julianna writhed under me and I altered my motion so my cock slid up along her clit with each thrust. She made quiet mewling sounds, and I slowed down my pace, thinking only of making her come. I had to please her, and nothing else in the world mattered. By pleasing this woman, all would end well. I was certain of it.

Finally, just as I thought I might die of exhaustion, Julianna stiffened and almost threw me off her in the throws of her orgasm. She clutched at my back as she jerked against me, urging me on.

"Harder, more," she yelled, her body hitching against mine, her pussy clamping down around my cock.

Without waiting for further permission, I thrust again and again, until she clamped her legs around me, holding me immobile against her. I emptied myself into her, collapsing against her completely worn out from the exertion. Andreas' come ran out of my ass and mingling with mine between her legs.

Andreas was the first to move. My gaping hole was bereft, wanting the fullness of him to return.

"That was not a bad start to things," he said.

He helped me off Julianna, and I stumbled against him, my legs weak. A coughing fit hit me then.

"Shit," he said, gathering me in his arms, and carried me to the bed. I could barely move, and my breath caught hard in my chest. I struggled to breathe.

"Oh dear," Andreas said. "Did we overdo things with you?" He ran a hand along my forehead and across my cheek.

Julianna sat on the bed near my legs. She had re-dressed in the luxuriant blue gown. "Andreas, he doesn't look good."

"No. We can't continue," Andreas said. "There's no way he'd survive it. I don't think he'll make it out of here. We should call an ambulance and get him out of here."

"Continue?" I asked, barely able to get the word out. "Not done yet?" What more would they want from me? Andreas glanced at the bondage equipment behind him, and I under-stood. We had merely gotten through a warm-up.

"I don't need to see more," Julianna said, her fingers caressing my thigh. "I want him."

My throat was dry, and everything ached with a sudden, breaking pain.

"We can tell the registry office it was an emergency," Julianna said.

Andreas shook his head. "The rules are very clear, my love. We can't turn him until the forms are official. Signed. With witnesses. If we turn him without his permission…"

"I'm well aware of the risks, Andreas. But, I want him. And I will have him."

"Please, Julianna. It's too risky."

Julianna leaned over me. "He's dying, Andreas. He doesn't have an hour left, let alone a week. Fuck."

I struggled to keep my eyes open, to take in any air. I breathed in hard, but it was as if there was no air to fill my lungs.

"Mercutio, look at me. I need you to ask me to change you. Andreas, record this."

I opened my mouth, but nothing came out. I couldn't speak, I was dry. Spent. Dying.

"Mercutio, do you want me to turn you now? Just say yes. One word."

I moved my lips, breathed out, tried again. I mouthed the word yes. I tried to nod my head and say the word. There was no air left in me to make a sound.

Please, I thought. Please. I was swallowed by a deep encroaching darkness.

# ABOUT THE AUTHORS

**Gustavo Bondoni** is an Argentine writer with over two hundred stories published in fourteen countries, in seven languages, and is a winner in the National Space Society's "Return to Luna" Contest and the Marooned Award for Flash Fiction (2008). His latest books are The Malakiad (2018) and Incursion (2017). He has also published two science fiction novels: Outside (2017) and Siege (2016) and an ebook novella entitled Branch. His short fiction is collected in Tenth Orbit and Other Faraway Places (2010) and Virtuoso and Other Stories (2011). His website is at www.gustavobondoni.com

**Rhidian Brenig Jones** lives in Wales with his husband, Michael, and French bulldogs, Coco and Cosette. He leads an adult literacy program and writes before work, when the three best things in his life are still asleep.

**Emily L. Byrne**'s stories have appeared in *Bossier, Spy Games, Forbidden Fruit, First, Summer Love, Best Lesbian Erotica 20th Anniversary Edition, Best Lesbian Erotica for the Year Vol. 2, First, Witches, Princesses and Women at Arms, Blood in the Rain 3* and *The Nobilis Erotica Podcast*. Her collections, *Knife's Edge: Kinky Lesbian Erotica* and *Desire: Sensual Lesbian Erotica*, are available from Queen of Swords Press. She can be found at http://writeremilylbyrne.blogspot.com/ and @emilylbyrne.

**Bill Davidson** is a Scottish writer of horror and fantasy. His recent work can be found in a number of publications from the UK and US, such as; Flame Tree Publishing's Endless Apocalypse Anthology, Terrors Unimagined Anthology, Dark Lane Books, Storyteller, Under the Bed, Emerging Worlds, Metamorphose, Enchanted Conversation, Tigershark publishing and Storgy Magazine. Find him on billdavidsonwriting.com or twitter @bill_davidson57

**Kiki DeLovely** (kikidelovely.wordpress.com) is a kinky, queer, witchy femme whose work has appeared in various publications, including *Blood in the Rain 2* and *3*, *Getting It: A Femdom Anthology*, *Corrupted: Erotica and Erotic Romance for the Modern Age*, and the award-winning *Unspeakably Erotic: Lesbian Kink*.

When not daydreaming about plot lines and characters, **Andra Dill** practices yoga, reads voraciously, writes, rewrites, and then writes some more. She lets her friends talk her into all kinds of nonsense and loves road trips. Follow her on Twitter @aedill

**Sara Dobie Bauer** is a bestselling author, model, and mental health advocate with a creative writing degree from Ohio University. She lives in Northeast Ohio, although she'd really like to live in a Tim Burton film. She is author of the paranormal rom-com *Bite Somebody*. Learn more at http://SaraDobieBauer.com.

**Cecilia Duvalle** lives near Seattle with her family, cats, and chickens. Her erotic shorts are found in a number of anthologies. Learn more about Cecilia by visiting her website at Ceciliaduvalle.com.

**Maria Duendí** lives in New York City with her husband and daughter.

**Ella G. Hoare** is a former belly and burlesque dancer in Salt Lake City, Utah. While she has hung up her tassels, she can't resist entertaining others. She loves writing poetry, erotica, horror, and speculative fiction. When she isn't writing she can be found supporting Salt Lake's thriving kink community.

**Erin Horáková** is a southern American writer, critic and academic who lives in London.

**Calypso Kane** lives in the cooking heart of Texas. She writes fantastical fictions about the fey and the fiendish. Her short stories have been published in anthologies such as, *The Odd and the Bizarre, Creature Stew, Strange Little Girls, Offbeat: Nine Spins on Song,* and *Dark Voices.* Between submissions she enjoys hibernation and telling herself she'll get around to her growing tower of unread books eventually.

**Jennifer Loring**'s short fiction has been published widely both online and in print. She holds an MFA in Writing Popular Fiction from Seton Hill University with a concentration in horror fiction and teaches online in SNHU's College of Continuing Education. Jenn lives in Philadelphia, PA with her husband, their turtle, and two basset hounds.

**Jeff Mann** has published five books of poetry, *Bones Washed with*

*Wine, On the Tongue, Ash, A Romantic Mann,* and *Rebels*; two collections of essays, *Edge* and *Binding the God*; a book of poetry and memoir, *Loving Mountains, Loving Men*; six novels, *Fog, Purgatory, Cub, Salvation, Country,* and *Insatiable*; and three volumes of short fiction, *A History of Barbed Wire, Desire and Devour,* and *Consent.* The winner of two Lambda Literary Awards and two Pauline Réage Novel Awards, he teaches creative writing at Virginia Tech.

**Jordan Monroe** is delighted to use her English degrees. Her short stories have been featured in *Best Women's Erotica of the Year, Volume 2, The Big Book of Submission. Volume 2,* and *Symphony Amore: Erotic Stories of Love and Music.* She lives within 25 miles of Washington, D.C.

**Delilah Night** (delilahnight.com) has published over a dozen short stories in anthologies such as If Mom's Happy, Nine to Five Fantasies, and Myths, Monsters, Mutations. She is the editor of a charity anthology, Coming Together: Under the Mistletoe. Her first solo title is Capturing the Moment.

**Iskra Ryder** is a graduate student living in the Twin Cities. When she's not writing or working magic, she's making jewelry.

**Mary Trepanier** writes fantasy, erotica, horror, and paranormal romance. You can find her short stories in the *Blood in the Rain* anthologies of vampire erotica, among others. *The Queen of Heaven's Daughter,* first book of *Tales of the End Times,* is her first novel.

# MORE FROM CWTCH PRESS

Thank you for buying Blood in the Rain 2. We hope you've enjoyed the second volume of Blood in the Rain series. If you enjoyed these stories, you'll love our other two collections!

Click the following for links to the more hot vampire tales:

Blood in the Rain: Seventeen Stories of Vampire Erotica

Blood in the Rain: Seventeen Stories of Vampire Erotica

Blood in the Rain 3: Nineteen Stories of Vampire Erotica

Gillian Bainbridge and Damien Grey narrate the first collection—it can be found on Blood in the Rain: Seventeen Stories of Vampire Erotica Audible (as well as at iTunes.)

Look for future releases by signing up for our newsletter at Cwtch Press.

Do you enjoy some human-centric erotica? You'll love If Mom's Happy; Stories of Erotic Mothers.

9 781947 234116